Francis Bennett was ed College, Cambridge, and has be.. .. is managing director of Book Data, the information pub.. .g company that he co-founded in 1987. Francis Bennett is married with grown-up children and lives in Twickenham.

By Francis Bennett
Making Enemies
Secret Kingdom
Dr Berlin

Dr Berlin

FRANCIS BENNETT

PHOENIX

A PHOENIX PAPERBACK

First published in Great Britain in 2001
by Weidenfeld & Nicolson
This paperback edition published in 2002
by Phoenix,
an imprint of Orion Books Ltd,
Orion House, 5 Upper St Martin's Lane,
London WC2H 9EA

A CIP catalogue record for this book
is available from the British Library.

ISBN 0 75381 345 9

Typeset by Deltatype Ltd, Birkenhead, Merseyside

Printed and bound in Great Britain by
The Guernsey Press Co. Ltd, Guernsey, C. I.

For Dominic, Elizabeth, Stephen,
Clare and Alexander

Radin's reaction was instinctive – he was too far away to see anything in detail – but he knew at once that something was wrong. He tried telling himself it was anxiety, an attack of nerves brought on by his condition, but something within him had sensed a fault and its message was unavoidable.

'Stop the car.'

He wound down the window, the blast of heat momentarily sucking the air out of his lungs and leaving him breathless, and reached for the binoculars on the seat beside him. His damaged hands fumbled clumsily with the viewfinder while he adjusted the focus. He swept past empty expanses of steppe, hardened and dusty grey in the morning light, until he saw the bleached concrete of the vast hangar where they assembled the machines. There, to the left, dwarfing the buildings surrounding it, was the launch tower, the metal arms of its gantries supporting a huge steel column that glinted in the sunlight. Wisps of evaporation hovered around the chambers of the auxiliary engines clipped to the base. The biggest rocket ever built sat cold and immobile over the concrete fire trench, pointing towards the stars.

Two years before this vast machine had sprung into being as an idea in his head. With his team of experts he had worked with manic energy to create a rocket powerful enough to lift two, even four men into space on journeys to the moon and back, and then beyond, perhaps one day to the planets. He had not spared himself, nor those who worked with him, as if he knew that somewhere within his body the cancer was stirring, and this project would be his last. Those first few lines on a piece of paper had been transformed into a craft of breathtaking power and beauty. Now it stood before him, in all its shining glory, ready for its first flight. In a few hours, thousands of gallons of nitric acid and hydrazine would be transformed by the five engines into a white heat powerful enough to lift his giant rocket clear of the earth's gravitational pull. He would watch it soar into the mysterious blackness of the heavens, its trail of fire and smoke tapering away into nothingness, the only clues to its existence the radio signals charting its progress into the unknown.

A steel basilica, *his* creation, *his* monument.

He looked again, this time with a more rational eye, carefully travelling the distance from the nose cone to the engine nozzles. There at the base, he detected a minute wisp of condensation, the tell-tale sign of escaping nitric acid. A fuel leak: easy to miss if you didn't know what you were looking for, impossible to ignore once you'd spotted it. A real danger. His inner eye had been right after all.

'Do you have a short-wave radio?' he asked his driver.

'No, sir.'

'Drive on as fast as you can.'

Nitric acid might be stable but it was corrosive. Keep it in the tanks for too long and you risked it eating its way through a valve or the lining of the fuel chamber. Start the firing procedure and a single spark could ignite a catastrophic conflagration. There was no question about what should be done. The launch must be stopped, the tanks drained, the process begun again.

The car raced down the rough concrete road that cut like an arrow through what remained of the scrubby grasslands. The poor suspension made his lower spine ache. Shifting his position gave him no release from the incessant burning that smouldered in his back. The two or three white pills he was prescribed each day granted him only temporary remission. Every morning he pleaded for the dose to be increased – ten, twenty pills a day, what did it matter how many, so long as they brought relief? But his doctors, standing by his bedside, wrapped in the immunity of their white coats, shook their heads and denied him what he craved. They were worried about side effects, they said. His kidneys might give out.

So what if his kidneys were destroyed? He was never going to recover from his illness, they all knew that, but the truth failed to change their mind. Some bureaucrat in Moscow, who'd probably never suffered anything worse than toothache, had given instructions to keep him alive as long as they could, and his doctors feared the consequences of failing. Damn them! Would no one assume responsibility for his death? Was he not meant to die?

The car came to a halt outside the control centre, a concrete building poorly conceived and badly built. The driver got out, opened the boot of the car, assembled the wheelchair and helped Radin into it.

'Where to?'

'The control room.'

Still clasping his binoculars, he was pushed through the automatic doors, into the lift and up to the top floor. He saw before him rows of faces concentrated on terminals whose screens flickered with telemetry read-outs as the countdown progressed. The fans suspended from the ceiling made little impression on the heat that had built up in the badly ventilated room. He was aware of its intensity on the surface of his skin, but his bones remained beyond the reach of warmth.

'Comrade Director.' His former assistant, Voroshilov, was unable to conceal his surprise. 'We were not expecting you. We were not told you were coming.'

What can they have said about his condition? He'd never missed a launch in the past. Why should he miss this one? He had been ill for a few weeks, and in that time they had forgotten who he was. How quickly absence robs you of your power.

'I want General Ulansky. Where is he?'

'Outside, sir.'

'*Outside?*' What the hell was he doing outside? He should be here, in this room, now. This was where you controlled the launch process, not standing on the tarmac apron like a policeman directing traffic. The man must be out of his mind to be away from his post at a time like this.

'Get me a radio telephone. I want to speak to him.'

Over the years he had watched Ulansky pilot his way up the military hierarchy, a politician more than a soldier, a man with few administrative abilities who had exploited every connection he had to gain control of this secret rocket establishment. The Cosmodrome at Baikonur was a temporary stepping-stone on his journey to the heights of power. How could Moscow support a man he wouldn't trust to tie his shoelace? It was insanity to let him loose on a project of this complexity. Radin had protested at his appointment, citing Ulansky's inexperience. Within days he'd received a reply from an official in some department in the Kremlin extolling the merits of General Ulansky, hero of the Soviet Union, a man of courage and vision, with a record of selfless service to the state. Radin had stopped reading at that point because he knew that the real message was that Ulansky had powerful support. No point in pursuing a battle you can't win. He'd thrown the letter in the waste-paper basket.

'Sergei?' There was a crackled acknowledgement at the other end of the radio telephone. 'This is Viktor. There's a leak in fuel tank B. The launch must be stopped at once.'

The reply was incomprehensible, a continuous ribbon of indistinguishable sounds crackling in his ear.

'I can't hear what he's saying,' Radin said desperately. 'Take me down to the launch pad.'

He was rushed into the lift once more, down to the ground floor and out into the raging heat. Ulansky was sitting in a folding chair, a director on a film set, the star of his drama the huge inanimate object on the launch pad. All he lacked was a megaphone and a camera.

'Sergei.'

'Viktor?' Ulansky sounded surprised. 'I thought you were in hospital.'

'Look over there.' Radin pointed urgently to the base of the craft. 'Tank B. Can you see the leak?'

'Where?'

Radin handed him the binoculars. 'You've got to stop the launch.'

The launch termination procedure was documented, and Ulansky knew that. In the event of a leak, the countdown is halted, the fuel is drained, non-flammable oxygen is piped through the tanks to clear the vapours. Later, technicians in protective suits are sent in to make the spacecraft safe. Only then can the refuelling process begin.

'Emptying the fuel tanks and refuelling will take at least forty-eight hours. I don't have that time at my disposal.'

'What difference does forty-eight hours make?'

'My instructions do not allow me to delay the launch by more than twelve hours, Viktor.'

Radin knew what that phrase meant. Over the years he had done his best to stop scientific research being used for political spectacle but it was a campaign he'd never been able to win. He heard the pride in Ulansky's voice and he despised him for it, just as he despised the source of the instruction, the belligerent, uneducated peasant who sooner or later would lead them into an unnecessary conflict with the West, the consequences of which would be disastrous, unthinkable. It was a good thing he wouldn't be around to witness it.

'I don't give a damn about your instructions,' Radin said angrily. 'I demand that you delay the launch. There's more at stake here than the reputation of a few politicians. If you don't act now, there's a huge risk of an explosion.'

Radin registered the concern on the faces of the officials who surrounded them, and sensed their relief at his presence. They had no doubts about the seriousness of the situation. 'You can't ignore the leak, Sergei. You must do as I say.'

'I'll halt the countdown for an hour while we investigate.'

'It's not enough time to complete the necessary test procedures.'

'An hour's all I'm giving you, Viktor.'

Reluctantly Radin let himself be wheeled back into the control room. His hope was that when the engineers saw how serious the leak was, they'd report to Ulansky that the craft wasn't safe to fly. Then he'd have no choice but to cancel the launch. That was the only prudent course of action: stop now before something worse happened.

'Would you like to sit here, sir?' Voroshilov was offering him an armchair near the window.

'I'll stay where I am,' Radin replied, tapping the arm of his wheelchair. He needed the protection of the sheepskin cover to prevent the sharp edges of his hip bones shearing their way through his thin buttocks.

'Can we get you anything?'

He shook his head. He wanted to say a lorry load of painkillers but even the faithful Voroshilov might mistake his joke and report his request to his doctors, and then he'd be given a lecture about responsibility or some other nonsensical subject. Sometimes he thought dying was the best way to escape all that pious rubbish . . . if only he could die quickly.

He was left, safe behind the reinforced glass of the window through which he could watch the launch of his rocket. He marvelled once more at its grace and shape. His creature was as beautiful as any cathedral, its dark nose cone pointing towards the stars like a spire, the bodywork housing the engines a buttressed tower, the only difference being that the power of his creation was there to glorify man, not an unknown and unknowable deity.

The excitement he felt, a mixture of awe and fascination at the rocker's scale and complexity, provided momentary compensation for the pain deep in his back that was now his permanent companion. He would not live to see the fulfilment of his dreams, the day when men would ride routinely into the sky perched precariously on top of his fiery monster, but at least he had set them on their journey. That much was secure. Whatever they did with his memory when he was dead, whether they vilified or glorified him, he knew what he had achieved and that was all that mattered.

Fly, he whispered to himself. *Fly for me.*

He picked up his binoculars and once more looked closely at his craft. To his horror, he saw ground staff climbing all over the base of the rocket, ant-like figures armed with spanners looking for valves to tighten. *What the hell was going on?* He'd assumed Ulansky would investigate the leak before trying to repair it. This was madness. Even the movements of the technicians betrayed their uncertainty with this appalling break in procedure. In the distance he saw a group of government officials, air-force officers and senior scientists, nearly a hundred of them, taking their seats in a specially constructed stand to watch the launch – more evidence of Ulanksy's reluctance to accept any delay. The show must go on because the audience had arrived. The launch of his rocket had a significance beyond the scientific achievement of getting so many tons of metal into the air: it was a lead part in a political drama, a gesture on an international stage, directed by the Kremlin against its enemies in Washington.

'Tell General Ulansky I want to see him now. At once.'

His words were lost in a sudden roar of sound. Through the metal and leather of his chair he felt a deep vibration as if a huge drill was working its way through solid rock directly beneath him. The world was shaking his chair, the floor on which it stood, the walls of the control centre. He heard a terrifying noise, a deep, thunderous roar. He saw a white flash and then sharp tongues of blue flame burst from the nozzles of the main engine. Somehow the lower stage of the rocket had ignited, rupturing the oxidiser tank. He saw the auxiliary rockets ignite, the giant pods straining at the clamps that held them to the body of the craft. Clouds of white smoke blasted into the fire trench, to be directed away from the launch pad

7

as his dream was swallowed up in its own fire. He saw terror and panic spread among the figures scattering around the base of the rocket as they tried to escape, only to disappear into the rapidly spreading inferno.

In seconds the great steel structure was straining and shuddering on its pad as the gantries, shaken loose by the contained thrust of the engines, toppled to the ground. He saw flames shoot up the outside of the lower fuel chambers; he saw the explosion at the base of the second stage shatter the steel cladding and the bolts and struts that locked the two halves of the rocket together. For a moment, the upper section shuddered and vibrated, then agonisingly slowly it fell sideways, crashing to the ground, its spilled fuel exploding into a raging torrent of fire.

It seemed to Radin as if he was watching the sun burst in front of him, explosion after explosion, each fire generating another in an endless chain of conflagration. The expanding fireball swept forward with a ferocious velocity, fed by thousands of gallons of rocket fuel, consuming everything in its path: steel, concrete, tarmac, human flesh. He heard the angry roar of a world exploding in a fury of destruction as the last of his dreams was swept away into clouds of billowing black smoke blown outwards with the force of each explosion, turning day into night.

PART ONE
Summer 1961

1

1

My dear friend *(the note from Viktor Radin reads),* come quickly. My uninvited guest is greedy. Soon there will be nothing left for him to devour. There are last things to be settled between us.

The car slows as the driver turns off the road and down an avenue flanked by maple trees. They round a bend and there is the house, remote, austere, but unlike so many Berlin has seen in his life there are no bars on the windows, no guards at the door. There is no security because none is needed. The dying have nowhere to escape to.

He walks into the building: deserted and shadowy corridors, the distant squeak of unseen rubber soles on shiny linoleum, a merciful coolness. A woman in nurse's uniform appears from an inner office. He presents his identity papers.

'You are expected. Come with me, please.'

She leads him through a darkened day room shuttered against the glare of the sun. Patients sleep in chairs, their mouths gaping open, or stare sightlessly at the walls, all waiting for their lives to end. This is a house of death. It is filled with old men and the inescapable smells of excrement, cleaning fluid and overcooked vegetables. He feels uncomfortable walking past the dying, but they take no notice of him and once he is out on the veranda, he can breathe again. Down wooden steps, into the garden and the brightness and heat of the afternoon revive him.

Viktor Radin is sitting in a wheelchair under an oak tree, apparently asleep, a rug around his knees. Always small, he is now a diminished, childlike figure, the pale waxy skin on his face barely concealing the sharp outline of his skull.

'He's been looking forward to your visit,' the nurse says as they walk across the grass. 'Don't be upset at his condition. This is not a good day. But then no day is good now. We see that he suffers no pain.' She bends down to whisper in Radin's ear. 'Your visitor is here, Professor.'

'Who?' Radin awakes with a start, uncertain where he is.

'It's me, Viktor. Andrei.'

'Andrei. At last. I've been waiting for you.'

A parody of a hand reaches out to his, the fingers swollen, misshapen and apparently boneless. Berlin takes it briefly, hating the soft spongy feeling that serves as an awful reminder of what Viktor suffered so many years ago. The skeleton breaks into a smile revealing pale gums and worn, yellow teeth between dry, flaky lips. 'Welcome to the last station on the line.'

The nurse settles him, adjusting his pillows, altering the position of his wheelchair so that it remains out of the sun. She looks at her watch. 'Half an hour,' she says to Berlin. 'He tires easily.'

'How are you, Viktor?' Berlin takes off his jacket and sits down on the grass. It is a question he hardly needs to ask. There is no doubt about Radin's condition.

'You find me as you see me, a man on the edge of the greatest mystery of life. As a scientist, I can say there is a certain interest in observing the process of dying at such close quarters. My only regret is that when it is all over I will not be able to write up my experience for the benefit of those who die after me.'

Berlin is shocked at his frailty. Since he last saw him he has

12

wasted to nothing. He seems lighter than air. One breath of wind and Radin would disappear.

Radin reaches for Berlin's arm. 'The truth is, Andrei, I do not like to witness my own decline. I wish it were over. But I am glad you are here. Thank you for answering my plea so quickly.' He struggles to change his position in his chair. 'I need a cigarette.'

Berlin offers one to Radin, who grasps it with both hands and carefully places it between his lips, where it will stay until he has smoked it down to a sodden butt.

'How are you, where have you been?' Radin smiles again, the skin stretching thin and transparent across his face. 'Tell me everything about yourself.'

'There's little to tell,' Berlin says. 'I teach, I lecture, I do research. What else does an academic historian do?'

'He writes articles in learned journals, he publishes books, and if he is lucky he goes abroad for conferences. Occasionally, I hope, he dreams.'

Berlin smiles. 'Leipzig in May. Since then, nothing, and nothing planned. No luck and no dreams either. Very barren in all departments.'

'No dreams? What's come over you?'

'What is there left to dream about, Viktor?'

'In my situation, I agree, there is only time for memories and regrets. But you're young, Andrei, you have a future to look forward to. Or are you afraid to dream about what may be?'

This is dangerous territory. The state of his mind is not a fit subject for a dying man's curiosity, even when that man is as close to him as Viktor. If he reveals that he has not dreamed for longer than he can remember, that he has written nothing for months, worse, that he has no desire to write anything, he will be subjected to a merciless interrogation. That must be avoided.

'You didn't get me here to talk about myself, Viktor.' For his own protection, he must steer Radin's interest back to the reason for his visit. 'Your note said we had matters to discuss.' He cannot bring himself to use the phrase 'last things'.

Radin nods in agreement.

'I want you to tuck in my blanket.' This is more like the Radin he knows, giving instructions, reordering the world. 'As you bend over me, I shall give you an envelope. You are to conceal it at once and you must show it to no one. Is that understood?'

'Of course.'

Berlin gets to his feet and hovers over Radin's wheelchair. He might be dying but he hasn't lost any of his reckless determination to outwit the system when it stands in the way of what he wants to do.

'Now.'

Berlin bends forward, tucks in the rug and receives the envelope. He slips it into his pocket. 'There – that wasn't difficult, was it?' He is humouring the old man out of respect for their years of friendship.

Radin ignores him. 'You now have in your possession a report from the senior flight engineer at Baikonur. You will find that its technical content lies far beyond the competence of a historian like yourself, but even a brief glance will confirm its importance as a historical document. Engineer Kuzmin describes more than a hundred faults in the equipment of my rocket, not one of which had been attended to by the time of the launch on 24 May. On that day my rocket did not fly to the stars as I had planned, it exploded on the launch pad, killing two hundred scientists, engineers, senior military and government officials, as well as the director of the Cosmodrome at Baikonur. Kuzmin was one of those who lost their lives.'

'This is the first I've heard of such an event.'

'That doesn't surprise me. Since when does bad news travel well in this country?' Radin coughs harshly. 'It was a disaster of huge proportions that was wholly avoidable. This rocket was twice as powerful as that which took Gagarin into space. It is the source of power that will take men to the moon well before this decade is out. The consequences of this failure are catastrophic for our space programme, which has been set back by well over a year, probably two. I will not be around to guide it to success. Are you surprised I am fearful of the future?'

'Has there been an investigation into the causes of the accident?'

Radin shakes his head. 'The official report, if such a thing exists, will blame the failure of this launch on mistakes of judgement by Engineer Kuzmin, to which he will have conveniently confessed before he died. That is a complete fabrication. Kuzmin is being made to shoulder the blame because he is unable to answer for himself. If I were not in the state I am, I would defend his memory. He was a good engineer, one of the best. Once more the guilty escape censure while the innocent stand unjustly condemned.'

The effort of speaking is visibly exhausting Radin. He slumps forward, his chin on his chest, his eyes closed, all his energies concentrated on the relentless need to finish what he has so carefully prepared.

'Kuzmin knew that the level of risk had long passed any point I would have considered acceptable. Had I known then what I know now, I would have delayed the launch, probably by weeks. But he and his team, all experienced professionals, did nothing. *Why?* That is the question to which we must find the answer. They could not come to me because I was in hospital in Moscow. They appear not to have raised their concerns with Ulansky. Was it because they knew the only voices he would listen to were his political masters in Moscow, who have no understanding of the processes of scientific development? Ulansky paid for his ignorance by dying in the disaster, but that does nothing to restore the balance. He should never have been there in the first place. For all I know, his successor may be equally inept.'

Radin falters. His mouth opens but no words come. He

looks momentarily panic-stricken, as if he has lost the power of speech. Then his faltering voice returns.

'How many times have good men known the truth and failed to act because they were afraid? How many times have men with no talent risen up our hierarchy of power to positions for which they are hopelessly ill-equipped? Answer those questions honestly and you will know how far we have allowed ourselves to be corrupted.'

Is this the madness of the dying who, as they slip beyond the sanctions of the reach of the world, no longer have any need of caution? Or is Viktor seeing the truth with the sharp clarity of a mind no longer troubled by the daily struggles of life?

'If we conceal what we know to be true because we are afraid to declare it,' Viktor is saying, 'then we are allowing self-deception to threaten our present and our future. We live and breathe lies because we are too tired, too cynical or too fearful to do otherwise. If lies are all we teach our children, then we will perpetuate the cycle. Where are the men and women with the courage to tell us what we know in our hearts to be true, that if we are to avoid disasters like the one I witnessed, we must change our ways or we will destroy ourselves?'

'Have you had a good talk, Professor?' The nurse, a smiling, motherly woman, has returned.

'My friend is tired of my ramblings, nurse. He has been waiting impatiently for your arrival.'

'You've been out in the sun long enough.' She stands behind the wheelchair and turns it towards the house. 'Time for your rest.'

'I will have long enough to rest when I am dead.'

'What nonsense,' the nurse says. 'You're not to talk like that. We'll have you back on your feet in no time.'

'We will not meet again, Andrei.' Radin extends his hand in a gesture of farewell. 'Goodbye, my friend. Goodbye. I have enjoyed our friendship. Remember my words when I am gone.'

For one brief moment, their fingers touch.

2

If Kate has slept at all, she is unaware of it. She has long ago lost count of the number of times she has looked at her watch. It is now ten past two. In twelve hours, she calculates, she will be on a plane, Moscow will be disappearing in the September haze and with it a whole year of her life will come abruptly to an end. It is hardly credible that by the evening of this day, whose dawn will shortly appear, she will be back at home in York, and the time she had fought so hard for will be no more than memories, and with each day that passes those memories will fade.

The body beside hers stirs, mutters a few incomprehensible words and turns over. She looks at his face, his pale skin, the blue veins on his closed eyelids, his fair hair that never behaves, the soft lobes of his ears. In her mind she sees them together at the departure gate, clinging to each other, holding on to that last warmth of contact before the terrible winter of parting, saying the only words that can offer any comfort – their lives are bound together for ever, their love is indissoluble, it will overcome any barrier that tries to keep them apart – distance, time, even the power of political ideology. Their love will never die, they will tell each other again and again in those last desperate seconds. *It will never ever die.*

Whatever she may say to convince herself now, she knows that the moment she says goodbye her heart will break and her life will be over.

*

'Moscow? I'm not sure I like that idea, Kate.'

That was where it had begun, in York, almost eighteen months ago. Her father had been dubious about the notion of Kate studying in Moscow, just as he had once been dubious about Kate leaving the local grammar school and enrolling in the Northern Musical Academy. Other people's children played musical instruments, but their ambitions went as far as a place in the school orchestra. None of them wanted to be a professional musician. Why should his daughter be different to other girls her age? What was so special about Kate? Over a lifetime Dick Buchanan had developed the habit of opposing what he couldn't understand and Moscow, like his daughter's musical ability, was well beyond the limits of his comprehension.

'I wouldn't go there unless I was pushed,' he said gloomily, in the hope that his response might put her off. He was afraid to oppose her wishes more openly. 'And it would have to be a mighty hard shove even to get me to think about it.'

The Moscow Conservatoire was superior to any similar music school in the West, Kate's teachers at the Academy had argued patiently on her behalf, after a tearful interview with Kate, who had made them well aware of the obstacles she faced at home. The closed society of Stalin's time was long gone, they added, in an effort to gain Mr Buchanan's support for their star pupil. The Soviet Union was beginning to open up. Western pupils were welcomed at the Conservatoire. Yevgeny Vinogradoff, who had heard Kate play in London and had expressed his wish that she become his pupil, was one of the leading cellists of the younger generation. He taught only a few specially chosen students each year. To be invited to become his pupil was a rare honour, a genuine recognition of Kate's talent. It was an opportunity she couldn't let pass, not if she was serious about her ambition to play professionally.

'It's not the teachers I'm against, I am sure Mr Vinogradoff knows what he's doing,' her father told Kate. 'It's the location. Moscow's a bloody awful place.'

'Not if you aren't Russian,' Kate had replied, her optimism invented that moment in response to her father's ignorance of a city she knew he had never visited, only imagined with his prejudiced eye. 'Anyway, I won't be away for long, just a few months, less than a year.'

Wasn't anything bearable for a year, particularly if you were working with a musician as outstanding as Vinogradoff?

The argument had ground on during the spring and early summer, Kate sticking single-mindedly to her wish to go to Moscow. In the end her father had relented because he didn't want to hinder the development of an ability he found so difficult to understand but of which secretly he was proud. It was unlikely, he maintained to her teachers when she was out of earshot, that his daughter would be good enough to become a concert performer, but if her heart was set upon it, then he didn't want to be the one to oppose her. Better she find out the hard way that she wasn't up to it.

'If you don't like Moscow,' he said after telling her of his change of mind, 'you can always pack it in and come home.'

Later, as they said goodbye at the airport, he had briefly held her hand and said: 'I shall miss you, Kate. Take care of yourself.'

It was the closest he had come since her mother had died to expressing affection for her, and she had tears in her eyes as she boarded the aircraft.

*

Ten to three. Kate turns over restlessly, the sheet tangled and uncomfortable.

If the man I love is in Moscow, her night mind suddenly proposes, then I should follow my heart and stay here with him.

Her more rational self, caught unawares by this unexpected idea, takes time to regain control. She has promised her father she will return home. There is no escaping that obligation. Her visa will run out soon. To pretend she could have a life here is self-deception, if not madness. The authorities will never let her stay, however hard she pleads. There is no more stony heart than the bureaucrat acting under instructions that allow no deviations from the rulebook, and in Moscow there are regiments of such heartless men and women. She dries her eyes on the corner of the sheet.

No, she must count herself lucky that in this year that is almost over she has discovered the love that will sustain her all her life. She will celebrate it in every note she plays, every concert she gives. She will dedicate every hour of practice to this man who is sleeping beside her. Every day her music will call to him across space and time and somehow – how? – he will hear her message. Even if she cannot speak to him or touch him, he will hear in the sound of her cello that she loves him still, loves him always. She will work tirelessly so that they can be together, even if only fleetingly for a day or two in some foreign city. Better a life of brief moments of intense happiness than to live without love.

In the darkness he reaches out and holds her. Her tears spill over onto his shoulder.

'Don't cry,' he says. 'Please don't cry.'

The tumult in her mind means she is unable to hear a word.

*

Moscow, she imagines as the plane lumbers heavily out of Heathrow Airport on a rainswept September morning and sets its course east, will be a dark and hostile city. The thought fills her with anxiety. She has in her bag a guide to the city that she has not dared look at, an unopened Russian phrasebook and a potted explanation of Marxist-Leninism, whose first page she has found incomprehensible. What the rest is like she daren't imagine. But she has brought them with her none the less. As the plane bumps its way through the last ragged edges of cloud and levels out, she stares at the brightest of blue skies, her preconceptions of the country she is heading for nourished by familiar images from films she has seen, books she has read, ideas she has accumulated from newspapers and the radio.

Will the buildings be ugly concrete boxes so huge that the streets are always cast in shadow? Will there be signs of industrialisation everywhere, vast factories, chimneys belching smoke, the boom and roar of the thunderous march of Soviet heavy industry? Will she see on all the buildings brightly coloured posters illustrating happy, smiling workers milling steel or digging coal miles underground? Fulfilment in the Soviet Union is derived from finding one's true identity through working for the great process of building a socialist state. What is good for the masses is good for the individual. She has learned that much, at least. Will the people walk by in the street, eyes averted, the women's heads covered in faded scarves, their children pale and subdued, a population walking on tiptoe, under the vigilant eye of the KGB, who watch aggressively for signs of errant behaviour that betray the malign intentions of the enemies of the state?

Sheremetevo Airport, an ugly building rising up out of the dusk as the plane taxies towards it, confirms her fears. It is a cliché of communist architecture, just what she has been expecting. An army officer comes on board the plane to collect passports – she feels immediately nervous giving up, even for a short time, the only proof of her identity. The officer senses her reluctance and snatches her passport from her. His angry expression makes Kate feel she has already committed some crime by wishing to enter the country. Her anxiety mounts.

Once through customs, her instructions are to look for a man holding a placard with her name on it. Nervously she searches the jostling crowd in the arrivals hall. Why do they stare at her so? Not many names are being held up – the plane was half-empty – but not one of them is hers. Has she been forgotten? What will she do if she cannot find him? Eventually she spots a piratical figure with a black beard and moustache, a cigarette stuck to his lips. He carries a small card on which someone has spelled her name incorrectly. He looks hopefully in her direction. Can she trust him? She has a sudden vision of being kidnapped, taken gagged and bound to an apartment in Moscow where she is drugged and forced to become the mistress of a bloated drunken communist official more than twice her age. For a moment she is paralysed, unable to move. She takes control of herself again and follows the pirate to the car. He neither smiles nor speaks English. She tries her elementary Russian but he chooses not to understand. It is growing dark, and the night air stings her cheeks with cold. Autumn in Moscow is already well advanced.

He drives her to the students' hostel in Malaya Gruzinskaya Street. The streets are too dimly lit to see much. Moscow under the cover of night retains its mystery. The morning will reveal it in all its expected awfulness. She is met by a Czech girl, Pryska, with limited English who has been deputed to show her round. She goes to bed that night in a room she will share with another student, a singer from Volgorod called Natasha who has not yet arrived, with her suitcases unpacked, her clothes hanging in the wardrobe leaving, she hopes, enough space for her companion. She lies in an unfamiliar bed, exhausted by her fears but still sleepless, wondering why she agreed to come here. Her father was right. Why did she listen to the siren voices of her teachers? She hears the noise of other students talking late into the night. Someone plays a piano. She is disturbed by sudden laughter. She sleeps uneasily. The fearful city inhabits her dreams. She is miserable and alone; her passport lost, she is unable ever to return home. She has got what she wanted but she is not sure of the wisdom of her decision.

The following day she is collected by the same unsmiling driver, still smoking what looks like the same cigarette. She trusts him now and greets him with a smile that is not returned. The morning is clear, the light sharp and the cold has gone. Her journey takes her through tree-lined boule-vards. The leaves are already on the turn. How many trees there are, and parks: so much more green than she had expected, though she is surprised by the lack of flowers. Where are the brutal buildings, the huge posters, the dark streets deprived of sunlight, the smoking factories she expected? The Moscow that she sees is unexpectedly a nineteenth-century city: there are very few cars in its wide streets. Occasionally she sees a gigantic lorry rumbling its way along the enormous highways of the city, or a black official car racing down the central reservation. A number of buildings are topped by an illuminated star; on others a hammer and sickle have been carved out of stone or made in brick, or a red flag hangs limply in the warm air. In the middle distance she spots three tall chimneys, painted in thick red and white stripes, gushing white smoke. There are no other signs of Soviet industry close by.

Suddenly she passes the ancient citadel on its hill, the Kremlin with its dazzling golden domes, its flags and stars, surrounded by its blood-red wall of swallowtail battlements looking out over the Moscow River. In the months that follow she will come to know these buildings that as yet have no name: the Trinity Tower, the Palace of Congresses, the State Armoury, the Patriarch's Palace, the Cathedral of the Assumption, and beyond, the Mausoleum in Red Square where Lenin and Stalin are buried. Her spirits rise. It is a magical vision, and she can imagine music being played inside these walls.

'Kremlin,' her driver says, pointing. It is the first word he has spoken to her. Still there is no smile.

Vinogradoff is as she remembered him, tall, grinning and dressed in a baggy black suit at least one size too big. He comes out to greet her on the steps of the Conservatoire. He holds out his arms and kisses her warmly on both cheeks.

'Welcome,' he says in English. 'We are so pleased you are here. This is a great day for all of us.'

He applauds her suddenly and a few others join in. A young

23

student, a girl her own age, comes forward and presents her with a bouquet of flowers. Vinogradoff grins possessively, puts his arm through hers and leads her into the Conservatoire. She hears a singer practising her scales. Someone is playing a violin. This is familiar territory. She is back in a world she knows. She feels at home. Her Moscow adventure has begun.

3

Gerard Pountney, ex-Foreign Office lackey, ex-leader writer on a national daily, briefly ex-Moscow correspondent for the same newspaper, sits alone in front of the editing machine and watches his reincarnation on the monitor. His former lives have mercifully been jettisoned into a past that, with each day that passes, slips ever further into a memory that can be harmlessly suppressed. On the screen he sees a reinvented and revitalised version of himself, and he congratulates himself on his good fortune. He experiences a pleasing glow of satisfaction.

'Behind me,' his screen image is saying, 'is the famous Brandenburg Gate that separates East from West in the divided city of Berlin. On one side is the Kurfürstendamm, a street of well-stocked shops, cafés full of people, cars, bicycles, a street teeming with life as we in the West know it. Plenty to buy, plenty to eat, plenty to do. Over there is the Unter den Linden, its buildings mostly empty, many still carrying the unrepaired scars of a war that ended more than fifteen years ago. Its streets have few shops or cafés, and fewer people. It presents a desolate spectacle. This is where East meets West, and it is not a happy encounter.'

The camera, travelling secretly in a car along the eastern sector of the city, records the empty streets, the uncared-for buildings blackened with age, fleetingly picks up huge and brightly painted posters with incongruous images of healthy young men and women striding towards the 'radiant future' of socialism, their example exhorting the local population to a life of ever greater dedication and sacrifice. It is a forlorn message playing to an empty house.

'Is this the socialist paradise that the posters proclaim? Is this the promised communist Utopia? Well, the citizens of the German Democratic Republic don't think so. They give their verdict each day by crossing the border to the West in their thousands, never to return. We are witnessing a massive migration. On this evidence alone, capitalism and democracy are an irresistible combination.'

Pountney is walking down the Kurfürstendamm now, and the camera retreats in front of him. 'Who are these people who are voting with their feet? They are drawn from the entire spectrum of East German society: scientists, teachers, doctors, labourers, engineers, economists, accountants, students, the very people on whom a modern economy depends. These men and women are the human resources East Germany can ill afford to lose. Between 1949 and today, nearly two million people have migrated west from the GDR. Nearly two hundred thousand have left in the last year alone. That is why the streets are empty, and why the national economy underperforms. The consequences of this stunning rejection of communism for the future of East Germany are grim.'

The camera sweeps past a line at the Marienfeld Camp in West Berlin, showing people of all ages, complete families in some cases, staring steadfastly into the lens, their patient expressions betraying none of their fears. They are in transit between one world and another. Their futures are blank sheets waiting to be filled with the hopes and dreams that drove them to gamble with their lives escaping from the GDR and which, for the present, they dare not allow themselves to revive. While they have no official identity, their lives are suspended. They are powerless to do anything but wait, the fate of refugees everywhere.

'These people are typical of those who have fled. Young

and old alike, disillusioned by the communist experiment, unable to see a clear future for themselves or their families, all now seek a better life in the West.'

He is standing in front of the crowd, talking to the camera once more. 'Imagine the agony of taking the decision to leave your roots and your possessions, in some cases elderly members of your family whom you may never see again, a decision based on the hope that what awaits you can surely be no worse than what you have left behind and will probably be much better. These people at this camp represent two million such decisions. For the courage of those decisions they must command our respect.'

The angle changes. The camera looks over Pountney's shoulder at a panorama of Berlin.

'If that is the personal story, what about the political? The people are demanding a better standard of living from their government. They will wait no longer. They want it now. That is precisely what East Germany's command economy is unable to deliver. Unless the East German authorities can stop this exodus of people on whose skills their future must be based, the situation can only get worse.'

He turns to the camera. 'The propaganda has failed. The poster platitudes urging you to sacrifice the present in return for the promise of a better future are no longer believed. How long before the GDR acts? Can the authorities close the border? Can those who want to leave be stopped by force? These are the questions preoccupying both the East and the West. The answers, when they come, could prove dangerous for us all.'

The programme's theme music rises as the image of Gerry Pountney fades under the closing credits. He stretches in his chair. Not bad. Not bad at all, even though he says it himself. He looks at his watch. Time for lunch. A good morning's work. He smiles to himself. He is indeed a fortunate man.

Second
Helpings

Simon
Brown

by the author of
Playing off the Roof
& Other Stories
"Bristles with anecdote, good
humour and vividly drawn
vignettes" – THE TIMES

Dear Jennie

This may not be your kind
of look at all! If not, give
it to Philip.

Much love

Frank

1 May 2021

Second Helpings
Simon Brown

ISBN 978 1 8383036 1 7
15 February 2021 | £18 | 176 pages
www.marblehillpublishers.co.uk

MARBLE
HILL

4

'I have to tell the committee that I'm not happy with the choice of Andrei Berlin,' Bill Gant said, making his first contribution to the afternoon's discussion. 'I'm not disputing his academic reputation. That, as we all know, is well established. It's simply that I find myself unable to shift the feeling that he's not the right man.'

Until his intervention, Marion Blackwell had assumed Bill Gant's brooding silence signalled assent, and that the meeting was going her way. After all, he'd supported her proposal when they'd talked about it last Wednesday, and she'd had no reason to suppose he'd shift his position in the days that followed. His sudden change of heart was unexpected and the damage to her case potentially great.

'You were in favour when we talked before, Bill. What's changed your mind?'

The hint of intimacy in her reference to a previous conversation was a slip that Michael Scott's sensitive antennae would not miss. He gave her a sidelong look. She must be more careful in future. Especially where Bill was concerned.

'When all's said and done, the man's a communist.' Gant was looking down at the table. Was he deliberately avoiding catching her eye? 'He stands for everything we oppose. That's what I'm wrestling with. Berlin's a risky choice.'

'Isn't that the point?' Marion addressed her appeal to the other members of the committee. 'We want to revive these lectures, not send them to an early grave, which is where they'll end up if we don't do something about them. Let's have a speaker who'll stir up a bit of controversy. Let's have someone whose ideas will make us sit up and test our own beliefs. Isn't that why we're all here? To kick some life into this event?'

'Bravo, Marion.' Michael Scott smiled mockingly at her. 'Very passionate, dear. Very con brio.'

She'd known all along that Michael Scott would be difficult. She hadn't expected him to take pleasure in her discomfort. She felt herself colouring. Her neck always went red and blotchy when she was angry. She should have worn a scarf with her shirt.

'Am I alone in being sceptical of his academic distinction?' Scott continued. 'I see it as a smokescreen intended to obscure the fact that Berlin is a loyal apologist for a vile regime. We're fooling ourselves if we imagine his hands are clean.'

'How can you say that, Michael? Berlin's an academic with a growing reputation who's not regarded as an apologist for anyone.'

'A successful historian in the Soviet Union who is *not* in thrall to the regime is a paradox, Marion, and as you know better than most, having attended my lectures when you were an undergraduate, paradox became a casualty of Soviet society in 1917 along with irony, compassion, freedom of expression, truth and so many other attributes of the civilised world that Lenin took exception to. Bill's got it right for once. Berlin is as much a part of that obnoxious regime as the head of the KGB or the governor of one of their slave camps. Why should we invite a spokesman for a political system we openly condemn and provide him with a platform to preach Bolshevism to our impressionable young? It's asking for trouble.'

Her scheme was disintegrating before her eyes. It wasn't difficult to do the mathematics. Two definite votes against. She had to get Bill to change his mind or her position was desperate. Her candidate would be voted out.

'You're keeping your counsel close to your chest, Peter,' the chairman said, turning to Peter Chadwick. 'Where do you stand on this issue?'

Chadwick drained his cup of tea with a theatrical gesture. She didn't know him well enough to be sure of his support. He was an elusive man, a medievalist, with a couple of good books to his name. Their paths had hardly crossed. Where he stood on the Berlin issue was hard to predict.

'Michael's theory about contaminating the young doesn't hold water for a moment,' Chadwick replied dismissively. 'I think we can trust our pupils to know their own minds and judge Berlin accordingly.'

He was on her side. She could have kissed him for it. Michael Scott was furious. He leaned across the table in his anxiety to put Chadwick right.

'If you'd been at this university as many years as I have, Peter, you wouldn't fall into the trap of making a generalisation that can be so easily refuted. The point to remember about the young is that that is precisely what they are. To be young is by definition to lack judgement. Take them too close to the fire and they will always burn themselves.'

'Marion's position is valid, Michael,' Chadwick replied. Beneath his unemotional demeanour, she sensed his deep dislike of Scott. 'We must either have a speaker who'll put the Blake-Thomas lectures back on their feet, or we must drop this event from the university calendar, dissolve this committee and call it a day. Berlin's a courageous choice and I commend Marion for proposing him. I don't agree with his ideas but that doesn't mean he shouldn't be heard. Surely we're all strong enough to cope with a challenge to our beliefs, particularly from a Marxist historian? You make it sound as if we'd crumble after a paragraph, Michael. I can only assume you're being mischievous.'

'Bill?' The chairman turned to Gant. Marion could tell from Gant's expression that he hadn't been swayed by Chadwick's arguments. Her heart sank.

'Nothing I've heard makes me want to change my mind,' Gant said nervously.

'I think we know where you stand, Michael.'

'I've said all I need to say, Chairman.'

They were split down the middle. Two for, two against. The casting vote would go to Eastman as chairman. This was an outcome she hadn't banked on. Well, if you're going to go down, better to go down fighting.

'Andrei Berlin would be a splendid choice,' she said, addressing her remarks to Professor Eastman. 'Michael and Bill are showing a great lack of imagination. I think we'd find undergraduates queuing all the way up Mill Lane to get in to hear him. Why not create a little controversy for once? Why not challenge a few beliefs? Where's the harm in that? Perhaps some of us have become too comfortable in our habits of thought' – this looking at Michael Scott – 'and a bit of stirring up might be good for the system.'

Bill wouldn't like that, but so what? She'd show him she wasn't going to be crushed by the reactionary opinions of men like Michael Scott.

'Marion's right,' Chadwick said. He was doing his best to get Eastman into Marion's camp. 'It would do the Department good to have such a controversial speaker. Show the world that historians are not all deaf to contemporary issues.'

The clock in First Court struck four. Eastman reached for the leather-bound minute book which lay in front of him. He opened it and flicked through the pages. Marion knew he was looking for the Articles of Association.

'Well, Chairman,' Michael Scott said sourly, 'it looks as if the future of the Blake-Thomas lectures lies in your hands. What do you say to that?'

Professor Eastman was approaching eighty. He remained chairman of the committee because he was the last surviving member of the university to have known Blake-Thomas's daughters. They had lived in spinsterly splendour in a sandstone mansion in Madingley Road, devotedly protecting their father's reputation. They had entrusted their father's bequest to Eastman's care because, before his death more than fifty years ago, Blake-Thomas had declared that the then youthful Eastman was the best historian of his generation, which meant he was nominating Eastman as his heir. Time had not been kind to Blake-Thomas's approach to social history, nor to Eastman's reputation. He was now regarded as unfashionable. Therefore hardly likely to support Berlin. Marion felt depressed.

Eastman took his pipe out of his mouth and looked thoughtful.

'The Blake-Thomas lectures are an important platform from which over the years men of all creeds and beliefs have spoken their mind. In this university we are rightly proud of our traditions of independence of thought and freedom of speech. We have the intellectual courage to listen to unfamiliar arguments with an open mind, submit them to rigorous scrutiny and to judge them on their merits. I've followed your positions with great care this afternoon. It cannot be denied that Berlin is a Marxist, nor that he is one of the leading younger historians in the Soviet Union. His work is coloured by the dubious philosophy, not to say dogma, of a regime to which we are totally opposed. Although I don't agree with much of it, I consider Dr Berlin's *Legacies of History* to be a major interpretative work, and I am not alone in my verdict.'

He paused for moment, drawing as much drama as he could out of the situation.

'I am persuaded that Berlin is a serious candidate. Asking him to speak is in the true Blake-Thomas tradition. Therefore I cast my vote, which under Article Twelve of the Rules and Regulations I am constitutionally allowed to do' – here he held up in full view of the committee the minute book – 'in support of Marion Blackwell and her candidate, Andrei Berlin.' He looked round the table, pleased with his judgement. 'And that, I think, takes care of the business of the day, does it not?'

1

Berlin sat enclosed in a pool of light cast by the reading lamp on his desk, his mind floating in an unfamiliar world of acronyms, technical terms and baffling scientific calculations.

Engineer Kuzmin had painstakingly assembled information on each incident that had occurred in the construction of Radin's rocket: spring clips that did not spring, hatches that did not close, sealants that did not seal, screws that did not fit flush as they were designed to do, engine clips that broke under stress. He had logged every fault, the date and time of its discovery; he had described the nature of each malfunction and marked the failure of each test; he had recorded estimates of the time needed for repairs or the process necessary to get the equipment to work. He gave the dates for his submission of each of many reports detailing his findings.

Reports of these malfunctions, Kuzmin wrote, had been persistently ignored by senior officials in Baikonur. Requests for re-testing when vital components had failed were rejected so often that his staff no longer considered such requests worth making. Repeated appeals to extend the launch schedule to allow more time for the completion of essential tasks had been dismissed out of hand. The Ministry in Moscow had issued its instruction. The launch was to take place on time as planned. Kuzmin's fear was that it would be a disaster.

Even in Kuzmin's flat scientific style, Berlin could trace his deep dejection at a situation over whose solution he could have no influence. His response was mirrored by his account of the reaction of his staff, their initial concerns rapidly turning to incredulity at the indifference of those in authority to what they reported, then despair as the list of untended faults grew larger, and finally resignation at the impossibility of doing what they knew needed to be done. What was the point of reporting anything? Kuzmin asked helplessly, when the pleas of his team went unanswered because no one in authority was prepared to listen to voices from below, except to damn them unjustly as reactionary saboteurs.

'Unless some action is taken to reinstate essential control procedures and recognise the difficulties of working on new technologies that cannot always be made to perform faultlessly on time,' he warned finally, 'and unless we allow ourselves more time for testing, we will put our space programme in jeopardy. We will suffer disasters in future as we have done in the past, and we will lose our lead in space technology to the Americans.'

He was writing this account solely for the Chief Designer, who, he knew, would be disheartened by the evidence of the decline in standards that had set in so quickly since his ill-health had taken him away from Baikonur. Had he still been present, Kuzmin was sure that none of this would have happened. The new directorate appeared to have little understanding of or sympathy for the complexities of building a rocket on this scale. In desperation, Kuzmin was begging Radin to use his influence to intervene to ensure that the launch was postponed until every detail had been fixed.

Berlin admired the man's courage. Such outspoken remarks were rare. No wonder he had written the report only for Radin. Who else would believe him? It was a bitter irony that the disaster he had predicted had taken his life.

Only one mystery remained. Why had Radin given him this report? Information of this kind was an unwelcome gift. It could prove dangerous to know too much. A warning bell rang in Berlin's head. He may have known Radin for years, he may have loved him like a father, but he must still be careful. Viktor did nothing without a purpose. Even on his deathbed he was capable of ensnaring Berlin in some hare-brained scheme.

Where are the voices of truth, Viktor had asked, *the men and women with the courage to tell us what we know in our hearts to be true?* If Viktor was appealing to some better self that he imagined lived within him, then he was mistaken. Berlin was a historian. Historians recorded events, analysed motives, made judgements, debated their importance. They were not actors in their own drama.

That was a concept Viktor could never understand because his life was a perpetual drama and he was its leading player. He was driven by a vision that never released him from its grasp. His imagination might soar to the stars but it never stretched far enough to accept the plain fact that not everyone was like him – had it done so, Berlin believed, his achievements would have been much less. If Viktor was appealing to him to do something, he had chosen the wrong man. Berlin felt relieved. He could not respond because he had no ability to do so. Action lay outside his competence. Therefore he should feel no guilt for ignoring a dying man's appeal. He was off the hook.

2

At first Kate had hated Moscow. In those early days, a week in that gloomy, heartless city seemed an eternity, a year a sentence without reprieve, even though the Moscow she found was not what she had expected. The heart of the city was not ugly concrete blocks as she'd imagined: its buildings were well proportioned, there were wide avenues and parks, churches, museums and libraries. The metro stations were like underground temples. What depressed her was the neglect, the disrepair, the tawdriness of the place. Was she the only one who longed for restoration and a coat of paint? Did the citizens of Moscow really need the ever-present icons of Stalin and Lenin and the ubiquitous red stars perched on the top of building after building to remind them they lived in the Soviet Republic? Wouldn't they respond to other colours in their lives, other icons?

If the path to socialism brought universal benefits, why were there daily queues of women and old people outside the shops? Why were there so few goods for sale? One week you might be able to buy milk but not butter, the next some scraggy meat but no vegetables. And fruit – how infrequently she found any fruit. She was not surprised by the sad demeanour of the people in the street, but why were they reluctant to look you in the eye – what did they think she might do to them? Why were their clothes so shabby, their skin so pallid? When she went on the tram, why did the old women point at her blonde hair and move away? In her letters home she concealed her unhappiness from her father. Every day she wondered how she would see out the month, let alone the year.

*

'That wasn't right. I'm sorry.' Kate breaks off before he can say anything, her voice petulant and troubled. 'I'll play it again.'

She is playing the second movement of Dvořák's Cello Concerto. She knows she should let Vinogradoff comment on her performance but in her irritation at the quality of her playing she can't help herself. Better that she should tell him she knows she hasn't got it right than let him assume she thinks any different. She goes back a couple of bars and repeats the phrase, but the effect is no better. Despondently, she waits for his comment. She is sure it will be critical.

'The mistake was in your head, Kate. You play fine the first time. Sometimes, I think you are hard on yourself without reason.'

Her lessons with Vinogradoff take place each week either

alone in his cramped apartment, where they are now, or with other students at the Conservatoire. To her surprise he refuses to play the cello with her. He prefers to make his points on the piano.

'If I play for you on the cello,' he explained at their first lesson, 'perhaps I will then hear myself in your performance. That is not why you are here, is it?'

Just as well, she thinks. I can copy anything you do, I can mimic you to perfection. One night in her third week at Malaya Gruzinskaya Street she had drunk more than she should have and made the other students laugh by giving a 'Vinogradoff performance'. Not only had she played like him, but she had reproduced his physical mannerisms as well, the nervous pull at the lips, the way he bowed forward over the instrument one moment and then leaned away from it the next. Afterwards, she was ashamed of what she'd done, and she hoped it would never get back to Vinogradoff. But it had made her life a little easier, and had diminished the suspicion with which the other Eastern Bloc students regarded her.

'Just for an evening,' she wrote to her father, remembering the laughter and applause, 'the ice between us seemed to thaw a little.'

'I don't seem able to make it sound the way I hear it in my head.'

The admission is made with more passion than she has intended. Will he understand her irritation with her own performance? She is desperate to show him what she is capable of. Why can't she feel at ease in his presence? In the few weeks since her arrival in Moscow, Vinogradoff has not heard her play as he did when he came to London. Something is lacking and it frustrates her, making her lose confidence. She blames this on the strange city she has chosen to study in, so very different to anything she has encountered before.

'You are trying too hard to show us what you can do, Kate,' he tells her in his slow, accented English. 'Please understand, you have nothing to prove. You would not be here if we did not believe that you could become a true musician. Have confidence in yourself. Trust the musicianship you carry inside you. When you play, you must release this gift you have been given so we may all share in it.'

'It is so much harder to play here than at home,' she tells him in a sudden moment of confession. In this alien city, the familiar certainties of her life have deserted her. Her mind is permanently in turmoil.

'It never ceases to be hard for any of us,' Vinogradoff says, assuming her comment is philosophical. 'You must work at the talent you have. You are among friends here. That is important. We are your musical friends.' He smiles encouragingly at her. 'Do you feel ready to play this at your recital?'

Each student is encouraged to play in the informal recitals that take place in the Conservatoire every fortnight. So far she has avoided performing before an audience on the grounds that she has not yet settled in. Vinogradoff has endorsed her refusal. She must play only when she feels she is ready. She knows he does not want her to play in public until she has overcome the inhibition he senses in her. This is the first time he has brought up the subject.

'Do you think I should?'

'It's a difficult piece; it demands courage,' he replies. 'Why not show them you are brave enough?'

'I'm not sure I am at the moment,' Kate replies, knowing this isn't the answer he wants. 'My courage seems to be in short supply these days.' Vinogradoff says nothing. He looks at her with his sad, hooded eyes. How she hates to disappoint him. 'May I think about it?'

'Please,' he says, 'think positively. It is an important step.'

Whatever encouragement he gives her, she is not yet the master of this music. Something in it still escapes her. Vinogradoff is right. She must find the courage to play before an audience if she is to win his approval. First, she has to overcome her own fears.

'He was smiling, Gerry.' Julius Bomberg was working himself up into a rage of indignation. 'The bastard was actually *smiling* as he said it.'

They were lunching in the staff canteen. In his passion to express his views, Bomberg had upset his glass of water with a flamboyant wave of his arm. The plate of shepherd's pie that he had hardly touched now appeared to be floating on his tray. He seemed not to notice. He cared little for food and he resented the time it took to eat it. His energies, fuelled by cheroots and his own noxious brew of black coffee, had greater ambitions to satisfy than filling his stomach.

'He wasn't smiling, Julius. He was grimacing.'

'Same thing,' Bomberg said dismissively. 'A colonel in the British Army sat there in front of the camera, cool as you like, and said that if we have to go to war with the Soviets over Berlin, we will do so and damn the consequences.' Bomberg looks for a response but Pountney says nothing. 'You can't deny he said that, can you, Gerry?'

'How can I? It's there on film.'

'The man *wants* to go to war, Gerry. He *wants* to fight. He's typical of the military on both sides. Bursting to get their hands round each other's throats and damn the rest of us. How can you possibly drop something as good as that? You're crazy. You're cutting the best bit.'

When he had shown his film to Bomberg that morning, he had not received the endorsement he expected. He was dismayed to discover Bomberg's determination to make him include the quote from the officer in the British Zone of Berlin. Changing his mind was going to be difficult.

'The context is wrong, Julius. My piece is about economic migration, not the risk of war with the Soviets. How the GDR will survive if this exodus continues. Talking about the likelihood of a conflict is out of place. The quote doesn't fit.'

'Sooner or later their government has to put a stop to this migration. They can't sit back and do nothing while the country empties, can they?' Bomberg was in full flow now, arms flailing, voice loud, caught up in the energy of his own indignation. 'So they swallow Berlin into East Germany. Then what happens? The Western presence in Germany is challenged by the Soviet Union. Threat and counter-threat. Neither side will budge. East and West bid each other up in a war of nerves, each side pours in tanks, troops and high-powered generals, until armed to the teeth they stare at each other across a street in Berlin. Meanwhile, the world holds its breath. Someone sneezes. A trigger is pulled, and within seconds a shooting match begins. Each blames the other for starting the war. By the end of the first day one side threatens to explode a nuclear bomb if the other doesn't pull back. Neither yields an inch. Next day a nuclear bomb is exploded and that's it. There isn't a third day because the world came to an end the day before. In a matter of moments and without thinking about it, a thousand years of European civilisation has been reduced to dust and millions are dead. And this smiling officer says keeping our troops in Berlin is worth the risk of destroying Europe and murdering its citizens. The man's insane.'

'He didn't put it like that, Julius.'

'Tell me I heard it wrong.' Bomberg's mockery was tangible.

'What he said was, "If the Soviet Union denies the Allies their legal access to West Berlin, the West will have to find some way to convince them that on this issue we mean business."'

'Game, set and match,' Bomberg said furiously. 'That's what I'm talking about. The Allies are preparing to go to war over Berlin. Doesn't that terrify you? Doesn't it make you think that maybe you should do something to try to stop it, like draw our audience's attention to what's going on?'

'The man's a soldier, Julius. That's how soldiers think. It's not policy. It's his opinion, which isn't unreasonable given the aggressive behaviour of the Soviets.'

'The way he's talking, Gerry, we could all wake up dead tomorrow and no one would know why. You've got to include that quote.'

'If the situation deteriorates, there'll be plenty of other opportunities to get the military view. We can use this clip then.' His knowledge of Bomberg told him that if you let him bully you once, he'd never leave you alone after that. If you wanted to work with him successfully, you had to defend your corner or be swept away in the storm.

Bomberg was silent. The storm wasn't over, it had temporarily blown itself out.

'Look, hurry up and finish, will you, Gerry?' Bomberg took a cheroot out of his pocket and tore off the cellophane wrapping. He put it in his mouth unlit. 'I want to smoke this thing. We'll carry on upstairs.'

Bomberg was calling time on lunch. Pountney hated eating with him. He'd take a couple of mouthfuls of what was on his plate, and that was that. When he was done, you were done. Pountney pushed his tray aside unfinished. The cod may have seen better days, but the sponge pudding with hot treacle sauce looked enticing. Oh well, too bad.

*

Over the previous decade, Julius Bomberg had made his reputation pushing forward the boundaries of current affairs on television. He was responsible for a number of innovations that were now setting the agenda. If there was a theme to the choice of subjects on his programmes, it was the need to expose the devious strategies the powerful used to conceal the truth from those they governed.

This national obsession with secrecy, Bomberg argued, eyes blazing behind tinted spectacles, suggested that there was something rotten in the vital organs of the government, and his job, *their* job – here fingers stab at Pountney and his colleagues – the *raison d'être* of a current affairs programme like theirs – was to prevent this sickness spreading by telling their audiences what was going on.

'Ignore what sociologists tell you about class distinction in our society, OK? There are only two classes that matter,' he maintained, 'the few who are in the know and the many who aren't. In this country, secrecy divides us even more than wealth or birth. It is the great enemy of democracy, the means by which governments of all colours exploit the governed. Secrecy is an unrecognised crime perpetrated every day against the men and women of this country by those they vote into office. Our task is to oppose by all means within our power the bureaucratic machinery of government that tries to conceal its activities from public scrutiny. Our watchwords must be scepticism, vigilance and persistence. We believe in a transparent society. We're here to show the buggers up for the liars they are. OK?'

Pountney and Julius Bomberg had met on their first day at Cambridge. Their names were painted in white, one above the other, on a black square at the bottom of C staircase in Milton Court. Bomberg J. T. (Julius Timothy, as Pountney discovered) and Pountney G. R. (Gerard Raymond). They had rooms opposite each other, 3a and 3b, on the second landing, though Pountney saw little of his neighbour. Bomberg's life was lived outside the college. If he slept at all – and Pountney had little evidence to suggest that he did – then it was only occasionally and during the hours that others were awake. By the end of their first term, pieces were appearing in *Varsity* under Bomberg's byline.

By the end of his first year he was widely recognised as the thinly disguised author of a regular social column in the undergraduate newspaper in which he reported mockingly on the antics of what he described to Pountney at a rare meeting on their staircase as 'Pitt Club monsters with more money than is good for them'. Those he sought to ridicule saw the appearance of their names in his column as reinforcing their status. They bayed for more. Bomberg's success brought him the notoriety he sought. His ability to put a name in a column gave him a power over his fellow undergraduates that he relished. The scholarship boy from Hackney Downs had successfully created a persona that gave him credentials his background denied him.

'Look, at Cambridge, you can do anything you set your mind to,' he told Pountney as he returned late one evening from the *Varsity* office. 'That's what makes it so intoxicating. I wasn't anybody before I came here. I wasn't breathing. I wasn't alive. Now I can reach for a world I never knew existed and make it mine. It's better than dreaming.'

Pountney watched enviously from the sidelines as Bomberg slipped the moorings of his origins and reinvented himself. If he was to make the same journey (he too had dreamed of Cambridge as the stepping-stone to a new life), he would have to do it in his own way and his own time. It would take much longer, he knew, because he lacked Bomberg's nerve and self-confidence. But with patience and care, he'd get there. He never doubted that. Patience had always been his strength.

Bomberg's ambition tripped up only once. In his third year he ran for President of the Union. It was a step too far. He suffered a humiliating defeat at the hands of a Tory with, he claimed, 'not an original thought in his head but the right connections'. Despite this baggage, or perhaps because of it, his victor ten years later had a safe seat in the Commons. The rejection hurt Bomberg because it told him the place he had engineered in Cambridge society was less secure than he had imagined. For once his dreams had been too heavy for the foundations he had tried so carefully to lay, and without warning they had collapsed.

He took his rejection hard. For a week he hardly left his room. Then, one night, unshaven, his eyes deeply ringed, his hair unkempt and wearing a dressing gown over a pair of old corduroys, he burst into Pountney's room and declared what he would do with the rest of his life.

'Look, Gerry, you go and fly the flag in foreign parts,' he said, knowing that Pountney was trying for the Foreign Office. 'For me, the future's in television. That's the land I'm going to conquer, OK? Then I'll get my own back on the bastards who did for me here.'

Pountney got a first, passed well into the Foreign Office and his own quiet adventure began. Bomberg scraped a third and disappeared from sight. He was last heard of working in television in Manchester or Glasgow – no one knew for sure – producing a children's programme, something to do with glove puppets. He was written off by his enemies as overambitious. 'Shot his bolt at Cambridge. The rest of his life will probably be an anticlimax. All that energy, to end up with puppets. Too bad, isn't it? No wonder he's gone to ground.' Pountney said nothing. He knew better than to underestimate Bomberg. He'd surprise them all yet.

*

By the mid-fifties, Bomberg had graduated from children's puppets to current affairs. The year after Suez – he had now risen to the role of editor of a weekly current affairs programme – he revealed that a group of councillors in a northern city had been lining their pockets for years by taking their cut on local building projects. The accused were put on trial on charges of corruption, convicted and sent to prison. A police investigation prompted by a television programme was the instrument by which justice was finally done. The verdict created headlines. Bomberg had triumphed. The apprentice years of painful obscurity and other humiliations were quickly forgotten. He was back in control, his reputation assured. This time the dream had been built on such solid foundations that it was soaring into the sky. The lesson of his humiliation at Cambridge had been well learned.

Three years later, out of the blue, he contacted Pountney, who by this time had resigned from the Foreign Office over

Suez and was working for a newspaper, having in the interval written a book about the crises of 1956.

'Look, Gerry, I read your book,' he said on the telephone, not bothering to announce himself. It was as if they had spoken to each other only ten days before, not ten years. 'Come and have lunch. I've got a proposition you'll find irresistible, OK?'

They met in a restaurant in Audley Street. Nothing had changed over the years. Julius Bomberg was recognisably the same man he'd known at Cambridge, only more confident, harder, more ambitious.

He handed the menu to Pountney. 'I can't be bothered to read all this. You choose, OK? I'll have whatever you're having, so long as it's not offal.'

They talked briefly of the years since they'd last met. Bomberg questioned Pountney on his resignation from the Foreign Office: 'Getting out was the best thing you ever did, Gerry. You were wasted in that organisation. God knows why they don't abolish it', on his book on the Suez Crisis: 'Not enough anger, Gerry. The writer is still trapped inside the civil servant. You must learn not to be afraid of your feelings so we can know where you stand on issues. Still, I enjoyed it. Who'd imagine Gerry Pountney fighting the establishment?' and on his divorce from Harriet and his new life with Margaret. Bomberg had already been through two wives and was now on to his third: 'I pay more in alimony in a month than most people earn in a year.' Finally Bomberg came round to Pountney's reinvention as a journalist.

'Are you happy in Fleet Street?' Bomberg asked. There was an aggression in his question that unnerved Pountney.

'The newspaper's been good to me, Julius,' he replied, the defiance in his voice a response to Bomberg's unstated challenge. 'I like the people and the job. It's something I do well.'

'I thought the anti-establishment Gerry Pountney was braver than that.'

'Braver than what?' Pountney was bemused.

'Look, you resigned from the Foreign Office because you thought their policy towards Nasser and his henchmen was wrong at a time when we should have been helping the Hungarians. You wrote a book to give more permanent form to your arguments. Does it end there? Has Gerry Pountney, harrier of those more powerful than himself, shot his bolt? Is he a one-hit wonder? Does he retreat under the skirts of a newspaper whose leaders read like a government press release? Come on, Gerry. You're worth more than that, aren't you?'

Had Bomberg suggested lunch so he could attack him for accepting a job that had nothing to do with him? The mystery about the invitation deepened.

'Look at it another way, Gerry,' Bomberg continued. 'Print's finished, OK? Hot metal, thundering presses, restrictive practices and out-of-control unions – they've had their day, thank God, and not before time. The newspaper industry has begun its fatal slide to a watery grave and it's not worth saving. Ten years from now there won't be a newspaper business to speak of. When the ship is sinking, my advice is take to the lifeboats fast.'

'The ship seemed pretty buoyant when I left it an hour ago.'

'Remember what I told you all those years ago, Gerry? I was right then and I'm right now, OK? The future's in television. Come and join the future. Come and work with me.'

Mystery solved. Lunch was a job offer. Julius was handling the subject with all the sensitivity of a charging bull.

'I don't need a lifebelt, Julius. I'm quite happy where I am.'

'Look, I'm talking to you from the future. I'm offering you the chance to sail in a ship which is not only seaworthy in every department but is now beginning to get up speed and make waves.' He paused for a moment to draw breath. 'I want a new kind of presenter, Gerry. I want a journalist with

46

experience of foreign affairs who can work in front of a camera, OK? You've been overseas, haven't you?'

'Moscow. For a few months. That's all.'

'Good enough. You'd fit the bill as well as anyone.' Bomberg lit a cheroot and contemplated Pountney from behind a cloud of blue smoke. 'But I get the impression you despise our brave new world. I'm right about that too, aren't I?'

'How can I despise what I don't know?'

'Show me a more self-satisfied organisation than a national newspaper.' Bomberg laughed. 'Most journalists I know would bite my hand off to come and work in television. They ring up every day begging for jobs. What's holding you back?'

'You think I bought the wrong ticket. I'm not convinced I did.'

'The cosy confidence of Fleet Street. How I hate it. All right, I can take that argument head-on. Is television a serious medium? Can it deal with news, facts, current affairs? You may think the jury's still out on that one. I maintain there's no case to be answered. Television can do the job a damn sight better than most newspapers, and a damn sight quicker too. That's the point, OK? The speed of news-gathering and broadcasting will change the world and put newspapers out of business. The power of television as a popular medium is awe-inspiring. Gerry, come and make your name with the rest of us as we pioneer this extraordinary revolution.'

*

'Coffee?' Bomberg was already at the machine, pouring himself a cup of what was known at the Centre as Bomberg's 'black poison'.

'No thanks.' Last time he'd drunk Bomberg's coffee, he'd felt ill for days.

The office was a cramped and chaotic affair. Bomberg himself, a small, unprepossessing man with a sallow pock-marked face and a shock of stiff black hair beginning to grey, sat in the only armchair, an ancient cane-backed affair, out of keeping in scale and style with the rest of the office, but to which he was devoted because, he said, it was all he had inherited from his much-loved great-aunt Bella. Pountney sat in a chrome and canvas contraption, a design that was as out of date as it was uncomfortable. He had to press his outstretched feet against the table leg to prevent himself pitching onto the floor. He wondered if designers ever sat in the chairs they created.

'OK. Let's look at that interview again.' Bomberg wasn't going to give up without a fight. He set the machine and sat back to watch.

The short extract began with a shot of a uniformed colonel in the British Occupation Force replying to Pountney's question about the future of the Allied presence in West Germany.

'The Soviets are threatening to change the status of West Berlin by merging it with the German Democratic Republic. That would mean the Allies would be able to enter Berlin only with East German permission. Such a situation is wholly unacceptable. Not surprisingly, we would interpret such a move as an aggressive act. If we don't oppose the Soviets on issues as fundamental as this, we will be pushed out of Berlin and possibly out of Germany. If we are to stop the Soviets having their way, we must convince them that on this issue we mean business.'

'You mean stop them by force,' Pountney asked from behind the camera.

'If we have to, yes.'

The camera held the officer's face for a moment. Was he smiling? Certainly not, Pountney concluded. He was showing the proper distaste for the possibility of conflict. Then he was gone, and Pountney once more filled the screen. He looked troubled, perplexed even. He held the microphone in front of him like a torch.

'In a few weeks or less, the Soviets say, they will bring their sector of Berlin under GDR rule. The West cannot accept such a move without destroying its own position. In America and the Soviet Union, military budgets are suddenly being substantially increased, the first moves in the inevitable game of political brinkmanship that may bring the world ever closer to an East–West confrontation. Suddenly we are hearing talk of war. The question is, now we've got on this treadmill, how do we get off again?'

The clip ended. Pountney turned off the monitor.

'That was a smile, no question,' Bomberg said excitedly. 'The man was enjoying himself. That's what I object to. The British Army threatening war on the Soviet Union off its own bat is news so good that we've got to keep it in. You can't possibly cut it out, Gerry. We're going to be headline news tomorrow. God, what a bloody shambles.'

Behind the indignation, Pountney sensed Bomberg's excitement.

4

Marion was in the bathroom when she heard the key turn in the front door. She ran quickly into the bedroom and got into bed, pulling the sheets up to her neck. It was absurd, but she still felt embarrassed if he saw her naked when he was dressed.

'Bill?'

She knew who it was – who else had a key to her flat? – but that didn't stop her calling out.

'I'm late, I'm sorry. I got held up.' He came in, carrying his jacket and eating a sandwich. 'The bursar collared me after my supervision. Some nonsense about wanting me to join the wine committee. Of course I refused. He must know by now I've never joined anything in my life.' Gant, sitting on the end of the bed, put his bicycle clips on her dressing table, a habit which always irritated her, and began half-heartedly to untie his shoes. 'How was your morning?'

She'd had a sleepless night, debating whether to ask him why he had suddenly turned against her at the Blake-Thomas meeting. She had watched the dawn light spread across the rooftops of Cambridge and had sworn she would say nothing, but now he was here in her bedroom her irritation at his lack of any greeting – not even a perfunctory kiss – coupled with those bloody bicycle clips, pushed out of her mind the promise she had made to herself.

'Why didn't you support me yesterday, Bill?'

'Berlin's the wrong man, Marion, and it would have been dishonest to say otherwise.' He sounded weary, reluctant to debate the issue further.

'You were in favour when we talked last week.'

'I said he was an interesting candidate. I wasn't unequivocal in my support. I remember telling you that I had some reservations about Berlin and I needed time to think before I reached a decision.'

That wasn't her recollection but she wasn't prepared to argue about it. She hesitated. Should she close it now, forget about it, or risk a quarrel? She'd already gone too far to withdraw.

'Why didn't you tell me you'd changed your mind before the meeting? I'd been counting on your support. You could have telephoned me or left a message.'

'My opposition can't have surprised you, surely.'

'It was a shock to hear you were against me.' She noticed he had stopped undressing. 'What have you got against Berlin? I don't understand why you're so opposed to him.'

'I think his book was overrated.'

'Oh, come on, Bill.' Was this professional jealousy talking? Berlin's achievement highlighted Bill's failure to make anything of his academic career. '*Legacies of History* got a wonderful reception, here and in the States. We can't all be wrong.'

'I can't shake off this feeling that somehow he's fooling us. He isn't who he wants us to think he is. He's a phoney.'

They argued then, bringing the unhappy debate of the previous day into the bedroom. She put on her glasses so she could see him properly. He sat hunched on the end of the bed, an exhausted, defeated figure. She felt a moment's regret at her outburst. Then she saw that while they'd been talking Gant had put his shoes on again.

'Bill, if you'd rather not.'

'What?'

'There's no rule that says we have to make love. We can just have lunch if you'd prefer.'

'Are you sure?' The relief in his voice was undisguised. 'I don't want to disappoint you.'

She slid out of bed, wrapping herself tightly in the sheet. What kind of inhibition made her hide herself from him?

'Go and see what's in the fridge while I get dressed.'

She stared at her reflection in the bathroom mirror. Was that it, then? Was this how it was going to end? In the early weeks of their affair she had allowed herself to rewrite the truth about Bill Gant. His academic promise had fizzled out, she told herself, because the demands of his invalid wife were destroying him, and he either couldn't or wouldn't see what was happening to him. He needed rescuing and she had felt an overwhelming need to reinstate the man she believed still existed somewhere behind the exhausted mask he presented to the world. Ideas don't die, she told herself, nor does real talent, and Bill had had ideas and talent when he was young. It is energy that fades, especially when drained away through impossible emotional demands, and with it that special self-confidence so necessary to sustain academic theory. Poor Bill.

She would restore his belief in himself by rebuilding him through love. She would make no demands on him, except that he make love to her once or twice a week. From that the relationship would grow. She would watch over his steady recovery. In time, they would write history together. They would make their reputations, and she would laugh at deriders like Michael Scott, who claimed there was never any way back up the slippery slope of academic advancement once the downward slide had begun. They would build their lives together. That was her unspoken dream. She took Bill Gant in her arms once a week on Wednesday lunchtimes and tried to work her magic on him.

How she had longed for him in those first weeks of their affair last autumn, an intoxicating time when she had still believed her dreams were possible. Each Wednesday morning she'd had difficulty concentrating on her supervision. The moment her students had gone, she'd rush off on her bike to buy something savoury from the French delicatessen in Petty Cury, then to Fitzbillie's for a treacle tart – Bill had a sweet tooth – before racing back to the flat to await his arrival. Sometimes the tension of the minutes until she heard him put his key in the door was almost unbearable. Why was she always so afraid he wouldn't appear? Why did she always fear that in her letterbox one day she'd find a note ending the affair? Couldn't she have more confidence in herself? Sometimes, after he had gone, she would lie in bed crying.

No notes came. He kept their appointments every Wednesday. But the magic didn't work because magic cannot be one-sided. Bill Gant remained what he was, a tired man whose reserves of life had been wrested from him by the demands of a mad wife. He could not be revived because there was no longer anything left to revive. He came to Marion for comfort and relief, for someone with whom he could share the misery that was slowly destroying him. He made love to her with a clumsiness that upset her, as if he was careless of her feelings. He slept in her arms, not peacefully, but twitching and sometimes calling out. Too late she learned that Bill Gant was a lost soul, and that lost souls have nothing to give. They can only take. The relationship, she realised, was indeed one-sided. She felt empty and resentful. That he needed her was clear. That she had made a mistake in believing they might have a life together was also clear. She was trapped in an affair she now wanted to end because she had overestimated her own powers. In his fragile frame of mind, wouldn't rejection destroy him?

She continued to let him come to her flat; she allowed him to make love to her; she dreamed of ways of breaking off the relationship but on each occasion, as Bill described the worsening of what he called 'this business with Jenny', her nerve broke and she said nothing. She had fooled herself and now she was caught in a plot of her own making.

No, this wasn't how it would end because it wasn't ever going to end. There was no way out. Her life would be an endless cycle of Wednesdays, dreary apologies for late arrivals, bicycle clips on the dressing table, clumsy grapplings with each other's bodies and endless stories about Jenny, each one worse than the last. She felt a sudden desperation spiral up inside her, bringing tears to her eyes. Only with an effort was she able to control it.

Bill Gant was eating a piece of cheese when she came into the kitchen. He'd put plates on the table and cut some bread.

'All I could find,' he said. 'The cupboard is bare and so is the fridge.'

No thinly cut French ham today, no mushroom salad with a sweet French dressing, no treacle tart. She'd not had time to go shopping. The truth was, she hadn't even thought about it. She'd only got back to the flat ten minutes before he arrived.

'You'll be all right,' she said, more sharply than she'd intended. 'You've already had a sandwich. Here—' She handed him his bicycle clips. 'You forgot these.'

She brought out an opened bottle of white wine from a cupboard and poured him a glass. Bill looked uncomfortable, shifting his weight from one foot to another.

'Marion.'

'Yes?'

'The thing is . . .' He stopped in mid-sentence, at a loss for words. It was bound to be more bad news about Jenny and her regular visits to the local sanatorium. 'I had to take Jenny into Fulbourn last night.'

Poor Bill. No wonder the years of coping with Jenny's bouts of mania had run down his energies and come close to finishing him.

'I'm so sorry.' She wrestled with her guilt. She could imagine the strain he was under because of Jenny. Had she been too hard on him earlier when she'd attacked his opposition to Berlin? All she had done was make his mood worse. No wonder he hadn't wanted to make love. 'You should have told me at once.'

'She'd complained of not feeling well all this past week.' The words burst from him with an intensity that defined his misery. 'I tried to convince myself that there was no danger of something brewing up. When I got home yesterday, she was sitting in a corner, crying. She wouldn't let me come near her. I tried to reason with her but she wouldn't listen. Eventually I had to call an ambulance. She screamed when they took her away. Said some terrible things, all of them without foundation. Everyone in the street heard her.' Suddenly he burst into tears. 'I can't take much more of this, Marion. I'm at the end of my tether.'

She held his head against her as he wept, patting him gently until his tears stopped. She'd met Jenny once, a couple of years ago, at a faculty do, a pale, silent, vacant figure who had clung desperately to Bill's side, wouldn't talk to anyone, drank a glass of water and asked to be taken home early.

'Forgive me. I don't know what came over me.'

She waited while he slowly pulled himself together, her arms around him protectively, feeling guilty at her outburst, comparing her selfishness with his desperate need for sympathy which she had all but denied him.

'I'm not going to desert you,' she said. The moment called for convenient lies. Truth would have to wait for another day.

'Thank you.' He looked up at her soulfully, smiled briefly and touched her hand. 'I knew I could rely on you.'

She looked at him with compassion in her eyes, wondering if he knew that compassion isn't love and, if he didn't, how she would tell him.

Poor Bill? Poor Marion.

5

Viktor Radin's hands were burning. The pain brought him reluctantly out of the warm, enveloping mists of unconsciousness, forcing him to open his eyes. The same white-walled room, the same bed, the same saline drip keeping him reluctantly alive. If only he had the strength to tear it from his arm he could be done with the process here and now. The glare of the day had gone but it was not yet dark. While he'd been asleep the blinds that had earlier been lowered against the sun were now raised so that he could see into the garden as the shadows lengthened. No clocks anywhere – he had asked for them to be removed. Another day was passing. How many more would he have to endure before the darkness came?

His looked at his hands, swollen and useless on the sheet, a cruel cartoon image of hands, misshapen and broken, the relic of the time of madness that he tried so hard to forget and never could. A fire was burning in his fingers, spreading across his palms, into his wrists and up his forearms. Only once before had he experienced pain like this, and he had buried that time in his life years before. Why was it all coming back to him now?

★

They came for him before dawn, as Elza had warned him they would. Why had he never listened to her? Why had he always mocked her anxiety? They banged on the door of his apartment, shouting his name. Confused and frightened, he had got out of bed and let them in. When he thought about it afterwards, it seemed like a dozen policemen or more but it was probably only two or three. They ordered him to get dressed, giving no explanation. He obeyed automatically. Elza stood by the door of the bedroom, a worn dressing gown over her nightdress, white-faced and terrified, crying silently as he hurriedly gathered a few clothes into a holdall. Before he could say goodbye, they pushed him out of the apartment, down the stairs and into a waiting car, Elza too terrified even to touch him as he passed. The noise had woken Olga, and his last memory before the door of their apartment was slammed shut was the voice of his daughter calling for him out of the darkness. Its poignancy nearly broke him. Were those the last words he would hear his daughter speak? Would he ever see her again?

'Why are you arresting me? Where are you taking me?' he asked repeatedly, as the car raced through the deserted city, the street lights dimly reflected in what remained of the snow. His captors gave him no answer. His mind refused to imagine what might happen to him. He was hustled into the Lubyanka, an officer on either side holding his arms in an iron grip, down in the elevator to the basement, along a corridor and finally into a cold, windowless room furnished only with a desk, a chair, a table and a lamp.

'Why have you brought me here? I demand to know.'

He was bound to his chair with ropes that tore into the skin of his wrists and ankles and he quickly lost any feeling in his hands and feet. His interrogation began at once. He was accused of betraying the Soviet people by giving secrets to German spies. He denied the accusations, saying he had given away no secrets: he was a loyal Soviet citizen. They appeared uninterested in his defence. They held photographs in front of him and shouted the names of his colleagues who, they claimed, were traitors too, working for the enemy. Who else belonged to this secret organisation? Where did its meetings take place? Who was its leader?

There was no secret organisation, he told them, no meetings, no leader. His captors refused to believe him, calling him a fascist spy, and threatening that, unless he confessed his crimes, he would be taken out and shot.

He had given secrets to no one, he repeated, his voice betraying his desperation. He was an engineer, he worked in a laboratory, dedicated to the task of designing a missile that would transform the Soviet war effort. He went home at night to his wife and children so tired he could hardly think. He had no opportunity to betray secrets to anyone, and no reason either.

They ignored his denials – did they even hear the words he used? – and taunted him with what they would do to Elza and his children if he didn't tell them what they wanted to know.

He broke down, sobbing, unable to exercise any control over himself now, repeating again and again that he had done nothing wrong. His accusers were mistaken. He was innocent of any charge against him. He was part of a team of engineers and designers, working on rockets whose power would help defeat the German invaders. He was not the man they were after. It must be a mistake. They should let him go. He had important work to complete. *They must let him go.*

Their response was to strike him in the face and kick his legs, knocking over the chair so he lay helpless on the floor, where they kicked him again, telling him they'd do worse to his wife and daughter, but still he had told them nothing because he had nothing to tell. How do you confess to crimes you have not committed? Or blame men you know to be innocent?

Later on – is it minutes or hours, is it still night or has the day dawned? – at a nod from his interrogator, they untie him. For one hypnotic moment he imagines he is being released. He is unable to move because he has lost all feeling in his arms and legs. He is lifted from the chair and taken to the back of the room. They roll up his sleeves, remove his watch and force him to kneel before a table, palms down on the wooden surface. They pull off his leather belt and lay it over his wrists. Then, with hammer and nails they secure the belt so that he cannot move his hands. Behind him, one man holds his head, another his shoulders. He cannot imagine what they are about to do.

While his interrogator continues to shout more questions to which he has no answers, another man systematically shatters first the ends of his fingers, then the joints, the knuckles and the bones in each hand, hammering them with a wooden mallet. With each question he cannot answer, another bone is broken. Radin experiences pain of an intensity of which he has never dreamed. Unconsciousness is the only relief from his suffering but every time he loses himself in merciful oblivion, they throw icy water over him. When he revives, the questioning and the hammering continue.

Give us the answers we want, they say, *and you will save your hands.*

For one brief moment in his ordeal his mind escapes from the pain, travelling outside his body, and he sees with great clarity what is happening to him. He is aware of the bleeding mess of his hands, the bloodstained table, the marks of blood on his forearms, his shirt, his face and neck, the twisted expressions of his torturers, who stand so close to him, and the overpowering stench of their bodies. He senses their anger against him, an anger whose origins he cannot comprehend; he hears them shout again and again that he and his colleagues are traitors who should die for their crimes against the state.

He sees a way out of his torture. Why not identify one of his colleagues as a traitor? Someone must have betrayed him without cause – why should he not do the same to another? For a moment he is attracted by this escape route. He will reveal that one of his fellow scientists has betrayed secrets to the Germans and that will be it – a lie but the pain will cease. They may even let him go. It is tempting, to end his terrible suffering.

Somewhere within him a voice that he recognises as his

own but he is unsure where it comes from tells him that if he lies, he will become an accomplice in their crime, a new link in an endless chain of lies and corruption. Once he goes down that path, if he is lucky enough to survive, he will have lost himself and become their creature. At that moment the life he has always dreamed of will be at an end. He knows that he has been born to build rockets that will reach the stars. Whatever else he does, he must resist the temptation to give in or he will never realise his destiny. *He must resist.*

Then he slips into unconsciousness.

*

Two weeks later he arrived in Kolyma at the start of a five-year sentence for anti-Soviet activities. Blood seeped through the crude bandages someone had wrapped around his shattered hands. The bones were set by a prisoner who claimed he had been a medic in another life, but he did it badly and without any kind of anaesthetic, and again the pain was intense. Some bones mended, others didn't, and the swellings reduced but never disappeared. His hands had been beaten permanently out of shape. They no longer had much feeling or mobility and little strength. He was the prisoner with two enlarged fleshy gloves that could hold little on their own. He was unable to work in the mine, dig trenches or cut trees. He saw the danger of his uselessness. To save his life, he suggested that they put a harness around him and use him as they would a horse or a donkey to pull carts or haul logs. For months, before they moved him from Kolyma, his life was little better than that of an animal.

Eight months later his case was re-investigated, his sentence cut to two years and, after the intercession of his professor, he was moved to a *sharaga*, an open prison where, with other scientists, also prisoners like himself, he worked on the designs of aeroplanes. For a time he was brought to Butirskaya prison in Moscow, where he was visited by Elza and his children, Olga and Kyrill. On these rare occasions, he felt he was looking at his family through the wrong end of a telescope. Increasingly they were people he did not know, growing older without him, lives that hardly touched his own. When he was in their presence, he kept his hands out of sight, behind his back or in his pockets. Elza knew what had happened to him. His children, he told her, were too young to understand. He found it hard to resist the temptation to take them in his arms.

After the war, he never revealed what he had suffered. He made no complaints about the waste of human resources, nor of valuable research time while he was serving his sentence. Nor was he heard to question the authority that had so cruelly disabled him. When he was told about the great advances made by German rocket scientists in the time he had been away, as he called it, he was not surprised. He studied engineering journals, listened to reports of his fellow engineers who had been to see the V2 factory in Peenemunde, spent hours poring over the spoils with which they returned, and later more hours in conversation with German scientists who had been brought to Moscow to work on the development of Soviet rockets. He settled back into the work he had begun before the war, the task of designing spacecraft that would eventually take a man to the moon and beyond.

His disfigured hands provided long moments of anxiety for the authorities. Radin was now vulnerable because his disability made him an identifiable target for the enemies of the state. Members of the Space Administration Committee feared that he would become a magnet for American agents, that in a desperate effort to reduce the Soviet lead over US technology, they might kidnap or even kill him. Soviet doctors, they learned, could not disguise what had happened to him because they had no cure for the damage he had suffered. The man whose genius was now recognised had to be kept out of sight, the Committee instructed. In the interests of his own safety, they argued, he was to become invisible.

The executive action to remove the evidence of his

existence was carried out with clinical efficiency on instructions from the Kremlin. Radin was deprived of a home address, a telephone number and any official place of work. There was no longer any record that he had ever been born, that he married and had children or that he was divorced. His name could no longer be found on internal memoranda, on the circulation list of the minutes of meetings, even on the door of his office. There was no record of his conviction and sentence or of his incarceration. He was forbidden to travel abroad for conferences. His photograph was removed from all newspaper archives so it could never be reproduced. There was no reference to him in any edition of the *Soviet Encyclopedia*. He was not allowed to appear at any public event, nor to receive public recognition for any of his exploits. When he was awarded the Order of Lenin, the medal was presented to him at a secret ceremony in his office, with only two of his senior staff present, and they were sworn to secrecy. In the Kremlin, in the state-owned military-industrial organisations that built spacecraft and missiles and at Baikonur, the secret cosmodrome where Radin's energy and vision directed the space programme, he was known only as 'the Chief Designer'.

If within the Soviet Union Viktor Radin had become invisible, in the West his reputation, based on his invisibility, outgrew even his considerable success.

*

Why is he experiencing pain again now, when he has felt nothing in his hands for years? Why, when he closes his eyes, can he see the face of his interrogator and hear his harsh voice shouting at him? He can even smell the sour sweat on his body and his foul breath. Why is this event from so long ago suddenly so close?

At that moment he has the sense that his hands have been touched, that they are no longer burning. They feel as if they have been plunged into ice-cold water. The feeling of coolness and the strength have been restored. He looks at his hands. They are again as they once were, white, with long fingers and well-manicured nails. A transformation has taken place. He has been healed. A calm descends on him as his memory drains into the distance. From somewhere in the room he hears a voice calling softly, *Viktor, Viktor.*

It sounds like his mother but it can't be. He hasn't seen her since she died years ago. How can she be here with him now? He turns towards the voice, and there she is, standing by his bed in her familiar grey apron, a thin, worn figure, her white hair in a bun, smiling at him.

Viktor, Viktor, she is saying. Her hands are outstretched in greeting. He knows that it is her touch that has healed him.

Mother, Mother. Is that smiling young man next to her his dear son, Kyrill? *Kyrill. Is that you?*

As he reaches towards the faces he loves his eyes close and he falls slowly and willingly into a soft and endlessly enclosing darkness.

IVAN'S SEARCH FOR HIS FATHER

It was film night. The decision had been taken three days before: they would not use the official cinema. The nights were far too hot to be shut up in a room without proper ventilation. They'd set up an open-air cinema. Rig up a screen. Bring chairs, rugs for the children. And the film? By popular demand, *Ivan's Search*. What else?

For Andrei, the day passed too slowly. Seconds were like hours, minutes like days. He wanted to help with the preparations but was told he couldn't, he'd only get in the way. The fathers would build the cinema for a night, while the mothers sunbathed and swam. The children played on the beach, except for Andrei, who hung around, watching the construction of the makeshift cinema from a distance.

'It won't be dark till much later,' his mother said. 'You must eat now. You'll be hungry if you don't.'

'Where's Father?' he asked.

'He's coming soon.' He caught the bewilderment in his mother's expression. She had no idea where his father was. 'I'll save him something for later.'

He ate reluctantly and tested the state's denial of religion by secretly praying for the sun to fall out of the sky and bring night sooner. His prayers were not answered. He was not sure whether to be pleased or sad. Would nothing make the time pass?

His elder brother Anton teased him. It was just a film, he said. Films were nothing but light projected onto a screen:

illusion, make-believe, stupid dreams. What was Andrei getting excited about?

Don't get angry, Andrei told himself. He wants you to lose your temper so he can demonstrate his superiority.

'Leave him alone,' his mother said wearily.

Andrei caught his mother's eye and said nothing. She knew what he felt because she felt it too. Anton was talking nonsense. Films were real, adventures that sucked you into their stories so that you became the people you were watching. Anton spent too much time trying to attract girls to want to believe in anything but himself. He couldn't understand that intoxicating feeling of being another person living in another world – a world of dreams, but what dreams, what adventures. He could be a pilot flying his plane through a blizzard on a mercy mission to save a dying mother-to-be; or a soldier single-handedly defending his elderly parents' home against the enemy; or a young boy taking his sick father's place in the shift at the mine to earn money to keep the family alive. These were the adventures he watched on the screen, and these were the dreams he wanted in his own life. When the film was over, he relived them again and again in his mind until he became the heroes whose exploits he so admired.

He left the communal dining room to find the open-air cinema. It was still hot. He took the long route so as not to get there too soon. He walked along an endless corridor, passing door after door. He counted the numbers. Seventy-two. Seventy-four. Eighty-six. Eighty-eight. One hundred. How many people were staying here? He knew that in this vast building there were many more corridors like this, and that outside in this seaside resort there were many more accommodation buildings, say, four hundred rooms in each building. Families of four shared rooms. Perhaps sixteen hundred people at any one time were all here for a holiday. All, like his father, had been rewarded with a Black Sea trip for their efforts in building the Soviet state of which they were so proud.

He continued down some stairs, along another corridor,

past the entrance to the open-air swimming pool – deserted now, the water stilled and waiting for the morning, the slowly darkening sky reflected on the smooth surface of the water, the smell of chlorine making his eyes smart. On he went past the gym, also deserted, past the cinema, its door closed.

Why did he go in? Was it to pay homage to the heroes whose thrilling exploits he dreamed of at night? Or did he hear hushed voices inside, curiosity making him creep into the darkness? Later, when he tried to remember, his memory played tricks and he couldn't be sure what had made him do it. Whatever his motive, he pushed open the door and slid in silently, waiting for his eyes to become accustomed to the dark before he moved. He was aware at once that someone else was in the cinema: he could hear a man's voice whispering, then a woman's. Why anyone would want to talk in the dark in an empty cinema when everyone knew that tonight the film would be shown out of doors escaped him. He crept into the auditorium, keeping low between the seats, and listened.

'Please.' A man's voice, pleading.

'We can't. We simply can't.' A woman's voice. A firm denial.

'Why not?'

'Someone will see.'

'It'll be dark. They'll all be staring at the screen.'

Silence. A sound like kissing, then a sigh.

'That's unfair. I said no, I meant it.'

'No, you didn't.'

'You're a pig.' Another silence. More kissing? This time he wasn't sure. 'I won't do it. I won't come.'

'You will. I'll be there, waiting. You won't be able to resist me.'

'That's what I'm afraid of.'

Then, from outside, a whistle, the signal that they were ready to begin. Without thinking he ran for the door and the noise alerted the speakers. He didn't think they could identify him in the darkness, but it was always possible. He ducked between the rows of seats to hide himself. Only at the last moment did he look back, and then only for an instant. As he opened the door, a shaft of light cut through the darkness. He saw two heads, close together, eyes staring – no time to identify them before they too ducked out of sight. Were they frightened of being seen, or was that his imagination? He ran for his life.

It was almost dark outside, the sky completely clear, the stars distant pinpricks of glistening light. Lanterns had been lit, and one or two people had torches. A sheet had been suspended between two trees to serve as a makeshift screen. The projector was rigged up on a table, its front resting on a pedestal of books so that it would throw its image high onto the screen. Benches and chairs had been brought out of the main building, with rugs spread on the ground at the front for the children.

It was cooler now. A breath of air was occasionally blown from the sea by the light evening breeze. The air smelled sweet. His mother, he saw, was already seated, keeping the chair next to her for his father. She waved at him and pointed to the rug. Anton was with his friends at the front, a group of boys noisily pretending to be uninterested in what was going on. Suddenly someone shouted, 'Lights out, we're ready,' and one by one the lanterns were extinguished.

All was darkness and quiet. These was not a sound, even from Anton. Andrei rested his chin on his knees and looked up at the screen as a light began to flicker across it. He was momentarily disturbed by a child standing up in front of him and playing his torch on the audience before his mother reached forward to snatch the torch from him.

He had that familiar feeling of excitement in his stomach as the film began. *Ivan's Search for His Father*, the children around him murmured aloud. The sound rattled from an old loudspeaker that had been placed under the screen. Occasionally it played tricks with the words, making the dialogue hard to hear. Occasionally, too, the night breeze rippled the oblong screen, making the images dance and distort, at which the children giggled, to be hushed by their parents. But none of that mattered. Andrei was transfixed by what he saw.

Into his view, there appear a wide prairie; trees, birch and oak; a river snaking its way through a field; a village going about its daily business, the men in hats and boots, smoking pipes, some on horseback, others in shirtsleeves, working in the fields harvesting, stacking sacks of corn in a barn. The women, scarves around their heads and wearing full skirts, nurse children or wash clothes. A boy about his own age, with huge eyes and cropped blond hair, Ivan, is in the fields with his friends helping with the harvest. There are shining faces, old and young alike; images of contentment, of time suspended, of life as he had read of it in story books at school.

Then the picture changes. Horses thunder across the plain, throwing up dust and stones, a posse of men with hard faces and guns in their saddles is riding somewhere. He sees again the village he has only just left but now the faces are full of fear as the peasants scatter, mothers clasp their babies, dragging their younger children by the hand as they try to escape the marauders. He sees burning brands being thrown into houses, men being shot in the street, women falling and being cut down where they lie, vainly protecting their children with their bodies. Ivan runs as his mother and brothers are trapped in their home. The barn alongside their house is set alight. Smoke forms a huge column in the sky, blacking out the sun. Night falls, the village burns. Flames fill the screen and his imagination. The village dies.

3

1

Berlin sat in the back of the Zil as it raced through the empty streets of Moscow. The telephone call had woken him from a deep and dreamless sleep. The message was brief and direct: he was needed now. No reasons were given. The anonymous voice had instructions to issue orders, not explanations. He knew it would be like this because murderers, thieves and informers always meet their destiny in the anonymity of night.

The car came to a halt in a courtyard inside the familiar building. He was escorted through a side door into a world of artificial light where day and night no longer had any meaning, past the security guards, across the marble hall, into the elevator and up to the third floor. Not a word was spoken. The hand that guided him might have held a gun such was his ready obedience to the slightest pressure on his back.

This was the fortress within the fortress of Soviet Russia. In the offices that led off this brightly lit corridor the lives of his fellow citizens were ceaselessly monitored. His was among them, he was sure. The records of who they were, what they did, what they said – what they thought even? – were assembled, annotated, analysed and archived in endless shelves of indexed files hidden in guarded cellars deep in the bowels of the building. This was the great state machine of secret bureaucracy, whose rumoured existence was the source of the universal fear so essential to the exercise of absolute power. This building that was never in darkness was both the engine and the symbol of Soviet power. Its inhabitants were the guardians of the socialist ideal, who kept a permanent vigil against those who threatened to destroy the greatest experiment in engineering human nature the world had ever seen.

'In here.'

The room was no different to so many he had entered over the years. The walls were bare except for a poorly reproduced black and white photograph of Lenin, arm raised, fist clenched, mouth frozen at the moment of command: 'Forward, Comrades, forward', a familiar icon of power. Next to it on the wall was the dusty outline of another picture, long since removed, of Stalin, the now disgraced former leader. How naive of someone – Lenin presumably – to assume that the repetition of such tawdry images would exhort the population at large to believe what their own eyes told them was not true, and yet at the same time how inspired. How had he known that the empty rhetoric would work its dangerous magic and the deceit succeed? Berlin would never understand the gullibility of the masses. Their thought processes mystified him.

He waited. However urgent the summons, you were always kept waiting. Then a voice would say, *Thank you for coming at such short notice.* That was how every interview began, with a cynical disregard for what both he and his interrogator knew to be the truth. After so many years and so many visits, why maintain the pretence that he had any control over his presence in this room?

'Thank you for coming at such short notice.'

His interrogator was not one he had seen before. He was a man of his own age, scrubbed and shining, uniformed and eager, the familiar outward skin of the ambitious officer – he'd met his kind before. He disliked zealots as much as he disliked new faces. Hadn't he earned the right to a single controller by now, someone whose idealism had been worn down by the realities of Soviet life? No doubt it was a rubric of the system that it was dangerous to allow any degree of comfort into the relationship. Hence, tonight he was facing the Zealot for the first time.

'You visited our Chief Designer recently. How did you find him?'

Berlin was continuously surprised at the way these people felt it necessary to disguise their intentions. They were not remotely interested in his assessment of Radin's health. They had more urgent questions. They had summoned him to this building in the middle of the night because they wanted to know what Viktor had said to him.

'He was failing. That was obvious. He can't last much longer.'

'He's outlived all his doctors' predictions,' the Zealot said. 'Either he is stronger than we thought, or his doctors are poor judges of the progress of his disease.'

If only these people were more sympathetic, how much easier their job would be. But sympathy and interrogation do not lie easily together.

'Tell me, what did you talk about? Were there any last things to be settled between you?'

Last things. The echo of the sentence in Radin's note was deliberate. They would have intercepted his letter, and now they were curious about its consequences.

'He seemed very tired. His mind wandered. What he said was inconsequential.'

He concealed the truth without thinking. Why he did so he was not sure. Usually, during these official interrogations, his life was suspended and he was transformed into someone else, a man who told his questioners what they wanted to know because he had no moral strength to resist them. In rooms like this one he had betrayed his students, his colleagues, sometimes even his friends.

Now, for reasons he could not fully determine, he had given a reply that meant while Radin remained alive, he would keep his secrets safe. He had taken a stand. *Why?* His refusal was an unexpected act of dissent, of resistance to the idea that he should betray Radin because he had betrayed others. Now there was no going back. He was trapped in his own lie. He would have to sustain the deception.

'What did he talk about?'

'His childhood, his early interest in rockets, the death of his son.'

That was risky. Viktor had told him once how his son had died but he couldn't remember any details now. Stick to what you know. Don't elaborate.

'Did he mention Baikonur?'

'Not that I recall, no.'

'You're sure of that?'

'Quite certain.'

The Zealot was writing on the pad of paper. Berlin craned forward. With an eye skilled from years of practice, he was able to read the name of his interrogator: Colonel Medvedev. A name he would remember, along with so many others.

'You spent over forty minutes in his company. You must have spoken about something.' Behind the impatience was the scepticism that his interrogator would have been trained to employ. It was a trap, of course. He must be careful.

'I listened to the ramblings of a dying man. It was a disturbing experience. So little of what he said made sense. I was shocked at his deterioration since my previous visit. Much of the time he seemed not to remember who I was.'

Was that going too far? When you wanted to reveal nothing, the trick was to stay as close to the truth as possible because you could never be sure what additional evidence your interrogators might have collected. It was always dangerous to give them information they could check the moment you had gone.

Radin's son had been a pilot. He remembered now. Hadn't his MIG fighter crashed while trying to take the world air-speed record from the Americans?

'The nursing staff reported that he was confused after you left.'

Good old Viktor, fooling them to the last. He'd put on an act and they'd fallen for it.

'That doesn't surprise me.'

'Did he give you anything before you left? Any letters or notes?'

His interrogator stared at him. This was the simplest test of all. Berlin knew that if he looked away they would take that as a sign of guilt and know that he had lied. Then the atmosphere in the room would change, the questioning would take on a more aggressive tone. He was prepared for that. He accepted the challenge and returned it.

'If he had, it would be in your possession by now. I would have handed it over immediately.'

That is the language of the man who has sold his soul, the syntax of lies and subservience, of pretended humility and compliance, as he buries his moral identity in sordid moments of betrayal to secure his own survival.

'Where would our space programme be without our Chief Designer?' His interrogator took out a cigarette and lit it. He looked reflectively at the ceiling, as if declaiming what he had been ordered to memorise. 'He put the first satellite into space, then the first man. He invented the super-rocket that will allow us to colonise the moon. He is the author of all our great achievements in space. Without him, we would certainly not have the pleasure of humiliating the Americans so frequently.'

Radin as great servant of the state, whose successes in space caught the imagination of the world on a scale no one had imagined. How dramatic the newspaper headlines had been, proclaiming Soviet superiority over the Americans after Gagarin's flight. How quick the politicians had been to catch on to the idea of space spectaculars to promote the virtues of the communist system. How cleverly the First Secretary, the Politburo, the Central Committee had been to promote Radin's achievements as their own. Viktor could do nothing. He had neither public face nor voice. He was the invisible genius on whose back others were shamelessly riding. Men who don't exist can't protest.

Yet this is the man, a voice inside Berlin was bursting to say, whose professional life you frequently made a living hell because of the pettiness of the restrictions you placed upon him in order to shore up your own power, and by the lack of imagination you showed when asked to approve his new plans. How often were his ideas rejected by men without the competence to judge what he proposed? How can you dare to exploit his successes as your own when, within living memory, you tortured him to betray his innocent friends? You systematically smashed his hands, finger by finger, bone by bone, while he screamed in agony, leaving him with a disfigurement that is a permanent monument to bureaucratic insanity sanctioned by a power gone mad.

Radin's achievements will last for ever, while yours, whatever they are (and they can't be more than sordid secrets which will one day be exposed to the world's scrutiny), will end up as a catalogue of crimes for which, if there is any justice in the world, you and others like you will be made to pay.

That was it. He had found his answer. If Radin could remain loyal to a system that had treated him so badly, then he, Andrei Berlin, must remain loyal to Radin. That was how Viktor had come to terms with his injuries. They were the living reminders of his refusal to be broken.

'It will be a relief when his sufferings are at an end,' Berlin said.

'That moment has come.' The Zealot stood up. 'The Chief Designer is dead.'

'When?' It was the only word he could bring himself to say.

'A few hours ago.'

Viktor dead. That great mind that had created so much silenced at last. That extraordinary source of inventive energy, stilled for ever. Berlin was overwhelmed by a sense of loss. Tears welled unexpectedly in his eyes. He looked away to conceal his distress.

'I am sorry to have to give you this news.' The Zealot had

seen his reaction. What would he make of it? How would he record Berlin's distress in his report on their meeting? 'You and he were close, weren't you?'

'He was closer to me than my own father.'

It was a lie, of course. He had hated his own father. But to a man like the Zealot it sounded right, and that was as good a reason as any for saying it.

★

The ghosts of his secret past came hunting for Berlin that night, and he found nowhere to hide from them. Was he dreaming? Or had he been swept into a surreal world where people he had hardly known crowded round him in silence, staring at him with their accusing eyes? The boy who had defaced a portrait of Stalin in a textbook. The schoolmaster caught with his hand up the skirt of one of the girls in his class. The goalkeeper in his football team who had declared that American jazz was superior to any popular music in the Soviet Union. The engineering student accused of spying for the West because he had photographs of the latest MIG fighter in his briefcase – his passion was to make model aircraft. The woman who had stolen some rubles from his overcoat pocket while cleaning his flat. The researcher he had feared was trying to get him removed from his job. He had invented some charge against him and made sure of his departure from the Department. So it went on. The living history of his betrayals, ghost-like figures from his conscience facing him with the terrible truth of his actions.

Denial was impossible. What he had done, he had done knowingly. He had ruined other lives to protect his own. The system to which he was captive had demanded to be fed, and he had obliged, caring not whether his victims were innocent or guilty, nor whether they had dependants, nor whether their work was valuable to the state. That was for others to judge. His role was to point the finger.

Then he saw another face, familiar to him. The face of his

75

father, looking at him in horror and astonishment, and saying, 'You betrayed me too. Why? *Why?*'

When he woke, hours later, he found his pillow was stained with tears.

2

By ten o'clock, the rumour that the Chief Designer was dead had swept through the Space Institute. By midday the rumour was officially denied when a typewritten statement was issued to all Departments from the Acting Director. The Chief Designer had been seriously ill, he said, but his illness had been successfully treated and he was now back at work, building the new generation of spaceships that would extend the leadership of the Soviet Union over the West.

The brazenness of the invention was greeted on each floor of the concrete building with private disbelief and passive acceptance. If Viktor Radin was back at work, as the official statement declared, then he would either be visible in his office on the second floor, or they'd all be running around in response to the usual string of telexed instructions from Baikonur. Throughout the day his room remained empty and the telex machine silent. Neither was his secretary visible. She had gone home early, reported to be feeling unwell – a diplomatic illness, Valery Marchenko assumed, so she could grieve in private. Radin *was* dead. The Acting Director's denial was proof enough. Why not come clean and admit it?

The seriousness of Radin's condition had been widely known for some months at the Institute but never discussed openly. When he'd first gone to hospital, there'd been whispers that his doctors had tried an experimental therapy because his life was so valuable. When he didn't return to work as the doctors had predicted, it was assumed the treatment had failed. The Institute struggled on in an uneasy state of suspension, its progress mutating into inaction. Radin's continued absence and the accompanying silence about his condition unnerved those who worked for him. On the surface little changed. The sign on the door of his empty office still read 'Chief Designer' – he was referred to by name only behind his back and out of hearing, and then always as Viktor – the door between his office and that of his secretary remained open as if he was ready to call for dictation. On the few occasions that Valery had asked about Radin, she had reassured him that the Chief Designer would be returning tomorrow, the day after, soon. She had spoken to him on the telephone only a short time ago; he sounded cheerful, he was looking forward to coming back to work, he had asked for his papers to be brought to him. But he never appeared. Each day she bore her disappointment with a stoicism born of careful instruction.

Decisions waited for Radin's return, budgets for his approval, schedules for his authorisation, changes to the design of an engine or a space capsule for his agreement. At the Institute in Moscow or at the Cosmodrome in Baikonur no one dared to step into the vacuum created by his absence and assume responsibility for his programme. The inactivity continued, unquestioned, unchallenged, its poison spreading a slow paralysis throughout the organisation. Without his galvanising presence, the machine that Radin had set up was beginning to run down. With Radin's death, the Soviet space programme was leaderless.

What would happen now? Whispered speculation was rife. Who would they appoint in his place? What changes would be made? There were no obvious successors – certainly not Grinko, now Acting Director in Radin's 'continued absence'. He had made too many enemies: that was the problem. The Politburo had relied on one man for too long. They had never allowed themselves to assume that he was mortal. They had never insisted that he train successors, and now so much of what Radin had achieved was likely to be lost because of the government's short-sightedness. Valery's frustration and anger took another turn. Did no one ever think ahead?

The official denial of what everyone knew to be true followed a familiar pattern – truth disguised as rumour, followed by a denial couched in some transparently false explanation because the truth was politically unacceptable. Did those who manufactured these statements no longer have any regard for the people they governed? Did they truly imagine that their fabrications were believed? A quick survey of his colleagues would show (if you could overcome the impossible task of getting them to reveal their thoughts) that they knew these statements had no foundation at all. But what could be done about it? The system might make a fool of itself, verifiable truth might be officially denied, but there'd be no complaint, no protest, no shared sense of outrage – hardly even a sly comment on its absurdity. A passive, mute acceptance would be the only reaction to events, characterised by an instinctive retreat from any possible conflict, in the interest of one's own survival. Always keep your head down. Never show yourself above the parapet.

We are no longer a society, Valery thought. We are a collection of individuals looking out for ourselves. How great our rulers' contempt must be for the people they have emasculated so successfully. How low we have sunk.

'When he heard that Viktor had died,' a colleague whispered to Valery as they went downstairs for lunch, 'the First Secretary was so angry he ordered the Politburo to bring him back to life, which they did. Another Soviet first to celebrate. We can now raise the dead.'

3

'Come and have tea,' Stevens told Marion Blackwell on the telephone. 'Any time after four. We can talk then.'

Geoffrey Stevens was a legend to the undergraduate population, a professor of nuclear physics who, a couple of years after the war ended, had lost faith in the atomic bomb he had been helping to build. In an act of madness or courage, depending on your viewpoint, he had gone to Moscow to try to convince the Russians to outlaw nuclear weapons. He'd failed, of course. The Soviets had humiliated him, effectively ending his public career. On his return from Moscow, Stevens had resigned from all his government appointments. He had retreated to Cambridge, where he was ostracised by a number of senior members of the university, who condemned what he had done. Some of his most vocal opponents were in his own college. They had been outraged by his flight to Moscow, which they considered an act of treachery. His subsequent adoption of the anti-nuclear cause confirmed – as they saw it – the rightness of their verdict. If Stevens was hurt by the rejection of his colleagues, he never showed it. He remained an icon to those he taught and to many others who shared his convictions, and a formidable opponent to those who advocated the building and use of weapons of indiscriminate destruction.

'Marion.' She took his outstretched hand. 'Come in.' He ushered her into the kitchen, where tea was laid. She saw one of Celia's cakes on the table, dark with raisins and dried fruit.

'I need your help, Geoffrey.' Stevens had little capacity for small talk. It was best to get to the point quickly.

'Shouldn't you be asking someone else?' He demurred out of habit, but she knew he was delighted to be approached for advice. She suspected he had the opportunity all too infrequently. 'I'm hardly classed as respectable these days.'

'I'm on the Blake-Thomas committee,' she said, ignoring his objection. 'We selected this year's speaker months ago but very inconveniently he recently died on us. We've had to find a replacement. That's what all the fuss has been about.'

When she'd come up with the idea of proposing the Russian historian Andrei Berlin, she told him, she had never imagined she would run into such fierce opposition. After some fearful wrangling, the issue had been decided by

Professor Eastman's casting vote, which didn't make her at all popular with her opponents on the committee.

'In the end I won, after a split vote.'

'Congratulations.'

'The trouble is, I've been having sleepless nights ever since.'

'If you're asking me to support your candidate, Marion, I'm not sure your chairman would approve. Eastman and I haven't spoken for over a decade.'

'No, it's nothing like that. I want you to tell me if what I've done is mad.'

'Mad isn't the epithet I'd choose,' Stevens said. 'Brave, yes. But then that's what I'd expect of you.'

'I don't want flattery, Geoffrey. This is too important. I want to know what you really think.'

Stevens took out his pipe and began to fill it from a yellow oilcloth wallet. 'Berlin's reputation is growing. I've not read him but that's what I hear from those who know about these things. One can only gain from trying to understand how one's opponent's mind works, however discomforting the process might be. Berlin would give the Blake–Thomas a good shake-up, which is just what it needs.'

'I should stick to my guns and stop worrying?'

'Do you have an alternative?'

'Michael Scott keeps muttering about Professor Astruc.'

'Astruc starts hares running and then drops out of the hunt – never finishes anything,' Stevens said dismissively. 'I'm surprised Michael doesn't agree. He ought to know better.'

'I began to think I was wrong and everyone else was right.' She smiled at him. 'I feel relieved. Thank you.'

Stevens laughed. 'You don't need me to bolster your convictions, Marion, though I'm flattered you think I could.' He poured her some more tea. 'Who else was against you? Not Peter Chadwick, surely?'

'No, Peter's an angel, backed me all the way.'

'Who then?'

She hesitated. 'Bill Gant.'

'Poor old Bill. Doesn't surprise me at all. When has he ever been *for* something? Such a shame. He was an able undergraduate – best historian of his year. Great things were expected of him but our high hopes never came to anything. Bill ran out of steam before he was thirty. The charitable explanation is that his career is a casualty of his wife's illness. He's never been able to concentrate on anything for long enough, he's always had to have half an eye on her. How well do you know him?'

How well indeed? Here come the lies.

'Our paths cross from time to time.'

'Don't worry if he's against you. He's a fading influence now. His opposition doesn't count.'

'I can deal with Bill,' she said. 'It's Michael Scott I'm worried about. He took me aside afterwards and told me that in all the years of the Blake-Thomas, there'd never been a decision on a casting vote before. He made his disapproval quite plain. In his opinion I should have withdrawn before Eastman intervened. I've got to make Berlin's visit a success or Michael isn't going to let me forget it. This is a bad time for me to make an enemy of him. I'm up for a university lectureship.'

'You'd better make sure Berlin's visit *is* a huge success, then Michael won't dare raise a whisper against you.' Stevens reached for a piece of paper and wrote a telephone number on it. 'If you think you need more ammunition, talk to my son, Danny. He's Berlin's publisher. I'm sure he'll be able to help you. The pair of you should be able to put paid to any thoughts of revenge Michael Scott may have.'

4

Kate watched the dawn creep into the room through the break in the curtains, its soft light flooding into the bedroom like an incoming tide, illuminating first the chair with the stuffing coming out of its arm, then a section of the wooden floor (how uneven the floorboards were), the end of the bed and up the sheet that covered them, until finally it painted the face that she loved so much with its grey light. At that moment, she wanted to wake him with her kisses, hold him in her arms and tell him that she was his and that nothing could ever separate them.

Had she spoken, he would have opened his eyes at once and stared at her with that troubled look that hurt so much. The world is a prison, he would solemnly tell her, in which we are all trapped and from which there can be no escape, no happy ending. Her mind translated his words to mean we have no future together, only a number of days and nights together, and each day that number is reduced by one.

'When you leave Moscow,' he had told her once, 'we will shed tears, we will make promises to each other as we say goodbye, but in our hearts we will know that when we part we will never meet again. From that moment on, we will be simply a memory to each other that over time will fade and die. That is how our love will end.'

She refused to believe him. If she left Moscow, she said, in the knowledge that she would never see him again, her life would end. She loved him with a certainty and a passion that meant there was nothing she wouldn't do to keep him. He was hers and she would never let him go.

'Such dreams are impossible,' he had replied. You must not hope for a future that cannot be realised. We must live in the real world. Dreams are dangerous deceptions, creatures of darkness, which is why they vanish when you wake.'

She called that his Russian pessimism and dismissed it. He had smiled sadly and looked away, accepting what he saw as his fate, *their* fate, with a resignation that infuriated her. In moments like that, when he tried to rationalise their situation – he called it bringing her back to earth – she felt that he was as far away from her as he could be. Sometimes her pain was so intense that she wondered if he still loved her.

Somehow, in the weeks before her return home – a day she

refused even to imagine but which was coming closer with an unwelcome speed – she had to find the answers that would convince him that their parting would be temporary, not for ever.

What she found impossible to make him understand was her sense of her own determination. It was what had got her to Moscow when the obstacles seemed insurmountable. Now she would use it to save the man she loved. She *would* not let him go. They *would* spend their lives together. It might sound absurd – of course it sounded absurd – but in her heart she knew it was possible. What she didn't yet know was how it could be done.

★

Six weeks after her arrival in Moscow, one of the students at the Conservatoire – a Bulgarian violinist whom she hardly knew – had insisted that Kate listen to a recording he had of a Russian composer she had never heard of. It was a cello sonata, and she was at once entranced by its playfulness and humour, so different from much of the contemporary Russian music she had heard. Where, she asked, could she learn more about Khutoryanski? The Conservatoire appeared to have neither a biography nor any of his music.

'Try the Lenin Library,' the Bulgarian told Kate. 'It has thousands of scores. You're bound to find Khutoryanski there.'

Two days later, she walked up the steps of the library and flashed her student card at the elderly woman guarding the entrance, to be rewarded as usual with the traditional angry Muscovite stare. Why were there so many cross people in this city? She could not get used to the Russian sullenness – or was it Soviet sullenness? The library was a crowded palace of culture, with marble halls and reading rooms of polished wood, and the inevitable photographs and busts of Lenin wherever you looked, in a permanent state of oration.

She submitted her request for the score of Khutoryanski's

Third Cello Sonata to an unsmiling girl not much older than herself, who disappeared through a glass door into a catalogue room filled with pale wooden bureaux with endless drawers containing thousands of tightly packed library cards. Kate watched her search through two boxes, find nothing, then engage in conversation with an older woman who snatched the request from her, read it and shook her head.

'We have no score of this name,' the assistant told Kate a moment later.

'I know it's published,' Kate began. 'You must have it somewhere.'

'We have no score of this name,' the girl repeated. There was no apology, no explanation. Only that stubbornly closed expression signifying a bureaucratic triumph in denying her what she wanted. She had met this before when her way was barred or her request refused.

'Please will you look again. I'm sure the score exists. I need it for my studies.'

'There is no composer of this name in our catalogue.'

'You must be mistaken,' Kate said.

'No,' the girl replied emphatically. 'I am not mistaken.'

'I've heard his recordings. I've seen his name on the label of the record. Why would I ask for the music of a composer who doesn't exist?'

'There is no composer of this name.' This argument was beginning to attract attention. She was aware of people staring at her.

'I don't believe you. You must have it. Please look again.'

'Is something the matter?'

Kate turned. A fair-haired Russian man was standing beside her. She responded to his sympathetic voice. She was a student at the Conservatoire, she told him. She was here to borrow a score that she needed for her studies, only to learn that the library had no record of either the composer or the score. That couldn't be true. She had heard one of his recordings only a day or two before. She had read his name on the cover of the long-playing record. It was absurd to deny that neither the man nor his music existed.

The stranger listened carefully and then spoke to the library assistant. She replied too quietly for Kate to understand.

'Let me buy you a cup of tea.'

'Please – I want to understand why—'

'I think it is best to leave now,' he whispered in English. She was so startled that she allowed him to take her arm and lead her away.

'Of course Khutoryanski exists,' he told her as they left the building. 'As does the score for his Third Cello Sonata, though I have never heard it myself. I am certain that there is a copy in this library. That young woman you spoke to knows it too.'

'Then why won't she find it for me?'

'If you look in the library's catalogue, you'll discover that there is no record of any Soviet composer by the name of Khutoryanski nor any of his music. Officially, neither exists.'

He took her arm as they dodged the traffic and pointed to a restaurant. 'Getting tea there will demand a negotiation worthy of a summit meeting, but perhaps we may be lucky. The quality will not be good, but there is nowhere else nearby. Shall we try?'

They were lucky. A sullen waitress reluctantly brought them some tea and a plate of biscuits that looked – and tasted – as if they were made of compressed cardboard. As they sat at a table in the empty restaurant the young man continued to talk as if they were in danger of being overheard. Sometimes she found it hard to catch what he was saying.

'Khutoryanski fell out of favour in the thirties. Who knows why? In this country, actions are not accompanied by explanations. Perhaps one evening Stalin was in a bad mood, and he complained that he did not like some piece of music he had heard on the radio. His colleagues identified Khutoryanski as the composer, which may or may not have been the case, we shall never know. A single telephone call to the Musicians'

Union, that most compliant of organisations, and Khutoryan-ski's music is banned. It displeases the Father of the Nation. It is decadent, not sufficiently socialist, altogether too frivolous and light-hearted. No one may play or conduct or teach any piece by Khutoryanski again. The composer is stripped of all his privileges. His work is suppressed. His entry in the *Soviet Encyclopedia* is excised, his name mysteriously eradicated from the list of prizes he has won. You won't find any record of his time at the Conservatoire, yet everyone knows that's where he studied. In desperation, Khutoryanski appealed to his fellow musicians but they were deaf to his entreaties. Probably, they were threatened with similar treatment if they intervened to support him. The poor man became so distressed that, in protest, he tried to defy the state that had taken away his livelihood. He set up a music stand outside the gates of the Kremlin one morning and played a piece he had written for solo violin which he dedicated to Stalin. He was arrested, tried and given a savage prison sentence on charges of anti-Soviet activities that were evidently false.'

'What happened to him?'

'Who knows? He disappeared, like so many thousands of others, into the secret universe of prison camps that exists in this country, and was never heard of again.'

'Did he die there?'

'Probably.'

'Was his music destroyed too?'

'Not destroyed, no. Removed from public access, which is as good as being destroyed. It was as if he had never existed, and therefore he had written nothing. His wife was made to give up all her husband's possessions, even the pencils and paper he used. I'm sure his scores are held under tight security on the top floor of the Lenin Library, with all the other prescribed texts which none of us may see for fear of their powers of contamination to weaken our resolve to build the socialist paradise.'

His demeanour, she noticed, was not hardened and cold

like that of so many Russians she had seen, but open and generous. He had deep-set eyes which seemed to look at you from a safe distance. There was, she told herself, a mysterious un-Russian quality about him, though she was unable to identify what it was. Then she realised that such a thought was absurd – how could he be anything *but* Russian?

'How did you hear of Khutoryanski?' he asked.

'One of the students at the Conservatoire played me a recording he'd found.'

'May I give you some advice?'

'Please.'

'Avoid contact with that student. Whether you like him or not, from now on you must regard him as untrustworthy. I can't believe he played that record to you without an ulterior motive.'

'Such as what?' Kate asked. The Bulgarian violinist had been at the Conservatoire for two years. He must have known that the composer's music was censored. Why would he want to get her into trouble with the authorities?

'How can I know?' He smiled at her. 'I know nothing about you.'

'I'm sorry.' She felt herself blushing. 'How rude of me. My name is Kate Buchanan. I am English, and I'm here studying the cello under Vinogradoff.'

'My name is Valery Marchenko,' he replied solemnly, offering her his hand across the table. 'I am Russian. But I think you already know that.'

He was older than she was, in his late twenties, she imagined. In repose, he had the soulful expression she had seen on so many Russian faces that lit up the moment he smiled or laughed.

'If Vinogradoff teaches as well as he plays, then you are lucky.'

'He is a wonderful man,' she said. 'I am lucky. I know it.'

★

It was her hair that first attracted him, long, thick, blonde hair falling over her shoulders like a rippling golden fan. He had noticed her as soon as he came into the library, sitting on a chair waiting, her music case on her knees. He had seen the young assistant librarian summon her, and he had instantly recognised the arrogant triumph of minor authority. The girl with the fair hair had no idea what was in store for her. He had gone across the room to help her without knowing why he had done so.

'What do you do?' she asked. It was an innocent question but his defences sprang instantly into action.

'Me?' he said with studied nonchalance. 'I'm an engineer.'

'I've been here long enough to know that I should ask no more questions.'

'If you know that, you're halfway to becoming Soviet.'

She laughed for the first time, tossing her head back, closing her eyes and pulling her hair away from her shoulders. He saw her long pale neck, and wanted to touch it with the tips of his fingers so that her eyes would remain shut and he would see her eyelids flicker with pleasure.

'Where did you learn English?' she asked.

If he said 'at school', she would know that wasn't true. She had probably been in Moscow long enough to know that very few people were taught English. If he said 'by listening secretly to the radio', she might blurt it out to one of her friends and betray him unintentionally. If he told her the truth, she probably wouldn't believe him but that wasn't a risk he was prepared to take.

'My mother taught me.'

'She must have been a very good teacher.'

'Or I was a very attentive pupil.'

Once again she laughed.

'Thank you for rescuing me,' she said, getting ready to leave. 'And for the tea. I really enjoyed it.'

'It was undrinkable,' he said apologetically.

'If it was I didn't notice.'

'May we take tea together again?' If his request were to carry any conviction, he would have to give her some reason. 'I would like to practise my English. It is hard to do so here. I would like to improve.'

'And you think I would be a good teacher, do you?' He couldn't make out if her smile was mocking him or not.

'I am sure you would be excellent,' he said solemnly.

'Then, Valery Marchenko, there is only one way to find out. I hope we can arrange the first lesson soon.'

5

Colonel Koliakov's decision to wear uniform was a mistake. The material was too thick to disperse the heat of his body even though he had taken off his jacket, loosened his tie and occasionally fanned his face with the agenda. He wiped his forehead with the edge of his finger, shaking off the sweat below the level of the table. The sodden back of his shirt was sticking to the fabric of his chair. Every time he moved his belt chafed the skin around his midriff into a boiling rash. Discomfort had given way to irritation. He had been sitting here for an hour already and nothing had been achieved. How much more would he have to suffer before he could be released? He longed for a bath.

The emergency meeting of the Disinformation Committee had begun soon after seven on a humid July evening in a badly ventilated room on the fourteenth floor of the Foreign Ministry. In the distance, unseen by the nine men around the table, the clouds built up, threatening thunder. Occasionally, hot spots of rain fell in the streets like exploding bullets, but there was no storm and no thunder, nothing to clear the air that became more humid and oppressive as the night wore on. Because of the secrecy of the agenda, the doors and windows on the fourteenth floor were kept firmly shut. Jackets had been rapidly discarded, sleeves rolled up, glasses of water poured. So far, that was all the committee had managed to accomplish.

The chairman, in his opening statement, had come straight to the point. 'It is my sad duty to report that our distinguished colleague, the Chief Designer of our space programme, died yesterday. He was sixty-two.'

There was an immediate outbreak of expressions of grief around the table. Koliakov watched the reaction of feigned sorrow as the members of the committee extravagantly praised the Chief Designer's achievements – even in death his identity remained concealed – and vied with each other in their demonstrations of distress at his passing. One man held a handkerchief to his eyes, and when it was his turn to speak, waved away the privilege, too overcome to say a word.

Had any of them known Radin intimately? Unlikely. Most had probably never met him, let alone spoken to him, yet they were behaving as if he were a close member of their own family. How Koliakov hated Moscow and its self-enforced play-acting. Was nothing real here? Nothing genuine? Was there only ritual posturing to conceal a cold and empty heart? If the members of the political elite of the country could put on so cynical a performance, what hope was there? Was this the 'radiant future' their leaders had promised, and for which so many millions had sacrificed their lives? The descent from those distant days of heady idealism was steep and sickening, and the sharpness of the fall had accelerated in the months he'd been away in London.

A small man with a narrow face stood up. 'This committee wishes to express its deep sorrow at the death of our valiant and much-respected colleague. The shock of his passing is too sudden for us yet to express in words our true gratitude for a life lived in service to the ideals we all share. Please convey our sincere condolences to the First Secretary on this great loss to the nation.'

Vadim Medvedev looked around for approval and sat down

to murmurings of assent. He was pushing himself forward, as usual. No change there. Koliakov had forgotten how intensely he disliked him. Throughout his previous stint on this committee they had frequently clashed. Medvedev had often taken a contrary view to his. It dismayed him now to see that he remained on the committee. Why hadn't someone seen fit to remove him? Or had he become too powerful for that?

Apart from two others in uniform – both suffering from the heat, Koliakov noticed, as much as he was – and their chairman, the men around the table were bureaucrats with neither imagination nor courage, in whose hands lay the true power of the system because they drafted the documents that their ministers saw, and they knew how to make their way through the bureaucratic maze and manipulate what their ministers did. How he despised them for their small-mindedness and for their concern to protect themselves. How wrong it was that men like Radin – geniuses without whom there would be no future – had to argue their case for resources in front of men like these.

In two more days Koliakov would be back in London, where it would certainly be cool and probably raining and there would be play-acting of a different kind, that effortless snobbery of the English where schools and breeding and accents created a social hierarchy whose intricacies he would never grasp. Once there, he would cease to be a KGB colonel. His uniform would be put carefully away to await his next visit to Moscow. He would once more assume the identity of the friendly Soviet diplomat, mixing with friends in Congress House, Fleet Street, Whitehall and the House of Commons. In order to gain the confidence of those he mixed with, he had even tried to master the rules of that ludicrous game of cricket, though without success. He was regarded as a 'decent' Russian, not a raging communist; a man you could leave your grandmother or your daughter with and who'd treat both with the utmost respect. Another deceit, another hypocrisy, all part of the trade he'd been trained in. One day, when the need for all these different incarnations was over – the radio journalist in New York, the quiet, solitary passport official in Budapest, the clubbable diplomat in London – when he had time to be himself once more, would he still find some trace of the man he once was? Or would he have lost his taste for the true self he had disguised and suppressed for so many years?

The voices around him were arguing about formal issues of procedure – nothing he needed to take account of. He allowed his mind to transport him to a mews house in Knightsbridge, to tease him with the smell of Chanel No. 5 and tempt him with memories of a young body lying invitingly naked on a white linen sheet, softly calling his name. Not his real name, he felt ashamed at that, but some lies were necessary even when he was being himself. Was there one corner of an invented life where, whatever role you were playing, you could shed the disguise and, for an hour or two, become who you really were? How nearly his powers of deception came to an end in her embrace! Every time he held her, he wanted to confess his lies, to cleanse himself for her, but some mechanism planted in his training years before restrained him. How hard it was to break the resolve that had been forged in his youth.

And the girl? His obsession with her was absurd, impossible, reckless. How could he have allowed it to happen? If Smolensky or anyone at the embassy found out, the consequences would be disastrous. But until that moment came, he knew he would not let her go. He would risk everything for her, his beliefs, if he had any beliefs any more, his career, his future – and why? Because she gave him freedom from the pain and deception of his life that he had not experienced before. Remembering her now, he felt the heat in his body rise still further. He was lucky that this visit to Moscow was so short.

'Our enemies in the West,' the chairman was saying, 'recognise the Chief Designer as the inspiration and guide of all that we have accomplished in space, a man whose efforts have given us such a significant lead over the West. They know him through the results of his work, the huge power of his rockets which sent the first satellite and then the first man into space, triumphant events which demonstrate unequivocally before the world the superiority of the Soviet system.'

Here he paused, as if the emotion of what he had to say was getting the better of him. There was no movement around the table. All eyes were on the speaker.

'Throughout these years of triumph, we have successfully kept his identity secret. The West knows him only by reputation, not what he looks like, nor where he lives, nor in which department he works. That policy has served its purpose well. Our Chief Designer's success has cast a long shadow over Europe and America; his invisibility has increased our enemy's fear of him. His genius is a formidable weapon in our undeclared war with the West, and a strategic asset of great value.'

The chairman stubbed out his cigarette and immediately lit another.

'And now his tragic early death puts all those gains at risk,' Medvedev said.

'Your assumption is correct,' the chairman agreed.

The timing of the interruption was too neat to be anything but rehearsed, Koliakov was sure of it. Medvedev's contribution was too slick, too seamless to be anything else. The stubbing out of the cigarette must have been his cue. If he was that close to the chairman, his power *had* increased in the time Koliakov had been in London. Better to be wary of him.

'The success of our space programme,' the chairman was saying, 'has advanced the socialist cause faster and further than any other event since the defeat of the Nazis in 1945. The originality of vision that characterised the Chief Designer's work, and which is the source of his achievement, must continue to play its part in the heroic task to which we have dedicated our lives — the achievement of the global socialist revolution.'

Transparent hypocrisy, though you would not think so if you looked at the expressions of the men round the table. Perhaps Medvedev had written the text.

'Our instructions are that death must be no obstacle to the Chief Designer's continuing contribution to the superiority of Soviet achievements in space. Though he is no longer with us, we must find ways to deceive our enemies into thinking that the Chief Designer *is* alive, so that we may continue to benefit from his influence. That is our task, and the reason we are gathered here tonight.'

To pretend Radin was not dead . . . to conceal his death from the world! Koliakov was incredulous. Had the Central Committee finally lost its senses? Such an idea was not only impossible, it was nonsense, the product of minds that had lost all connection with the real world. He felt sickened and angry.

What about the Chief Designer's funeral? someone asked. Will the state not want to honour him publicly, given the significance of his contribution to Soviet leadership over the Americans in the space race? Will these events not tell the world that he is dead?

There would be no official funeral, no obituaries in the papers, no public memorial of any kind, no announcement of any successor. The chairman could reassure his colleagues on that. There would be no reference to his death anywhere.

'Officially, the Chief Designer is not dead. He has been seriously ill – that much is known by the West – but the skill of our Soviet doctors is such that he is very much alive today and restored to his former strength.'

Why are we being asked to find strategies to conceal the death of our leading scientist? What truth are we trying to hide? Perhaps Radin's death has revealed a weakness in our armoury for which there is no other defence than deceit? He could guess what that weakness was, though the chairman had, Koliakov imagined deliberately, made no reference to it in his opening remarks. *Radin had no obvious successor.* Without him the space programme was leaderless. This policy of deception was born out of desperation. Behind the scenes, there would be a bitter battle to inherit Radin's mantle. It is always the self-important who struggle for power. The genius, like Radin, waits for the call.

If the Americans were to learn of his death, he imagined, they would whoop with delight at their good fortune and redouble their efforts to eliminate the Soviet advantage. Within months Moscow would see its lead over the West rapidly eaten away, and with it so much of the widespread political influence that its recent space successes had brought. Such a prospect was unacceptable to the bald, diminutive and impulsive peasant who now guided the fortunes of the state. Which explained why nine men were sitting around a table in a small room on a hot night uneasily searching for answers to an impossible question: how to bring Radin back from the dead.

He shifted his position in his chair and felt his body ooze moisture as he did so.

'You are asking us to come up with a plan that will deceive the West into thinking that the Chief Designer is still alive?' Medvedev asked, playing the chairman's straight man again.

'It is essential that the West believes that the Chief Designer's work continues. It is imperative that they do not learn about his death.'

The discussion quickly ran onto the shoals. Tea was brought, and later plates of caviar and blinis. More fans were asked for. A search in the adjoining offices, long since emptied for the night, found two, only one of which worked. Its addition was powerless to bring down the temperature in the room which had noticeably risen since the meeting had begun. Twice the chairman called for breaks in the proceedings to allow members to stretch their legs, in the hope that movement or the emptying of bladders might stimulate creativity. Despite these usually helpful devices, success continued to elude them.

Koliakov, tired and irritable, looked around the table at the equally tired and irritable faces of his colleagues. Finding an answer was a task well beyond the energies and competence of all of them. They were in for a long night.

Soon after midnight, the chairman reminded the committee of the importance of its task. His message was uncompromising. They would not be released until they had come up with a proposal. The smoke in the room thickened, and once or twice a roll of thunder could be heard but the longed-for storm held off. The temperature rose, brows and necks were mopped more frequently. Creative thinking remained at a low ebb. Somewhere a clock struck one.

That was the moment that Koliakov decided to break the stalemate. He did so not out of conviction or belief. His ambitions were more mundane – he was impatient at his continued discomfort. Anything to get out of this stifling room and end this absurd meeting, to escape the numbed minds of men for whom he had so little regard, to throw off his wet clothes and immerse his boiling body in a long cold bath.

Was his proposal serious? Did he intend that the committee take up his suggestion? The only question that concerned him at the time was: could his proposal fool the committee for long enough to get the chairman to close these pointless proceedings? Or would one empty vessel recognise the emptiness in another? He never gave a thought to the consequences of his scheme beyond his own need to get out of that suffocating room.

He raised his hand to catch the chairman's attention. He had said little during the evening but now he reminded the committee that he was attending as an observer, having been a full-time member during his last posting in Moscow, as no doubt some of them would remember. Would they, though? In the interval since he'd last attended regularly, the make-up of the committee had largely changed. He knew few well and none intimately, apart from Medvedev, who, he noticed, was eyeing him suspiciously.

His posting in New York and now in London had given

him, he said, some insights into the workings of the Western mind which might now prove of benefit to the committee's task.

'Very few Westerners have ever met the Chief Designer,' he continued, 'and none since the war. He has not left our borders. No Westerner has been allowed to meet him here. As our chairman has made clear, scientists in the West are certain he is the author of our successful space programme. I know that to be true from conversations I have had in London. The First Secretary is right when he says the Chief Designer's reputation is of inestimable value in our ideological conflict with the West. His formidable achievements strike fear into the hearts of our enemies.'

Here he paused for effect, looking round the table at his colleagues, using his apparent hesitation to increase the impact of what he was about to say. So far, so good.

'I propose that we make public what we are planning to do in space,' he continued. 'As their experts study what we say we will do, they will recognise the ambitious signature of our Chief Designer. That will convince them, if they need convincing, that the Chief Designer is still alive because there is no other engineer in the Soviet Union who is capable of being the author of such a programme.'

His idea was greeted with frowns of puzzlement and a moment of silence before a barrage of questions burst on him.

Was he seriously proposing that they release secrets of their space programme to the West? Surely that went against every precept they'd ever followed? How could their cause benefit from revealing their plans? Surely maintaining secrecy must be a paramount consideration?

'We could invent plans for the purpose.' In his desperation for a bath, Koliakov was now giving his imagination free rein, hardly caring if his inventions were convincing or not. 'Plans which to our enemies will seem all too credible.' He paused again to look round the table. 'I would remind this committee that our task is, after all, *dis*information.'

The room was still not with him. He was the butt of another barrage of questions. What kind of invented plans? How could they be sure they were not confusing imagination with reality — was there not a risk that they might give away vital information unwittingly? Koliakov feigned irritated impatience, as if bored by the slow-wittedness of his colleagues in not seeing the neatness of his plan.

'Let them believe,' he said, inventing another idea on the spot, 'that we have built a much bigger and more powerful rocket than that which enabled Gagarin to fly his single orbit around the world. Let us tell the West that we are preparing this new giant machine to launch into orbit above the earth a satellite from which we will be able to fire nuclear missiles at any target in the United States of America.'

The room was stilled by the audacity of the deception. A nuclear arsenal in space from which the West could not hide — unquestionably daring, undoubtedly provocative, and consistent with the innovations the world had come to expect from the Soviet space programme. The slow strands of cigarette smoke, curling upwards above the heads of the committee, vanished into the darkness above the level of the lights. The fans creaked angrily. Through the window Koliakov could see the dimly lit city spread before him. A flash of lightning split the sky for an instant but there was no thunder. The idea was taking root. Silence is always the first staging post on the way to acceptance.

'Only by telling the world what Radin is going to do,' Koliakov said, 'will we stimulate the belief in the West that he is still alive. In that way we will maintain their fear of our dominance in space.'

There was a moment of silence in the room as his listeners withdrew into themselves to wrestle with a dilemma that might affect their careers. Had Koliakov taken leave of his senses? Or had he found a breathtakingly simple answer that would satisfy their chairman and his masters? He watched them face the agony of decision-making.

'Which is preferable?' he continued, the silence pushing him further than he had intended to go. 'To let the West discover, as soon enough it surely will, that our greatest space engineer will build no more rockets?' He paused to light a cigarette. 'Or to deceive them into believing that he is still here, more powerful than ever, making his dreams come true?'

He looked around. There were one or two nodding heads. The chairman had taken off his glasses, always a sign that he was prepared to listen. Medvedev, without a personal signal from the chairman, was shaking his head. It was always better to express your doubt first. Becoming convinced by an argument – especially once you had seen which way your chairman would vote – was a decent excuse for changing your mind.

'Perhaps,' Koliakov added recklessly, letting go of the restraint that he had so valiantly kept in check so far, 'this will be Soviet proof that there is indeed life after death.'

There was no reaction to his remark. Clearly, it was too late in the night for jokes. Worse, the chairman had completely missed his point. Mercifully, there was no harm done.

'Can we be sure such a deception will work?'

'Of course not,' Koliakov replied. 'The success of any scheme of disinformation can never be guaranteed. If the choice is between using every weapon at our disposal to maintain our lead over the West's space technology, or doing nothing, surely we know in which direction we should move?'

Would the West fall as easily as Koliakov was suggesting for these grandiose schemes? Medvedev asked. On what evidence did Koliakov base his assumption? That was Medvedev – even from where he was sitting he could feel the heat of his scorn. Was he alone, Koliakov wondered, in sensing the hostility behind Medvedev's question? Time, it seemed, had settled none of their differences.

'Fear of the unknown prompts belief in the unlikeliest of

phenomena,' he replied. What was happening to him? Was this how he would sound when his posting to London ended and he returned to work in Moscow? 'Given what we have achieved so far, and with a convincing tale to tell, their fear of what we might do in the future will force them to believe what we tell them.'

The chairman let the debate drag on for another half an hour. Koliakov's position slowly gathered support. Even Medvedev, seeing that the mind of the group was moving towards Koliakov, was nodding in agreement. By now, even if he had wanted to, the process had gone too far to allow him to deny that what had begun as a frivolous diversion to bring a meeting to an end was being engineered into policy. With any luck, helped by his return to London, someone else – Medvedev, perhaps? – would claim the idea as theirs and his ownership of it would be forgotten. *Meanwhile, Comrade Chairman, please let us go home.*

Shortly before three in the morning his proposal was accepted, not least because it was the only proposal with any kind of feasibility that, in their long and sometimes irritable hours of deliberation, the committee had come up with. When it finally came to a vote, it was passed with weary unanimity. The Chief Designer might be dead, but Koliakov's moment of madness had ensured that Radin's ghost would now live on, his powers apparently undiminished.

4

1

The letter from Olga Radin, Viktor's daughter, described how in his last days her father had given strict instructions about what should happen after his death. Any offer of an official funeral – not that he expected any such offer to be made – was to be rejected. It would be hypocritical, he said, to accept any show of public honour that had been denied him when he was alive. He asked instead to be buried without ceremony next to his son Kyrill, whose early death had left him stricken and wounded.

After the disposal of his body, the dispersal of his possessions. 'My good companion, Andrei Berlin, is to be the first of my friends to be given the key to my apartment, so he may choose something of mine to remind him of our conversations, which, over the years, have brought me so much pleasure.' Anything that his friends and family did not want was to be burned.

Did his friendship with Radin deserve this privilege? Being singled out in this way both embarrassed Berlin and made him fearful. He had known Viktor for many years. But didn't he have other friends whom he had known better and longer? Weren't they more deserving of this honour? Then there was his irrational fear that Viktor might be trying to hook him into something. He was quite capable of wanting to control Berlin's life from beyond the grave, though why he should want to do so Berlin had no idea. He looked again at the statement in Olga's letter. Viktor was unequivocal in his assertion of their friendship and in his instruction that Berlin should be the first to select a personal memento from among his possessions. That left him no choice. He must do as he had been instructed.

★

The lift was, as usual, out of order for 'summer repairs', and Berlin had to climb the stairs. Viktor always complained that they were lucky if it operated for six months in any year, and it never worked between June and September. Berlin had once found him on a hot July day, sleeves rolled up, trying to mend the machinery himself, a hopeless task given the injuries to his hands. As he put the key in the door of the apartment, Berlin was aware that this was the very last time he would do so. He felt a moment of regret for a man he had truly admired. Whatever their differences (though they had often argued, they had never quarrelled, even when Viktor overplayed his curiosity about Berlin's life), he was diminished by the loss of a brave and inventive man.

The air was stale, the place unlived in. Viktor had been taken to hospital some weeks before, and had lived a lot longer than anyone expected. Berlin wasn't surprised. All his life Viktor had stubbornly worked to his own timetable. Why should his dying be any different? No wonder the authorities had found him uncomfortable to deal with.

He went into the bedroom, pulled the curtains and opened a window. The room was as he remembered it, with a chair, a table, a bookcase, a vase for flowers, empty now, bare, white-painted walls, a wooden floor, a bedside table on which a bottle of pills had been left behind and a single bed that had been stripped, the red blankets folded on the mattress. A pungent smell of disinfectant hung in the air. It was an anonymous, functional room, containing enough to suggest its owner only if you knew who he was, and if you didn't, you'd never be able to guess.

The study revealed Radin's personality. Framed blueprints of his earliest designs were on the walls, and a collection of photographs stood on a bookshelf: a young Viktor Radin with a head of wiry blond hair, beside the base of one of his first rockets; an early picture of the Cosmodrome at Baikonur; Viktor with members of his staff celebrating a successful launch; an older Viktor on different occasions in the great hangar where his rockets were assembled; Viktor standing with a succession of Soviet leaders. How sour he looked in all the official photographs. Berlin remembered his resentment of official visits. Why waste time posing with politicians, he complained, when there was so much to do if they were to keep their lead over the Americans?

A model of a rocket stood on his desk beside a photograph of his daughter taken when Olga was much younger, but even then she was the image of her father. Pinned to the wall behind his chair was a series of sketches, of futuristic spacecraft and drawings of space stations, speculations on what one day might be. Berlin studied them carefully. Radin had dated each of them – these had been done in the last two months. Even as he was dying, Viktor continued to dream. The drawings expressed his sense of wonder at the world still to be explored, how he always wanted to venture beyond what was known. His life had been dedicated to breaking down conventional barriers. Whatever else he may have been, Viktor's nature was that of the true explorer. Berlin envied him the certainties of his vision.

On the table beside a worn leather armchair was the framed portrait of a good-looking young man in air-force uniform whose smile, frozen for ever in its youthful innocence, called so painfully across the emptiness that his tragic early death had inflicted on Radin.

The words of the letter resonated through Berlin's mind, their mystery unresolved. Why had Viktor insisted that he be the first? Could there be a coded message that only he would understand? Was there somewhere in this apartment some possession that Radin wanted him alone to find? It was an unlikely theory, but while he stood in Radin's study, no other took its place.

Berlin scanned the tightly packed bookshelves – he recognised none of the authors except for Tsiolkovsky, the renowned father of the Soviet space industry, though he had never opened any of his books. Viktor had *The Investigation of Cosmic Space by Reactive Vehicles, The Theory of the Jet Engine*, and his final work, *Space Rocket Trains*. Then there were yellowing scientific journals and the records of symposia arranged meticulously in date order. *Space Science and Engineering, The Soviet National Space Engineering Symposium, Space Exploration*. There was nothing here that interested him – he was a historian, not a scientist – and he had no intention of writing a history of the Soviet space effort, nor of Radin's contribution to it.

He unlocked the filing cabinet with the key Olga had given him and searched through personal correspondence meticulously organised, so typical of Viktor. There were the texts of speeches he had given in the order he had given them and academic diplomas from his youth: Radin was a professor of aeronautical engineering at twenty-four. There were letters of commendation from his professors; his official citations for the decorations he had received – these were unexpected signs of vanity. Berlin found a copy of the judgement that had sent him to Kolyma and the identification tag he must have worn there; the official letter telling him of the death of his son, and a newspaper cutting with a photograph showing his son's widow receiving the posthumous award of Hero of the Soviet Union from the First Secretary; letters from different medical specialists over the years about the state of his hands, with the same message that the damage was too great for anything to be done. Each had Radin's courteous reply pinned to it, except for one from a specialist in Boston, who thought he might be able to reconstruct Viktor's hands, but he would need at least a year or more of his time to do so. That offer Viktor had refused. No doubt the politicians to whom he was accountable would have suspected some CIA trick behind the invitation and prevented him from going to America.

With difficulty, Berlin shifted the cabinet from its position against the wall. Nothing had fallen behind it, nor were there any secret compartments, though he hadn't expected to find any. He went through the drawers of the desk, carefully removing each one in turn and feeling behind it for concealed papers. All he retrieved were some ancient crumpled envelopes, a torn piece of blotting paper and a broken pencil.

Angry with himself for imagining even for a moment that Viktor might have acted as crudely as that, he sat down at his desk and surveyed the room. Perhaps his interpretation was wrong; perhaps he had read into the words a meaning they couldn't support. Forget the fantasy of a coded message. Read the sentence as the generosity of a dying man, and accept it for what it is. What would he like to remind him of Viktor? The drawings of spaceships, an old man's last speculations about a future he would never see? A blueprint of an early rocket? But wherever he looked, the thought wouldn't leave him alone. Was that really why Viktor wanted him here?

He could hear Viktor's voice in his ear, he could feel the presence of his energy in the room, the small, neat man talking, gesturing, arguing, directing, driving those around him to levels of achievement they didn't know they were capable of, a continual source of inspiration to anyone who came in contact with him.

Anything of mine to remind you of our conversations, which brought me so much pleasure.

Radin must have calculated that he would puzzle over that sentence, that he would worry away at it until he had found the code to unlock its meaning. He knew then that his first response had been right. There *was* something here that Viktor wanted him to have, which was why he wanted him here first. He was sure it would not be found in the bedroom or the sitting room, nor would it be trapped behind a cabinet or simply left in a desk drawer. Viktor wasn't like that. He was a meticulous man, an engineer for whom order and organisation were everything. He could sit at his desk and lay his hands on any piece of information he wanted because he knew exactly where it was.

'The future of civilisation is to be found in our ability to tame chaos by imposing order. Order is the mark of man's ingenuity.' How many times had he heard Viktor say that? He must look out for anything that disturbed the patterns Viktor had established. He looked again at the arrangement of photographs, the correspondence on his desk, the drawings pinned to the wall. They yielded no clues. Nothing jarred. Nothing was obviously out of place. He returned to the bookcase to examine the journals again. The titles were listed alphabetically by author or by date of issue, as might have been expected. A familiar precision was there, too.

Then he spotted it. Every so often the number of an issue of *Space Exploration* was repeated. There were two copies of issue 39, two of 50, two of 58. Why keep a second copy? He pulled one out. The covers were genuine, but inside each issue the printed text had been cut out neatly with a razor blade, and inserted in its place were a few pages of manuscript in Radin's neat and careful handwriting.

He pulled out all the second issues, and withdrew the manuscript concealed within each one. Together they added up to more than fifty pages of closely written text. He looked at the title-page. *An unofficial report into the space flight of Cosmonaut A. Alexandrof.*

He sat down at the desk and opened the manuscript. The only Soviet cosmonaut who had flown in space was Yuri Gagarin. He'd never heard of Alexandrof. What was Viktor on about? He began to read.

★

How strange to imagine *(Viktor wrote)* that when you read this you will be hearing a voice from the grave. Olga will have written to you, you will have puzzled over my instructions. You will have wandered around my apartment racked with indecision. I can see your reaction in all its stages of confusion. Flattery: that I should have chosen you before all my friends. Self-doubt: why you before others? Suspicion: what was the reasoning behind my instruction? Dismissal: this can have nothing to do with you, you are imagining it. Until finally that dogged, rigorous curiosity which makes you worry away at a problem until you have discovered the truth, drives you to find the manuscript I have crudely concealed for you. You see, my friend, I have observed you closely. I have come to know you well.

So, now you have my manuscript in your hands. Prepare to have your faith tested. I shall lay siege to your beliefs. Defend them well. Cling hard to the myths that have framed your life. I will shake them to their foundations. Hang on to your cherished illusions. Before you finish reading, you may find them slipping from your grasp.

Now read on, my friend.

★

Antonin Alexandrof was always the one for me, right from the beginning. I never liked the farm boy Gagarin, whose sweet smile has become the embodiment to the world of the superiority of the Soviet ideal, and will help to extend the life of this intolerable regime by at least another generation. How subtle our rulers are in their choice of hero. Alexandrof shone out among the rest. Manned space flight was more than an adventure to him. He had the intelligence to see that it was another step in the unending confrontation between man's ingenuity and courage and the dangers and mysteries of the unknown.

Not only was he the right physical size – medium height, slim, athletic – he was articulate, and he had genuine intellectual curiosity. He wanted to know everything about my spacecraft: how it was constructed to withstand the huge stresses it would encounter on its journey, the extremes of heat and cold; how the engines worked, how much thrust they must generate to throw the capsule out of the earth's gravitational pull; how many litres of fuel were consumed in a second; the effect of this acceleration upon the human body; how the stages of the rocket separated one from another; the dimensions of the spherical capsule; the layout of the cockpit and our reasons for it; the temperatures the defensive shield would have to resist if the capsule were to survive the intense heat generated by its re-entry into the atmosphere. Always questions and more questions in his search for knowledge. There was hardly a detail he wasn't curious about. He was the only one of that group of twenty cosmonauts who wanted to do more than inspect the capsule to see if they could fit inside it. I spent many hours with him, showing him my drawings and plans, sharing with him my ambitions and my dreams, while he listened, always giving me his full attention.

I cannot say I got to know him well. I satisfied his thirst for knowledge, and I had to be content with that. He did not seek my companionship, nor, as I discovered, was he close to anyone in that first group of cosmonauts. There was some part of him that he held back from his relationships. I wanted to know more about him, but he cleverly avoided talking about himself. I learned from his file that he was born in Leningrad, the son of a doctor and a primary-school teacher; that he had attended university at the Institute of Aeronautical Engineering in Moscow; when he joined the air force and what aircraft he had flown – there were many hours on MIG 17s and 19s. He told me he had a wife and two small sons, but I learned little more about him from his own lips.

In many ways he reminded me of my son Kyrill: he had that same eager innocence, that same trust that said 'give me your machine and I will fly it for you', never doubting that the machine would fly, nor that he would return to earth safely. I once asked Alexandrof if he had known Kyrill. 'I knew of his exploits,' he replied, 'though I was never lucky enough to meet him. He was an inspiration to all of us.' Kyrill, you may remember, had briefly snatched the world air-speed record from the Americans a few weeks before his death.

Alexandrof had never seen action, he told me in a rare confessional moment, and he regretted that. Flying in space was the closest parallel he could find. That was the only clue he gave me about what drove this quiet, almost scholarly man to undertake the extremes of physical testing that our scientists demanded – often mistakenly, in my opinion, but that argument is for another time – or what made him want to outshine his colleagues. You could not spend an hour in his presence without being made aware of the extraordinary inner drive that fuelled his ambition. I was never in doubt that he wanted to be the first man in space.

We met at the top of a 28-storey lift shaft in the Moscow State University. I am sure Lev Rudnev, Stalin's architect, who designed this unbelievably ugly building, never imagined the use to which our medics would put his lift shaft. I had gone to review our training schedule. Can the human body operate effectively in a state of weightlessness? That was what the doctors had been asked to investigate. We knew by then that dogs could survive the stresses of space flight and the ordeal of life without gravity, so why not humans? I wanted to see for myself what the weightlessness training consisted of, whether we were not wasting our time in an experiment that told us little or nothing. In my experience, medics become obsessed with the data from their experiments, and only unwillingly can they be persuaded to part with the results. All I wanted was a young man strong enough to sit inside my rocket, remain conscious during the flight and return to earth alive.

Our people had rigged up a special cage that fell down the lift shaft. For a second or two of their descent, our cosmonauts would experience something akin to weight-lessness. It told us nothing and was a foolish waste of time. Send them up in a MIG fighter, I argued, they will learn more there. But the doctors would not listen to me. That situation has not changed. Only a few moments ago in this bedroom where I am secretly writing this text, despite my protestations my own doctors have once again denied me painkillers, fearing the damage to my kidneys. What does it matter? I tell them. I will be dead from other causes long before my kidneys give out. But they are not persuaded.

They were all there, Alexandrof, Gagarin, Titov and the others. One by one they climbed into the cage, which was then released to drop down the lift shaft, coming to rest on compressed-air buffers. Alexandrof was the last to go.

'I have some questions, Comrade Director,' he said to me while he waited. He was a serious, dark-haired man, who seldom smiled. He was a little taller than the others, and he reminded me more of a teacher than a pilot.

'Have I time to answer them now?' I asked.

He wanted to have an hour or so of my day, he said, if I could grant him that. He indicated the sort of questions he would ask. I was intrigued, and we agreed to meet later that week. He would drive the forty kilometres or so from Zvyozdny Gorodok, the compound that was being con-structed to house the cosmonauts' training programme, meet me in my Moscow apartment and then return.

We followed the same routine whenever I was in Moscow. How many precious days of my life have I wasted in meetings with the supervisors of the State Planning Committee, with its absurd five-year plans that any child could have seen were doomed to fail? How many more hours in the offices of the Space Flight Commission, arguing a case with men who had little idea of what I was talking about? Bureaucracy is strangling hope in this country, and smothering dreams of adventure. This country's future is being held to ransom by men without courage and having too much power. I despair.

Alexandrof would telephone to arrange a time to meet. We would sit in my study and he would produce his notebook, where he had written down what he wanted me to explain. He would take notes as I talked. When the interview was over, we would have a drink, never more than one, which he always took standing up, then he would thank me and leave. There was no intimacy in the relationship. He never called me anything than 'Comrade Director'. But I looked forward to his visits: they became a regular feature of my trips to Moscow. In that city, these were rare moments of engagement with a mind that interested me.

What did he want to know? The precise details don't matter, at least, not in the context of what I am trying to tell you. Nor would you be able to follow our technical language, that is quite beyond your competence. I want you to understand that I came to respect Alexandrof. He was not another reckless fighter pilot who wanted to show off his courage by going further and faster than anyone had ever gone before. There was a rigour about him that I liked. He was thoughtful, his questions were well prepared, his observations often· useful. I began to trust his point of view. I made a number of important modifications to the interior layout of the capsule as a result of his comments.

Our meetings continued uneventfully for some time. Then one evening, two days after I had been summoned to return to Moscow for a series of planning meetings which were to last ten days, when in fact, with a halfway decent organisation, the work could have been done in three, Alexandrof telephoned me and asked if he could see me at once. If I detected any stress in his voice I put it down to the progressive effects of the training programme. I agreed that he should meet me at my apartment that evening at the usual time.

'We are hearing persistent rumours,' he told me as soon as I had shut the door, 'that the launch date has been brought forward.' He was referring, I knew, to the date for the launch of the first manned space flight.

I had not authorised any change in date, and told him so. I was the director of the project, nothing could be altered without my consent. To my surprise that did not satisfy him. He urged me to find out if the rumour was true. Bringing the launch date forward by six weeks would mean cutting short the cosmonauts' training, and that, he believed, was a mistake. I agreed, though not for the reasons he gave me. The new launch date would also deny us vital testing time on some of the brand new technologies we were using on the craft. We were at that time experiencing a number of serious difficulties, particularly with the parachute spring releases. Unless they functioned properly, the descending capsule would simply plunge to the earth, killing the cosmonaut. I would not agree to send my rocket into space until I was sure that it was likely to return with its human cargo unharmed.

Again I tried to reassure Alexandrof that he was mistaken, but without success. When he had gone, I thought about the visit. He had shown great personal courage. After all, I could have been the one who had changed the launch date. He had made it clear that his concern was for the project and the benefits its success would bring to the country. There was nothing personal in his anxiety. There never was with Alexandrof. He was not trying to save his own skin. If I was further convinced in my assessment of Alexandrof as the ablest of our group of cosmonauts, I was equally mystified at the rumour about the changes in the schedule. But I knew that my authority could not be overridden and thought no more about it. Rumours about everything were a daily occurrence, as they are bound to be in a world that is nourished on lies.

The following day I received a telephone call from my

assistant, Voroshilov. It had been a struggle, he said, but the rescheduling task had been completed and was now ready for me to review. There were still some details of the new arrangement that worried him, he confessed, in particular the reduced time for testing some of the more advanced equipment. The spring release on the parachutes persistently malfunctioned in test after test. Perhaps we could talk about these issues when I returned.

'I have not authorised any rescheduling of the launch date,' I said.

There was a stunned silence. Then Voroshilov said, 'I have in my hand an instruction signed by the Central Committee that the launch date has been brought forward by six weeks. We are to reschedule the entire programme. That is what we have been doing over the last forty-eight hours. We have hardly slept.'

My own authority had been overlooked. Indeed, I had not even been consulted. The project to put a man into space had been taken over by the politicians in Moscow for their own reasons. I feared the worst, and I was right to do so.

★

The reason for the rescheduling (*Viktor Radin's manuscript continued*) was scandalous. Moscow wanted the launch brought forward to coincide with the general election in Italy. The appearance of the first man in space would be seen as another significant victory for the communist world, and the intensity of the worldwide celebration of this achievement would create an emotional wave that would dramatically increase the communist vote, if not sweep the Italian Communist Party to power, furthering the advancement of the socialist revolution in Europe. It was political propaganda masquerading as scientific achievement and scientific achievement taken hostage to politics.

You can imagine my fury. I flew first to Baikonur to

assess the impact of the changes. I went through the revised schedule line by line. Not only had the engineers found no solution to the problem with the parachute releases, but there were also, equally worryingly, a whole range of other technical tests for which we would now not have the time to complete satisfactorily. The risks, already enormous in an enterprise of this complexity, had now grown to an unacceptable level. We had to resolve these problems before the launch, and the pressure to do so was bringing my team to breaking point. They were working excessive hours. I saw too many examples of small mistakes made through exhaustion, any one of which could have caused a disaster in the launch. The success of a major scientific experiment was being held to ransom by the need to support the Communist Party in Italy in its bid for power. It was an absurdity, and had to be stopped.

I flew back to Moscow and entered that graveyard of optimism, the Kremlin. I tramped the endless corridors, losing myself in the secret arteries of power; I attended committee meetings, made representations to ministerial officials, lobbied senior members of the Politburo and got nowhere, and achieved nothing. Why was it so hard to convince these people of a cause whose rightness was self-evident, even to a child? No one would listen to my plea for a return to the original launch date. They were afraid to do so, which told me where the order had come from. My repeated requests for a meeting with the First Secretary were refused. With each day that passed I became more despondent.

Then I remembered some advice Peter Kapitsa had once given me. In the difficult times in the late thirties, after Stalin had prevented him from returning to Cambridge, and he had established a new research laboratory in Moscow, he used to write letters to Stalin which set out the consequences of certain actions that 'the Great Father' had authorised, the unmentioned 'actions' being, of course, the elimination of members of Kapitsa's team on trumped-up charges. In all the years he wrote, Peter Kapitsa got only one reply, a line and a half thanking him for his letters and expressing the hope that he and Stalin might meet soon. They never did. I know Kapitsa saved the lives of a number of distinguished scientists by explaining to Stalin that without them a major scientific scheme would be halted in its tracks. I would follow his example.

I spent a day composing the letter. I argued that while I recognised the importance of the expansion of the communist ideal in other countries, I was deeply concerned by the impact the change of date would have on the first ever launch of a spacecraft with a human being on board if we did not complete all the proper tests and checks in our own time. The success of the mission, which I saw bringing enormous worldwide acclaim to the Soviet Union, asserting the now invincible superiority of the communist system over any other, was being jeopardised by the demand that it coincide with the Italian elections. If we went ahead on the revised timing, we risked our success turning into an appalling disaster. I pleaded that, in his wisdom, the First Secretary authorise a return to the original date. I decided to read the letter once more in the morning before sending it.

That evening I had dinner with Marshal Gerasimov. Have you come across him? He is a great old warrior, now in his seventies, a lean, grey man, endlessly tall, full of wisdom, a survivor of the 1917 Revolution who still wields enormous power. We had got to know each other over the years, though we were never close. There was, I like to think, a certain mutual respect between us. During the evening I was struck by how outspoken he was. I suppose he imagined he was invincible by then, having survived the worst that Stalin could do to him: for a few days of his life in October 1940 he had been under sentence of death before being reprieved and sent to a gulag, only to be released to help in the defence of Stalingrad, where he, like so many others, distinguished himself by his selfless bravery. Either that, or he no longer cared about himself. I call him the Iron Man, hard but honourable, difficult because he has his own ideas and does not suffer fools gladly but is deeply loyal to the ideals of our socialist revolution. His military record is outstanding.

Our conversation was a monologue. The present leadership, he said, was a catastrophe. Policy was no longer the subject of debate and agreement, it was made up on the spot, often the judgement of one man. You can guess who. At best it was contradictory, at worst its aggression and belligerence were dangerous. He had looked for but could see no restraints on the First Secretary. The Politburo was made up of time-servers obsessed with protecting their own interests. The civil servants were too terrified of losing their jobs to do anything but ensure that their ministers took the safe decisions. No one had any time for the military any more. They had lost their power base within the governing body. The KGB, jealous of their position at the very heart of the state, had seen to that and had outmanoeuvred them politically. He feared for the future and hoped he would die before his worst fears were realised.

'We have lost the spirit of the revolution,' Gerasimov told me. 'That is our tragedy. We have lost our way as a nation. We live in the present. We no longer pioneer a new future for ourselves.'

We drank excessively that evening. Alcohol gave me the courage to explain my dilemma. I told him about my plan to write to the First Secretary.

'You are too innocent for this place,' he laughed. 'Your letter will never reach its destination. It will be intercepted long before it reaches the First Secretary's office and held on file. Some time in the future, when the occasion demands, it will be produced by your enemies *as if* it had reached the First Secretary, and used as evidence against you.'

'Then what can I do?' It was a rhetorical question, meant

to express my disillusion and despair. I was surprised that Gerasimov didn't take it like that.

'Work to the original launch date,' he said. 'Ignore any changes. Pretend the demand for the new launch date never happened. Destroy the evidence of the forged note.'

I must have looked astonished because he continued: 'What can they do to you? Imprison you? If you don't run this project, who can? What other sanctions have they? Always look for the power that rests in your own hands. Understand it and then use it carefully. Never rashly, never unwisely, never too often. But when the moment comes and you have run out of other options, do so fearlessly and with courage.'

That is how we returned to the old schedule for the launch. I tore up the new schedule and waited. Nobody removed me from office. Nobody tapped me on the back and poked a pistol in my ribs. Nobody screamed abuse at me or charged me with anti-Soviet activities. I escaped untouched. We resolved the issue of the spring releases for the parachute. We established that our other difficult technical devices worked effectively. A formal note was sent to the Party Central Committee for their endorsement that a huge programme of scientific testing had been completed both on the ground and in simulated flight conditions, that our spaceship was now ready to put the first man into space, fly for a single orbit round the world and land again in the USSR. The note was signed by all present.

What happened at the Italian elections, I can hear you asking? Well, the elections came and went, and the Italian Communist Party did not get into power. If anyone should ever say to you it was my fault, please deny it on my behalf.

*

I had two deputies, Grinko and Ustinov. Grinko was officially my Deputy Chief Designer. He was many years younger than me, able and ambitious, and I disliked him intensely. He was a political appointee, imposed on me against my will. I had no interference in the appointment of the rest of my team. I made sure that I concerned myself not with their political opinions but with their abilities as scientists and engineers. It was this policy – one I have always defended – that made the authorities impose Grinko on me, to ensure that I did not stray too far from the norms of Marxist-Leninism. In my early days of directing the space programme, I had done my best to get rid of Grinko, but without success. He had powerful protectors in Moscow who watched over his interests. Some time later Grinko discovered what I had tried to do. I was betrayed by someone in my own office – I never discovered who it was. Thereafter he never lost an opportunity to report to his superiors on my mistakes in the hope that I would be removed and he would take over. When my illness made it impossible for me to continue, you can imagine my pleasure when Grinko was not confirmed as my successor.

Ustinov was in charge of administration. He was one of those rare men, endlessly loyal, hard-working, believing selflessly in a cause to which he dedicated his life – the success of the Soviet space endeavour – someone who exercised power over an ever-expanding organisation with a light but expert hand. Without his considerable skills, both political and administrative, I sometimes wonder if we would have had the successes we did. I quickly became devoted to him. He had my complete trust.

I had flown back to Moscow for the final selection committee, at which the cosmonaut would be chosen for the first manned flight into space. I was in bed when the telephone rang. It was well after one. Ustinov apologised for waking me. He sounded worried.

'Have you read the papers for tomorrow's meeting?' he asked.

I told him I hadn't had time, I'd be getting up early to do so.

'You will find that in a few important areas Alexandrof's test results have been substituted for someone else's, and his own results suppressed. This is because in almost every test he scores higher than Gagarin.' He didn't have to tell me that this had been done in order to secure Gagarin's selection.

'Do you have your hands on the correct version?' I asked.

'All being well, the papers should be with you tomorrow morning. One of our own people is on his way to Moscow now. He will bring them to your apartment.'

The rumour had grown during the day, he told me, that Gagarin had the firm endorsement of the Kremlin and would therefore be the chosen candidate. Earlier in the evening, Ustinov had been tipped off that the results of some of the tests that the cosmonauts underwent might have been tampered with. He had taken the authority upon himself to rescue Alexandrof's originals from the safe.

Gagarin had a sweet smile and an engaging personality, but he was little more than a fighter pilot. He lacked higher aspirations. The other leading candidate was Titov, a more able man than Gagarin, but less likeable and a less obviously popular figure. I had never had any doubts that the first man into space should be Alexandrof. I had expected a hard fight. I had not anticipated that the selection would be fixed.

There were nine of us on the selection committee, with General Leonov, head of the Space Commission, acting as chairman. We had been given files with the details of each candidate on the shortlist, testimonies to their psychological and physical health, detailed accounts of their very different backgrounds, their educational records, their flying experience, and summary sheets showing comparisons between their performances on all the measurable tests. The debate began on orthodox grounds, with the rapid elimination of all but the three leading candidates, Alexandrof, Gagarin and Titov, followed by a close debate of their claims. It was immediately clear that Gagarin was out in front.

'Comrade Chairman,' I said. 'I am in a position of some confusion. Your summary of the medical history of Cosmonaut Alexandrof differs dramatically from my own.' I held up the paper Ustinov had sent me and read from it. 'May I ask if those words appear on your report?'

General Leonov looked disconcerted. 'No, mine reads quite differently.'

He looked around the table to receive nods from the other members of the committee. Theirs too were different from mine.

'How strange,' I said. 'I can only assume that there has been a mistake and you have been issued with the wrong papers.'

'They carry Alexandrof's name at the top,' Leonov said defensively.

'Are they signed?' I asked.

'Signed?'

'Does the medical report bear the signature of the candidate in question?' I already knew the answer to the question.

There was some hurried scuffling through papers, an embarrassed silence. Then General Leonov said, 'No. There is no signature on Alexandrof's report.'

'As we all know,' I explained carefully, 'each of the test results is made known to the cosmonaut, who then reads and signs the paper. Unless that rule is obeyed, the report is deemed unusable because of the possibility, however remote, that it may not be authentic. We are being asked to make our assessments on the basis of unsigned pages, which must be wrong.'

It was a small mistake by the forger but it is on such small points that the history of the world revolves. It was easy after that. I got them to destroy the forged documents, replaced them with copies of the authentic medical reports, and by the end of the afternoon, my candidate, Antonin Alexandrof, had been chosen as the first man to fly into space, with Gagarin as his back-up. Our general left the room without even a nod in my direction. He had failed in the task he had been given, to select Gagarin whatever the cost. I was quietly triumphant.

★

The night before the launch I was unable to sleep. I sat on the narrow bed in my cabin, smoking, and stared out of the window, waiting for the dawn to appear, wanting the day to be over before it began. I was sending a man into space for the first time. Within hours I would know whether my reputation as an engineer would be confirmed, or whether I would be condemned as a murderer, guilty of sending a brave young man to his death before his time. I felt confident in the design of my craft to perform the task, but I also felt a terrible responsibility for Alexandrof's life. In those hallucinatory moments between sleep and wakefulness, Alexandrof became my son, Kyrill, and with all the super-reality of a nightmare I saw repeatedly the image of a fireball streaking across the sky, crashing to earth and burying itself deep in the ground.

At six o'clock, I checked the medical reports on both Alexandrof and Gagarin, who was acting as the standby cosmonaut if, for some reason at the last minute, Alexandrof would be unable to take up his role. They were perpetually wired up, so the doctors could test their reactions to everything. The record showed that during the night they both slept a few hours. I find it hard to believe, even now, how much calmer they were than I was.

I won't bother you with the details of the launch. We had two moments of concern when we had to halt the countdown for half an hour, but that is not unusual. The ship blasted off into the sky and disappeared on its single orbit of the earth. We were in radio contact with Alexandrof all the time, and he appeared to be suffering no ill effects, either from the terrible stresses on his body as the rocket accelerated to break the grip of the earth's gravitation, or from weightlessness once he was in orbit. He reported that the capsule had separated from the main booster engine – he could see it drifting away, he said, in the mirror we had attached to the sleeve of his protective suit so he could see out of the porthole at the back of the capsule.

He described his emotions as he looked down from his position so many miles up. The earth, he said, was mysterious and blue against a deep black sky: he was seeing it as no other man in history had seen it. He was travelling higher and faster than anyone had done before. He was proud that a Soviet cosmonaut was the first person to have this privilege. He had with him a small photograph of Lenin, to whose memory and revolutionary achievements for the furtherance of Marxist-Leninism he now dedicated his journey. I remember feeling a sense of elation combined with enormous anxiety. We had succeeded in getting Alexandrof into space. Now we had to get him down again.

It was Voroshilov who alerted me that we might be in difficulty. 'We're getting a worrying read-out,' he said. 'We're trying to verify the information now. It's always possible it could be caused by a faulty transmission.'

He showed me the telemetry printouts. The problem was deeply concerning. When Alexandrof had released the catch that fired the mechanism to separate the booster from the capsule, one of the spring releases had malfunctioned. The booster engines had failed to disconnect cleanly. For a few moments the booster had swung from one unreleased cable connector before its weight had torn it free from the capsule. In the process it had damaged the left rear retro-rocket, which is so necessary for altering the capsule's angle of flight so that it may re-enter the earth's atmosphere as it begins its descent.

The capsule I had designed had four retro-rockets. One no longer existed. I asked Voroshilov if the remaining three were operational. He thought they were, but he added that it was possible that firing them might set the capsule spinning uncontrollably. That would have only one result. Alexandrof would no longer have the ability to alter his current trajectory. He would be unable to return to earth.

Could we not turn the capsule on its axis, in effect turn it upside down and use the top two rockets to power the change in direction? I suggested. It was a complicated manoeuvre, I admitted, but surely worth trying. Voroshilov went away to test this solution on a computer model. Even at this stage I did not think that all was lost.

He returned within five minutes. 'It cannot be done,' he said, tears now in his eyes. 'The damage is worse than we thought. In addition to one retro out of action, another is malfunctioning. We have lost the ability to manoeuvre the capsule. There is nothing we can do to bring Alexandrof back. He is flying towards certain death.'

It was an appalling moment. Nightmare and reality became one. In the background I could hear Alexandrof's voice relaying information over the radio. On the wall was a huge electronic map on which we tracked his orbit. He had travelled more than halfway round the world by now. As far as he knew, everything was going well. Yet here, in our control centre, we were in possession of information that would transform his triumph into a death sentence. At the appropriate moment, we would press all the switches to fire his engines in preparation for re-entry. Instead of beginning his descent, his capsule would start to spin uncontrollably. He would know immediately what was happening. He would attempt to take manual control of the craft, punching in the code that allowed him to fly the capsule himself. He would go through all the emergency procedures we had rehearsed. But nothing would stop the spinning. His efforts would be futile. We would hear his questioning voice, asking for advice. We would be forced to tell him there was nothing we could do. He would be beyond rescue, his capsule would have become a steel coffin from which there was no escape as it went spinning off into space, every moment flying farther and farther away until his radio was out of range, knowing all the time that his oxygen was running out.

We discussed Voroshilov's calculations. He was a meticulous and careful man, of great humanity, and I had no doubt that his analysis was correct. In the short time available, I confirmed to my own satisfaction that what he was telling me was true. I checked the telemetry reports. I saw for myself that the rocket had lost its essential ability to navigate. It was now no more than a missile with a human cargo hurtling through space. There was nothing Alexandrof could achieve by any attempt to override the automatic control system manually. He was lost.

'Ten minutes to re-entry,' the flight controller announced.

'We must tell him,' I said. 'We must warn him what is about to happen.'

'Is that wise?' Voroshilov asked.

'It may not be wise, but what choice do we have? He must know his situation.'

I was given the microphone. The control centre had fallen silent. All eyes were on me. I was about to tell a man who, over the months, had discussed every aspect of my design with me and who trusted my engineering ability that he was about to die because of a mechanical failure I could do nothing about.

I cannot remember my exact words now. I told him that we had a serious problem. One of his navigational rockets was lost, the other wasn't working. That meant only one thing. We could not change the direction he was flying in, and nor could he.

There was a long silence, then he said: 'Are you telling me I am unable to return to earth?'

'Yes.'

'Is there nothing that can be done?'

'We have investigated every possibility. We can find no solution to the problem.'

'If that is your judgement, Comrade Director, then I must believe you.' Silence again. 'How long have I got?'

I looked at Voroshilov. 'Eight minutes until we start the re-entry procedure,' he said.

'How much oxygen?'

'Another two hours.'

Silence.

'Please fetch my wife and sons. Bring them to the control centre. I wish to say goodbye to them.'

'Very well.' Voroshilov was weeping openly now. Three minutes later Alexandrof's wife, Marina, and her two sons, both under five, were brought into the control centre. Voroshilov had explained why Alexandrof wanted to speak to her. Marina was pale and shaking, somehow managing to hold back her tears. I suspected she was too shocked to cry.

We listened as Alexandrof told her that because of damage to the rocket sustained in one of the separation procedures, his craft had lost the ability to navigate. He would be unable to reposition the capsule for the re-entry procedure. That meant he could not return to earth. In the few minutes he had left, he needed to tell her how to bring up their sons, what she should tell them about their father, his life and his death. As far as money was concerned, he was sure she would be given a state pension, so she would have no worries on that score. He asked her to remember him tenderly, to think back on their love and the years they had spent together, the happiness she had brought him. Then, after a decent interval, he begged her to marry again.

She broke down at that point. 'No,' she screamed. 'Never. Never. I love you, Antonin. You are my husband. You will be my husband for ever.'

The two little boys were crying now, not understanding what was happening but upset by their mother's distress. She was kneeling against one of the long desks, her head in her arms, crying uncontrollably, repeating her husband's name as if by intoning the name of the man she loved she could save his life and spirit him back to earth. I noticed that Voroshilov had thoughtfully turned off the microphone she had been holding so that Alexandrof could hear nothing of her distress.

'I would like to speak to Director Radin,' Alexandrof requested.

'I am here,' I said.

'This is not an eventuality we discussed at one of our meetings,' he said calmly. I did not know how to reply. 'I have switched the craft to manual control,' he continued. 'Please give me the instructions at the correct moment. I will fire the rockets. It is always possible that something will happen.'

Voroshilov, his arm around Alexandrof's wife, looked at me anxiously. I shook my head. 'If you wish to do that, you have my authority to do so.'

'Thank you for the time we spent together, Director. I enjoyed our conversations. I am sorry we will not have the opportunity to discuss this flight in the detail I had looked forward to.'

Then, as the moment to begin the countdown for the re-entry procedure approached, he fell silent. The only sound was the crackling of the radio connection, the voice counting down in the background and the sobbing of his wife.

'I am going to fire the retro-rockets,' he announced, as if everything was working as planned. I admired the man's coolness. I waited, suspended, to see if all our calculations were wrong and in fact Alexandrof was able to control his capsule. If I had known how to pray or believed that there was any point, I would have done so. At that moment I would have willingly sacrificed my own life to save Alexandrof.

'I'm spinning,' he shouted suddenly. 'The craft is out of control. Goodbye, Marina, Josef, Yevgeny. Goodbye.'

For a long moment his self-control held. Then I heard the most heart-rending sound of my life. Alexandrof was crying. The sound of his tears was coming across the ether to us as every second he spun faster and farther away from the earth.

'Marina, Marina, Marina,' he shouted between sobs.

'He's venting his oxygen tanks,' someone said.

Unable to bear the concept of a slow death by asphyxiation, he was killing himself deliberately now. Then there was a curse, a scream, confused noises. The radio connection with the craft went dead. We were left in silence, the only sounds the sobbing of Alexandrof's wife and the whimpering of her children. Alexandrof had killed himself.

★

Now do you understand that Gagarin was not the first man to go into space? Yes, he was the first man who went into space *and* returned. How strange fate is. If a small mechanical process had worked as it was intended to, Antonin Alexandrof would be alive today. He would be fêted all over the world as Gagarin is, and his name would be in the history books. Instead, you will find no record of Alexandrof as a member of that first group of cosmonauts; you will not find him in any of the photographs taken at Zvyozdny Gorodok; you will discover no mention of any Alexandrof in any training reports or in the minutes of the meeting at which the first man to go into space was selected – the debate is limited to a discussion of the merits of Gargarin and Titov. Nor in any of the files at Baikonur will you find any record of the launch of that rocket with Alexandrof on board. It is our practice to give no name to rocket launches that fail. As far as history is concerned, Cosmonaut Alexandrof does not exist.

Yes, you will find his air-force record, that is still there if you know where to look, but you will be surprised to learn that Flight Lieutenant Alexandrof died in a flying accident when his MIG 19 crashed out of control during a training flight. If you find his gravestone in a cemetery far from Moscow, you will never discover the true date of his death. The date of his accident is one month before he started his training as a cosmonaut. We have falsified the evidence of his life, but in death we are courageous enough to provide him with the honour he is due. Only on a headstone in the silence of an obscure cemetery, where no one will see it, is some small recognition of the truth of Antonin Alexandrof's life allowed to be known. You will read the words: *Hero of the Soviet Union*. It is an honour justly earned by a good man.

*

That is my story of Antonin Alexandrof, cosmonaut and Hero of the Soviet Union, a brave man who died well before his time. Why did it happen? Was it chance, misfortune, bad luck? Or was some more malicious force at work? I asked for the test records of the release mechanism. I had checked these myself before taking the decision that we were ready to launch. The documents showed unequivo-cally that the system worked. We built a mock-up of the capsule and repeatedly tested the explosive bolts that were intended to force apart the capsule from the final section of the rocket that would hurl it out of the atmosphere. Again and again we tried to re-create the circumstances that had led to Alexandrof's death. On each occasion, the explosive devices worked as they were intended to. The cable connectors separated as they were meant to. I was mystified. What could have gone wrong?

I asked Voroshilov for the original designs. At first he appeared reluctant to give them to me. When finally he produced them, I saw what had happened. There was a flaw in the design. Although I could find no record of it, I suspected that the explosive charge had never worked properly during its testing phase. Despite that, it had been cleared for the launch, in the hope that it would work. The system I tested after the disaster was not the same as the one that had been on Alexandrof's craft. It was the second version, in which the problem had been solved. The records had been falsified to show that version one had tested successfully.

What was I to do? A man I respected had died unnecessarily and I was responsible for his death. Had we been honest with ourselves and accepted that the component design was faulty, we would have delayed the flight until the problem was solved, Alexandrof would have survived and the flight would have been a triumph. But we had done none of these things. Someone on our team had suppressed knowledge of the mechanical problems. He had falsified the report on the trials of the detonator that separated the capsule from the rest of the craft. Why? Out of fear of the consequences that an important component in the design of the craft could not be made to work on time? Out of terror that to reveal a design fault would have intolerable personal repercussions for the technician who blew the whistle because it might have led to unacceptable delays? *Why?*

Is it better to lie than to speak the truth, Andrei? Better to deny than to admit responsibility? Better to conceal than to expose? What kind of people have we become when we reverse the order by which the world works? What kind of political belief upholds the turning inside out of the sense of personal responsibility that is at the heart of all morality? The unnecessary, avoidable loss of Alexandrof taught me how far this process of self-deception has sunk into our hearts and minds. We are deceived, every minute of every day because we can no longer recognise what is true and what is not.

If this is true of our space programme, where else should the finger point? What about our much-vaunted weapons systems? Do our tanks really work? Can our machine-guns fire? Our cruisers float? Our submarines swim noiselessly under the oceans of the world? Will our aircraft fly? Will our missiles reach their targets? Or are we fooling ourselves with illusions about our military superiority? Are we promoting dreams about ourselves that cannot be maintained in reality?

I fear for all of us, Andrei, because we are all deceived. We have come to believe our own myths, to honour false gods. The people of our country have been misled all their lives. We are victims, not of a conspiracy, but of a terrible arrogance and a brutal cynicism, the attributes of a power that has utterly corrupted those who rule us. Take away the patriotic flag-waving, the endless parades of marching men and machines of war; the boastful statistics of our soldiers under arms, how many bombers and fighters we have, how many tanks, artillery, missiles; ignore the belligerent speeches from our politicians that demonstrate the inevitable superiority of anything Soviet; destroy the conspiracy of silence that binds us all, and what do you find? Emptiness. Nothingness. A void. A moral vacuum. The genius of the Russian people is being betrayed once more, as it has been so often in the past. Our revolution has changed nothing. We are slaves still, as we always have been. Perhaps slavery is our destiny: I hope not. All I know is that I will not live to see our nation's emancipation.

*

There was a time when I feared that if I spoke candidly, I might be betrayed. Now I am dying and such cares no longer worry me. I am beyond pain and punishment. I have determined to trust you, and I will do so.

There must be others who believe as I do, Andrei, people who see the truth but who, for their own reasons, are afraid to speak or act. In these weeks of my illness many people have come to me and confessed their doubts, their anxieties, their fears for the future, knowing that I will take their secrets to the grave. These men and women are the future of our country. Seek them out, Andrei. I would ask you to be one of them yourself but I have never thought that courage was one of your qualities.

I ask this not for myself but for those who will come after me. One man alone cannot save a nation. But one man can set in motion a movement that in time may attract others, and together you may salvage something of value out of the riches both human and material that we have so cruelly squandered in the last forty years.

This country is dying, Andrei. It takes a dying man to recognise the truth. That is my legacy to you. Open your eyes to what is happening around you. Help to save us from those who govern us. Find your own route to redemption. Above all, act. Act before it is too late.

Goodbye, my friend. Goodbye.

IVAN'S SEARCH FOR HIS FATHER

As Ivan walks away from the devastated village, there is the sound of an explosion. He is suddenly consumed by fire. Flames curl around his body. The images on the screen disappear, and the sheet is a blank rectangle of light once more. The projector is smoking. The broken reel of film clatters helplessly against the metal spool. There are expressions of anger and dismay. Children stand up to see what is happening. The projectionist bends over his machine, doing his best to douse the fire while others inspect the damage by the light of hastily lit lanterns.

'How bad is it?'

The projectionist shakes his head. 'We'll have to show the rest tomorrow.'

'It's nearly at the end of the first reel,' someone says. 'We didn't miss much.'

There are groans and cries as the illusion is lost. Secretly Andrei is pleased. Now he can dream of what Ivan will do next, amid a feeling of delicious anticipation, waiting for this time tomorrow.

On the morning after the breakdown, a number of the fathers gathered in one of the family apartments to inspect the projector. Andrei hung around on the off chance that they might show some of the second reel to test their repairs. He listened patiently to the theories for the breakdown – a faulty fuse, a surge in power, poor connections on the cable – a lot of head-shaking and advice but no agreement on the cause. The projector was stripped down and reassembled. He dozed at one point, to be awakened by cheers when the machine was working again. Someone had spliced the broken film together, and he was able to watch the last few moments on the reel projected onto the white wall of the common sitting room.

The day dragged by. He went down to the crowded beach, swam with his mother, walked to the end of the concrete groyne and dangled his feet over the edge. His mother gave him some sandwiches and fruit for lunch and urged him to play with the other boys his age. He hated football, he told her. Surely she knew he was no good at it. Anton appeared soon after with his friend Igor Orenko, and did his best to persuade Andrei by kicking him to get up off the red towel he shared with his mother as they lay on the sand.

'He's got a headache,' his mother declared, defending Andrei with lies. For once Anton believed her and left his younger brother alone.

'You're thinking about Ivan,' his mother said later, as they made ready to leave the beach.

'Yes,' Andrei said. 'What else is there to think about?'

'I've seen the film before,' she said, giving him a hug.

'I don't want to know,' Andrei pleaded.

'It's all right, I won't spoil it for you.'

As they climbed the steps towards the huge building, Andrei took his mother's hand.

They didn't see the film that night nor the next day because it rained, a light, incessant veil of warm rain that made the dry countryside green. Andrei spent much of his time by himself lying on his bed. He avoided the other boys, especially Anton. In his mind he relived Ivan's adventures as if they were his own. What would he do if his mother, father and brother were suddenly killed? Where would he go? How would he survive? His impatience to learn where Ivan's journey would take him forced him to beg his mother to tell him what happened. She laughed at his curiosity, saying he must wait and see.

Two nights later Ivan's adventures began again.

Ivan wakes, desperate with hunger. It is more than a day since he's last eaten and he is almost too weak to move. The pall of smoke that only a few hours before had turned day into night has gone. Only the acrid stink of burned houses remains now, smouldering fabric, charred corpses. The smell brings back terrifying memories of the horror of what had happened only a few hours before, and he feels tears welling in his eyes.

His companion of the previous day is still asleep. He appeared from nowhere yesterday afternoon. He said nothing about where he came from, nor who he was. A refugee, probably, from some neighbouring village that had been burned to the ground just as his had been. Together they had escaped the fighting by hiding under a pile of sacking in a coal cellar. Once they heard shouts and a woman's screams in the room above, followed by a single shot. They had clung together from fear that they might be discovered, dragged from their hiding place and killed. They had waited until well after dark before they ventured out. By then, they had been surrounded by silence for hours.

The village is deserted. The only light comes from the flickering flames in the houses that are still burning. No building has been left untouched, no door unbroken, no window unsmashed. They see a headless body in the street and a dead donkey lying on its back. They search in the ruined houses for something to eat but find nothing. The village has been ransacked. What couldn't be stolen has been destroyed. Then, exhausted by their ordeal, they find shelter in a ruin and fall asleep.

Ivan knows it is early because his breath is visible in the morning air. His nameless companion lies a few feet away, wrapped in an old coat he must have salvaged, his arms around his face to keep out the light. He can hear the rhythmic sound of his breathing. He creeps towards him and feels carefully in the pocket of his overcoat. His fingers close on something hard. He pulls out a lump of cheese. He'd had it on him all the time yesterday, the bastard, and he hadn't once talked of sharing it.

Carefully he removes his prize. The lump is old and stale, with green bits of mould around the outside. He rubs them off with a stone and eats hungrily. It doesn't taste good but it is better than nothing. He gets to his feet, brushing yesterday's coal dust off his arms and legs. The morning sun is low in the sky. There is the smell of smoke everywhere. The village where he has spent his entire life is unrecognisable. He has got to go somewhere but where? He has no idea. All he knows is that he must escape. One life has ended, when his parents and his elder brother were dragged away, their screams finally silenced by three pistol shots. That was the past. Survival means forgetting about what happened. Today a new life is about to begin. Where that might take him, whether he will survive, he has no idea. All he cares about now is food, how he will quell the raging demands of his stomach. He hopes he ends up where they have plenty to eat.

'You bastard. Come back.'

The stone hits him on the back and he turns to see his companion chasing after him. He puts up his arm to protect himself from more missiles.

'You stole my cheese.'

'No, I didn't.'

'Lying bastard. You did.'

The boy is running towards him, shouting angrily. This, he knows, *is* about survival, the primitive urge to stay alive. He runs away, but not fast enough. The next moment he is rolling in the dirt, fighting for his life.

The demented boy's hands are around his throat, squeezing the life out of him. He is going to die, he is sure of it. With one desperate movement, he grabs a piece of broken brick and cracks it on the skull of his assailant as hard as he can. The fingers around his neck relax their grip. Ivan chokes and breathes heavily, filling his starving lungs with air. The boy is unconscious, blood leaking through his hair and down his cheek from the wound in his head. He is still alive because blood is bubbling out of his nose.

'One more,' he says to himself. 'One more for safety.'

He hits the boy again, as hard as he can. He feels the skull give under the force of the blow and blood bursts from the wound and covers his arms. He is disgusted by this and drops the brick.

'Serves you right.' The boy has stopped breathing. He looks at his open, sightless eyes. 'Your cheese was stale.'

He walks off without a backward glance.

1

The small, barrel–like figure of the First Secretary, wearing a crumpled suit and holding a panama hat, emerges smiling from the Parliament building. He waves his hat in salute at the crowds of onlookers kept at a safe distance behind steel railings and ranks of helmeted security police. As he walks towards the microphones erected on the forecourt, to face journalists and photographers, he is followed by the nondescript figure of the Romanian president. Pountney, watching the film on the television monitor, is sure that the little man is enjoying all the power of the moment.

'Addressing a special session of the Romanian parliament today,' the Soviet commentator intones in English, 'the First Secretary pledges a series of economic measures in support of the Romanian five–year plan.' In an echoing voice that gives his words an eerie metallic edge, he reels off figures for annual coal production in Romania and the quotas that will be exchanged for Soviet oil.

Impatiently, Pountney presses the fast–forward button on the editing machine. For a few seconds, the bald man becomes a manic puppet, gesticulating wildly, his expression changing from smile to grimace and back again, while the commentary squeaks unintelligibly.

Restored to normality, the Soviet leader nods towards the Romanian president as if to say, 'That's it, that's enough', and walks back towards the Parliament building. Suddenly he stops. He returns to the microphone as if there is something he has forgotten to say. In those few seconds, his expression changes. Gone is the familiar geniality, and in its place is an anger whose sudden and unexpected appearance Pountney finds frightening. His face and his body bristle with aggression as he barks out what he has to say.

'The First Secretary reminds the West,' the commentator says, 'that the Soviet lead over American space technology is widening with each day that passes. The Soviet Union was the first nation to put a satellite into space, followed by a historic orbit of the earth, both events proving the superiority of the socialist system.'

The First Secretary pauses to assess the effect of his words. The crowd waits in obedient silence. Then, his hand stabbing the air in front of him, he continues.

'Soon, the Soviet Union will have the capability of firing nuclear missiles from a satellite orbiting above the earth. That will be the moment when the West will have to recognise that the Soviet Union has won the arms race. No military installation, no airport, no arms factory, no garrison, no home, not even the bunkers deep in the White House, nowhere in the world will be beyond the reach of Soviet missiles. The West should take good note of the unassailable power of the Soviet Union, and bear this in mind when reviewing Soviet intentions for the absorption of the city of Berlin into the German Democratic Republic.'

The camera dwells on his frowning, aggressive expression as he issues his threat to enthusiastic applause. The little fat man nods angrily at his audience and walks away.

Pountney reaches for telephone. 'Julius,' he says. 'I've got something here you ought to see.'

2

The sign hanging over the front door showed two links on a chain painted gold above the letters 'F. S.' in dark blue, signifying the commercial marriage of Fischer and Stevens. If what she'd heard was to be believed, the marriage had prospered, an impression strengthened by the newly painted exterior of the elegant Georgian building. Marion Blackwell pushed open the door and went in.

'Mr Stevens is expecting you. His secretary will be down in a moment.'

She was in a low-ceilinged, oak-panelled room, one among what appeared to be a warren of rooms, all leading off this hub of the building. On a table to her right, under a Joan Eardley painting of a soulful waif outside a tenement building, was a large display of copies of a book on whose green and blue jacket a warship was plunging through raging seas. Who on earth bought novels like that?

'Dr Blackwell? Mr Stevens will see you now.'

She was taken upstairs into a well-proportioned study with a bow window looking out over the tiny square off St James's Street that, until a few minutes ago, she hadn't known existed.

'Hello. I'm Danny Stevens. Good to meet you.'

He was younger than she'd expected, late thirties she guessed, and very like his father: tall, fine-looking, fair hair already turning grey. He greeted her warmly and talked about his partner, whose portrait behind his desk she had remarked upon.

'George Fischer escaped from Czechoslovakia when the communists took over after the war. He arrived here penniless, hardly able to speak a word of English. Over the years he made a fortune from property, and then he took a punt on me. Mercifully, it all worked out before he died. In his will he asked me to remove his name from the masthead because he said it made him a ghostly impostor in a world he would never understand, even if he were to live two lifetimes. I won't do that because of the debt I owe him. He was a great man. I'm proud to have known him.' He turned towards her, smiling. 'Now, after that potted history of the origins of Fischer Stevens, how about some tea?'

While they waited for the tea to appear, he told her about a novel he was publishing – she might have seen copies of it displayed in the hall. Not literary at all, he said; it was an adventure written by a former naval engineer with, he claimed, real storytelling ability. It would sell in its thousands, he predicted, and they'd got a good book-club deal. The question now was what would happen in America? He was going to New York in a fortnight, where he hoped to auction the American rights. Wasn't that exciting? He talked to her, she noticed, about what was uppermost in his mind.

'My father tells me you're involved with Andrei Berlin,' he said, as soon as their tea came.

'We've asked him to speak in Cambridge at the beginning of the Michaelmas term, and I'm looking for support,' she said bluntly.

'Not financial support, I take it?' Was it her imagination, or did she sense his uncertainty?

'No, no, nothing like that.' She explained the circumstances of her invitation to Berlin. 'Blake-Thomas was a rich man. The trust that supports these lectures is very well endowed. We can cover all travel and accommodation costs. My concern is that I want to make Berlin's visit a success. I want to prove to my colleagues that my choice was right.'

What she didn't say was that by going out on a limb, relying on Eastman's vote, she was taking a huge risk. If the visit were a disaster, Michael Scott would not be the only one dancing on the grave of her career.

'I suppose what I'm after is moral support.'

'That's the kind we're best at.' Was Stevens smiling with relief? 'We'd be thrilled if he came over. It would do the house good to remind literary editors that we're Berlin's publishers. They tend to think of us as popular publishers and nothing else, because we're better at selling books than many of our competitors. We like to remind the trade that we can also make a success of books by distinguished academics like Berlin.'

He finished his tea. 'I must confess, I found *Legacies of History* rather over my head, though it goes on selling steadily, I'm glad to say.'

'May I count on your support?'

'Of course.' He wrote something in a notebook. 'We'll get our rep to set up some window displays in Heffer's and Bowes & Bowes, and our publicity people will meet him from the airport. We'll put him up in the hotel next door for a day or two. I'm sure we can get him some interviews with the press. We'll see he gets to Cambridge on time. All you've got to do is tell us when. Is that a deal?'

'You're very kind.'

'Not at all, we're delighted to help.' He smiled again at her. 'Now, Dr Blackwell, I'm very interested to hear what you do, exactly. My father tells me you're a historian. He's been singing your praises. What's your period? Are you writing anything at the moment? We have a very strong history list, and we're always looking for new authors. I'm sure there must be something you're burning to say.'

3

The air is already warming up. Kate knows these Moscow days, when the sky starts clear blue and it gets hot too soon, then heavy grey clouds progressively threaten the city, intensifying the heat with no prospect of the relief of rain. A languid day stretches ahead, when every movement demands too great an effort, when it is too hot to do anything except wait for night and hope it will bring some relief.

Tomorrow she will wake up in her bedroom in the house

in York. It will probably be cool or raining – her memories are always of rainy days – and Moscow will have become a dream once more. She tries to picture what her life will be like, but quickly gives up because the thought of returning home makes her want to cry.

★

Two weeks after her visit to the Lenin Library, Kate received a note from Valery Marchenko, asking if she could help him translate an article from an American scientific journal. He suggested that they meet outside the Conservatoire the following Thursday at five. The note had no address or telephone number to which she could reply. It assumed that she would be available. She shrugged her shoulders. If she was free she would meet him. A few days later, she stood in Gerzen Street as he'd asked. She waited in the October cold for an hour before deciding that he had either forgotten or had found something better to do. Either way, soon after six she gave up and made her way home, cold enough to wish she had never met him, and miserable that he had failed to turn up. She was disappointed that he could have treated her like this. He had seemed so different when they'd met. She was determined to put him out of her mind.

★

Valery sat at his office desk, his chin resting on steepled fingers, a sheet of calculations and a series of sketches of a mechanical moon excavator in front of him, an untouched cup of tea rapidly cooling by his side. If anyone in the Department had bothered to look they would have recognised the posture – the leader and inspiration of the robotics project, lost in thought. Best not to disturb him.

Had they been able to look inside Valery Marchenko's head, they would have questioned their assumptions. He was thinking about neither the design of the excavator nor the merits of different solutions to the problem of the weight of

142

the digging arm that was still too heavy for the robot platform it would sit on. He was in fact dreaming about the English music student he had met in the Lenin Library.

He found he had no way of controlling her presence in his life. She travelled with him on the metro in the morning and evening; she would interrupt his concentration on his work; she was present in his dreams at night. However hard he might try, he was unable to shift her out of his life, and after a few feeble attempts he gave up. She had invaded his mind, and her presence delighted him.

She sprang unexpectedly into his consciousness when he least expected it, pushing aside any other thought until he was willingly overwhelmed with images of her – Kate listening, talking, laughing, looking earnest, worried, amused, relieved, concerned. How was it that in the space of little more than an hour he had seen her in so many guises? Was that really true, or was he inventing images to suit himself? That was the problem. She was a mystery – he knew next to nothing about her. Until he saw her again, he would have to work like a detective and make deductions from the little he knew.

Coming to Moscow for a year told him she was a brave woman. Her reason – that the chance to work with one of the country's leading cellists was one she could not pass up – told him that she was ambitious and dedicated. She was also a realist. She must have weighed up the advantages of studying under Vinogradoff against the awfulness of a year in Moscow. So far so good. Then the process of deduction skidded to a halt as he remembered her fair hair, her dark blue eyes, her long neck that he had so much wanted to touch, how her eyelids flickered sometimes when she talked. Her laugh, the sheer uninhibited gaiety of it, her shyness – or was it innocence? – that would suddenly appear like a blind being drawn down. Her reserve – was it English reserve? – that perhaps hid some kind of unexpected passion waiting to be discovered behind it.

Five days ago he had written her a note suggesting a

143

meeting. He had invented a reason – the translation of a technical article into Russian – one he could read perfectly well in English, but he would make sure she never knew that. He could not give her either a daytime contact address or telephone number. The building where he worked had no official street address. He would simply turn up outside the Conservatoire at the appointed hour and hope she was there, though he wouldn't be surprised if she wasn't.

Throughout the day of their meeting he was unable to concentrate. What would she be wearing? Would she be as he remembered her; or should he prepare himself for disappointment? Memory, after all, can play tricks. Would he be able to recapture that extraordinary emotion he had experienced in the Lenin Library, when no power that he knew could have stopped him going to help her?

The day passed slowly. He achieved little. He was irritable with his colleagues. He put off two meetings on issues that only a day before he had been arguing were urgent. His poor excuses mystified the Department. Marchenko was in a bad mood – best avoid him. He saw their reaction and didn't care. Nothing was going to get in the way of his rendezvous, and in his mind he was already there.

At ten to four, Viktor Radin's secretary, Galina, put her head round the door.

'The Chief Designer wants you.'

'I have an external meeting. I'm leaving in five minutes. I'll see him tomorrow.'

Galina remained by the door, stony-faced. 'He wants you now.'

'It'll have to be quick.' If the meeting went on for long, he'd have to find some excuse to cut it short.

Radin was on the telephone when Valery went in. He motioned to him to take a chair. Why, Valery wondered vaguely, did he never wear a tie? Radin replaced the receiver and pushed a file of papers across to Valery. 'These figures don't make sense. Baikonur say they're correct but I don't think so. There's a flaw somewhere. Something wrong with the volumetrics. I want you to recalculate them for me.'

'By when?'

Radin looked at his watch. 'It's now four. You should be able to do this in four hours. Nine o'clock tonight at the outside.'

'I have an external meeting.'

'Cancel it. This is more important.'

The telephone rang. Radin motioned to Valery that he had said all he needed to say. He was to get on with his task.

★

There was nothing he could do. He could not leave the Institute, take the metro to the Conservatoire, make some hurried explanation to Kate and then race back to his office. What if Radin called for him and he wasn't there? How would he explain his absence? He couldn't telephone Kate at the Conservatoire. The operators on the Institute's switchboard had instructions to prevent the staff from making outside calls to any destination that had not previously received security clearance. The Conservatoire, he knew, would not feature on the list of agreed destinations.

As he ran through a series of mechanical calculations he imagined Kate waiting, her scarf around her face against the cold, impatiently looking at her watch, wondering what could be keeping him. He saw her stamping her feet to keep herself warm as the minutes passed and he didn't show up. He saw her confusion at his lateness growing into disappointment and anger before she gave up and went home. And all because some idiot at Baikonur was unable to complete a set of calculations correctly.

He tried writing notes of apology in his mind, but he could find no convincing words of excuse or explanation. What could he say? 'I work for a secret state organisation. I cannot mention its name nor tell you what I do. When I am at work I have no way of communicating with the outside world. Last

145

night, when I should have been meeting you, I was unavoidably detained . . .'

Whatever he wrote it would be far from the truth, and she was worth more than that. What could he say to her that bore some relationship to what had happened? In the end, he neither telephoned her nor wrote to her. He remained silent, using the secrecy of his work at the Institute as his excuse. He hated himself for it.

4

Hart had chosen a small French restaurant off Kensington Church Street where, he claimed, not only was the food good – he was sure Pountney would appreciate their liver and bacon – but it was never full at lunchtime. With luck they might have the place to themselves, which would give them a chance to talk. What they might talk about Hart didn't reveal on the telephone. But if he was prepared to break his habit of a packet of crisps, a sausage and a pint in one of his smoky pubs in Victoria, then it had to be something out of the ordinary.

Pountney had met Hugh Hart five years before, introduced by his publisher soon after he got the commission from Fischer Stevens to write his book, *Wrong Time, Wrong Place*, a critical account of the Suez catastrophe and the Hungarian uprising.

'You ought to meet Hugh Hart,' Danny Stevens had said one afternoon when Pountney was in his office discussing the outline. 'He was in Budapest with Bobby Martineau. They were both MI6, working undercover as members of the diplomatic corps. Hugh always maintained that Martineau had been sending warning signals to London throughout the summer of 1956, long before there was any hint of the explosion to come, and that Merton House deliberately ignored him. Whether he'll hold to that story now he's been promoted is anyone's guess, but it's worth a try.' He tore off a page from his notebook, on which he had written down a telephone number. 'Give him a ring. Tell him I suggested the two of you get together. You never know, he may be able to help.'

How a publisher was on close terms with an officer in the Intelligence Service defeated Pountney. Wherever he turned, Stevens seemed to have connections, and he showed no reluctance in exploiting them. Perhaps using your friends to further your own business was one of the characteristics of being a successful publisher.

Stevens was right. Hart had been unexpectedly forthcoming. His anger at Martineau's treatment was still raw. Whichever way you looked at it, he said, it was inexcusable. The man had been shamelessly ignored. Everything he had predicted had happened. Thousands of innocent Hungarians had died, and their blood was on the conscience of a number of his former colleagues who, he argued, had been wilfully deaf to Martineau's reports. If there hadn't been a clear-out at Merton House after the Hungarian Revolution had been crushed, Hart would probably have resigned.

Much of what he subsequently told Pountney during a few long and drunken evenings found its way into the narrative, suitably disguised. After the book came out, to generally favourable reviews, and Pountney began his new career as a journalist, they had lost touch. It was more than two years later, shortly before his departure for Moscow, that Hart unexpectedly reappeared in his life.

'We were wondering,' he said, as they dined in a Chinese restaurant on the outskirts of Richmond, 'if from time to time you could give us the benefit of your knowledge of Moscow and the Soviets.'

Pountney, anxious to do nothing to compromise his new position as a foreign correspondent, showed reluctance. Was he being recruited as a spy in all but name?

'No cloak and dagger.' Hart laughed at the thought. 'The days when we employed amateurs are long gone. What I'm suggesting is an informal relationship, nothing compromising. We're looking for occasional access to your wisdom, that's all.'

He was that rare commodity, Hart reminded him, a specialist on Soviet affairs who was there, on the front line. He could report on what he saw in the street, the amount of food in the shops, the demeanour of the people, the buzz, if there was one, on the diplomatic circuit. All they were asking him to do was keep his eyes open, and he was already doing that for his paper, wasn't he, and answer a few questions. 'Not exactly onerous, is it?' Hart concluded.

On that definition, Pountney had to admit that what Hart wanted him to do was neither onerous nor compromising. Should he have a word with his editor?

'We already have,' Hart added with a smile, 'and he has no objection.'

Hart had stuck to his word. Twice on leave Pountney had been given a decent dinner and was asked some questions, all of which he had been able to answer without compromising himself. It was all pretty harmless, Pountney admitted. He was glad to be of help.

*

His life as a correspondent in Moscow was not as he had expected, though on reflection he was not sure what he *had* expected. He had a room on the tenth floor of a decaying hotel whose lift was permanently out of order, where the food was worse than any he had eaten anywhere and the heating was either tropical or didn't function at all. All his attempts to interview members of the government or senior members of the civil service were turned down. Those whose names were supplied as official contacts seemed too frightened to give him any useful information. The press agencies were useless, providing government propaganda barely concealed as information. Good stories were hard to find. He met journalists from other countries and discovered that, like him, they depended upon Soviet newspapers and gossip. As the winter gripped the city in a cold whose intensity he found terrifying, he wished he were back in London. He viewed the coming months with gloom.

★

Soon after his return to Moscow in December from a short trip to visit his ailing mother, Pountney was taken aside at an embassy party by a diplomat he'd not met before.

'My name's Peter Wiley,' the tall young man said, grinning broadly. 'I'm new here. One or two people at home have suggested I look you up. You wouldn't be free, would you, to come and have a bite of supper when this shindig is over?'

Wiley had taken him back to his flat in the diplomatic compound and introduced him to his wife, Jane. She was walking up and down calming a crying baby when they arrived.

'Meet Bill,' Wiley said proudly. 'My son and heir. All of ten weeks.'

'The poor little man's got colic,' Jane said. 'If you're hungry, you'll have to fend for yourselves, I'm afraid, or wait until I've settled him.'

Pountney sat in the kitchen drinking bottled beer while Wiley made cheese omelettes. They gossiped about the embassy and the diplomatic community. Jane joined them later, and they questioned Pountney about the difficulties of living in Moscow. At ten she announced she was going to bed. Bill was going through a patch of waking two or three times a night, and she was exhausted.

'I should be going too.' Pountney got to his feet.

'Please, not on my account,' Jane replied.

'Have a nightcap, old man.' It was clear Wiley wanted to talk to him alone. Tempted by the offer of a malt whisky, and against his instincts, Pountney agreed.

'I think you might know a friend of mine,' Wiley said later. 'Hugh Hart. Ring a bell?'

Pountney felt as if a net had been thrown around him.

149

Wiley was not a diplomat, he was one of Hart's Merton House gang. He should have guessed.

'He said you and he go back a long way.'

'Not that far,' Pountney said, wishing he could deny ever having heard of Hart.

'Well, we won't argue about that.' Wiley smiled. 'Hugh's got a small commission. He asked me to sound you out.'

'What kind of commission?' Pountney's voice was full of suspicion.

'There's someone here we're beginning to think might be important. The trouble is, our fellow's a little shy about putting his nose out of doors. Hugh wondered if you could help.'

'What kind of help?'

'Research, really. That's the best way of describing it. We'd like to know a bit more about him. We thought you'd be just the man for it.'

'Who is he? Some politician?'

'Not a politician exactly, no.'

'Who then?'

'Bloke called Viktor Radin. Ever heard of him?'

'No. What does he do?'

'He's a boffin.'

Pountney brightened. An exit had suddenly become visible. 'You mean he's a military scientist, don't you?'

'Works on missiles and space rockets, yes.'

'Men and women who work for the military,' Pountney replied with authority compounded with relief, 'are invisible people, without addresses or telephone numbers. They live strictly supervised lives in secret cities that are given numbers, not names, not one of which appears on any map. They're miles from anywhere, surrounded by barbed wire, legions of security and God knows what else. To compensate for their lack of freedom, they are paid well, and their living conditions are much better than elsewhere in the Soviet Union. To disguise what they do, they are employed by ministries with strange-sounding names, like the Ministry of Light Engineering, which builds nuclear bombs.'

'That must explain our lack of profile,' Wiley said. 'We were hoping you'd be able to help us put some flesh on the bones.'

'Even if you could find them, which you can't, boffins like Radin are strictly out of bounds,' Pountney said with conviction, hoping to end a conversation whose direction he was increasingly uncomfortable with. 'Tell Hugh what he wants simply can't be done. It's impossible. Sorry.'

'He'll be disappointed.' Wiley looked put out. Clearly, Pountney hadn't reacted in the way Hart had led him to expect. 'Radin sounds an interesting man. He's the brains behind the Soviet space programme. Been obsessed with rockets since boyhood, apparently. That's about all we know about him, except that his hands don't work. They're damaged, useless, he can't do anything with them. We don't know how it happened. The rumour is that his own people did it to him years ago in the war, when they got it into their heads that Radin was working for the Germans. No evidence of that either, or none that our people ever found when we looked into it after the war.' He looked at Pountney sadly. 'I suppose nothing I can say would make you change your mind?'

'It's not my mind you need to change.'

'Pity.' Wiley surveyed his empty glass. 'But there we are. Worth a try. At least we all know where we stand. No hard feelings, I hope? Still friends.'

★

'You've got to come, Gerry,' Annabel Leigh was shouting excitedly down the telephone. 'I'm asking everyone I know and I won't take no for an answer. Vinogradoff's a rising star. Everywhere you go in Moscow people are talking about him. He's booked to play at the Festival Hall next summer, so you'll be way ahead of the field if you see him here first. You simply can't say no to me, can you?'

He'd never heard of Vinogradoff and he wasn't mad about Russian music – he didn't really know much about it – but Annabel Leigh was a formidable matron at the British Council in Moscow whom it was hard to refuse. There was also the enticing prospect of a decent meal. Her supper parties were renowned.

'You can count on me, Annabel.' He hoped he'd struck the right note of enthusiasm. 'I'd love to come.'

'You're an angel, Gerry darling. Bless you.'

In the interval of the concert, eating caviar and drinking excellent Georgian wine, he was talking to the bureau chief of the *Washington Post* and a man he vaguely knew from the American Embassy, when he was drawn to one side by Annabel Leigh.

'Gerry, I want you to meet a good friend of mine.' She had her arm through that of a tall, dark-haired Russian whom Pountney had never seen before. 'I don't think you know Andrei Berlin. Dr Berlin's a historian at the university. He's in my good books because he's always helping me entertain my visiting academics. Aren't you, darling? I'm sure you two have lots in common. Now don't let this lovely man escape, Gerry, while I'm looking after my other guests. He's promised to sit next to me in the second half and I shall be coming back to claim my prize.'

Berlin smiled indulgently at his hostess, then turned his attention to Pountney.

'Annabel tells me you're a journalist,' he said in precise but accented English. 'You must have committed a serious crime to deserve banishment to our Moscow winter. It gets very cold in this city, as bad as Siberia.'

Berlin, he had to admit, cut an impressive figure. He was tall, with long black hair pulled back from a high forehead and deep-set eyes that stared soulfully at you. When he talked he had the engaging habit of fixing his attention fully on you.

Was it surprising Annabel flirted so obviously with him, even though she was old enough to be his mother?

Berlin was full of questions. What did Pountney think of John Kennedy? Was he a serious presidential candidate or a playboy? Would the Democrats really nominate him? How close were the British to the Americans? Was the so-called special relationship between the two countries real, or simply a convenient piece of propaganda with which to threaten the Soviets?

Pountney was giving his opinion when an older man, small, with thinning spiky grey hair and a long beaky nose, approached Berlin. He reminded Pountney at once of a character from a children's book. Mr Weasel, perhaps? He muttered a brief apology in Russian to Pountney and then spoke to Berlin, who bent down to hear what he was saying. Pountney remembered a brief glimpse of the man's hand resting momentarily on Berlin's arm. It was larger than his physical size suggested, swollen and deformed, as if it had been made without bones, a parody of what a hand should be. Was this Wiley's man, Radin? He dismissed the thought and returned to Berlin's questions.

The bell rang for the second half of the concert. Annabel returned with a shriek and dragged Berlin off with hardly an apology. 'You're not going to escape me this time, darling. I'm having you all to myself for the rest of the evening.'

'I have enjoyed our conversation,' Berlin said, smiling warmly. 'We must meet again some time.'

Pountney took his seat once more. 'I often wonder,' his neighbour, an ageing member of the British Embassy, whispered as the musicians took the stage, 'whether Annabel gets to sleep with her trophies, or whether the relationships are purely platonic. I've always imagined making love to Annabel would be like riding a fire engine on its way to a fire.'

At the last moment Pountney saw the small Russian squeeze past others to sit directly in front of him, his arms folded, concealing his hands from view. At some point in the recital the Russian rested them briefly in his lap. Pountney saw their odd pancake-like shape, the splintered, discoloured nails, the misshapen fingers, the scars over the joints on the knuckles, the inflamed, puffy surface of the skin. He had the impression that his hands were hot, as if they'd been roasted. From what he could see, few bones had been missed, suggesting that the damage had been inflicted deliberately and precisely to create a maximum of pain and permanent disability. He noticed that, when each piece ended, the Russian did not clap or use his hands in any way. He nodded his head in appreciation. This was Radin all right: it had to be. And he was sitting less than three feet away.

★

A month later, very late at night, Pountney received a phone call in his apartment.

'Is that Mr Pountney? The English journalist?' His caller was a woman with limited, halting English.

'Yes. Who am I speaking to?'

'I have little time. Listen please. Today was killed Kyrill Radin, son of Viktor Radin. Kyrill is pilot on MIGs. He tries to make new world speed record. Now he is dead. You know Viktor Radin? He is Chief Designer of Russian spaceships. Kyrill is much-loved son. It is new tragedy for man who has already suffered much. Now he only has daughter, Olga. The father is good man. Not what you think. Thank you.'

His mysterious informant rang off. Pountney had received calls like this before, though usually from men. A woman was unusual. News was given to him anonymously in the hope that he would report it. It was without exception propaganda, and the method a transparent attempt by the authorities to control what appeared in Western newspapers. This, for reasons he found himself unable to explain, felt different.

Two days later he heard from a contact at the embassy that a Soviet pilot had been killed on a test flight of a new fighter. The plane had gone through the sound barrier and then had suddenly spiralled out of control before crashing into the ground and exploding. The name of the pilot had been withheld. In a small way Pountney had his first scoop.

★

The snow was falling heavily. Pountney, muffled against the cold as much as to hide his identity, stood beside a gravestone and watched as the coffin was lowered into the ground by four members of what he presumed was Kyrill Radin's squadron. They were too far away for him to make out the insignia on the shoulders of their greatcoats. Towering above them was the formidable figure of Marshal Gerasimov. He saw the grieving family staring down into the grave, the man he now knew was Radin with his arm round a weeping young woman he guessed was his daughter. A few paces away, an older woman stood by herself, presumably Radin's wife – estranged wife? As far as he could tell she did not appear to be crying. Perhaps this was one tragedy too many in a life full of sorrows. Perhaps she had no more tears left to cry.

The daughter threw the white flowers she had been carrying onto the coffin and turned away. Radin was searching for something in his pocket. He appeared increasingly agitated at his failure to find what he was looking for. His daughter spoke to him, taking his hand in hers, and put her face into her father's chest. He held her tightly. At first Pountney thought the father was supporting the daughter. But as they walked slowly away from the graveside, he saw that it was the father who was crying openly and the daughter who provided comfort. His wife, if it was his wife, a stiff, upright figure, followed a few paces behind.

If Pountney stayed where he was, the grieving family would have to pass directly in front of him. The temptation, despite the numbness in his feet and hands, was too great to resist. He remained fixed to the spot, a solitary mourner in a field of the dead.

The group was a few feet away when Radin stopped. He

pulled off his glove and put his hand into his overcoat pocket. Clumsily he drew out a large white handkerchief and put it to his eyes. As he did so, his scarred and broken fingers lost their grip and the handkerchief fell to the ground at Pountney's feet. Pountney picked it up and returned it to Radin. For an instant their eyes met, and he saw the expression of inconsolable grief in the Russian's face. He knew unequivocally that Radin's heart was broken, and he found himself touched by his sorrow.

He followed them at a distance out of the cemetery. Radin shook hands with the officers who'd attended his son's funeral, and spoke for a few moments to Marshal Gerasimov, before walking towards an official car. How terrible, Pountney thought, to lose your only son, for the child to die before its parent.

'Wait. Wait, please. I must speak to you.'

He turned. An old woman, dressed in black, was hobbling towards him. She was holding out her hand.

'You dropped this back there. I saw you do it. Please. This is yours.'

He held out his hand towards her. She gave him something metallic. He thanked her. Then he opened his hand. He was holding Kyrill Radin's cap badge.

*

This is madness, Pountney tells himself again, freezing to death to do something I don't have to do. He has repeated the same phrase a hundred times, but it makes no difference. He doesn't have to do this but he can't give up. Some nagging part of his conscience won't allow him to keep the cap badge. He must return it to its rightful owner.

The street lights gleam dimly in the dark. Pountney shivers. It wasn't difficult to find out where Radin lived. He followed father and daughter home after the funeral. But it took him a week to build up the courage to call on them. How to get into the apartment building? The entrance hall is under the watchful eye of an ancient witch who seems never to sleep. He's got no chance of slipping past her on his way to the lift. His only hope is to attach himself to a small group of two or three people as they enter the building, and trust that he can get into the lift before his presence is noticed. That demands patience. Well, being patient is what he's good at.

He looks at his watch. He has been waiting in the shadows for more than two hours. He stamps his feet to keep the circulation going. Twenty minutes later three men approach the building. One presses a bell and pushes the main door open. Pountney pulls his hat down over his face, slips out of the shadows and quickly follows them in. He crosses the hall as one of them nods in greeting to the witch. They wait at the lift, agonising seconds while it slowly completes its grumbling descent to the ground floor. Pountney is the last to enter. He pulls the iron grille of a door tightly shut. Someone stabs the button for the fourth floor. He touches six. The lift begins its slow ascent. So far so good.

He gets out at the sixth floor and waits. The lift descends at once in answer to a summons from below. The uncarpeted landing and corridors are deserted. Pountney walks quietly down the stairs to floor five. Radin's apartment is number 14. The sign indicates that 14 to 18 are to his left. He hears the mechanical grunts and growls as the lift ascends once more. He retreats up the stairs to avoid being seen. The lift stops at Radin's floor. A man gets out, walks the few paces to number 14, rings the bell. The door opens. Pountney hears an exchange in Russian. The door closes. Radin has a visitor. *Damn.*

He can't stay where he is. He must find somewhere to hide. He walks down the corridor, past number 14, looking for a door without numbers – a janitor's room, a store cupboard, anything. He finds an unlocked room and goes in. He sees a large lagged water heater with a stopcock. If he keeps the door ajar, he can watch the entrance to Radin's flat at the end of the corridor. He waits. An hour passes. It is warm in the cupboard, and feeling slowly returns to his frozen body.

It is well after ten when he hears Radin's door open. He listens. There are hushed voices. The man emerges – he wears the uniform of an air-force officer – and waits by the lift, repeatedly pressing the bell. It doesn't come, and after a time he decides to take the stairs. Pountney waits five minutes. Then he steps out of his hiding place and knocks on Radin's door. Mr Weasel – Professor Weasel – answers.

'Professor Radin?'

'Who are you?'

Radin looks up at him, realises he has never seen Pountney before, and immediately moves back into his apartment, trying to push the door shut with his feet as he does so.

'Please. I am not what you think. I would like to speak to you. Please.'

'I do not wish to speak to anyone.'

In that instant he sees the desperation in Radin's eyes. He is still lost in grief at the death of his son. Pountney feels an overwhelming compassion for the man.

'I have something for you.'

The door shuts. He hears bolts snap tight. Somewhere deep in the building an alarm sounds. Moments later the security forces arrive. Pountney has just enough time to conceal Kyrill Radin's cap badge in the lining of his coat before he is arrested.

*

Pountney's career as Moscow correspondent for his newspaper was seven months old when it was brought to an abrupt and unexpected end with his arrest on charges of spying. For four desperate days he was held in a Soviet prison, half starved, hardly allowed to sleep between interrogations, set upon by his fellow inmates on one occasion and beaten up, afraid that any trial would make a mockery even of Soviet lip-service to the idea of a judicial process, that he would be found guilty, as his jailers jeeringly told him, and either shot as a spy or sentenced to a lengthy period of imprisonment in a Siberian camp.

During the days of his incarceration, a deal was brokered in London between Gennady Koliakov and Hugh Hart, who had got to know Koliakov in Budapest shortly before the Hungarian uprising. In return for concessions to the Russians that were never revealed, charges of spying against Pountney were dropped. He was found guilty of the lesser charge of actions incompatible with his status as a journalist and expelled. By agreement the Soviet authorities let it be known that Pountney been arrested travelling without official permission outside the cordon sanitaire that limited the free movement of all non-Soviet personnel to within a narrow radius of Moscow. It was a lie Pountney was more than willing to support in exchange for his freedom. Twenty-four hours later, he was back in London, the news of his return a brief headline in his own paper. It had been, he admitted breathlessly to Hart, 'too close a call'. He'd done Moscow. He was never going back.

*

'Have a look at this and tell me if you recognise anyone.'

Hugh Hart nods at the waiter. He should go ahead and pour. Looking at the label on the bottle – a '58 Sancerre – Pountney knows the lunch isn't for old times' sake. Hart doesn't order wine like this usually. He's after something, all right. He produces a large brown envelope from his briefcase, and extracts from it a black and white print which he hands to Pountney.

'Be prepared. It may bring back unhappy memories.'

The photograph has been taken from a distance with a long-range lens, and judging from the angle probably from a first-floor window. It must have been magnified a number of times before the print was made, which explains the grainy tones and lack of definition in some of the detail. Despite that, the centre of the image is clear. An old man is sitting hunched in a wheelchair, a rug over his legs, shaded by the overhanging branches of an oak tree. He has a cigarette clamped tightly between his lips. His hands, Pountney notices, are tucked out of sight under the rug.

'It's Radin all right,' Pountney says. 'No question.'

'You're sure?'

'Quite sure.'

'What about the other man? Recognise him?'

Jacket off and sleeves rolled up, a tall man, many years Radin's junior, is lying on the grass beside the wheelchair, propping himself up on one elbow. He too is smoking.

'Yes,' Pountney says. 'Strangely enough, I do. I met him at a concert in Moscow once. Annabel Leigh was draped all over him. We had a talk in the interval. Intelligent man. Spoke very good English. I liked him.'

'Who is he?'

'His name is Andrei Berlin. Am I right?'

'You're the one who's talked to him, Gerry. I've never seen him before.'

'He is a historian. Teaches at the university in Moscow. Annabel told me so.'

'This Annabel Leigh woman – can she be trusted to get things like that right?'

'Where men are concerned. Annabel never gets details wrong.'

The photograph, he is sure, has been taken in one of the secure clinics outside Moscow. Berlin must have been visiting Radin. Pountney is impressed. Hart's sources are much better than he imagined. Perhaps the rumours of incompetence in Merton House were merely a smokescreen to fool the Russians. Or was that what they wanted him to believe?

'Radin looks in bad shape,' Pountney says.

'Our understanding is that he died a few days after this photograph was taken.'

'When was that?'

'About three weeks ago.'

'Are you sure?' Pountney asks.

'Why shouldn't I be?' Hart sounds less certain than he wants to be.

'There's been nothing on the wire service about Radin dying.' No photographs either, no adulatory articles in the Soviet press, no ceremony in Moscow, no procession of Politburo members following the garlanded photograph of the dead man into the cemetery.

'There's been no official announcement, I agree. But we've had a report from a usually reliable source that Radin is dead. If it's true, it could be of considerable importance.'

'Why does knowing whether Radin is alive or dead matter so much?'

'There's a lot at stake right now, Gerry. In the arms race, in space, wherever we turn, the Soviets are leading us by the nose. They got a man into orbit before we did, they've got an armoury of missiles many times larger than anything we have, and huge numbers of men under arms. Now they're threatening us with a satellite that will be able to aim nuclear bombs at any city in the West. Last of all and far from least, they want us out of West Berlin. A wrong political move now – particularly one based on false assumptions about the Soviets' military capability – could put us on a collision course that within hours could lead to war.'

'What's Radin got to do with all this?'

'If he's dead, then it's more probable that the First Secretary's threats about a new armoury of space weapons are bluff, which means time is on our side and we can play a longer game. We're pretty sure the Soviets have got no successors of Radin's calibre. Without him the space pro-gramme is likely to be less adventurous and slower to move off the drawing board, which gives us time to catch up with them. In that case it's a reasonable bet that this crisis over West Berlin won't end in a giant nuclear explosion.'

'And if Radin's still alive?'

'It's very worrying. The chances are that the Soviets may

well miscalculate over West Berlin and push too hard. If they do that, then there's a huge risk we might all go up in smoke.' Hart paused for a moment and fiddled with his napkin. 'If we're to make the right decisions and have a hope of coming out of this one alive, we need to know what the Soviets are up to. Their threat with Radin is very much greater than their threat without him. That's why we have to know if he's alive or dead.'

5

The letter explained what was expected of him. He was to give three lectures over a period of eight days, each of an hour in length, on a theme of his choice, before an audience of members of the university, both academics and students. Could he let them know the titles of his lectures, so that suitable announcements could be made in advance of his arrival? The Blake-Thomas tradition, the letter continued, was that each lecture was presented at a different location, beginning at the University Church – Great St Mary's, he knew that without having to look it up. This was a secular occasion. There would be no religious ceremony. How thoughtful of Dr Blackwell, secretary of the Blake-Thomas committee, to reassure him. The second would be at the lecture theatre in the Engineering Faculty. He racked his brain – where Fen Causeway joined Trumpington Street, opposite the Leys School, was that correct? – and the third in Mill Lane. That was easy, it was near the Anchor Inn, where Tolley's beer was served.

And Dr Blackwell? Who was she? A historian like himself, that much he knew. The rest was speculation. She would be a spinster in her sixties, probably, with glasses, hair on her chin and a shapeless dress concealing an equally shapeless body. Why did beauty and brains so seldom go together? Was that why he haunted the student canteens, patrolled the corridors of the lecture theatres, even forced himself to turn up at student parties? Was he searching for a beauty he would never find? Whatever Dr Blackwell was like – and he was sure his image was correct – he was deeply grateful to her. He would thank her properly when they met, and try to ignore the whiskers on her chin.

The invitation included a short historical biography of Norman Blake-Thomas and the endowment he had given the university so many years before. His expenses, he read, would be fully covered by the Trust. A list of previous speakers, in whose company Berlin was happy to be numbered, was also enclosed, and a message relayed from his publishers saying that they would be delighted to look after him while he was in London. A copy of the letter had been forwarded to the Home Office in London as a preliminary to obtaining his visa.

Dr Blackwell ended by saying how eagerly she and other members of the committee looked forward to welcoming him to Cambridge in a few weeks' time.

He had never been to Cambridge, yet it was present in his mind as if he had lived there all his life, a mysterious and ancient city that drew him to its heart. Since his first trip outside the Soviet Union more than ten years before, he had bought books on Cambridge and read them avidly, absorbing their details into his memory. He had only to take one down from his shelves and his dreams would be fired at once. He would travel in his imagination (by bicycle, of course) along the Backs, down Silver Street, then left along King's Parade, turning right in front of the Trinity Street exit towards Market Square, with Bowes & Bowes on his left, the English editions of his books displayed in the window, and beyond W. H. Smith, the market to his right and the famous David's bookstall where on Saturday you bought second-hand copies, Marshall's, Eaden Lilley, Joshua Taylor, and opposite, Heffer's the stationers. He had reached a point where he was sure he knew the topography almost as well as someone who lived there but an air of unreality clung to his images. In his mind, he had created a mystic city where some part of his destiny waited to claim him. Until that moment, his life would be unfulfilled and incomplete.

Now it was here, in his hand: the invitation to visit the city of his mind, to walk in its narrow streets, to be surrounded by its ancient buildings, to meet the destiny that awaited him. To his surprise, he felt little excitement. It was inevitable that he should be invited, inevitable too that he should go. A missing piece of the puzzle of his life was about to be fitted into place. A mysterious force was drawing him there and he could do nothing to resist it.

Cambridge. City of dreams set deep in the fenland of East Anglia. At last it had claimed him, as he had always known it would.

PART TWO
Late Summer 1961

6

1

Words are not necessary. The images on the television screen tell the story with convincing eloquence. East German workmen under armed guard lay the foundations of a massive barricade whose purpose is to isolate their people from the rest of the world. Protesting crowds in the streets of West Berlin angrily condemn the enforced separation from their families caught on the wrong side of a wall that, overnight and without warning, has sprung up between them. Elderly East Germans stare despairingly at ground that yesterday they could walk across but which today has become a dangerous no man's land, the pain in their faces a potent statement of their misery. Young American soldiers, machine-guns at the ready, look nervously across the artificial divide at young men like themselves, only yards from where they stand, equally armed, equally nervous.

These pictures flicker across the television and newsreel screens of the world as men and machines erect a wall of concrete and steel which is topped by barbed wire, flanked by minefields, illuminated by searchlights and guarded by soldiers with orders to shoot to kill. Overnight, East Berlin has become a prison.

2

'What we are looking at,' Pountney says to the camera, 'are the unmistakable images of confrontation. The Soviet Union is deliberately testing the collective nerve of the Western Allies as Berlin becomes once more the focal point of international tension. Suddenly the Cold War is in serious danger of overheating. It is frightening to think,' he adds, 'that when we went to bed last night we had no idea that a few hours later we would wake to a crisis that could lead the world to the brink of war.'

A studio panel has been assembled to discuss the implications of this dangerous development. Pountney turns first to Simon Watson-Jones, the Minister of Defence. What, he asks, does the Government make of these events?

'Building a wall to imprison your own people is an act of desperation from a discredited regime which has proved itself bankrupt of ideas.' Watson-Jones is contemptuously dismissive. The communists are no longer trying to conceal the failure of their social and economic policies, he says. The East German government and its Soviet masters are openly trapping their people behind a wall because they have no other way of stopping the migration to the West which threatens the economic existence of the East German state. He warns the communists that they should tread carefully. The world will hold them responsible for 'whatever happens in the future'.

'Crispin Thursley, do you agree that the building of this wall is the desperate act of a bankrupt regime?'

The Liberal spokesman on foreign affairs is a former geography lecturer at Liverpool University, a thin, pale man whose rimless glasses glint in the studio lights. He blinks repeatedly as he speaks.

'This is a public admission of defeat before the court of world opinion,' he says. 'The East German regime must be condemned by the international community for ignoring the fundamental right of the individual to free movement. Building a wall to keep families apart is a barbaric idea dragged up from the moral pit of the dark ages to which the Soviet Union clearly wishes to return.'

'It's damned dangerous,' Ken Oates, a Labour MP, comments angrily. His face is flushed and a lock of white hair has fallen across his forehead. 'The Government is going to have to move fast if it is to prevent this situation from running out of control.'

'What can the Allies do?' Pountney asks. 'How can we stop this wall rising any higher? That's the question in the public's mind.'

The Government is firm in its condemnation of this Soviet-inspired action against the citizens of both East and West Berlin, the Minister says. 'Make no mistake, this wall has Moscow written all over it.' He makes assertive noises about NATO's commitment to maintain the status quo in Berlin, but he refuses to yield to any direct questions from Pountney about the use of force.

'It's quite inappropriate to talk at this stage about military action,' Watson-Jones declares. 'Indeed, your opening comment that the world is sliding towards war is irresponsible scaremongering. We are facing a crisis that we must resolve. Our clear duty now is to sit round a table with the Soviets until we find a peaceful solution.'

'Words have never made the Soviets change their minds in the past, so why should dialogue be successful now?' The disdain in Oates's voice is evident. 'Talking to the deaf is a waste of time. Every hour spent round a table gives them another hour to build their wall. We've got to stop them now – before this monstrous monument is an inch higher.'

'How can we do that except by military intervention?' Pountney addresses his question to Thursley.

'Military action is unthinkable,' he replies. 'This crisis calls for cool heads. Ken Oates has got it wrong. The Allies must sit round a table with the Soviets, and the sooner the better. We have no alternative.'

'I'm glad that on an issue of such importance Crispin Thursley and I see eye to eye,' Watson-Jones says soothingly. 'Ken Oates, of course, is peddling his traditional response to any crisis: shoot first, ask questions later.' He pauses for a moment, closing his eyes in apparent concentration, resting his chin on the points of his arched fingers in a public gesture of contemplation. 'Force must be seen as a last resort,' he declares solemnly, 'only to be used when we have exhausted every other possible course of action. We are a very long way indeed from such a position.'

'The truth is, this crisis has taken the Government by surprise,' Oates says. 'Neither the Minister nor the Government has the first idea what to do. The Soviet leader is a bully. By not standing up to his threats, the Government is giving him licence to go on bullying.'

Watson-Jones denies vehemently that he is acceding to Soviet pressure. He is doing what he has to do, examining all options before recommending a course of action to the Prime Minister and his Cabinet colleagues.

'By the time the Government has made up its mind,' Oates says scornfully, 'the wall will be built and the Soviets will have proved once again that we're all bark and no bite.' He leans aggressively towards the Minister. 'The wall dividing Berlin will be a daily reminder to future generations of our failure to stand up to the Soviets. It's not Moscow's name you'll find written all over it, but the name of this Tory Government.'

'I am confident,' Watson-Jones says, 'that before long this wall will be reduced to nothing more than a brief memory, whether by diplomacy or other means.'

'What other means, Minister? Are you contemplating a military response if the East Germans don't agree to pull the wall down?'

Pountney's intervention catches Watson-Jones by surprise. For a moment he looks hopelessly lost, as if he cannot remember what he has said. Oates laughs openly at his embarrassment. Thursley blinks frantically. The colour on the Minister's cheeks deepens with anger as he tries to remedy his gaffe.

'The Government is considering all options, as it must. But I can say right now that military action will get no support. We will do what every responsible government does in times of international tension. We will consult with our friends and allies and act in the best interests of this country and the Western Alliance.'

'In other words,' Oates replies, knowing that the programme is about to end, and that he must have the last word, 'you're going to let the Soviets get away with it again just as they have done in the past. Shameful. Quite shameful.'

3

Moscow disappeared under a layer of cloud and Koliakov was not sorry to see it go. In the last few days he had spent too many hours in stuffy rooms listening to men for whom he had little respect deny facts they knew to be true. Once propaganda had been a legitimate instrument of the Revolution. Now lies were proclaimed as truth, and no one believed in anything any more. The distance between the governors and the governed had never been so great. Koliakov shuddered. How he hated Moscow.

Then there was Medvedev. In some unspoken way he knew that the battle between them had been joined again. His behaviour was strange, even for a man of his self-importance, on occasions verging on the imperious, as if he had been given some secret command. 'No,' Koliakov corrected himself, 'I'm allowing my dislike of him to colour my judgement.'

They had met as young recruits at KGB Training School 101. Even then, Koliakov had been aware of Medvedev's ambition, and of the lengths he would go to to promote his own cause. On graduation they had gone their separate ways, Koliakov first to the embassy in Warsaw and then Helsinki. Medvedev had disappeared into some internal security department.

Years later, in 1947, Koliakov had returned unexpectedly to Moscow for his father's funeral. The old man, he was told, had been killed in a fire that had consumed his block of flats following an explosion in a nearby laboratory. After the funeral, he had visited the apartment block, a scarred, shattered relic of a building, with no roof, no windows and no doors. A few days before his return to Helsinki, Koliakov had bumped into Medvedev on a staircase in the KGB building. Medvedev had insisted that they have dinner together. Perplexed at this unexpected show of friendship, and assuming he wanted an audience to marvel at his exploits since leaving Training School, Koliakov had agreed. Medvedev had told him an extraordinary story and asked for his help.

He claimed he had discovered a traitor at the heart of the Kremlin who, under the code name of 'Peter the Great', was betraying Soviet secrets to British Intelligence. Recruited in the last months of the war by a member of the British Embassy – it was Bobby Martineau, whom Koliakov was to come across years later in Budapest – 'Peter the Great' was the creation of a group of members of the government and senior military who had become disillusioned by the lack of social and economic progress under Stalin. A secret Soviet source within Merton House, the centre of British Intelligence, had warned Moscow of the existence of 'Peter the Great'. Tracking down the culprit had been difficult. A month after the war ended, a senior planner working closely with Marshal Zhukov had been arrested. He had confessed nothing before he died. Surprisingly, after his execution by firing squad, the flow of information to London and thence to Langley, Virginia, did not stop.

'What we hadn't realised,' Medvedev said, 'was that as one source was closed off, another stepped in to fill the gap.'

Consequently, more and more valuable information was passed to the West. For nearly two years British Intelligence was little more than a heartbeat away from the centre of power in Moscow. 'They were listening in to all our decisions. For a time they knew everything about us.'

He had been appointed, Medvedev explained, to hunt down the traitors and close 'Peter the Great'. None of those arrested so far had revealed any names before their execution. A number of arrests had led to suicide to avoid the perils of interrogation. But he had had a piece of luck and discovered that one of the links in the chain was none other than Koliakov's former boss, Vladimir Serov. He now wanted Koliakov to support his evidence against Serov.

Koliakov was horrified. He had worked with Serov for three years, he replied. He was a good and loyal intelligence officer. Nothing in his behaviour suggested there was any truth in Medvedev's story. It was impossible to imagine him as a traitor. He refused to betray a man he believed was innocent.

They had quarrelled violently, all the dislike that had built up in their training years finally coming out into the open. Koliakov had opposed Medvedev so vehemently because he saw his accusation against Serov as a crude device to allow the ambitious Medvedev to advance his career. That night he had tried to contact Serov to warn him but his telephone had been out of order. The following day, Koliakov learned later, Serov failed to appear at the office. By midday it was confirmed that he had been arrested at dawn that day. By the evening, he was dead, having confessed his role in 'Peter the Great' and betrayed others. More arrests, it was rumoured, would follow. 'Peter the Great' was now seen as an attempt at a *coup d'état* which had finally been uncovered.

Koliakov knew he had made a dangerous enemy. He was sure that in some malign way Medvedev had used Koliakov's refusal to cooperate to damage his career. His mistake, he recognised, had been not to realise that Medvedev had a long memory for those who impeded his progress, and a patient character.

★

The plane had been three hours late leaving Moscow, and by the time he touched down in London, Koliakov was thoroughly tired and irritable. His diplomatic passport got him through immigration easily enough – though not without a harsh look from the officer at the kiosk – but he had to wait forty minutes for his luggage to appear. He cleared customs and looked for Smolensky. Officially, Smolensky was registered as an embassy driver; unofficially he was a fourth-floor man, a code specialist, while secretly he was a political commissar who watched for signs of deviation in the embassy staff. His meticulous devotion to the rule book of Marxist-Leninism provided him with a measure of correctness that even the Ambassador failed to meet. What he reported to his bosses in Moscow Koliakov didn't dare imagine.

He was not at the meeting point. Koliakov waited for twenty minutes and then telephoned the embassy. No, he was told, Smolensky was not in his room. As far as they knew he was at the airport.

'If he was, I wouldn't be telephoning,' Koliakov said sharply. It was pointless getting angry with the clerks. They'd only make trouble for him later, forgetting to give him his telephone messages, failing to deliver his mail, whispering lies about him to Smolensky.

He had two more coins. One more call, or should he wait? He looked round. As far as he could tell in the crowded hall, he was unobserved. He doubted the British would wire-tap a public telephone. He dialled another number.

'Hello?' A sleepy, smoky voice answered, and at once he felt his blood draining away and a giddiness overwhelming him. He was on the deck of a ship in a stormy sea. He held on to the side of the phone booth as the world moved around him, and looked down at his shoes.

174

'It's me,' he said. 'I'm back.'

'Hello?' the voice came again, this time more urgently. He'd forgotten to press the button to release the coins. They weren't connected.

'It's me,' he said again. 'I'm back.'

He could think of nothing else to say. There was complete silence at the other end. The pips began to sound. He put down the telephone. Why hadn't she spoken? Hadn't she recognised his voice? The anticipation of this moment that had sustained him in Moscow now drained into despair. What a mistake. He should never have rung her. He had broken the power of his dream.

'I had a tail on the way out here,' a voice was saying to him, and he knew he should be listening. 'I decided to lose it.'

It was neither an apology nor an excuse. Smolensky, a cigarette between his thin lips, was standing beside him. No smile of greeting, only the barely concealed contempt of a threadbare explanation. Smolensky lied because doing so let him demonstrate his superiority. He was answerable to no one at the embassy, and he was daring Koliakov to challenge his reason for why he was late. No point arguing or making accusations. He'd get nowhere. Best to get back to his flat, have a bath, go to bed and try to forget this endless, frustrating, depressing day. He slumped in the back as they drove in silence through a haze of rain into a wet and shining London.

How the hell had he got himself into this mess?

*

'You boys must get lonely sometimes, don't you? All on your own over here.'

Noel Kennedy was leaning heavily on the bar. He was neither drunk nor sober, but in the only state he could tolerate, floating alone and bemused, far from any recognisable shore. Any other condition, he claimed, was unendurable.

'Lonely, Noel? Why?'

'Far from home. No women. What a life.'

'Sometimes.'

Koliakov was furious with himself. He'd not noticed that Kennedy was alone in the bar. It was too late now to think of escape. He ordered himself a glass of wine and another brandy for Kennedy.

'Prison, eh? Like being in prison.' Kennedy chuckled at the thought. 'Life without a woman, eh? Drives you round the bend, doesn't it? Christ, when I think back. The women I've had.'

Kennedy, he knew, was a man of social privilege and inherited wealth who had squandered his background and his money and every day was sliding deeper into the gutter. At night he lived in the bars and clubs of Soho, by day he would surface for lunch at his club, start drinking as soon as he arrived, and would grab anyone he knew as they appeared, especially if they arrived at the bar unaccompanied.

'How do you boys survive?'

'We have our beliefs to sustain us, Noel.' He hoped Kennedy wasn't too far gone to appreciate the irony.

'What use is Marx when you want a shag, old son?' Kennedy laughed too loudly. It didn't matter. The bar remained deserted except for the barman, and he was used to Kennedy. 'Nothing like a good screw to put some colour in your cheeks. What you need is a woman.'

He was leaning towards Koliakov now, bringing his face too close. He must have fallen and cut himself earlier in the day. There was a dark wound on the side of his face. It was bad enough to need stitches, but Kennedy had put a piece of cotton wool over it and hoped for the best.

'That would loosen you lot up, wouldn't it?'

His eyes, Koliakov noticed, were floating pools of bloody water and his cheeks were an unnatural red, a maze of broken veins and raw skin. 'Mate of mine's got a real corker.' His voice was hushed now, confidential. 'Broke her in when she was sixteen. Taught her all she knows. Very superior merchandise, he says. Trained to fly.'

'Broke her in, Noel? What does that mean?'

'Took her cherry, Koli. Get it? He was her first screw. He likes them untouched, you see. She's a year or two older now, so my old mate's looking for pastures new. That's why he gave me her number. Thought he was doing me a good turn but she's no good for me. Can't remember the last time I got a salute out of the old man.' More hoarse laughter. 'You can give her one for me, old boy. All right? How about it? Another drink? Your shout, old son.'

★

For two weeks the number burned in his pocket. Twice he threw it away, only to rescue it again before he left the office. Twice he went to a call box, only to replace the receiver without dialling. On the third occasion, he dialled the number and this time he waited until his call was answered.

★

The house was in a mews off the Cromwell Road. There were window boxes on the upper floor but the geraniums were languishing for want of care. He rang the doorbell and waited.

'Hello. I'm Georgie.'

He stared at her, unable to move. She was as young as Kennedy had said, with a strong body and thick auburn hair. She wearing a black peignoir, which she held closed with her right hand. In her left she held a cigarette. It was uncanny, disconcerting. He found himself falling dizzily back into the past.

'Let me make you comfortable, shall I?'

She helped him off with his jacket and carefully placed it over the back of a chair. She stubbed out the cigarette and took off her peignoir. She was naked now except for a pair of high-heeled shoes. She showed no embarrassment in front of him.

'Can I get you a drink?'

177

Vodka, he wanted to say. Wasn't that what they'd always drunk together?

'Whisky, please.'

The cut of her hair was different. But the shape of her face, her eyes, the colour of her hair, the shape of her body were mysteriously the same. It was like seeing a photograph that was almost but not quite in register.

'That's better, isn't it? Now the shoes.' She knelt down in front of him and untied the laces. 'What's your name then?'

'Alexei,' he said. His voice sounded as if he were speaking from another room. Why had he chosen the name Alexei? It brought back a flood of bad memories.

'Alexei,' she repeated. 'Foreigner, are you?'

'American.'

'Over here for long?'

'For a time.'

'I'd love to go to America. My girlfriend's been to New York and Hollywood. Skyscrapers and stars, she said. That's what America is. Wonderful, eh? Perhaps one day, when I give all this up. Who knows, eh? Dreams. That's what keeps us alive, isn't it, darling?'

All the time she was talking she was working on him, taking off his tie, unbuttoning his shirt. Her words were a magician's patter, a stream of inconsequential phrases to distract you from the trick that is about to be performed on you.

'That's better, isn't it? More comfortable after a long day, eh?'

He said nothing because he was numbed into a frozen silence. Her body had the pubescent roundness of a girl becoming a woman, thin legs, a flat stomach with only a small light triangle at the groin, strong breasts on which a necklace, a golden chain with a single heart, rested carelessly. *Only I never saw her naked.* Her skin was as pale as marble and he was struck by the desire to touch her, to see if she was real. *I never touched her once.* Horrified and excited, he reached forward.

Eva Balassi.

He had met Eva in Moscow, during the war, when they had both been students. She'd arrived in 1939 as part of a small intake of Hungarian communists – though he was never convinced that the beliefs she professed were real. Her studies were disrupted by the outbreak of war, which prevented her return home. He had thought she was the most beautiful woman he had ever seen, and all his life he had never had reason to change his mind. He had fallen in love the moment he set eyes on her but in Moscow she had preferred the military cadet Alexei Abrasimov, and she had had his daughter. Years later, during his posting to Budapest, he had come across her again, older now but still as beautiful, a young widow with her teenage daughter. He had wanted her as desperately as he had before. This time he had lost her to the Englishman Martineau. Had she ever understood what he felt about her? Most nights he was sure she hadn't. There were some moments, rare occasions when he felt optimistic, when he managed to convince himself that she knew only too well of his devotion to her.

Now the reincarnated image of the woman he had worshipped for years was standing before him. He was touching her breasts and she was smiling at him.

'They're nice, aren't they?'

Suddenly she pushed her breasts together and squeezed them so that her nipples brushed his mouth. It was a vulgar, assertive gesture that immediately upset him.

'Don't do that.'

'Don't you like it?'

'Stand there,' he said, 'quite still. Let me look at you. You are very beautiful.'

She laughed in acknowledgement of what he had said but he knew she was untouched by it. She must be used to being told she was beautiful. It meant nothing to her because she felt nothing for those who said it.

Suddenly she was sitting on him, her hands working to arouse him. He lay back and let her do what he had paid her to do, knowing that this was not what he wanted, part of him wishing he had never come.

★

'You all right, dear?' she asked later. 'You're not a talker, are you?'

'You remind me of someone I knew once,' he said. He was lying on his back on the bed, smoking a cigarette. Outside he could hear the afternoon sounds of the street.

The girl laughed. 'There's always someone, isn't there? Someone you've lost and want to be reminded of.'

'Is there?'

'Tell me about her. Did you love her?'

Inside him some restraint burst and he wanted to tell her everything, to confess the misery of his infatuation for a woman who had never seen him as more than a friend but whose brief appearances in his life had led to a torture he could never escape.

'From the first moment I saw her.'

'Did she love you?'

'Not as I wanted her to.'

'Why not?'

'I never told her what I felt.'

'You should have done that.'

'How could I? She went off with someone else.'

'You've got to be bold and tell a girl what she wants to hear. It makes us melt inside.'

'It was all a long time ago.'

'Where is she now?'

'She disappeared. Perhaps she's dead. Who knows?'

'You can't live in the past, dear, can you?' She kissed him suddenly on the cheek and got up. In that moment he saw her for what she was, a woman who had allowed him to use her body. She would wash away the signs of his presence and prepare herself for the next man. How could he have imagined she was like Eva? He felt sickened at his weakness.

'See you again, will I?'

His head ached badly. Moscow had got on his nerves this time – too much tension, too much bureaucracy, and the business about Radin. Absurd! The man was dead. What was the point pretending otherwise? The world would find out soon enough. He could see a Smolensky lookalike giving the instruction: 'The Chief Designer is dead. We will deny his death and the world will believe us.' Didn't Moscow understand the scepticism the West brought to every statement they made? You cannot lie every day and then expect to be believed when it suits you.

He closed his eyes. Smolensky was well over the speed limit. The car had diplomatic plates. He smiled bitterly to himself. Nothing to worry about.

4

'He was a man who achieved what he was capable of, and there are too few who do that in this country,' Ruth Marchenko said. 'He was only a year or two older than me. Sometimes I think this nation is damned. Why do we lose those we need most?'

She turned to face her son, tears in her eyes. Valery held his mother as she sobbed. He'd had no idea that Radin's death would affect her in this way. Perhaps their friendship all those years ago had been more intense than he had understood.

Early one summer, when he was thirteen, Ruth had taken Valery aside and instructed him that he was never to mention the name of the man who was coming to their apartment that evening. He was to wipe from his memory what was about to happen. Valery did not understand, and Ruth gave him no explanation, but he obeyed willingly. He was too devoted to his mother to think of doing anything else. For a few months a small man with thinning spiky hair, a beaky nose and damaged hands was a regular visitor to their apartment. He would arrive in the evening, stand in the doorway of their minute kitchen and talk to Ruth while she cooked. Some nights he would eat with them. His concentration was always on Ruth. Valery was ignored as if he did not exist.

Sensing her son's mute hostility, Ruth talked about Radin. He was a wonderful scientist, she whispered, a visionary who could see beyond the confines of the world they lived in. He was planning to build huge rockets that would one day take men to the moon. Valery was impressed by this account of Radin's ambition – how could he fail to be? But it did not make Radin into a man towards whom he could feel any instinctive sympathy. Was it his hands? He remembered the first time he'd seen them. They reminded him of uncooked pastry. He could hardly hold a knife and fork. He noticed his mother cutting up Radin's food before she served it to him, as if he was a cat. A man to command respect but not affection.

Behind the glowing account of Radin's achievements, he sensed his mother's ambivalence. He was sure she had discovered qualities in Radin that she did not like. His presence in their apartment made Ruth unsettled, anxious, not herself. His conclusion was that Radin posed an unformulated threat to him and his mother, and he resented his presence and the secrecy that surrounded it.

Then one day Viktor stopped coming. His mother offered no explanation. Valery did not dare to ask why. His impression was that in some unexpressed way Ruth herself was relieved.

'I was at school with his wife, Elza,' Ruth was saying. 'I knew Viktor before she did. She and the children stayed with us for a few weeks when their marriage broke up. You probably don't remember, you were too young. I felt sorry for Elza. Viktor changed after his awful experiences in the war. The man who returned from prison was not the man she'd married. In his suffering something had been taken from him and its absence broke Elza's heart. I respected Viktor, but Elza was right. He was impossible to live with. He was a driven man, obsessed by his work, frightened that he would never have enough time to complete the tasks he'd set himself. He lived every day expecting that he'd be snatched away before his work was finished, which is why he drove himself and those who worked for him so hard.'

After her friendship with Viktor was over she had told Valery how, during the war, he had been wrongly imprisoned and tortured. His hands had been broken deliberately to force him to betray his colleagues, but somehow he had endured the pain and said nothing. His disability was proof of his remarkable courage but also a sign of the mental wounds that never allowed him to forget what he had suffered. His terrible experience explained his driven nature, his restlessness, his sudden outbursts of anger at the Institute when his high standards were not met by those who worked with him, and his overwhelming drive to succeed as if he knew that he would not live to any great age.

'And now he's dead.'

'If only I could believe that,' Valery said.

*

'How did your presentation go?' Ruth asked later. 'What did the Project Committee say?'

The meeting had taken place at the offices of the Space and Technical Commission. This was the first such occasion over which Grinko, as Acting Director of the Institute in Radin's absence, had presided. Valery and his small team had taken weeks to prepare their presentation on the advantages of using robots to explore space. He had told his audience what his robots could do if they were landed on the moon. He explained how they could travel around using solar power, take photographs and send the images back to earth, excavate the surface of the moon or those of planets, extract samples of rock and dust and bring them back to the mother ship; how they could measure the chemical content of the atmosphere; how they'd be cheaper than people and more reliable.

His audience had listened to him in silence. When he had finished, Grinko had risen slowly to his feet. He was speaking, Grinko stated, a sneer never far from his expression, on behalf of the Chief Designer, who unfortunately was not able to attend this meeting and for whom he was deputising. Men were essential to the discovery of other worlds. No machine could ever take their place. It was folly, if not a dangerous waste of scientific resources, to propose that machines could do the same work with even a small degree of success. Why were precious funds being wasted on robotics when the space programme would never agree to go down that route? The work of Marchenko and his team was valueless. It had no part in the Soviet space programme, as laid down by their esteemed colleague, the Chief Designer. He sat down to a standing ovation from the same scientists and engineers who had privately encouraged Valery, and who had criticised the waste of resources on a project they considered would bring little reward.

The audience's ovation underlined the point that Grinko was representing the beliefs of the Chief Designer. They all knew that Radin was dead, yet they preferred to believe the myth of his absence. Valery was the victim of a policy whose course could only be changed by a man who was dead. The conclusion was as clear as daylight: *the policy would never change.* He left the chamber bruised and depressed.

'Grinko made it clear that our work has no place in the space programme. As long as the myth of Radin's return to life remains, nothing will change.'

'Will you challenge the decision?'

'Where would it get me?'

'If you don't do something Grinko could force you to disband your team.'

'If no one will listen to me, what choice do I have?'

'You can't let them destroy your work,' Ruth said. 'You can't drop what you've done, it's too valuable.'

'What do you suggest I do?' He was angry. Her demands on him were unrealistic. Surely she of all people should understand the pressures he was under. 'As long as Radin is officially alive, his colleagues will cling to the orthodoxies of his position even more tenaciously than before. They're all much too frightened to make even a slight deviation from the path he chose in case that reveals to the world that Viktor Radin is dead.'

'Where does that leave you?'

How could he answer her? Was this a setback or a defeat? That was the question he had asked himself as he walked down the boiling street to his mother's apartment. The decision against him had no justifiable basis in science. Radin was a great man, his contribution enormous, his courage beyond belief – that was undeniable – but he had played his part and now he was gone. It was the turn of others to develop new ideas, to challenge the assumptions of the past. They could not fool themselves that Radin was still alive and directing the space programme. The dead could not be allowed to design the future. That way would lead to catastrophe.

Yet the lie had won, as he had seen it win so many times before.

'If I knew, I'd tell you,' he said.

IVAN'S SEARCH FOR HIS FATHER

It is time to change the reel on the projector. Some of the children in the front stand up and watch the process. Andrei closes his eyes so that the images of what he has been watching are not lost. He opens them only when he hears the familiar ticking of the projector and he knows that the next part of the story is coming.

*

There are six of them, probably all about his own age though they seem bigger. They catch him scavenging for food in dustbins, and they mock him, shout insults, call him a gypsy. They are on a spy hunt, Ivan learns, searching out strangers in the neighbourhood and reporting them to the authorities. He is a stranger, therefore he must be a spy. They must arrest him, they say. He runs off to escape because he fears they might beat him up. He is too exhausted to go far. He has eaten nothing in two days. They do not seem to be starving, they do not have hollow cheeks and sticking-out bellies. He decides to follow them; perhaps they will lead him to where he will find food. He tracks them carefully, keeping his distance, hiding in doorways or ducking into alleys so they won't notice him, but never losing touch.

They are exploring an old derelict house that has collapsed through neglect when the quarrel begins. Ivan is too far away to hear what it is about, but he can see them gesticulating at each other and he can hear their shouts, though not what they are saying. He watches the pushing and shoving that go on before the group divides. He creeps closer. Reds against Whites, the new against the old. It is not the first time he has seen that game.

It quickly becomes apparent that it is more than a game. The Reds run back towards a pile of broken masonry left at the base of a wall which provides their armoury. A hail of stones forces the Whites to scurry for safety. A council of war takes place. One of the Whites points to the other side of the building. Keeping low, the three boys race away as fast as they can. Dismayed by the sudden disappearance of the Whites, the Reds emerge from their citadel. They have stuffed their pockets with as many stones as they can carry, and they have stones in their hands. They advance warily, searching for the enemy: no sign. On, on they go, bravely, towards the line where they have last been seen.

Ivan can guess what will happen next. The Reds will be surprised by the Whites who will have gone round behind them and captured their armoury, leaving the Reds exposed. It is a clever trick. Cautiously, the Reds peer round the wall, expecting White opposition. As they do so, there is a yell behind them and a new hail of stones begins. The Whites have established themselves by the armoury and are celebrating its capture by pelting their opponents with anything they can lay their hands on.

The Reds take shelter behind the wall as pieces of brick and cement shatter on impact, sending dust and sharp pieces of stone in all directions. There is a small return of fire − the ammunition the Reds had brought with them quickly runs low − and then a hurried consultation. Ivan can imagine what the discussion is about. Should they stay and fight to the end, or should they escape to fight another day? It is clear that there is a disagreement over tactics. The leader wants to stay and fight, his troops to retreat. Punches are thrown and suddenly two of the Reds run off, leaving their leader isolated and alone. He peers round the end of the wall to be greeted with another bombardment and triumphant shouts as his opponents catch sight of the deserters, now out of range.

From his vantage point Ivan can see that one of the Whites has detached himself from the others and is creeping undercover to cut off any possibility of the Red leader's escape. If the remaining Red doesn't get out now, he will be captured and then what will happen? Three against one? Impossible odds. He has seen the effect of that in his own village on the night of the attack. Terrible memories boil within him.

Ivan runs across the street and enters the deserted building. It is cold and damp inside, and smells of rotting vegetation and excrement.

'What are you doing here? Go away.' The tone is aggressive, commanding.

'They're cutting off your retreat,' Ivan says. 'I've come to help you.'

'I don't need any help.' The defiance of the would-be hero.

'You won't get out alive on your own.'

As if to support his statement, more stones are thrown, this time from a different angle. The Whites are growing in confidence. Ivan and his would-be ally duck for safety behind the wall.

'I don't need you. I can defeat them on my own.'

The Red is filling his pockets with the remains of the stones that have been thrown at him. More jeers come from the other side, closer now: they are becoming bolder knowing the odds are stacked in their favour.

'Don't try it,' Ivan begs, but it is too late. Red emerges from the shelter of the wall to race towards the enemy position in a display of insane courage, hurling stones as fast as he can. He is halfway across when he is hit, a large missile striking him on the temple. Red falls. The missiles stop. The Whites emerge from behind their defences. Red doesn't move.

Ivan runs out. Red is lying on his side, unconscious, blood pouring from the wound, discolouring the stones. He kneels down and puts his hand on Red's neck. He can feel something. He is alive still.

'Stop,' he shouts. 'Stop fighting. He's badly hurt.'

The Whites come forward, fearing a trick. Ivan picks up Red in his arms. He is heavier than he imagines but he has done it now, there is no going back.

'Where does he live?' he asks. 'We've got to get him home. He may die.'

'I'll take you there,' the leader of the Whites says.

Stumbling under Red's weight, Ivan carries his wounded comrade across the battlefield and behind the lines. Across a street, down another, through an alley, up some steps, into a hallway, up the stairs. Red's parents live in a dormitory in Old Arbat. A door opens, a woman screams, a bearded man in glasses appears.

'What's happened?'

'He's had an accident,' Ivan says. 'He's been hurt.'

Red is taken from his arms by his father and laid gently on a bed. His mother gets a bowl of water and a towel and bathes her son's head. Ivan can hear Red murmuring dazedly in reply to his mother's questions.

'Did you do this to him?' the father asks Ivan.

'No, sir.'

'He rescued him,' the White leader says. 'He carried him home. I helped him because I knew where he lived.'

'What happened?'

'We were talking,' Ivan says. 'Some boys appeared. They attacked us with stones. Your son was hit. We brought him home as quickly as we could.'

He turns to see that he is alone. The White leader has disappeared.

'He was on the other side, I take it?'

'Yes.' Ivan hangs his head.

'You look pale,' the father says. 'Would you like something to drink?'

'Something to eat, please,' Ivan says.

The meal that he eats alone in the kitchen is the first of many over the years.

That is how Ivan came to have a roof over his head, and to become like a son to Boris Chernevenko.

7

1

Outside, the rain hammered down in First Court. Marion Blackwell could hear water gushing from an overflowing gutter. In the distance there was a long, low growl of thunder. It was early afternoon but already the room was dark.

'In the face of this deliberate act of provocation,' Michael Scott said, 'which has the handprint of the Soviet leadership all over it, I can see no good reason for any debate. Berlin's visit must be cancelled. Surely we can't disagree on that?'

He looked expectantly round the table. For a moment no one spoke. The sound of the rain filled the room.

'I disagree for one,' Marion replied. 'I think the present crisis makes it even more essential that we go ahead with the visit.'

'Given the misery the Berlin Wall has already generated, and the threat it poses to all our futures, I find your response hard to fathom.' Scott's mockery was undisguised. 'Perhaps you could elaborate on your reasoning.'

How hard it was to keep her composure before Michael Scott's incessant provocation! Did he oppose her because she was a woman? Or was there some deeper reason – as if the question of her gender wasn't deep enough? If she was to keep alive the prospect of Andrei Berlin's visit, she had to resist all Scott's attempts to unsettle her.

'The political tension created by the building of the wall is nothing to do with Andrei Berlin. Therefore why should he be made to suffer because of it?'

'Nothing to do with Andrei Berlin?' Scott repeated her phrase slowly, as if a careful repetition would increase his understanding of it. He looked perplexed. 'Am I not right in saying that Berlin is a citizen of the Soviet Union?'

'Of course he is.'

'Then by definition, in an unfree society, he must support the government, right or wrong. Surely we cannot come to blows over that, can we?'

He stared at Marion, daring her to disagree. She said nothing.

'In which case, I don't want to sit down in my own house to listen to a man whose government gave the instruction to build this terrible wall. I don't imagine there is more than a handful in this university who would not endorse that sentiment.'

'How do you know he doesn't want to use his visit here as an opportunity to condemn what his government has done?' She knew at once she should have said nothing. Her naive response revealed the poverty of her arguments in defence of the visit, and she was sure Michael Scott would spot that. She was letting her anger get the better of her.

Scott laughed. 'When you defend Berlin's appearance here on the grounds that he might want to use the occasion to act independently, you're allowing yourself to be manipulated by the Soviets into defending their cause, which is what Berlin will certainly do when he comes here, at least he will if he wants to return home and carry on as before. You seem to forget, Marion, that altruism does not exist in the Soviet Union. Every word, every act has a single purpose: to push the Soviets ever further towards their goal of so-called socialist domination. As a Soviet citizen, it is inevitable that Berlin is tarred with the same brush. Whatever you may think, he is their creature and therefore inevitably hostile to us. His presence could be seen as a potential danger.'

'So your assumption is, he's coming over here as an apologist for this wretched wall?' Marion hoped that she was matching Michael Scott's aggression with her own.

'How can I possibly know? I'm not privy to the Politburo's deliberations. But I am sure that Berlin's influence cannot be other than malign. That is why I am asking this committee to have the courage to rescind our invitation. At a time like this, we cannot have such a man here as our guest. His presence among us would be intolerable.'

The rain had eased and the torrent from the overflowing drainpipe had diminished to a trickle. It was still dark. A flash of lightning briefly illuminated the room, and was followed by a closer rumble of thunder.

'What Michael says may be true, but I hardly think it matters,' Peter Chadwick said. 'The present situation – the building of this wretched wall – is abhorrent to all of us but it is irrelevant to the question Michael is asking us to consider. If we withdraw Berlin's invitation, we risk being seen to act politically. At worst, the interpretation could be that we are under the Government's influence. There is a precious tradition in this university of independence of mind and judgement. We must be careful not to jeopardise that. We offered an invitation to Berlin because we wanted to listen to what he had to say. I see no reason whatever for changing our minds. The same reasoning applies now as it did then. Our task in this crisis is to hold our nerve.'

'You're looking very thoughtful, Bill. Where do you stand?' The chairman was determined to test the strength of Michael Scott's support.

Gant's face was drained and pale, his shoulders hunched. Marion had met him on their way into the building, and she'd been shocked by his appearance. The news wasn't good, he'd told her. Jenny had tried to kill herself on two occasions in the last week, and was now under sedation at Fulbourn. The crisis had clearly pushed him to the end of his reserves. She had felt sorry for him and squeezed his hand.

'I think Peter Chadwick's right,' Gant said. 'We're committed to Berlin's visit. It's too late to back down now. We must show our independence of mind and resist all influences to the contrary.'

Bill was deserting Michael Scott. It was unexpected but she welcomed it. A sudden thought struck her. Was Bill changing sides because he imagined that by doing so he could win her back? Surely he couldn't have read more into her gesture of sympathy than she had intended?

'Has there been any pressure from the Government for us to change our mind?' the chairman asked.

'None that I know of,' Marion replied. 'We've heard nothing from the Home Office, either officially or unofficially.'

'Nor will we,' Scott said with weary authority. 'Whitehall won't interfere. That's not their way. They will leave the decision to us. That said,' here he paused for effect, looking round the table, 'my sources tell me that they do expect us to withdraw the invitation. If we don't, we could be regarded as "unsound", and that could lead to limitations on our freedom in future. It's a dangerous game we're playing here, and the stakes are higher than I suspect some of us realise.'

It was a threat without teeth because he'd lost the support he needed. Bill's defection put Michael Scott in a minority. It was too late to use scare tactics to try to change minds. There wasn't even a need to put Michael Scott's objection to the vote. He'd failed to command a majority. Berlin's visit would have to go ahead. That wouldn't be the end of Michael's objections — she must expect a backlash of some kind — but it was a significant victory none the less. She felt pleased with herself. The storm had passed without damage.

2

At first glance, the back-projected image looks like a child's drawing, a large spherical object with horns, a huge steel mine made not to float in water but to fly in space.

'This is our artist's impression of the latest Soviet weapon of war,' Pountney says to the camera, 'the satellite they claim can fire nuclear missiles from space. It is, apparently, invulnerable to any counterweapon the West may possess. We have neither the missiles nor the artillery to shoot it down.'

He points to the sphere. 'We estimate that, to have put such a weapon into orbit, the Soviets will have needed a rocket at least twice as powerful as the one that in April lifted Gagarin into space. The question is, do they have such a rocket?'

Behind him, the slide of the satellite is replaced by a blurred photograph of a Soviet rocket held in its gantry. 'What you see behind me is Gagarin's rocket, itself a huge machine, on the launch pad at Baikonur, the Soviet Cosmodrome. We know the Soviets have now built the largest rocket in the world. It is the brainchild of the man who inspires and guides the highly successful Soviet space programme, Professor Radin. We also now know that last May it exploded on the launch pad before lift-off, with devastating consequences. News of this disaster has only recently come to light, but we know it has been a severe setback to Soviet ambitions. What we don't know is whether they have solved the reasons for the explosion and built a new rocket. They certainly have the ability to do so.'

The photograph of Baikonur is replaced by a drawing in cross-section of the satellite. Pountney points at different sections of the drawing. 'Here is where our experts think the navigational equipment might be housed. These hornlike projections are the retro-rockets that correct the satellite's trajectory once it has achieved orbit. Here are the storage zones for the payload of four nuclear intercontinental missiles, each of which carries its own navigational equipment in the nose cone.'

The lighting in the studio dims. The image of the satellite fades. Pountney walks towards the camera. He is no longer the instructor giving details at a seminar, he is now the seer foretelling doom. 'It is worrying enough to describe such a terrible weapon, against which we appear to have no defence. But there is another aspect, which is equally terrifying. Soviet missiles are notoriously inaccurate. While it is entirely reasonable to speculate that Professor Radin may have solved the problem of lifting this dreadful weapon of war into space, it is hard to see how the Soviets will have solved the problem of how to make their missiles hit their target. That, perhaps, is where the greatest danger lies. Aim one of the missiles at a military target, miss it by a hundred miles, what then? The chances are it may well explode in a highly populated urban area. The effect on civilian life will be catastrophic. The greatest threat the West faces from this new weapon is what happens if it fails to perform properly? The likelihood of that happening are, the experts believe, very high indeed.'

*

Koliakov watches Pountney's image fade as the programme's portentous theme music plays over the closing credits. He turns off the television. Is it possible that what began as a stupid device to get out of a hot room and into a cold bath has led to this? Surely not. But the thought won't leave him. He invented the idea of an orbiting satellite armed with nuclear missiles on the spur of the moment. Is it possible that he anticipated reality?

He has seen on the embassy television the statement made by the First Secretary outside the Romanian parliament, and he remembers smiling inwardly that his plan was working. What he invented on that boiling night was a policy of threatening words and ideas whose sole purpose was to intimidate the West. He had taken the most extreme idea he could think of because that was the only way to end the meeting. He never imagined that such an idea would have an independent life.

Now this.

What he has learned from the television programme terrifies him. The idea of inaccurate weapons falling on civilian targets and killing indiscriminately fills him with horror. In his mind he sees a bleak, desolate place, a clearing in a forest in winter, the branches of the fir trees bending under the weight of snow. There is no wind, no sound, only a bitter cold. The darkness is lit by the headlights of two lorries. The smell of diesel mixes with the smell of cordite. He sees the body of an old man, his only protection against the bitter night air an overcoat thrown hastily over nightclothes, lying face down on the recently dug earth. Around him are other bodies, of men and women, all old, all dressed as if they had been roused from their sleep and given only moments to leave their homes. All are dead, brutally murdered.

Koliakov sees himself, as he has so many times over the years, holding the machine-gun that has killed them. He can feel the effect of the recoil in his arms, the heat of the barrel; he can smell the burning oil. It is an all too familiar nightmare. He can taste the salt of his own tears.

He knows that the idea that he is responsible for such an outrage is an invention of a powerful subconscious. He has never fired a shot at a human target in his life, and he cannot imagine himself doing so except in the direst moments of self-defence. Yet the haunting refuses to leave him. Nor will it, he knows, until he can rid his conscience of the fear that he will be the cause of death of innocent people, like the frozen bodies in the clearing.

Kate got out of bed and stood by the window. The early morning light made the roofs shine. The streets were still deserted. Silent people, silent streets – she had noticed that in her first few days. Moscow wasn't a noisy city – was it the lack of cars? Or the cowed nature of the people? How strange it was here. Even after a year there were so many mysteries she would never solve.

'What are you doing?'

'Looking at the view.'

'Come back to bed.' She didn't move. 'Come back to bed.' More urgently this time, and she responded.

★

'Is it always like this?' Kate asked, struggling to reach an empty seat.

'What did you expect?'

Almost every row in the lecture theatre was already filled. Students were standing in the aisles and at the back of the auditorium. From the numbers in the audience, she assumed many more had turned up than those studying the course.

'He's the most popular man in the faculty,' Yelena said, unwinding her scarf. 'His lectures are always full. Some of us come because we have to, some because we want to. I wonder which category you belong to?'

Kate had met Yelena Aronovitch, a second-year student at the Institute of History, at a party to which some of her fellow musicians at the Conservatoire had insisted on taking her. She was a plump, plain girl in her early twenties. In a sudden rush of confidence a few nights before, while making tea for Kate in her hostel, she had confessed her infatuation with her history lecturer.

'When he's speaking, you hang on every word he says, as if your life depends upon it. You can't help yourself. He seems to have this power over all of us. He stares at us as if he's searching for someone he's lost. Whenever he looks at me, even though it's only for an instant, I think I'm going to melt.' She laughed nervously. 'Why don't you come and see for yourself? You might learn something, mightn't you?'

More laughter, this time less nervous.

'That would be my excuse, would it?'

'Why not? He's worth it, he's so good-looking, you'll see.'

'The morning is our time for practising.'

'An hour away won't harm your career.'

Her Russian wasn't up to it, Kate replied. She wouldn't be able to follow what Berlin was saying. All those abstractions would wash over her head. Perhaps some other time, when her command of the language was more assured. What she meant was that she hadn't come to Moscow to listen to communist propaganda, however attractive the speaker might be. She was letting Yelena down gently.

Yet here she was, a few days later, in a crowded lecture room at the Institute of Contemporary History, captive to a curiosity whetted by Yelena's persuasive and unyielding enthusiasm and what she had learned about Berlin from some of the older students at the Conservatoire. Yelena was by no means the first to have been swept off her feet.

'What's the lecture about?' Kate asked, once they were settled in their seats.

'The Great Patriotic War.'

'What's that?'

Yelena looked surprised. 'When we defeated the Germans at Stalingrad and saved the world from fascism. Don't they teach you history in England?'

The conversation that filled the room hushed quickly to silence as a tall, thin man in his early forties made his way slowly down the stairs to the stage. He was older than Kate had imagined, with long black hair greying at the temples and dark eyes shining out of a pale, high-cheekboned face. He looked more like a poet than a historian, she thought. Did historians have a look? He settled his notes on the lectern and looked up at the ranks of students facing him. He had long fingers, she noticed, like a pianist.

'Had the defenders of Stalingrad not heroically resisted the might of the Nazi invaders,' he began, 'the commander of the German Sixth Army, General Paulus, would have crossed the Volga, destroying our armies in the process, Hitler would have got his hands on Soviet oil and the war might have ended very differently. The Soviet army under General Zhukov's command joined forces with the people of Stalingrad in one of the greatest acts of resistance the world has ever witnessed.'

If Stalingrad was what Berlin was going to talk about, she should never have let herself be persuaded by Yelena's infatuation. Wars and battles didn't interest her. Hadn't Hitler, like Napoleon before him, tried and failed to conquer Russia, and hadn't hundreds of thousands of German soldiers been left to die in the terrible cold? Perhaps, if she left now, she could explain her late arrival at the Conservatoire with some possibility of being believed. She looked round. Far too many people in the row to squeeze past, and then there were students sitting on the stairs. The lecture theatre was packed. If she tried to get out, she'd make an exhibition of herself. Nothing for it but to stay put. She tried hard to suppress her guilt at the practice she was missing, and the lies she would have to tell to explain her absence. If only her truancy had been for some purpose.

The sound of Berlin's voice drew her back to his lecture.

'The long, brutal struggle for control of the city, waged through a boiling summer and a winter of desperate cold, was finally won by the unshakeable courage of our own people, tens of thousands of whom preferred to die in defence of their homeland rather than yield precious Soviet territory to the enemy. Though the cost in Soviet lives was enormous, the ultimate reward was victory. No Soviet death was in vain.'

Berlin spoke simply and directly, not in the abstract terms Kate had come to associate with the political indoctrination with which one or two of the students at the Conservatoire had tried to engage her. (A Polish violinist had taken her aside recently and warned her in whispers to avoid them, saying that they were KGB stooges.) Almost against her wish she found she could understand most of what he said. His voice, she realised, was musical. She wondered if he could sing.

'The battle for Stalingrad was the first major defeat Hitler experienced, a defeat from which he was never to recover. Fascism was stopped in its tracks by the power of the Revolution and its citizen armies. It was the true turning point in the war.'

Could that be true? Some instinct told her it wasn't what she had been taught at school. What *had* she been taught? If only she could remember. She felt defenceless, wishing desperately that she had the knowledge to resist the Soviet case that was so convincingly laying siege to her beliefs. Was she betraying her own side by not having these arguments at her fingertips? She felt suddenly vulnerable and exposed to the confident assertions of the man she was listening to.

'The legacy of that great conflict is alive in this country today. Sixteen years after the end of the war, our suffering continues.'

Berlin was suddenly silent. In the lecture theatre, his audience tensed. Not a cough, not a whisper was heard, not a movement made as they waited for him to speak again. Abandoning his notes, he stepped forward to the edge of the stage.

'Today, as we rebuild our devastated cities, as we plough the fields over which our people fought so bravely for so long, again and again we come upon the unburied remains of our own citizens, the whitened bones of our nameless brothers and sisters, fathers and mothers, heroic countrymen and women who sacrificed their lives so that we may be here today. The wound of that war lives on deep and unhealed in our national psyche, and it will continue to do so for years to come. It is a vivid scar reminding us that we must be vigilant against our enemies, who would try to steal our motherland from us. We must never forget the threat that Nazi Germany posed to our country, nor how narrow was the margin by which we defeated them. We must be on our guard, now and in the future, against a revival of German militarism and those in the West who would promote it. To all of us, this great battle is a living symbol of the need for sacrifice on the way to ultimate victory. The lessons and experiences of Stalingrad must live in our memories for ever. They must never be forgotten.'

Berlin stopped speaking. Kate held her breath. His eyes were sweeping the rows of students in front of him. What was he searching for? Some kind of approval from his audience? Wasn't the enthralled silence indication enough that they had absorbed what he had told them? She knew instinctively that it was deeper than that. There was a desperation in his expression that told her he wanted something that his audience could not give him, though what it was she could not guess.

Kate looked up to find that his eyes had settled on her. Confused and embarrassed, she looked away, knowing that the colour was rising in her cheeks. Of all the people present in this room, he had discovered the one who was an impostor, who had no right to be there. She felt shamed, humiliated. She put her hand to her cheek. Her face was on fire.

*

The canteen was crowded and noisy. Berlin, she noticed, was eating by himself. The only available seat was opposite him. The other students, perhaps overwhelmed by his reputation, seemed reluctant to join him. If she wanted to have her lunch sitting down, she had no choice.

'Do you mind if I sit here?' she asked in Russian.

'Of course not.'

He moved his tray to make room. For a moment he stared at her, as if trying to remember where he had seen her before. Once more she felt the force of his penetrating gaze and her cheeks begin to redden. Perhaps he would put it down to the effect of the heat of the canteen after the bitter cold of the street.

'You've been to my lectures, haven't you?' he said. Out of the mass of people in that vast room, how could he possibly know that? 'I don't recognise you as one of my students.'

'I'm studying at the Conservatoire.'

'I thought music students were never allowed out into the real world.'

'We are sometimes,' she replied, smiling. 'With special permission, of course. Provided it's for something our teachers think is important.'

'My lectures qualify, do they?'

For reasons she didn't understand, she felt she had to explain her presence. 'I'm very ignorant of Russian history. As I've come to the Soviet Union to study, I thought I should know more about the country I'm living in. You can't understand the politics until you understand the history, can you?'

It was a phrase her father had used once, though not about Russia. Berlin looked pleased. 'I wish more of my students thought as you do.' He was staring at her as if there was no one else in the world. She felt frightened by the power of his concentration. Then, in English, he added, 'I am flattered. You are my first English student.'

'How did you know I was English?'

'Don't all English girls look like you?'

She felt the colour rising in her cheeks again and she was furious with herself for imagining his reply was a compliment. To distract him, she asked: 'Have you been to England?'

He shook his head. 'To America, yes, France, yes, Italy, Switzerland, Sweden. But your country? Never.'

'One day perhaps,' she said.

'One day I hope,' he replied, smiling. 'Very much I hope.'

*

'You sat at the same table with him?' Yelena said in amazement that evening. 'How could you?'

'What was I supposed to do?' Kate replied. 'The place was full. It was the only seat that wasn't taken. All the other students were avoiding him.'

'Did he ask you out? Did he make a pass at you?'

'Of course not.'

Yelena found her expression of surprise amusing. 'How innocent you English are. Why shouldn't he want to sleep with you? You are a young woman and our handsome historian likes young women. He is famous for seducing many of his students. He won't have changed his tactics just because you are English. You must have missed the signs. Or ignored them.'

There'd been no signs, Kate was sure of that, but she said nothing. Instead she made Yelena talk about Berlin – not, as it turned out, a difficult task. He had written books, she said, though she had yet to read them. She spoke as if writing books put you on a different level of existence, definitely higher than those who had not. Sometimes he went overseas to lecture: he'd been to America, she knew that, to Harvard and somewhere else in California she couldn't remember, so he must be in favour because permission to travel was so hard to obtain.

'Will you have lunch with him again?' Yelena asked.

'I don't imagine so,' Kate said. 'Why should I?'

★

Moscow shivered on the edge of winter. Snow, ice, low cloud, falling temperatures, all were on their way, she was told. Life in the city would be reduced to a struggle for survival. In preparation she bought a fur hat and coat and a pair of lined boots, and as she set out for the Conservatoire each morning, she wore two pairs of gloves in order to retain some feeling in her fingers. It was already as cold as anything she had experienced. She couldn't imagine it getting colder.

Once or twice she remembered the fair-haired Russian she had met so briefly in the Lenin Library, but slowly his image faded and she forgot about him.

★

She skipped the next two lectures deliberately. She wanted to see if Berlin noticed her absence. When she queued for lunch after her return, he came and stood beside her.

'Have you been ill?'

The question was direct, as if now he expected her to be present at all his lectures. She imagined those dark eyes relentlessly searching the crowded rows of students. Was it possible that he was looking for her? Surely not. But if he had looked for her and failed to find her — what then?

'The times of my classes changed.' Surely he wouldn't believe a lie that was so obviously transparent?

'And now they have changed back again?'

'Yes.'

'How convenient. Now you can continue your studies of our history. Are you learning much?'

Was he mocking her? Did he want her to stay or go? If only she understood the game he was playing. He nodded at an empty table and they sat down together. He began to question her. Why had she come to Moscow? At whose suggestion? Who had told her about the Conservatoire? Weren't there suitable music schools in England, or America?

She told him how, during a visit to London, Vinogradoff had heard her play and soon after had invited her to study with him for a year. It was an extraordinary offer, one that she had never dreamed of.

'Naturally, I leaped at the chance — who wouldn't? I'd never heard anyone play the cello like that before.' She described the difficulties she had had to overcome, particularly her father's concern at the prospect of his only daughter spending a year alone in Moscow.

'He was afraid I'd be unhappy here.'

'Was he right? Are you unhappy?'

She hesitated. She found it impossible to deceive him. 'Sometimes, yes.'

'Why?'

She was confused, unable to frame a reply. He saw her confusion and laughed, touching her hand briefly. 'I am sorry. That was unfair. Of course you are unhappy sometimes. We are all unhappy. These are unhappy times. Moscow is an unhappy city. Tell me about the life of a student musician at our Russian Conservatoire.'

She talked about the pieces she was studying – by Bach, Tchaikovsky, Dvořák – about Vinogradoff's teaching techniques, the hostel where she lived with other music students. At some point she mentioned a concert that was to be held at the Conservatoire at the end of the week.

'Are you playing?' he asked. Should she feel flattered that he wanted to hear her? Or was he saying that out of politeness?

'No, not yet,' she replied. 'It's too early.'

'Too early?' He was puzzled by her reply. Was it her imagination, or did she sense his disappointment? 'Too early for what?'

'Vinogradoff wants to be sure I have settled down in Moscow before he lets me perform in front of an audience.' It wasn't quite true, but the story would do for now.

Berlin laughed. 'I'm sure he knows what's best for you.'

Was he mocking her? She had no way of knowing. 'There's a student concert this Friday. A young Czech pianist is playing. We all think he is going to win the Tchaikovsky Prize, and Vinogradoff is also playing a short piece. He is always wonderful.'

'If that is an invitation to your concert, then I accept.'

She dreamed of Berlin that night. She was alone in a huge concert hall, playing her cello, and he was an audience of one, sitting at the back of the auditorium. She was no longer a student: she had become the woman of her dreams, elegant, seductive, assured. She was dressed in a dark blue satin dress whose folds caught the light as she played; she had her hair up, and wore her mother's pearl necklace. With each note, she drew Berlin slowly but inevitably towards her. Whenever she looked up he was in a different seat, gradually getting closer. She felt no fear, only a rare confidence that he would be unable to resist her so long as she went on playing. There was a power in her music that she had not to experienced before. She felt it with every note. She was drawing him towards her, ever closer, until he was beside her and still she was playing. Then, as he reached out to touch her hand, the music came to an end and she woke up to a silence broken only by the beating of her heart.

Was it a dream of seduction? How awful. Impossible! He was so much older, he would never find her interesting. How could she keep the attention of a man like him except for a few brief moments in a queue at a student canteen? What could she have been thinking of when she told him about the concert at the Conservatoire? Perhaps he hadn't meant it, he'd only agreed to come to please her, and on the day he would fail to turn up. Was that to be her fate with Russian men? She would not feel disappointment, only relief that she had not made a fool of herself.

She settled her mind by telling herself that he wouldn't come.

*

She wore her best black dress and put her hair up, using tortoiseshell combs she had inherited from her mother. It made her look older, her father had said when she'd worn them once before. Seeing them again, she realised, brought back painful memories. Tonight she wanted to be the woman she had been in her dream, and the combs were an essential component in the image she was creating. She waited in the entrance hall of the Conservatoire, prepared to lie, if anyone asked, that she was expecting her friend Yelena. To her relief no one did.

'Hello.'

Berlin was beside her, kissing her on both cheeks, his lips cold from the night air. Smiling, he complimented her on her dress, and apologised for keeping her waiting, greeting her as if they had been friends for years.

'The faculty meeting was endless. I am sorry. You must have thought I had forgotten.'

She saw the astonished looks of her fellow students as Berlin greeted one or two of the staff at the Conservatoire as friends. She stood silently by his side while he talked to them, anxious that he might reveal that she had been attending his lectures. He'd come, he said, to hear the young English cellist whose reputation had preceded her arrival in Moscow, only to find that her teacher would not let her play. This was devastating news. Perhaps he should leave and come back some other night. Or should he speak to Vinogradoff and get him to change his mind? All the time she felt his hand tightening its grip on her arm.

The Czech pianist played first, not as well as she had heard him play in rehearsal. To her surprise, in front of an audience he seemed to suffer from nerves, and stumbled where on other, private occasions he had been so fluent.

'He is talented,' Berlin whispered, leaning towards her. 'But he is a teacher, not a performer.' She was sure his lips touched her hair. His breath smelled of smoke.

Vinogradoff played a duet with one of his pupils, and was then prevailed upon by the audience to play an unaccompanied Bach chaconne, which was received triumphantly. There were shouted requests that he play again. He refused shyly, saying that this occasion was for the students, not the teachers.

In the interval, Berlin slipped from her side. She saw him talking animatedly to Vinogradoff. From the way they greeted each other, it was clear they had met before. Why hadn't he told her he knew Vinogradoff? She couldn't have said anything critical of him, could she, which Berlin was now reporting?

'Time to eat,' Berlin said, taking her arm.

'Aren't you going to stay for the second half?' she asked.

'If you aren't playing, then I've heard all I want to hear this evening.'

Without knowing why, she had imagined that a group of them would eat together, and now she was alone with him, walking in the streets of Moscow. It was cold, and for the first time she felt uncertain. The evening had taken a direction she had not expected. Being alone with him had never been part of her plan. Come to think of it, there'd been no plans for after the concert because in her heart she hadn't imagined he would turn up.

They entered a restaurant, a place of endless unoccupied chairs and tables, soulless decorations and grim lighting. A group of sullen waiters stood around doing nothing. One of them was reading a newspaper. In the gloom she made out two solitary figures hunched over their plates.

'We are full,' she heard one of the waiters say. 'There are no free tables.'

'They are too busy reading the paper and smoking to attend to us,' Berlin said in English. She caught a momentary look of indecision on his face.

'I'm quite happy to go home,' she said.

Berlin said something to the waiter, who gestured resignedly towards the stairs. Kate was guided into a smaller dining room on the first floor, smoke-filled and crowded. As they sat down, he briefly acknowledged one or two smiles and waves. He chose dishes for her – she was too overwhelmed by what was happening to concentrate on what to eat – and filled her glass repeatedly with a delicious white wine.

'Better than some of the student places you must have been to,' he said. 'I hate student parties. The wine always tastes like rocket fuel and the songs and poems are so dreary. When I was a student we worked hard but when we relaxed we laughed a lot. We had fun. Today everyone is so serious. What's happened to your generation? Why have you lost the ability to let your hair down?'

It was after midnight when they left. As she emerged into the night, the street revolved around her, and for a moment she had to lean against Berlin. He put his arm round her shoulder. The rush of cold air cleared her head and her nagging conscience, silenced for so long, sprang into life. What was she doing alone with a strange Russian whom she hardly knew – a man more than twice her age? Was this why she had come to Moscow? She was a music student, studying under one of the world's greatest cello players – she should be in bed in her hostel, or preparing for tomorrow's lesson. But her ability to listen to her more rational self receded with every step she took. She had no idea where she was going, nor did she care. She had submitted herself willingly to powers beyond her control. Tonight she was bidding farewell to the prudence that had governed her life. She was no longer the shy student who played truant from her music to attend his lectures. Berlin's presence beside her transformed her into the woman in her dream. But now he was playing the tune and she was the one being drawn ever closer to the music.

An official car roared past and disappeared. The street was deserted and silent – that Moscow silence again. She clung tightly to Berlin's arm.

★

His flat was high up in a huge modern building and full of books, a few paintings – she liked one of a young soldier, in a greatcoat and hat, holding an unfamiliar rifle in his hand, waiting anxiously to board a train that would take him away to the front. There were some photographs – his parents, she imagined: his mother was a tall woman with thick blonde hair. Berlin, she noticed, was very like her – and a bronze head and shoulders of his mother, sculpted when she was young. Kate was struck by the innocent beauty of the portrait of a young woman on the threshold of life, her expression open and trusting before the cruel secrets of life in the Soviet Union were revealed to her. She was reminded of the faces she had seen on the public statues in the city, usually a young man and woman striding determinedly towards the much-promised 'radiant future', their hands held high, one holding a hammer, the other a sickle.

'Is that your mother?' she asked Berlin.

'Yes,' he replied. 'Before she married my father.'

'She's very beautiful,' Kate said. 'Who did the portrait?'

'My father was a sculptor.'

'He must have loved her very much.'

'Why do you say that?'

'Look at the face. She's so full of life, so eager, so hopeful.'

'For a time he loved her. At least I think he did.'

'I know I've seen her face before,' Kate said. 'Why does it seem so familiar?'

Berlin laughed. 'My father sculpted many of the public statues in this city, and elsewhere. My mother was his model and his inspiration.'

He had a cream-coloured Deccalian gramophone like her father's, with its familiar egg-box speaker – surely he couldn't have bought that in Moscow? – and next to it stood his collection of long-playing records.

'I thought jazz was forbidden in Russia,' Kate said teasingly, skimming through his albums.

'There are ways of bending the rules.'

'And sometimes you do?'

'Not everyone lives like this.'

'Will you play this for me?' She had chosen a record at random. He took the vinyl record out of its cover and inspected it lovingly for the presence of dust, wiping it carefully with a special yellow duster he kept in a plastic wallet. He put the record on the turntable. 'This is not your kind of music, I know. But listen. It will touch your heart.'

The sound of a sad trumpet filled the room, a solitary lament which slowly possessed her with its mournful magic.

'I discovered Miles Davis the first time I went to California,' Berlin was saying. 'I'd never heard of him before. He is a trumpeter of genius. On this recording, he plays with his great friend, the pianist Bill Evans. Discovering this music was a revelation to me. The moment I heard it, I entered a world I did not know existed.'

Berlin was right. This was music she was aware of but had never listened to. She found it touched her in a way she had not expected – it was music of emotion, sadness, poignancy; of fate as something that could not be altered, of raw passion that flared but did not last, and yet from whose demands there could be no escape, not if you were true to what you felt. There is only one voice you must listen to, each note was telling her, the voice in your heart. Listen to it carefully. No evasions, no dissimulations, no resistance. Live for the moment because there is nothing else. Be true to who you are. It is all you have, and it is soon gone because youth is short. As the music played, she became the creature of its impulses, obedient and trusting.

She sat on the sofa, her shoes off, her legs curled under her. Was it one o'clock? Two? Who were they listening to now? More Davis? Count Basie? Ellington? The Modern Jazz Quartet? She no longer cared. The boundaries between dream and reality had broken down, and she no longer knew if she was awake or dreaming.

She remembered her glass being refilled, once, twice, how many times? She listened to Berlin without hearing what he was saying. Probably it was about the musicians. He had met them in jazz clubs when he had visited California. In the dimly lit room – why had he only switched on one lamp? – she was transfixed by the intensity with which he spoke. His voice, his eyes, his face seemed to envelop her, defining the limits of her world, allowing her no escape. Wherever she looked, he was there, gazing back at her, this strange and beautiful Russian man who had swept so unexpectedly into her life.

At some point he got up from the chair to sit beside her on the sofa. She remembered letting him kiss her, putting her arms around him. How thin his neck was, how strong the body under his clothes! Then she pushed him away dreamily when his hands were on her. She knew then that he wanted her, and she felt not fear but a mixture of delight and confidence that she was the one he had chosen. If she wanted she could say no or yes to him. As the music played, the idea of saying no seemed a betrayal of herself, impossibly remote.

*

It was still dark outside when she woke. She looked at her watch. Five forty-five. She got up to look out of the window. In the hours of night the world had been transformed. The first snow of winter was settling on the pavements and streets, on the tops of the street lights, on the window ledges and roofs of the buildings opposite, transforming Moscow into a magical city, a new world. It would not last, she knew. Soon boots would tramp across the snowbound pavements, cars and trams would throw up explosions of snow as they passed, blackening them with soot and oil and grime, and Moscow would become its grim old self again. But for this short time, as the world stirred before waking, the city was hers, transformed into a pure white landscape of temporary but infinite beauty.

'Andrei?' No answer. She prodded him awake. 'I've got to go home.' She dreaded the idea of leaving him even for a moment.

'What time is it?'

'Nearly six.'

'It's too early. Go back to sleep.'

She looked at his face. The tension had gone from him. He seemed younger than he had last night, paler and more vulnerable. His eyelids quivered occasionally, responding to an inner tension she could only guess at. She bent down and kissed his forehead softly, then brushed his lips with hers. He didn't stir.

'Goodnight, my love,' she whispered. 'Goodnight.'

8

1

'Mr Hart is waiting for you, sir. Would you come this way, please.'

Pountney was shown into a small room on the first floor of the Oxford and Cambridge Club. Hart was talking to a man he'd never seen before.

'Gerry, thank you for coming.' Hart got up to greet him. 'I'd like you to meet an old sparring partner of mine. Gennady Koliakov, counsellor at the Soviet Embassy.'

So this was Koliakov: medium height, orange hair beginning to thin, pale face covered in light freckles, the kind of man whose sensitive skin kept him out of the sun. Not unsuitable for his profession, lived out, Pountney assumed, mostly in the shadows.

'Good evening, Mr Pountney. In some ways, I feel we have already met.' Koliakov spoke English slowly, as if concealing the remains of a childhood stammer, and with a pronounced American accent. 'I have seen you on television, of course, and I recall you were the subject of some lengthy conversations between Hugh and myself a year or two ago.'

'I don't think we want to resurrect the past, Koli,' Hart said quickly. 'All that's done and dusted long ago. We can safely leave it to the historians, don't you agree?'

'That was thoughtless.' He smiled disarmingly at Pountney. 'Will you forgive me?'

They talked undisturbed for half an hour before a member

of the club staff approached Koliakov to say that his driver had arrived. Koliakov got up and looked sadly at Pountney. 'I did explain to Hugh that I had another appointment.'

'It was good to meet you.' They shook hands.

'I knew we'd only got him for a while,' Hart said as soon as Koliakov had left, 'but I still thought it was worth it. I wanted you two to meet.'

Before Pountney had a chance to ask why, Hart was already explaining that he'd first come across Koliakov in a thermal bath in Budapest in the summer before the '56 Revolution. They'd ended up a few weeks later having a drunken evening together. 'Quite outside the Soviet rule book. God knows how Koli managed it. That's when he told me about Martineau's affair with Eva Balassi. I realised then that there was more to him than any of us had reckoned.' The outbreak of the Revolution within days of their dinner had prevented them meeting again. 'For a long time we'd assumed Koliakov really was a PCO.'

'PCO?' Pountney was hopeless with abbreviations.

'Passport Control Officer. Very lowly. In fact he was the senior KGB officer in the Soviet *residentz*. His job was to monitor the temperature of the local hostility to the Soviets and report back to Moscow on the city's state of health. We're pretty sure it was Koliakov who advised the Kremlin to send in General Abrasimov to crush the uprising. He went to ground somewhere in the Moscow hinterland for a while after returning from Budapest – there was a rumour he'd had a breakdown, though it's never been confirmed. Then a couple of years ago he reappeared in London, bright as a button if you please, with the rank of counsellor.'

Pountney wasn't listening. His mind went back to the photographs he had seen of the dead and dying in the streets of Budapest during the brutal Soviet repression of the uprising, of the harrowing stories he'd read in the papers or heard from the exiles he'd met, of the cry for help from a brave people which went shamefully unanswered by the West. Hungary was a tragedy that should never have been allowed to happen. Koliakov had had a hand in it – if Hart was right, he had set the whole terrible process in motion – and whichever way you looked, that hand was stained with blood. Now, over an indifferent glass of wine, they were talking as if their shared memories of that past didn't exist. How he hated the twisted morality of the intelligence community.

'After what the Russians did in Hungary, you're still prepared to deal with him?'

'Where would you be if I hadn't done so? Rotting in a Russian jail, most likely.'

Sensing Pountney's sudden change of mood, Hart hurried on. Koliakov's instructions for London were to get to know a wide range of contacts. Make friends; be seen around. Spend some money if you have to. Show the human face of Marxism. When you're in with politicians, trade union leaders, journalists and the like, listen and report. He was spying on us, Hart said, no question about it, but there was nothing Merton House could do. Koliakov hadn't broken any rules.

'Don't be deceived by the charm,' Hart continued. 'The spots on the soul of this leopard are a deep Soviet red. He's been at this game a long time. He knows all the tricks. He's a difficult nut to crack, a real hardline bastard when you strip away all the false sophistication.'

Why would Hart tell him this? Was there some unfinished business left over from Budapest? Had more gone on there than Hart was letting on, and were there old scores to settle?

'We've been watching him from the moment he arrived in this country, and we've not been able to pin so much as a parking ticket on him. Our Soviet friend is as clean as a whistle. He's been a model citizen.' Hart paused in his narrative. 'Until about a month ago.'

'What happened?'

'An indiscretion.'

Pountney laughed. Where would the Intelligence Service

217

be without human frailty? 'Tell me – was it a man or a woman? Or has he got his hand in the till?'

'A woman, but not the kind of woman you'd expect.'

'A duchess?'

'A call-girl.'

'Perhaps he's lonely,' Pountney suggested. 'Or he has certain specialised tastes that she satisfies.'

'Perhaps.' Pountney had the clear message that Hart wasn't interested in the possibility of Koliakov's sexual deviance. 'A long posting overseas can be quite a problem for some of them when they don't bring their wives with them.'

'Has Koliakov got a wife?'

'He's never married,' Hart said. 'The rumour in Budapest was that he had an unrequited love for Martineau's girlfriend, Eva Balassi, whom he'd met in Moscow during the war – I imagined jealousy of her attachment to Martineau was one of his motives in telling me about his affair with Eva. Anyway, our watchers are getting bored keeping an eye on Koliakov when, all of a sudden, he visits this girl. She's young, eighteen or nineteen, been on the game for two or three years. She works at the respectable end of the trade, you know, barristers, civil servants, the occasional bishop.'

'And now with her new interest in KGB officers,' Pountney said flippantly, 'she's moving into the rougher end of the market.'

'I'm sure our friend doesn't advertise his origins,' Hart replied sharply.

'Has he visited her often?'

'Our reports say he's becoming one of her regulars, yes.'

'It's not a crime to pay for sex,' Pountney said.

'That's why Koliakov is out of bounds to us. We can't lay a finger on him because technically he's doing nothing wrong.' Hart paused to stare at Pountney. 'We could of course turn the girl in, but we don't want to do that.'

'What will you do?'

'I'd like you to talk to him.'

'You're not serious, I take it?'

'Why shouldn't I be serious?'

'I remember you telling me before I went to Moscow that the days of the amateur were over.'

'I wouldn't ask if I wasn't desperate.'

'Come on, Hugh. Your people can do their own dirty work, you don't need me.'

'Koliakov's done nothing wrong, that's why we can't touch him.' Hart stared at Pountney. 'We think he may have the information we're so desperate to get our hands on.' Another pause. 'Look upon it as a favour, Gerry. I did the same for you once, remember?'

'That was a long time ago.'

'I've got a long memory.' Hart refilled their glasses. When he spoke again it was with a renewed intensity. 'This new missile-carrying Soviet satellite has put the wind up everyone. Whitehall's in a blind panic about what the Soviets will do next in Berlin. A war committee has been formed. The whisper now is that a general mobilisation is a real possibility. The Americans are sending a new division to reinforce their troops in Germany, and they've appointed General Clay to take charge. God knows what weaponry they're shifting into West Berlin. I'd bet my life on some of it being nuclear. The situation gets more serious by the hour. We've got to know whether Soviet aggression is based on bluff or reality.'

'I can't help you, Hugh. You know I can't. You don't need me to tell you why not.'

Hart ignored him. 'The key to what happens in Berlin is Radin. If he's alive, then it's more than likely this armed satellite exists and the Soviets will get it into orbit pretty soon. As we've no defence against it, we will need to get our reaction in first. If Radin's dead, then it's much more likely the Soviets are bragging about what they would like to do but probably can't, at least not in the next few weeks. Without Radin the threat doesn't go away but it diminishes. It takes the heart out of events right now, gives us a chance to sort this bloody mess out without so great a risk of blowing the world into a billion pieces. So we have to know for sure whether Radin is alive or dead. At this moment, we just don't know. Finding out the truth could make the difference between peace and war.'

'Why would Koliakov know if Radin was alive or dead?'

'Koliakov went back to Moscow for a meeting of the policy committee for disinformation around the time some of us think Radin died. That suggests he may know whether the Soviets are keeping Radin's death secret or not. He may even have had a hand in the decision.'

'It's a long shot, isn't it?'

'There's nothing else in the locker, Gerry.'

'What if I put the question and he doesn't play?' Pountney sounded dubious. 'You said it yourself. He's a tough nut underneath.'

'He's got a weakness now, Gerry, and we know about it. We've got times, dates, photographs of him visiting the girl. We've got a massive dossier on him. But it's worthless because we can't touch him. I want you to use what we know to squeeze him till it hurts enough for him to spill the beans.'

'What do you mean, squeeze him?'

'Tell him you'll inform the Soviet Commissar at the embassy, a man called, Smolensky, of his nocturnal habits if he doesn't tell you about Radin.' Hart paused, looking at Pountney. 'I know all the arguments you can use against me, Gerry, but I don't want to hear them. Time's running out. You've got to swallow your scruples and help us.'

2

He stirs and, mostly asleep, asks dreamily: 'Is it time to get up?'

'It's still early,' Kate says.

'I'll wake up in a moment,' he says, turning over.

She looks at him, this man she loves more than her own life. His hair is falling over his face, his lips are open and she can hear him breathing softly, rhythmically. How can I leave him? she asks herself. *How can I leave him and go on living?*

★

Moscow settled into the long winter, bound tightly in ice and darkness. The snow lay in blackened heaps by the side of the streets, the temperature fell to ten below zero and went on falling. If the sun rose and set each day, the city, trapped in a grey and gloomy half-light cast by daylight refracted through a low, leaden sky, knew little of it. None of this affected Kate. Berlin took her into a world she had never dreamed of, and she followed willingly. She knew she was seeing only what he wanted her to see but she no longer cared. Moscow, which only recently she had hated so much, now became an enchanted winter kingdom, brittle and glittering.

He took her to the ballet at the Bolshoi. 'No one else can dance like the Russians,' Berlin told her proudly. On the evidence of what she saw that was probably true. The women were graceful, the men powerful. What she found impossible to tell him was that ballet left her unmoved. How much more she would have preferred the opera, but Berlin had little time for what he dismissively called 'singers who can't act'. To avoid hurting his feelings, she learned to dissemble.

'You cannot come to Moscow and not see Chekhov,' he said, as they sat down in the Moscow Art Theatre to a performance of *The Three Sisters*. 'Tonight you will see to the last detail what Chekhov intended. This is the authentic version.'

The production was a lifeless ritual, over-respectful of the past. Little, it seemed, had changed since Chekhov's death, no gestures, no inflections, no movements. The actors appeared to sleepwalk their way through the evening as if they risked a penalty for breaking the rules set by the first director of the play so many decades before. Kate saw no instinct in the performance, only a rigid discipline coupled with a reverence for the past that smothered any emotional involvement. This was museum theatre, and she hated it. Faced with Berlin's enthusiasm – 'That's how Chekhov should be played, like a dream dance in the mind,' he whispered as the actors bowed to what she saw as ecstatic but undeserved applause – she did not dare to tell him how she wanted to leap onto the stage and shake the cast into some kind of life. Instead she smiled in agreement and clapped as hard as she could in order to please him.

Very occasionally he took her to the apartments of his friends, where she met journalists, actors and other academics. None, she noticed, were from his own Department – she sensed he had hand-picked those of his friends he could risk her meeting. Once there was a white-bearded film director with a reputation for making patriotic films about life in the Soviet Union.

'Many years ago,' one of Berlin's friends told her in an urgent whisper, 'when he was a young man, Grigor Penkovsky had a great popular success with his first film, *Ivan's Search for His Father*. If you saw it now, you'd laugh at its dated absurdities. For a while it was Stalin's favourite film. Poor Grigor! He let his early success go to his head. Stalin's praise destroyed what little artistic integrity he had, and for the rest of his career he went on making the same film over and over again, confusing patriotism with sentimentality, until his audience deserted him. Since Stalin's death, he's fallen right out of favour. He hasn't made a new film for years. We're spared his cloying stories about the exploits of heroes of the Soviet Union. His only claim on the present are his memories of the past.'

If they all despised him so much, why was Grigor here at all?

'In a country like this, Andrei says, you must cherish the innocent. He has a strange loyalty to Grigor that I've never understood.'

When she was introduced to Penkovsky he was sitting alone in a corner of the room, and was already visibly drunk. For Kate's benefit, he began reliving past glories, self-consciously playing the role of the great artist, telling her in a loud voice of the Western stars he'd met at film festivals in the fifties, and what he thought of them.

'Dietrich, Palmer, Bergman, Hepburn – beautiful, glamorous women. I knew them all. "Grigor," they would purr, "we admire your work, you are a great director, you must cast me in your next movie." At night they would come to my room to offer themselves to show how much they wanted me to direct them.'

She could find little that was innocent about the transparent exaggerations of his supposed success. If he did not actually mention Stalin, it was clear whom he meant when he knowingly talked of his 'important admirers at the highest level in the state'. What could Berlin see in someone so obviously fraudulent, so immodest?

When she mentioned Penkovsky's name later in the evening, Berlin said: 'Isn't he wonderful?' To her annoyance she found herself agreeing.

To his friends she remained an object of open curiosity. Why would a young English woman come to study music in Moscow? they asked her. Weren't there other places she could have chosen? What temptation could have drawn her to this dreadful city that they all dreamed of leaving but knew they never would?

'I'm Vinogradoff's pupil,' she replied. 'Isn't that reason enough?'

'She is a wonderful cellist.' Berlin would put his arm round her shoulder to demonstrate his belief in his verdict. 'One day she will be recognised across the world. Everyone will know she was trained in Moscow, that it was here, among us, that she found out who she truly was. When she is an international star, we will have something to celebrate.'

But didn't she hate Moscow? Wasn't it a dull and dirty city?

Wasn't she longing to return home? The implication was clear. What sane person would give up life in the West for a year in Moscow? Her reply was always careful, noncommittal.

'We are here to study, Vinogradoff tells us,' she said diplomatically. 'For his students, Moscow begins and ends with the Conservatoire. He doesn't allow time for anything else.'

She was surprised at the frankness of the criticisms she heard and told Berlin so. He laughed and said she mustn't mistake the Muscovite cynicism his friends affected for something it wasn't. How else was life possible in a country where saying what you believed was so dangerous? A little cynicism among friends was a necessary escape valve, it kept you sane and out of harm's way. It was as close as he had yet come to telling her about the true constraints under which he lived.

When they were alone, she accompanied him to GUM where she saw things for sale that were available in no other shops that she visited in the city. When she questioned Berlin about this, he smiled, put his fingers to his lips and whispered, 'There are ways of bending the rules, remember.' She did not pursue her questions because she didn't care what his answers were. Nothing mattered so long as he was beside her and she could feel his warmth, hear his voice and respond to the touch of his hand upon hers. In rare moments of self-appraisal, she admitted to herself that her understanding of Moscow, indeed of this strange country she had chosen to visit, was defined by her relationship with Berlin. Anything beyond what he chose to show her did not exist.

*

One night she asked: 'Tell me about the Great Patriotic War.'

'Weren't you there when I gave my lecture?' Berlin did not look up from the essay he was correcting.

'Yes, I was.'

'Then there's nothing more I can tell you.'

She was not sure if he was teasing her or if his dismissal of her request was more serious. She put down the score she had been studying.

'In England, we don't call it the Great Patriotic War,' she persisted.

'That doesn't surprise me.' He rubbed his eyes and stretched. 'I expect Stalingrad gets little more than a paragraph in English history books. The West has never accepted the role the Soviet Union played in the defeat of fascism. Our victory at Stalingrad changed the course of the war. If our resistance hadn't seriously weakened the Nazis, your invasion of France in 1944 might have turned out very differently.'

Didn't we make sacrifices too? she wanted to ask. Didn't we stand alone against Hitler when all Europe had crumbled? Why was Andrei being so maddeningly myopic in his views over this? She felt tears gathering in her eyes. A distance had opened up between them the size of a canyon. Any further pretence was impossible.

'I don't know what to think any more. Whenever you talk about the past, I feel confused.'

Berlin heard the distress in her voice and came over to her. 'What is it? What's worrying you?'

'Nothing, Andrei. I'm sorry. I'm being stupid.' She wiped away her tears and tried to smile.

'Tell me,' he said gently.

'It might upset you.'

'You won't know unless you ask me, will you?'

She hesitated. 'Your history is so different to what I learned at school. Sometimes the same events have utterly different meanings. Sometimes they don't exist. When I agreed to come to Moscow I never imagined the differences between us could be so enormous. Nothing in Russia is what I expected, nothing is what it seems.'

Would he understand that she was speaking in code? All she could see between them was an unbridgeable gap, one that got bigger with every hour that passed. Her anxiety kept her awake at night. If the differences were as big as she believed them to be, how could they possibly stay together? To imagine not being with him was impossible.

'What can I say? You come from the capitalist system. Here we live according to the dictates of Marxism. These are different worlds. Isn't it a rule of physics that there can be no reconciliation between opposites?'

'Do you believe that, in your heart?' She was unable to conceal her desperation.

'I must believe it. What else can I do? I live here.'

'I have been here three months, but I know nothing about what life in Russia is truly like.'

He lit a cigarette. 'That's how it should stay.'

'I want to know, Andrei. You must tell me.' Couldn't he understand her fears? Surely he knew her well enough to realise why she was upset?

'You must never know,' he said with a firmness that frightened her. 'Never.'

'Why not?'

'What few illusions you may have left are precious. I can't take them away from you.'

'You're protecting me,' she protested, tears of despair falling down her cheeks. 'You're treating me like a child. Don't I mean more to you than that?'

He looked thoughtfully at her. 'If I believed you needed to know the truth about us, then by now you would be familiar with the lies, the hypocrisies, the injustices, the betrayals, the cruelties and the absurd inefficiencies that make up our daily lives. But you are not a historian nor a sociologist nor a political reporter, nor indeed a spy. Therefore what use is that information to you? You are a musician with a wonderful talent. You have come here to nurture that talent. When you leave Moscow, I want you to take away a musicianship that will astonish those who hear you. When I hear of you playing in the concert halls of the world in years to come, when I listen to your recordings, I want to know that that is what we gave you. I want your success to remind me that something beautiful and unique and unspoiled can come from this city of the damned. Only your music matters. Anything else is of no importance at all.'

She wanted to throw her arms around his neck and whisper that she would never leave him, that she would stay with him for ever. Instead, she told him, 'You are keeping me away from the truth.'

'If I am, it is for your own good.'

'If I want to look—'

Before she could say anything more he had taken her hands and pulled her into his arms. As he kissed her he whispered, 'Trust me. Trust me, please. One day you will know I am right.'

*

Her letters to her father became shorter and more evasive. She doubted he would even notice. At the end of November, he wrote asking when she would be returning. He presumed the communists in the Conservatoire recognised such Western ideas as term-time and vacation, even if they ignored Christmas. She avoided answering for as long as possible. She felt a duty towards her father but if the idea of more than a few hours away from Berlin was intolerable, how would she cope with a fortnight apart? Would Berlin still be there when she returned? Would he want her still? Her rational self said yes, of course, a passion of such intensity would endure a short separation. But what if the passion were one-sided? The obstacle was not Berlin, it was her own uncertainty about herself and what she meant to him. The truth was, she was afraid to go away in case there was nothing to come back to, and that would break her heart.

She worried about how she would tell her father that she was not returning home for the holiday. What reasons could she give? Berlin had said nothing about her departure. Was that a sign that he wanted her to go? She longed for him to ask her to stay. She tried to engineer the subject but either he

227

misunderstood or he was deliberately avoiding the issue. She hung on for as long as she could, and avoided committing herself to any definite course of action.

'I have to go to Helsinki for a few days,' Berlin told her one night. 'Why don't you come too? You've never been to Helsinki, you might enjoy it.'

It was what she had been waiting for. Her heart raced. 'When?' she asked.

He had to give a lecture there on 20 December. They would leave on the eighteenth, and be back in Moscow by the twenty-sixth. Just over a week, no more. It was not for long.

She pretended to be disappointed. 'That's our Christmas,' she said. 'I should go home to see my father.'

'Of course you must see your father. How selfish of me to want you here. Forgive me. I should have said nothing.'

She leaned over and kissed him. 'Poor Daddy,' she said. 'He'll have to spend Christmas with his sister this year.'

3

The taxi pulled up, its lights shining brightly in the dark. Pountney watched Koliakov get out, pay the driver and walk off into the ill-lit mews. He followed at a distance. For a man who'd drunk as much as he had, his step was remarkably steady. He rang the bell of number 16, one short stab. Not a summons, a signal: it's me. The door opened at once. No caution, Pountney noted, even though it was well after midnight. For a moment a woman in a silk dressing gown was clearly visible. She put her arms round Koliakov's neck and kissed him, drawing him into the apartment as she did so. The door closed.

Hart was right. Koliakov had a dirty little secret. Her name, Hart had told him, was Georgie Crossman.

★

As Pountney drove home, memories swept over him of those fateful weeks in the autumn of 1956, when a brave nation had taken to the streets of Budapest only to be slaughtered in their thousands by their Soviet oppressors. At first the British had deceived themselves into thinking that nothing was happening in Hungary by ignoring Martineau's warnings. Then they had deceived their American allies and invaded Suez in a misguided attempt to regain their imperial role, or so he had argued later in *Wrong Time, Wrong Place*. Angered at what he saw as a betrayal of the moral position he had expected the Foreign Office to uphold, Pountney had resigned. Walking down King Charles Street for the last time, with no job to go to, no idea of what to do with himself, he'd had no regrets, only a feeling of enormous relief. No more buttoning your lip when you disagreed with policy. No more flattering ministers you despised. He was his own man now, free to do as he chose, even if he was experiencing a bewildering mixture of terror and excitement at this possibility. His future might be formless, but he knew his decision was right.

Within days he'd been contacted by Danny Stevens. He'd never met a publisher before. He was as impressed by Stevens's determination to track him down – he can't have been easy to find – as by his enthusiastic belief that Pountney had something to say that others might want to hear. Over lunch in his office in St James's, he convinced Pountney to put his anger to work in a book about Hungary and Suez.

'I don't want a balanced view,' Stevens had said. 'This is not considered history. It's a contemporary record. I want the reader to share your outrage at what you thought was morally wrong. Tell us what happened from your point of view. In this case, partiality is a strength. Hold nothing back. Give us the fever of the times and make us relive those shameful weeks in all their mayhem and madness. Tell us what it felt like to be there.'

Martineau. Eva Balassi. Abrasimov.

They were people from another time, another life. He remembered their faces, frozen in the black and white photographs that were included in his book: a youthful Martineau, dressed in white, in his college cricket team in Oxford; Martineau on his wedding day, looking not a day older, with the glacial, elegant Christine by his side, smiling with her face but not her heart; Martineau in fur hat, greatcoat and boots, photographed in front of the railings of some unnamed building in a wintry and desolate post-war Moscow, a stolen moment from his glory days, when single-handedly he ran the Soviet spy 'Peter the Great' who for a short but valuable time brought British Intelligence to within a heart-beat of the power in the Kremlin.

Then there was Eva Balassi – beautiful at sixteen, a smiling member of the Hungarian women's swimming team in a group photograph taken at the Dynamo Stadium in Moscow; Eva with her daughter, Dora, then aged four or five; Eva at the Olympics in London in 1948, shyly holding her gold medal; Eva acting as translator to a British mission to Budapest in a dark coat and hat, the days of her sporting triumphs long behind her, a new mature beauty apparent. No wonder Martineau had fallen for her.

The menacing features of Abrasimov in his general's uniform looked out from another, taken either on the podium at a May Day parade or at some other official function. Nothing, of course, with which to identify Koliakov or Hart. The secret players in the game remained invisible.

Hold nothing back, Stevens had instructed. In his researches Pountney had uncovered a story he'd wanted to tell. During that last summer before the Revolution, Martineau's wife had discovered her husband's infidelity and betrayed him to his bosses at British Intelligence. Martineau's 'unreliability' – 'How can you trust a man who betrays his wife and sleeps with the enemy at the same time?' – justified London's policy of ignoring his telegrams while they got on with trying to deal with Nasser. Somehow Koliakov had got to know of the affair. Pountney had become convinced that the source was a leak from inside Merton House, a Soviet spy who had somehow managed to escape the periodic slaughters of central office staff that the Director General deemed necessary to avert accusations that Merton House concealed a Soviet mole. One night during a drunken dinner at a restaurant in Moscow Square, he had told Hart that he knew.

Days later, Soviet tanks arrived in the streets of Budapest and Martineau had disappeared, last seen, so Pountney understood, marching with the crowd, holding high the Hungarian flag, Eva at his side. Merton House had refused to allow Pountney to make any reference in the book to Martineau's mysterious end. The idea that one of their own might have gone native was too much to swallow. The story was suppressed, on the instructions of the Foreign Office and Merton House.

'A well-tried Stalinist practice,' Pountney had complained bitterly when Hart told him unequivocally that the story had to go, 'painting someone out of the picture so you can alter history.'

Pountney appealed to Stevens to intervene with Merton House. Those men who had ignored Martineau's warnings were as much to blame for the thousands of deaths as if they had ordered the killing of the Hungarians themselves. Now they were trying to cover up the truth, using the need for the actions of the Intelligence Service to remain secret to conceal what they had done – or as Pountney maintained, had failed to do. For once Stevens appeared to be powerless. For whatever reason he had temporarily lost his influence. Pountney was forced to bury his indignation.

'Better you get the larger picture right, that's what counts,' Danny Stevens had told him with the pragmatism of a man whose money was invested in what Pountney was writing. Therefore he had settled for a largely fictitious Martineau, whose role in the drama was reduced and who, as the Hungarian uprising ended, had retired from the Intelligence

Service to cultivate roses in Broadstairs. There was no mention of Eva or her fate, and the icy Christine Martineau never once came into it.

How like the Soviets we've become, Pountney thought. Better to lie than tell the truth. As his anger settled, the idea that Merton House was harbouring a Soviet spy never quite went away.

★

Pountney parked the car outside his flat in Maida Vale. He looked at his watch. Well after one. The lights were out. Margaret would have been asleep for a couple of hours at least. He'd enter the flat, have a bath and creep into bed. If he disturbed her at all, she'd smile sleepily at him, whisper some endearment and turn over. How he used to hate coming home after working late in King Charles Street to find a tell-tale strip of light visible under the bedroom door, knowing that Harriet was there awake, waiting to question him. Who had he seen? Where had he gone? What had he said? What a fool he'd been, putting up with that for so many years. Thank God he'd face no midnight interrogation, only the warmth of a sweet welcome, a long kiss and open arms.

4

Candles. That was her first impression. Lighted candles were everywhere, on the mantelpiece, on the sideboard (on which a bottle of claret, glowing blood red, was being allowed to breathe) and in the middle of the table, two elegantly twisted silver candlesticks with endless swirling branches made the china on the white tablecloth blaze as if it was on fire.

'Marion. Come in.' Michael Scott took her shawl. 'It's just us. I hope that's all right?' He had his back to her as he wrestled with a cork. She watched him deftly pour champagne into a long glass. 'I always think an evening *à deux* is the best

232

way of reviving one's flagging spirits after a long day facing the young, don't you? I do find youth so exhausting.'

He made it sound as if he did this every day. There was champagne, smoked salmon, something simmering enticingly on a steam warmer, two pots of crème brûlée – the college kitchen's speciality – a bowl of fruit and nuts, grapes and a silver grape-cutter, and an alarming array of glasses. Marion Blackwell had stepped into the private world of the middle-aged academic with no dependants and the means to indulge his tastes. He had created in his rooms an intimate haven into which he could escape whenever he chose. How different it all was from the contemporary bleakness of her own small room, to which she had added a few cushions and a couple of prints without denting its institutional anonymity. No wonder Michael Scott and his cronies clung tenaciously to the life they had made for themselves, obstinately resisting demands from their younger colleagues that the college be brought up to date.

'Tell me about your pictures.' She recognised a Duncan Grant still life and a bright Julian Trevelyan seascape. There was one she couldn't place. 'Is that a Nicholson landscape?'

'One of his earlier paintings, done before the fall.' Michael Scott sounded surprised. She knew he wanted to ask her how she recognised it, and she delighted in his frustration at not being able to breach good manners and question her.

'The fall?'

'When he still painted what he saw, before he went all abstract and interior and became the critics' darling. I've never liked his lines and shapes, all so rigid and geometrical – God knows where they're meant to lead you.'

She knew she was meant to admire his collection, and it was no hardship to oblige. Recognising the quality of his taste was a test she had to pass – why, she had no idea, except that she knew he would think better of her if she was able to identify at least a few of the artists represented in the room. What else would she be tested on before the evening was over? How she

233

held her knife? Whether she drank claret with fish? She had to pass with flying colours, because she wanted him to change his mind about who she was, which was why she had so readily accepted his unexpected invitation to dinner.

'Beautiful images are lost on the young, don't you find?' His expansive gesture took in all the pictures on the walls. 'They're too impatient to absorb anything old-fashioned. They always want to move on to the next fad. That's why the real quality's to be found in my house in Cornwall. You must come down one day, Marion, and see for yourself.'

There was a certain notoriety about the house in Rock. She'd picked up stories about the all-male reading parties which gathered there during the long vacation; the games of canasta and whist that Michael Scott had to be allowed to win; the wonderful wines that he dispensed so liberally to his undergraduates; and then the infamous nude bathing. Could that be true? She couldn't imagine Michael Scott's soft, plump body skipping over the sands with nothing on. Perhaps he preferred to stand at the water's edge, fully clothed, and watch his boys cavorting. She didn't believe for a moment that he was serious about the invitation.

'I see you have something of an eye, Marion. One can learn the names of artists. What one can never learn is taste. That gift is given to you from birth.'

What is also given to you at birth, if you're lucky, she thought, are means, and Michael Scott had those means. Every spring he 'fled' to Venice: 'Such a delight to know that whatever happens in the rest of the world, at least there is one place where nothing changes, everything is just as it was the last time you saw it, even if it has sunk a millimetre or two further into the mud.' Then, the moment the summer term was over, 'I scoot off to Tangiers to recharge my batteries after the torments and tyrannies of yet another academic year. God knows why one does it, but one does.' Perhaps his financial security explained the chronic non-production that marked his more than thirty years at Cambridge – few articles, fewer books, only the occasional newspaper or journal review and an undistinguished record as a lecturer.

To Marion's delight, the dinner was exquisitely cooked, the wines as delicious as she had imagined they would be and Michael himself a wonderful raconteur, with a gift for mimicry she hadn't anticipated. It was a one-man show and she was his perfect audience, laughing at his scandalous stories of the college before and during his time as he brought to life a galaxy of colourful and eccentric dons. He was doing his best to lower her guard – she knew what he was up to all right – but the knowledge made it no easier to resist him.

It was after the nuts and a delicious Tokay, as he was pouring the coffee, that without warning he changed tack. By this time her defences were almost down.

'This business with Andrei Berlin,' he began. The unbidden guest at the feast had been brought to life, and Marion resented his intrusion. Why did Michael have to spoil what up to now had been a wonderful evening? She felt as if the cold point of a silver dagger was being pushed carefully and precisely between her shoulder blades. 'It's made waves in a few high places. You're probably not aware of that. How could you be? That's why we thought it was time you were brought in on our little secret.'

'Waves? Gracious, Michael. Where? Do tell.' Now wasn't the moment to undermine his image of her.

'Whitehall, dear. Where else?' He lit a cigarette and placed it in an ebony cigarette holder. 'Over the years,' he said, looking pleased with himself, 'I think I can claim to have established a certain usefulness to my masters. Nothing grandiose, merely running the odd errand, dropping a quiet word in the appropriate ear from time to time, keeping one's eyes peeled for the unusual. Always wearing a number of hats.'

Very special hats, she was sure.

'When summoned to perform a duty by the powers that be, one obliges if one can. One picks up secrets as the spoils of war, of course, but over the years one has learned to keep mum. Why do I heed the call, you might ask, when there is no reward? An over-developed sense of duty, at least by today's standards, and the desire, occasionally, to belong to a world larger than all this.' The sweep of his hand indicated, she presumed, the college and the university. 'Another perspective is so essential, don't you agree, if one is to keep one's sanity at Cambridge?'

Get on with it, she wanted to say. Don't try to impress me with your allusions to friends in high places and your secret tasks. Don't intimidate me with your pictures and your silver and your wine. Get back to the point, Michael. Explain the mystery. Tell me why you brought me here.

'You were going to tell me about making waves.'

'So I was.' He fidgeted unnecessarily with his cigarette holder. 'I received a telephone call the other day to tip me off that there was some disquiet at a high level – well, let me be frank about this, Marion, at a very high level – about your invitation to our Russian friend. Who is this woman? I was asked. Why's she so keen on having her Soviet pen pal visit these shores? Is she a red? Ought we to know more about her? There were other points, of course, but that was the gist of it.'

'How did you reply?' She was genuinely curious.

'I'm not very good at being brave, Marion. No thumb-screws were called for, you understand – when you've been around for as long as I have, there are always private pressures, weak points that aren't secret any more. I said Berlin was your idea, and that as far as I knew no one had put you up to it, that I'd tried to stop you but I'd been outvoted. Apart from that, I couldn't help. You'll have to forgive me, Marion.'

Was this the purpose of dinner? To ask for forgiveness for shopping her to his powerful friends in order to soften her up, and then jump on her when she was least expecting it? What a manipulative bastard Michael Scott could be. Instead of scoffing his smoked salmon, she should have thrown it in his face.

'Is that it?'

'They don't let go that easily, Marion.' A light laugh. 'Once they have their teeth in you, they're always greedy for more.'

'That explains the presence of two men with beards who have taken to following me wherever I go. What a shame. I thought they were admirers.'

'This is no laughing matter, Marion. These are powerful people.'

'If you're threatening me, Michael, with your hints that your friends are after my blood, I'm not much impressed. I've never believed in bogeymen, and I'm too old to start now. If you're trying to shake me, I have to tell you, I'm not shaken. Do you know why? I'm not important enough to worry anyone. I'm a woman academic, and women academics don't make waves. We're so insignificant we hardly trouble the radar. Sorry, Michael. If you're trying to frighten me, you'll have to do better than that.'

'I am trying to be helpful, Marion. You must see that.'

She laughed. 'Oh, Michael, please. Let's have a little honesty between us, shall we?'

'You're reading me all wrong. Truly, you are.'

His voice had changed. That certainty that had entertained her had slunk away, to be replaced by a less formidable Michael. He had feet of clay after all.

'I hardly think so,' she said, sensing her ascendancy. 'Berlin is an academic like us. He teaches students. He researches in libraries. Occasionally he comes to the West and gives lectures on erudite subjects of limited appeal. He's not head of the KGB, nor a member of the Politburo. He matters to the life of his nation as much as you or I to ours, Michael, which frankly isn't a great deal. Don't exaggerate his importance because you were voted down.'

'He's a Russian. We're not getting on too well with the Russians at the moment.'

'When do we ever?'

'The present political climate doesn't give you pause for thought, Marion? You surprise me.'

'Why should it? This isn't Whitehall, and it's certainly not West Berlin. This is Cambridge, a small university way out in the Fens, miles from anywhere, in case you'd forgotten.'

Michael Scott ejected the end of his cigarette from its holder and stubbed it out in the ashtray. 'The message from my friends is that, when Dr Berlin reaches Britain, they would like to have a quiet word with him.'

'Over my dead body. While he's here, he's mine and that's an end to it.' So that was what the evening was about. Mystery solved. The telephone call, the candles, the silver, the champagne – and there she was, thinking naively that Michael Scott had invited her because he wanted to kiss and make up. 'Sound her out,' his anonymous Whitehall friends must have said. 'See if she'll bite.' What a fraud Michael was, what a bastard! She felt angry and cheated.

'He's coming to Cambridge because we've asked him to give a series of lectures. When he's done, he'll go home to Moscow again, and that's all.'

'My friends think a quiet chat over a cup of tea might be useful.' She recognised a new insistence in Michael Scott's voice. Perhaps his friends in Whitehall had put him under pressure.

'I can guess how they define useful, Michael, and I don't like it. I'm not sorry to tell you that the answer's no. Berlin's agreed to come because I invited him on the committee's behalf. That's all there is to it. If Berlin thought for a moment that my invitation was a front for your seedy friends to whip him away to one of their country houses for a long interrogation session that could do him all sorts of harm when he returns home, he would never have agreed. He accepted because he trusts me, and I'm not going to do anything to betray that trust.'

'Is that your last word on the matter, Marion?'

'Yes, Michael, it is, and I hope it's loud enough to reach Whitehall either on its own or with assisted passage.'

Scott got up and poured himself some more brandy. 'Are you sure you won't?'

'No thank you.'

'Part of me sympathises with you, Marion. You may not believe that at this moment, but I assure you it's true. It would be wrong to betray Dr Berlin's trust. I admire you for that. But the other part of me, the part that is wise in the ways of the world and does not let my heart run its affairs, that part of me knows you are making a serious mistake. This is an opportunity we must take. These are dangerous times we live in. Berlin may have valuable information. Look upon it as *force majeure*, against which the likes of you and I have no defence – how can we? – and close your eyes. Then you won't see it happening.'

'I said no, Michael.'

'This is an opportunity we must take, Marion.'

'I'll say it again in case you missed it the first time: no.'

'Hear me out. You may not like what I'm going to tell you, but perhaps in time you'll thank me for saying it. My friends like to get their own way. They can be quite unscrupulous if they think they're being resisted. For your own good, please think again.'

'What can they do, Michael?' She hoped she sounded as dismissive as she felt.

'Perhaps I should remind you they don't play by our rules.'

'You're being coy, Michael. These allusions are lost on me.'

'They'll use whatever means they can to get their way.' One of the candles on the table guttered and he got up to snuff it out.

'Let them try,' she said.

'You may get hurt in the process.'

'How?'

'They tend to twist the knife in unhealed wounds.'

She was laughing at him now. 'I'm a pushy woman. I think there's too much dead wood in this university and much of it is male. I want to chop it out. Is that what you reported to your friends, Michael, when you told them all about my weaknesses?'

'No, as a matter of fact, it wasn't.' He lit another cigarette. 'Would it help if I prompted you by mentioning a certain name?'

'You're being coy again, Michael. It doesn't suit you.'

'Bill Gant?'

'What about Bill?'

'No need to play games, Marion. We both know what we're talking about.'

'No games, Michael. What about Bill?'

'You're sleeping with him.' Michael Scott looked pleased with himself. 'That's what I told my friends. I said you were sleeping with poor Bill Gant.'

'You can tell your friends that they must do better than that if they want me to change my mind. Their informant's not up to scratch. The news is old hat.'

'Old hat?' He looked as if he had been hit.

'What happened between Bill and me is over.'

'Since when?'

'God, does it matter? It's over, that's all. Ages ago.'

'Does Bill know?'

'What do you think?'

'I see.' He was gazing into the bowl of his brandy glass.

'If that's all your friends know about me, then they're not going to get very far, are they? I mean, what can they do? Tell the blessed Jenny that I went to bed with her husband? I doubt she's in a position to care about anything like that any more, poor woman. All she can hear are weird voices screaming in her head. Put a block on Bill's career? He's damaged goods already, Michael. Everyone knows that. That leaves me. Since when is adultery a crime? If they want to plaster the news about my brief affair with Bill all over the university, let them go ahead. I really don't care because I don't think anyone else does. But if your friends in high places think they've got enough dirt to make me buckle under and hand over Andrei

Berlin, then they'd better think again. One small move from them and I'll scream the house down and claim I'm being molested. So you see, Michael, I'm not interested in playing your little games, and there's nothing you or anyone else can do to make me. Is there?'

IVAN'S SEARCH FOR HIS FATHER

The rain has cleared, and the sky has been without even a touch of cloud all day. Now it is dark, parents and children have gathered once more in front of the makeshift screen. A light flickers. Andrei hears the familiar clicking of the celluloid over the gates and sprockets of the projector. Someone shouts: 'Reel three.' Once more Ivan's adventure begins.

*

'Where do you think you're going?'

The policeman holds Ivan roughly by the shoulder and pulls him away from the door of the police station.

'I want to see someone in authority. I have something important to report.'

'Not in there you don't.' Ivan is pushed roughly out into the road. 'On your way. Don't come back.'

The policeman glares threateningly at him. He had better not try that trick again. Disconsolate, he walks away. Yet again his plan has failed. No one will listen to him because he is a boy without an identity. He cannot prove who he is because he has no papers. They were burned when his first life ended. All he escaped with was what he stood up in. Isn't it enough to be alive? he asks himself each day as he gets out of bed. Isn't it enough to have survived the storm? In the eyes of official Moscow, though not in the eyes of the Chernevenko family, the answer is no. Why should I need pieces of paper to prove who I am? Why does no one believe me? He is at a loss as to what to do.

It is the same at school. His requests for help have been ignored by his teachers. They are suspicious of him. He is sure it is because they cannot establish to their satisfaction who he is because he has arrived from nowhere. Behind his back, in class, in the schoolyard at break times, he can hear them sneering at him. Who is the orphan Ivan? Where does he come from? Are his parents really dead? Is he hiding some grave crime? Perhaps he killed his own parents, or his brother. Were his parents imperialist spies who were executed for betraying secrets to the West? Perhaps the stories of the fire are Ivan's camouflage for what really happened. He has heard them say this. Until they can establish who he is and how he got to Moscow, they remain wary of him.

In the face of this reaction, he is helpless. There is nothing he can say or do that will make them believe his story. He can remember his parents: their names, their ages, where they lived, what they did, how they died, *when* they died, but he has nothing to prove that what he is saying is true.

Why should he invent the first part of his life? he asks repeatedly. Why should he invent such a brutal story?

'To be satisfied, we need more than you can tell us,' he is told.

'Everything was burned,' he replies, but the expressions on the faces of his listeners tell him they have heard that one before. Until the mystery is solved, he will never be accepted by his teachers or his classmates. He will remain an outcast. At times he feels so miserable he wants to cry, but he knows he mustn't.

He walks away from the police station, bitter with disappointment. How can he make himself into someone they can recognise, or respect, or even admire? How can he become a Soviet hero whom crowds will surround wherever he goes, at whom young mothers will smile while their young ones try to model themselves on him?

He knows these dreams of revenge are merely fantasy. The reality is, he can do nothing.

★

He finds no relief at home. In the days since his stepfather Chernevenko's arrest, his wife, Anna, has done little more than sit on the bed all day and weep.

'It's wrong,' she tells him. 'It must be a mistake. He's done nothing. Nothing at all.'

The words in her husband's defence pour out of her in an unstoppable flow. Boris is the victim of a conspiracy. Some of his colleagues at the Ministry, jealous of his recent promotion, have fabricated stories that he is a spy and passed the information to party officials. Of course the charge is nonsense. How could he be a spy? He is a loyal communist, an intellectual sprung from the working class. Boris is a man who has willingly and selflessly dedicated himself to a cause that he believes in and that has given him everything he has ever asked for. Those who've betrayed him, she says, are the old bourgeoisie, who resent the new breed of communists.

For days they wait for news of Boris Chernevenko. They hear nothing. It is as if he has dematerialised into the air. At school Ivan cannot concentrate. First him, now his stepfather. Two injustices have been committed. If he can do nothing to help himself, then he must act to help the man who, out of the goodness of his heart, took him in when he was starving. He has tried to talk to his teachers to explain what has happened at home, why he is so preoccupied all the time, but they either won't listen to him or are afraid to do so. He has been punished for inattention at school. He has spoken to the youth leader at the Komsomol, who has refused to hear what he has to say. Now he has tried the police station and once again he has been rejected. *He has to save Chernevenko.* But how?

It is while he is daydreaming in the classroom than an idea comes to him.

There are guards, he has expected that, but he is young, agile and still quite small for his age. For a moment he is tempted to see if he can dodge past them – but that would mean ditching the plan he has so carefully worked out. He manages to resist the temptation: it is simply too risky. Better to stick to what he has decided. He goes up to the guard.

'Please direct me to Comrade Stalin's office. I have a letter for him.' He clutches the envelope tightly in his hand.

The guard laughs. 'What makes you think he is here?'

'This is where he lives, where he watches over the children of Soviet Russia, where he guides our lives as we build the future.' He has been diligently rehearsing what he will say. He is surprised, when it comes to the point, how easy the deception is.

'Go and see that man over there.'

He is inside the Kremlin gate. He feels the first flush of success. Each time he repeats his request he is passed on to someone else. Each time he draws a little closer to his goal.

'Knock on that door and ask.'

Is this Comrade Stalin's study? His knees turn to water. He hesitates, then knocks. There is no answer. He knocks again and listens carefully: no sound. Could the room be empty? He turns the handle and goes in. He sees a large desk. Is this where Comrade Stalin plans the radiant future of the Revolution? He smells the bitter smell of old tobacco – the cigars Comrade Stalin smokes? There are papers on the desk, a reading light is on, there are telephones – why does someone need more than one telephone?

'Who are you? What are you doing here?'

It isn't Comrade Stalin. The man is too short, and he has a bald head and protuberant eyes partly hidden behind small round spectacles. He is wearing a waistcoat without a jacket. He has stains of sweat under his arms, and the musky smell of his body is everywhere in the room. Comrade Stalin is tall and well built, and he has a thick head of hair and a bushy moustache. Ivan knows that because he has seen photographs of the Great Father in the newspapers and magazines, and sometimes in newsreels.

Ivan stands frozen to the spot. There is something menacing about the man's appearance that frightens him. He is unable to speak.

'What are you doing in my room?' the man demands again.

Ivan finds courage from somewhere. 'I have come to deliver a letter to Comrade Stalin. I was told to knock on your door. There was no answer, so I came in.'

'You were wrong to do that. You should have stood in the corridor and waited until you heard the command to enter.'

'I'm sorry.'

'Give me the letter and I will give it to Comrade Stalin.'

'I cannot do that.' Ivan holds the letter behind his back.

'I said give it to me, boy.'

'I have promised the young pioneers that I represent that I would give this letter to the Father of the Nation in person.'

'If you want him to read it, you must hand it to me first.'

'I hold this letter in trust for the children of the nation, the citizens of the future. My instructions are to hand it over to the Great Leader myself. I have no authority to give it to anyone other than him.'

'What if he refuses to see you?'

'I will wait outside his study until he does.'

'What if he doesn't come out of his study for days, for weeks? Winning the world for communism demands his full attention. It is an endless task.'

'I will stay at my post for days, months, years if I have to.'

The bald man with the bulging eyes laughs. 'Brave words, young man. Wait there.' He dials a number and speaks quietly, grinning as he does so. He turns to Ivan. 'You're in luck. Come along with me. Our Great Father has agreed to see you.'

They go along another corridor, up some stairs, wide and

carpeted now, with pictures on the walls of battle scenes from history. Russian victories, he guesses. Then through two huge gold-embossed double doors, past secretaries at desks who look up amazed as he walks by, to another double door. The man with the bulging eyes knocks. The doors are opened at once.

'Is this our young friend?'

Stalin comes towards him. He is dressed in a simple khaki uniform without insignia. He is shorter than Ivan imagined. His face is more weather-beaten and pock-marked than he would have guessed from the official photographs, his hair thinner. In real life Stalin is somewhat less than Ivan has expected.

'I gather you have written me a letter on behalf of the young people of Russia.'

'My instructions are to speak to you alone,' Ivan says.

'I have a few moments.' Stalin nods at the bald man, who leaves the room. The doors close. Man and boy are alone in the vast room. Suddenly Ivan's courage deserts him. He stands before the Great One, speechless.

'Well, I am here and so are you. What is your letter about?'

He feels tears pricking at his eyes. He struggles to maintain his composure.

'This letter.' He stumbles over the words. 'This letter is not from the young people of Russia. Nobody has asked me to bring it to you. I wrote it myself. I lied because I wanted to speak to you about an important matter.'

'Your envelope is empty.' Stalin is puffing at a pipe and sitting on the arm of a chair. 'There is no letter in it?'

'None.'

'I see.' Stalin takes the pipe out of his mouth and inspects it. 'Then you had better say what you came to say, and make it quick.'

'It is about my stepfather, Boris Chernevenko. The man who took me into his house when I was orphaned, and who has always treated me like his own son.'

'What has happened to your stepfather?'

'He has been arrested.'

'Has he committed a crime?'

'No.'

'Can you be sure of that?'

'He is a good communist. He has taught me to be a good communist. He is your loyal supporter. He works for the Revolution every day. He would never commit a crime.'

'Then why was he arrested?'

'His colleagues invented charges against him. They are not good communists and Chernevenko knows this. He has criticised them for their lack of effort. They are lazy. He has worked twice as hard as they have in order to conceal their laziness. Now he has won a promotion. They are trying to put him in prison to protect their own easy way of life.'

'What can I do about that?'

'You can release him and punish the guilty for their crime.'

'Suppose you are wrong, and your stepfather is as guilty as his comrades suppose?'

'He is not guilty.'

'How do you know? Show me your evidence.'

'I have only the evidence of my heart. I cannot prove what I say. But I know he is innocent. If he is freed, I will dedicate my life to the socialist revolution.'

There is silence. The Great One puffs at his pipe. His eyes seem pale and distant. Suddenly he smiles his famous kindly smile, reserved especially for the children of the Revolution.

'Write the names of your father's colleagues on this paper.' Ivan does as he is instructed. 'If you tell me he is innocent, then your stepfather shall be freed.'

Stalin writes something else on the paper and rings a bell. A secretary enters and he gives her the folded note.

'You are a brave young man. Tell me, what is your name?'

'Ivan.'

'Come with me, Ivan. Together let us tell the world how

248

the love of a child has saved an innocent father from wrongful imprisonment.'

The Great Leader holds out his hand. Ivan takes it gratefully. They walk towards the double doors, which open before them as if by magic. At that moment, lights come on around them. Comrade Stalin is illuminated, and the effect is to make him appear not of this world, but somehow divine, a god on earth, a man mightier and more powerful, more compassionate than any other. Ivan looks up at him in wonder. If only his friends at school, his teachers, the policeman who chased him away – if only they could see him now.

'Come,' Comrade Stalin says.

Ivan takes his hand again, and together they walk towards the arc lights and the cameras.

'Do you know what is happening?' the Great One asks.

'No,' Ivan replies.

'This moment is being recorded on film. Tomorrow the world will see evidence of your courage – the true courage of the youth of the Soviet Union, our hope for the future.' The Great One smiles at the camera. 'This,' he declares, 'is Ivan, who has come to ask my help to save his stepfather. His courage against huge odds earns him the right to be a youthful hero of the Soviet Union. Let him be an example to the young people of today. It is on the backs of young men like Ivan that the future of our great country will be built.'

Comrade Stalin turns towards Ivan and smiles. Ivan smiles back because his heart is bursting with happiness. He has found his true father at last.

9

1

Four weeks after her father's death, Olga Radin held a party in her flat. Officially it was to celebrate her birthday. In fact, her intention was to use the occasion as an opportunity to celebrate her father's life, though she told no one about this. On the day of the party, she put a framed photograph of Viktor on a table in the hall next to one of her brother, Kyrill, and beside it a small vase of white flowers. Around the apartment she placed some of the many photographs of her father that she had collected over the years. With no words spoken, the message would be understood by her guests, and they would react accordingly. She had no fear of betrayal. Within her closed circle she knew that this secret ceremony to honour her dead father would remain safe.

The cramped apartment was thick with cigarette smoke when Berlin arrived. He recognised Generals Melnikov and Orenko, Ustinov, a senior member of Radin's team at Baikonur, and two cosmonauts, one of them Titov, the other whose face he knew but whose name he couldn't recall. Towering above them all, his lean frame upright and dominating, the shoulders of his dark green uniform covered with the embossed gold that marked his rank, was the elderly Marshal Gerasimov. No members of the Politburo were present; no party officials, no politicians, no administrators. Berlin could imagine Viktor smiling. He may have gone to his grave but the faithful Olga would ensure that his prejudices would not die with him, in much the same way that she would not let his death go unnoticed.

It was an occasion without formality. There were no speeches, no toasts, no formal words about Radin or his achievements, though his spirit, Berlin felt, was everywhere in the room and was given further life by Olga's photographic record of her father.

The conversation throughout the evening centred on Viktor; there were stories about working with him, about bruising encounters with his refusal to climb down when he thought he was right. Anecdotes were recounted of his eccentricity and his courage, particularly his inability to conceal his dislike of those who lacked the scientific under-standing to recognise the importance of what he was doing, yet who had sufficient political power to thwart his plans. Berlin felt a certain comfort in the presence of those who had known and admired Viktor in a life where, he imagined, his advocacy of his own rightness must have made him many enemies. He had survived on the strength of his achievements but he must also have had powerful protectors, some of whose identities he was probably unaware, yet without whom he might well have been abandoned years before. In the Soviet Union, achievement was no guarantee of survival.

Listening to stories about Radin and telling his own, seeing photographs of that familiar face at different stages of his life: the domed skull, the piercing, attentive eyes, the way he pushed his head forward when he talked to you, replaced Berlin's memories of the shrunken figure in a wheelchair in a hospital garden outside Moscow. However briefly, the Viktor Radin he had known and loved was restored to him. Perhaps, after all, the state had got it right. Radin wasn't dead, only absent.

'Will you do something for me, Andrei?' Olga had taken his arm. 'Will you talk to Natalia Kuzmin? She's Peter Kuzmin's widow,' she whispered. 'Over there. By the window.'

He'd noticed her when he arrived, standing alone, looking down at the street below. She had a glass of wine in her hand but she had hardly drunk from it. Her face was pale and drawn, her thin hair pulled back in an untidy attempt at a bun. She radiated a quiet desperation. Berlin had seen no one approach her or recognise her presence.

'Peter worked with Father at Baikonur,' Olga explained. 'He was killed in an accident a few months ago. Since his death, there've been all sorts of stories about his failures. He's been made the scapegoat for everything that's gone wrong. The authorities are using these rumours as a reason to deny Natalia a state pension. She no longer has my father to protect her, and it seems no one else has the courage to take his place. She has two young children to bring up. Go and talk to her, poor woman. She's so desperate. People hear these rumours about her husband and avoid her.'

Olga was distracted by one of her guests wanting to say goodbye. Berlin was relieved. He had no stomach for a conversation with Kuzmin's widow. It was cowardly, he knew, and he felt guilty. She was an innocent woman, suffering for losing a husband whose death was used by those more powerful than her to conceal their own shortcomings. Facing her desperation would be like meeting his own, and he had no wish to do that.

'Andrei, my friend,' a deep voice boomed across the room. Berlin was embraced by a man in a general's uniform. General Orenko's large frame was now covered with loose flesh. The athlete's body that Berlin had admired when he was a schoolboy had become overweight in recent years and was now paunchy and soft. The muscles that had once hurled the javelin so far had slackened and turned to fat. Igor Orenko had been his brother Anton's friend. He had not aged well.

'I hear a whisper about a visit to Cambridge. Is that so?'

'Not from Anton, I trust?'

Orenko smiled. 'Unless my information is wrong, Anton is

somewhere beneath the Polar ice cap, guarding us while we sleep against threats of war from the West.'

'Who then?' Berlin asked.

'A good general never reveals his sources.' More loud laughter. 'Shall we just say a little bird told me?'

'I've been invited to give a series of lectures in October.'

'Autumn in England. What better time to be there?' Orenko smiled. 'Viktor always said you were a fortunate man.'

'If Viktor told you that, he was mistaken.'

The general produced a leather wallet filled with cigars. 'Would you care for one of these?'

Cuban cigars. He hasn't seen one for years. 'Thank you, no. I prefer my own.'

'I saw Viktor the day before you did,' Orenko said between puffs as he lit his cigar. Berlin noticed that he had carefully steered them into a corner of the room. 'He told me he intended to give you Engineer Kuzmin's report predicting the disaster at Baikonur. I presume he did so?'

'Yes.'

'Did you believe what you read?'

'Not at first.'

'What made you change your mind?'

Berlin hesitated. Should he speak openly to Igor? They had known each other for most of their lives. It was a risk but one he was prepared to take.

'Some days later I read Viktor's account of the death of Cosmonaut Alexandrof. There were undeniable similarities between the two accounts.'

'How did you react to what you learned?'

'I was shocked. If both accounts are true—'

'I have had both documents checked for authenticity. They are genuine, I can assure you of that.'

'It appears we are living through the history of an illusion.'

Orenko studied the end of his cigar. 'You are not alone, my friend. All of us are victims of the same illusion, though too few of us are aware of the risks we run.' He paused for a moment. 'Viktor was one of the few who understood what was happening.'

Berlin had never heard Viktor speak about the general, yet Orenko was giving him the impression that there had been intimacy with Radin. Was that true? Or was Orenko trying to convince him that he and Viktor had been close? If so, for what purpose?

'When the First Secretary made public the revelations about Stalin's crimes at the Twenty-second Party Conference,' the general continued, 'many of us – and I was one of them – imagined that our society would become more open, that the constraints imposed on our lives would be relaxed. We were deceived: little has changed. We are paying a high price for that deception. Viktor predicted what would happen if significant changes were not made, and he has been proved right. The destruction of his rocket and Alexandrof's unnecessary death were caused by a malaise that is the inevitable consequence of our corrupted system. Its effects are not limited to Baikonur. They are increasingly visible everywhere.'

He knocked the ash from the end of his cigar with his finger and examined its glowing tip.

'Now Viktor Radin dies, and within a few days of his death we have the First Secretary, on a visit to Romania, promising to build an orbiting satellite from which we will launch nuclear missiles against America. Where did he find that idea? It's nonsense. We'd need ten Radins and double the resources to make that work. It isn't going to happen. At the same time the Kremlin insists that Radin is not dead. Such a lie is unsustainable. Sooner or later, the West will penetrate our illusion, discover how weak we are and perhaps then take their chance to strike against us. That will force us to move quickly to our only defence, nuclear weapons, which will destroy us as much as those we fight. Does that prospect not terrify you?'

'Of course it does.'

'How can we stop it happening? Unless we do something, we will be dragged into a conflict we cannot avoid.'

Olga suddenly appeared by his side. 'Igor,' she says. 'Your driver has arrived.'

'Thank you.' Orenko turned back to Berlin. 'That is the question that deeply concerns some of us. How do we stop the inevitable happening?'

2

They are alone in Vinogradoff's apartment. Today Kate is playing as she played when he first heard her in London, and she doesn't need to look at his expression to know that Vinogradoff is pleased. She has caught the mood of the music, the light, delicate touches when the notes seem to be dancing; the solemn, soulful moments that banish any thoughts of joy or pleasure, and then the powerful movements up the scale as the theme struggles to reach a bridge into a new world of hope and contentment, to complete its harsh and difficult journey from the pain of the present towards the hoped-for peace of future redemption. She has found a musical voice in Moscow, and she knows it is her own.

The last note vanishes in the silence of the room. Vinogradoff suggests she play another piece for him and she does so, relieved that the gift she thought she had lost has returned, and that now she can justify his faith in her. When he tells her finally it is time to stop, she is reluctant to end this wonderful morning of discovery.

As she gathers her music from the stand, she is aware of an unusual nervousness in Vinogradoff's manner, as if he has been dreading the moment of her departure. He remains silent. She is sure he wants her to stay but she does not understand why. He stands some distance from her, watching her put away her music, his expression full of anxiety, struggling to find words, when usually he is full of gossip from the private world of Moscow music. A muscle in his cheek twitches involuntarily, dragging at his eye. He is a highly strung performer, and wrestling with inner tensions is to be expected in a man of his temperament but somehow she senses that the source of his anxiety lies elsewhere.

'If you have the time,' he says, his voice suddenly conspiratorial, 'there is one more thing I would like you to do. Of course' – this said backing away from her – 'I would not want to delay you if you have somewhere more important to go.'

She has no idea what he wants, but he is her teacher, the man who will make a musician of her. How can she refuse?

'You are under no obligation,' Vinogradoff says. 'This request is outside the arrangement we have made. If you would prefer not to, I would understand.' He puts his hand through his hair. 'Perhaps it would be better that way. Perhaps I am asking more than I have a right to ask.'

'Of course I'll stay. What could be more important?'

For a moment he is frozen by her decision, as if he cannot believe her reply. Then he unlocks his briefcase and takes from it some music which he gives to Kate.

'Please play this for me.'

She is pleased he wants her to play again because her head still swirls with the exhilaration of the piece she has just finished. She looks quickly at the score. It is a solo cello part, the music handwritten. It has no title, there is no composer's name, nothing she recognises.

'Who wrote this?' she asks, taking her place on her chair once more.

'Play it for me.' The command in his voice startles her. He has never issued an instruction before. 'Now. This moment – before I lose my courage.'

She does not understand what he means but she responds to the urgency in his voice. She settles the music on her stand and begins to play, long, sweeping notes in the lower register.

Vinogradoff listens intently, his eyes closed in concentration, his fingers covering his face. Almost immediately she is inside the music; she is a river flowing sedately through green meadows on a warm summer afternoon. The sound she is creating is the life of the river – brightly coloured butterflies playing over the surface of the water, a kingfisher waiting for its prey, a dragonfly hovering, a trout leaping out of the water to catch a fly, carp resting from the afternoon sun in the shadow of the river bank, the green stems of reeds bending gently with the stream.

But the music is more than description, it is the fate of the river itself, unstoppable, inevitable, life-bearing and life-threatening, slow here, faster there, eddying or racing over stones as it pushes its way inexorably towards the sea.

It is music that she can instinctively understand, about struggle and survival, about journeys, the joy of arriving, the pain of leaving. About coming to Moscow and the difficult process of finding out who she is, of falling in love, of the fear of losing that love for reasons that she can never hope to overcome.

The last note fades like a view losing itself in the distant haze of a summer afternoon. When she looks up, Vinogradoff is staring at her, his eyes wet with tears.

'Thank you, thank you,' he says quietly. 'You played it as if you had known the piece all your life.'

'It's wonderful,' she tells him. 'I am grateful to you for letting me play it.'

'You have given me great pleasure.' He bows before her, a gesture she has seen him make only to his audience. 'That was your best performance since you arrived here, and it is music you have never seen before.'

'It is yours, isn't it? You composed it.'

She is whispering, as if they might be overheard. Vinogradoff doesn't answer at first. She knows why. He is weighing up whether he can trust her with his secret.

'Yes.'

'Was that the first time you've heard it played?'

The question seems to take him aback. He clearly wants to say as little as possible, to close the incident as quickly as he can, to get on with his life as if the last few minutes had never happened.

'I have heard it in my head many times but never before played by someone else.'

She is astonished. 'Why did you give me the privilege? I'm your newest student – I'm not even Russian.'

'I thought you might understand it,' he says. 'I did not know it at the time, but the way you played, I might have written the music for you.'

'How can I thank you?' she asks.

'By telling no one. *No one.* By keeping my secret.'

He has taken a huge risk letting her play even this small part of his composition, and now she has to convince him that she – a foreigner – knows the importance of what he is saying to her, that his secret is safe with her. In this strange society that she is struggling so hard to come to terms with, she has discovered that there are harsh penalties for private acts that would go unremarked at home in England. Betraying a secret can lead to arrest, trial, years of imprisonment or worse.

'Promise me you will tell no one that you have played this. No one, however close.' There is a desperate appeal in his eyes that she has never seen before. 'This must remain our secret. In this strange country, one can never be sure who one's friends are. If people learned about what we have done this morning, it might be difficult for both of us.'

She looks away, unable to absorb the probing intensity in his expression. How can music, the pure, gentle sound of a cello, pose any kind of threat? What kind of madness rules their lives?

'I promise I will never tell anyone,' she says. 'You may trust me to be silent.'

The tic in his face relaxes. He returns his composition to the depths of his briefcase.

'If I had not believed that, I would never have taken the risk of letting you play my music.'

He takes her hand and kisses it. How terrible that playing a piece of music can make them conspirators. In this world of secrets, she now has a secret too.

3

Avoiding Bill proved more difficult than Marion had imagined. She hadn't anticipated his frequent telephone calls, nor the frantic notes he left in her pigeonhole. She found the increasing volume of his appeals painful to ignore.

I have to see you, Marion, he wrote. *It is very important. When can we meet?*

She imagined her silence was sufficient reply. She had not allowed for his persistence nor his desperation. Early one morning, she answered a ring at her doorbell and there he was, a tired, unshaven figure, looking as if he hadn't slept for a week.

'I'm sorry, Marion. I know it's early. Please forgive me. But I must see you.'

'Come in.'

She led him into her small sitting room and drew the curtains. He sat down. She perched on the arm of the sofa, pulled her dressing gown tightly around her and waited. When he spoke his words burst out of him. What he was telling her, he said, he had told no one else. She felt cold at the thought of how central to his life she remained.

'They told me last night that Jenny's never coming out of that dreadful place; she's been declared insane. She has no understanding of the present any more, she's lost all connection with reality. She doesn't even recognise me when I come to visit – she screams when she sees me and tries to hide. She thinks I'm someone who's come to kill her. Her doctors have asked me not to visit for the time being because my presence so upsets her. She's vanished into a fantasy world of her own invention, and she's never coming back.' He paused for a moment to catch his breath. 'I felt like an executioner, leaving her there on her own. I know it's for the best but that doesn't stop me feeling guilty.'

'I'm sorry it's come to this, Bill. It must be awful for you.'

He reached for her hand and held it against his cheek. 'Marion, please—'

'No, Bill, don't. It'll only make the pain worse.'

'You must hear what I've got to say.'

'Of course.' She hated herself for agreeing, but how could she not?

'I'm going to divorce Jenny. She won't know anything about it, thank God. I signed all the papers a few days ago. I will be free soon, Marion. We can have our life together, the life I've dreamed of. We can help each other write the books we've always wanted to write. Without Jenny I can rebuild my career. I know I can – but only if I have you, Marion. I must have you beside me. You're my hope, my strength. I can't do this without you. You're the only one who can bring me back to life.'

He stared at her, tears filling his eyes. She slowly removed her hand.

'Bill, Bill.' What could she say? How to break it to him without destroying him?

'Listen to me. We'll get married as soon as the divorce is through. I love you, Marion. You know that. I'll always love you. What more can I say?'

'Please don't go on, Bill.'

If he heard the note of rejection in her voice, he took no notice. 'You can save me, Marion. You can help me resurrect my career. Everyone thinks I'm finished but you know I'm not. You're the only one who still believes I've got something original to say. You've always known the truth, that until this terrible situation with Jenny was sorted out, there was nothing I could do. Well, Jenny's gone now. That part of my life is over, done with. I'm ready to start again. I want to come back. I want to do all those things I promised myself when I was young that I would do, and never got round to because of Jenny. Now we can do them together. Can you understand what that means to me? You're the only person who can bring me back, Marion. You must help me. You must.'

It was breaking her heart to see his anguished face, the desperation in his eyes. He knew she would never agree. He'd known when she didn't answer his notes, before he had rung her doorbell. He knew as he spoke to her now, pleading with her to change her mind. All she could do was pity him and hope he would survive the pain she would inflict on him.

'Oh, Bill, Bill,' she said softly. 'Oh, Bill.'

She held his head against her and drew her hand slowly through his hair.

*

Had she ever been in love with him? She was walking home through the quiet evening streets after dinner in hall. In the very early days the illicit nature of their relationship had increased the emotional excitement. She had thought of little else but Bill; she had waited for his visits with an uncharacteristic expectation. If he had to cancel their date, she would be plunged into despair. But once they had started meeting regularly, that excitement had quickly evaporated. Their commitments – he to his sick wife, she to her career – meant their affair could make no demands on either of them beyond the stolen hours they spent together each week. It meant an hour and a half on Wednesdays at lunchtime, and occasionally on Fridays between tea and dinner, hasty lovemaking, a snatched conversation usually about faculty business while they bathed afterwards, a bite to eat or a quick drink, a moment's careful consultation of their university diaries to plan their next encounter (a simple cross and a time, no names) and he was gone, while she was left to remake the warm, crumpled bed. The relationship was doomed, she saw that clearly now, because what they had together simply wasn't enough. At least, not for her.

She opened the door to her flat. This was home, her sanctuary, where she could be what she was. Thank God her aunt had left her enough money to afford the place. She hadn't liked living in college, it had never allowed her the independence she craved.

Since her arrival at Cambridge as an undergraduate, her experience of love, she conceded, had been both limited and perfunctory. There had been a research student in her third year, a historian like herself, who had wanted to marry her. The physical side of their relationship, she remembered, had been a series of embarrassing blunders. When he told her excitedly that he had been appointed to a research fellowship in Tasmania and would she come with him, she demurred. She had an elderly widowed mother in Northampton. Hobart was too far. She felt no regret in ending the relationship, but out of guilt she went to Southampton to see him off. She didn't bother to stand and wave a handkerchief as the ship moved slowly away. In that crowd he'd never have seen her anyway. She hurried to the train and found herself a seat. He'd promised to write once he'd settled in, but she never heard from him again. His absence made no more impression on her life than his presence had done.

She had been teaching for more than two years when one of her students made clear his feelings for her, but she had never been interested in men younger than herself. To avoid embarrassment, she arranged for him to be farmed out to one of her colleagues who was teaching the same subject. There had been one or two short-lived brushes with romance since, and a wild and unexpected weekend in Barcelona with a visiting Spanish academic, but until Bill the emotional side of her life had been largely barren.

Now Bill had gone. They would see each other across a

table at faculty meetings; perhaps they would be on the same examining board. But their relationship was over, it had ended this morning. Why did she not feel more distress? Her heart had never been truly touched, not by Bill, nor, if she was honest, by anyone. That was the truth she had to face. Perhaps it never would be.

4

'This is Koliakov.'

The voice on the other end of the telephone was hoarse and tired. Perhaps he was suffering from a hangover. If there was any justice, then he should be feeling decidedly ill this morning.

'Gerry Pountney.'

'Ah, Mr Pountney. Good morning. What can I do for you?'

'I was wondering if we could meet.'

'That would be a pleasure. Though—' his voice suddenly faltered. 'If this is about appearing on your television programme, I shall have to refuse.'

'No, no,' Pountney reassured him. 'It's nothing like that.'

'Very well. When would you suggest?'

They had dinner in a restaurant in Sidney Street. By the time they had reached the coffee, they'd exhausted Pountney's list of subjects: the reasons for the uprising in Budapest, British colonial policy in Africa, growing tensions between East and West in Berlin. Time to get down to business.

'I gather you know Georgie Crossman.'

If Koliakov was surprised by the remark he didn't show it. 'We have known each other for a little time. Is she a friend of yours too?'

Pountney shook his head. 'Aren't you playing with fire?'

'You will have to explain that expression. I am sorry. I do not understand.'

The atmosphere had suddenly gone cold. Pountney was

certain the Russian knew exactly what he was driving at. Asking for explanations was simply a way of buying time.

'I think your Mr Smolensky would be very interested to hear about your new friend, wouldn't he?'

'Smolensky is my driver.'

'He's registered as your driver. But we both know what he does for a living. He's the Kremlin's man in your camp. He reports on your behaviour to Moscow, those moments of weakness when you slip from the high standards that are expected of you, those indiscretions you would rather no one knew about, like your visits to a certain mews house in Knightsbridge. We don't mind you sleeping with Georgie Crossman, what we worry about is how you're paying for the pleasure. Miss Crossman's favours don't come cheap.'

Koliakov lit a cigarette. 'I have a sense, Mr Pountney, but correct me if I am wrong, that you are trying to put me under pressure. Could that be because you want something from me?'

'Shall we say, I have a proposition for you.'

'In my experience,' Koliakov said, 'such a phrase means you are proposing a bargain. Am I right?'

'I won't give Smolensky details of your habits, if you tell me what I want to know.'

Koliakov took his time in replying. 'Isn't there a word for what you are proposing? Isn't that word "blackmail"?'

'If it is, I suspect you're more familiar with the practice than I am.'

It was as if they were the only two people in the restaurant. Koliakov played with the spoon in the sugar bowl.

'What is it you want?' he asked.

'Information.'

'Information I presume you can get in no other way.' Koliakov was talking to himself. 'Therefore information my country does not want you to have.'

He looked up at Pountney. His eyes were ice cold. His

expression confirmed Hart's verdict that beneath the sophistication lived a very different man.

'What do you want to know?'

'Is Viktor Radin alive or dead?'

'Viktor Radin? Who is he?'

'The time for games is over. You've got forty-eight hours. If I don't hear from you by then, I will be forced to send those interesting details to your colleague at the embassy. Is that clear enough for you?'

10

1

He was fully awake now, and his arms were around her. He was kissing her again and again, whispering that their separation was only for a time, that there was no force strong enough to keep them apart for ever, no obstacle they could not overcome. He would find a way for them to be together.

'Yes, yes,' she murmured, wanting to believe that his words were true, while her tears fell on his face.

'You mustn't cry,' he said, 'we must be strong for each other.' Nothing could defeat them, not politics, not ideology, no physical or mental barriers, not even their time apart now. Love bound you together so completely that your identities merged in the mystery of making love, he told her, and out of that something glorious and wonderful and everlasting was created that no power on earth could destroy, not even death.

She knew he was using his passion to bury the consciousness of loss that was making her cry, just as she knew that to comfort her he was saying the opposite of what he believed. But little by little his words worked their magic, and she slipped from the brightness of the morning sun that flooded the bedroom into a waking dream of love, where he showed her that she was the centre of his world and that nothing would ever shift her from that place.

'To find your one true love,' he told her, 'is to discover yourself. You have given me the strength to know who I am.'

'Yes, yes,' she cried, not knowing what he meant. After a while, her tears stopped.

★

As the train steadily gathered speed out of Kirov Station, Berlin lifted the blind in their compartment so that Kate could see the lights of Moscow disappearing in the distance. The billowing snow disturbed by the movement of the train caught the illumination from the carriages and looked like stars flying around them. He stood with his arms around her as they passed through ghostly birch woods, the branches laden with snow bending under the weight. When they had left the city far behind and the dark night had turned the window into a mirror reflecting the image of a young woman leaning against her lover, he took her to the restaurant car and gave her dinner. Afterwards in their compartment he made love to her.

She lay awake listening to the sound of the train while he slept in the bunk above her. Of course I love him, she told herself. How could I not? But does he love me? Will I ever I know?

As the train raced through the icy December darkness, her question remained unanswered.

★

'Helsinki,' she told Berlin, 'is like living in a painting of a winter night.'

They sat at a table in the Kapelli Restaurant, a delicate nineteenth-century pavilion of wood and glass, a fragile galleon floating in a sea of snow in the Esplanadie Gardens. Kate looked out at the mysterious world of lights that danced before her eyes, flickering candles that, reflected in the window, appeared to stretch far into the snowy terrace beyond, and street lamps that emerged in the darkness like illuminated balloons. Now she understood the fixation with light in this city of winter darkness. Candles in windows were a reminder of days past and days to come; living symbols of summer light and life in the depth of winter, when the world seemed to have halted its progress towards the vernal equinox, when these northern people believed they were trapped in darkness for ever.

'This is a little-known city at the crossing point between East and West,' Berlin told her as she ate reindeer meat for the first time, or *poronliha* as he taught her to call it. How like her father he was, always giving her history lessons, explaining what he thought she needed to know, never letting her find out for herself. Now he was recounting the history of Finland, a country that was without a national identity until the middle of the nineteenth century, when Elias Lonnrot wrote down the local folk tales that he published as the *Kalevala*, the myths and sagas that gave Finland a sense of its own culture from which the nationalist movement grew. It triumphed in 1917 when the Revolution gave Finland the opportunity to declare her independence from Russia and become a country in its own right. He told her about the poet Runeberg – on their way to the restaurant he had pointed out his statue – about the architects Aaltonen and Saarinen, who had given the country a style and a sense of itself. He told her how General Mannerheim had returned from the Russian army to lead his country; about the Winter War in 1940, when for a hundred and twenty days the small Finnish army in Karelia had resisted the vastly superior Soviet forces before Mannerheim had surrendered to save further loss of life. He recounted how the Finns had declared their neutrality after the war and now trod a delicate tightrope between independence and subservience to the Soviets, honourable brokers of the possibility of dialogue between East and West.

He respected the Finns, he told Kate. They were a little-understood people who deserved to be more highly valued. He loved this city, and all its secret delights that the world knew so little of.

Outside it had begun to snow again.

Berlin awoke. The bedroom was flooded with a pale light. He got out of bed and went to the window. It must have stopped snowing some hours before, and an icy wind off the sea had driven away the clouds, transforming the sky into a huge cavern illuminated by sparkling points of silver light, like the decorated ceiling of a vast basilica. Wherever he looked, the snowbound city was illuminated by moonlight, everything tinted with shades of blue – blue roofs, blue buildings, blue streets. Helsinki, city of night, had become a city of dreams.

Was he mad to have brought her here? How much easier it was to conceal their relationship in Moscow. By day, she studied at the Conservatoire and he at the Institute of Contemporary History. After dark, she came to his apartment. Occasionally they went to the cinema or theatre together. Sometimes he introduced her to those of his friends he could trust. It was an uneasy, circumscribed relationship, and he struggled to keep her in ignorance of the dangers she ran associating with him, and out of sight and knowledge of those who might disapprove of the relationship.

Suppose her presence here was betrayed? Perhaps there were spies in the hotel – the hall porter, the chambermaid – who had reported Kate's presence in Helsinki. Perhaps instructions had already been cabled from Moscow to arrest the English girl. They'd wait until the early hours, then they'd force their way into the room. She would scream his name as they led her away. He would struggle to save her and they would hold him back, threatening to shoot him if he moved. He would stand there listening to her cries for help and his heart would break.

These were night thoughts, running out of control. He refused to allow them supremacy over his reason. For a few moments he stood by the window admiring the view in an attempt to calm himself. Then his fears for her safety – and his pain at his own guilt in putting her at risk – reinserted themselves into his consciousness by a different route, and his wild speculation set off again.

Kate would be accused of any number of invented crimes – spying for the British Government, attempting to sabotage the Soviet state – it didn't matter how absurd the charge might sound, they could convict you for anything. This beautiful English girl who slept beside him now in complete innocence of the possible dangers he had led her into, who played the cello so wonderfully, would be dragged before the world's press and humiliated, the innocent victim of *his* selfishness.

They would use *her* to hurt him – that would be his punishment for daring to bring her to this winter city. Her suffering – and they would make sure she experienced extremes of pain and shame – would be intended to remind *him* that you can never challenge the authority that controls your life. Her punishment, ultimately, would be expulsion from the country, and he would never see her again. All she would remember, perhaps for the rest of her life, was that he had broken the trust she had so willingly given him. Her love for him would turn to hate because all she would remember was that he had betrayed her by bringing her here when he knew the risks. He would be denied the chance to explain what had happened. He would have to live with the guilt of his selfishness for the rest of his life.

Why had he got involved with this English girl? He was attracted to her – how could you fail to be? She had thick blonde hair that covered her shoulders, blue eyes, soft full lips, a sweet, captivating smile, a long beautiful neck. There was an innocent optimism about her that reminded him of the expression on his mother's face in the first portrait that his father had sculpted. Was she just another student, or was he truly in love this time? Had she stirred in him those deeper feelings that told him existence without her was impossible? Had she taken over his mind so that he could think of nothing else?

The overwhelming emotion that wouldn't allow him to

imagine a moment without her remained as elusive as ever. He wanted her for her smile, her eyes, her innocence, and because she reminded him of what he might have been. But even when he was with her he remained in control of his own destiny when he desperately wanted to lose it, to offer his life to a force stronger than any he had encountered. Once more he had failed to find what he was searching for. He felt a familiar shadow of sadness settle over him.

He had never truly been in love, not even with the beautiful Zinaida all those years ago. He had married her imagining that they would live happily in a dream of love, only to discover that physical attraction can never bridge the gap when two minds live in different worlds. He understood too late that he had nothing in common with Zinaida, and what a mess that caused. The intimacy he had dreamed of became a nightmare from which he could not escape fast enough. Now he could look back over his life and say without fear of contradiction that he had chased dreams of love again and again, his heart full of hope, only to be disappointed when those dreams had disintegrated.

Kate's innocence touched him. He knew she had committed herself and that he held her happiness in his power. Knowing that, how could he risk everything by bringing her to this city on the border between the two ideologies that divided the world? A more prudent man would have recognised the dangers and left her behind. He shivered. How could he have been so irresponsible? He was racked by guilt at what he had done, yet he was unable to imagine sleeping in this room without her.

He got back into bed. The girl stirred and sat up. He lay still, watching her. She went to the basin to pour herself a glass of water. On her way back to bed, she too saw the transformation outside. She walked to the window and looked out. The blue light fell over her naked body, transforming her pale skin into shimmering marble. She became in that moment a being of infinite beauty, delicate and mysterious, hardly of this world. Once more he felt overwhelming desire for her.

★

The lecture was due to start at five-thirty. Despite the cold he decided to walk. He left Kate at the hotel. She was tired, she told him, and wanted to rest. She had not asked where he was going nor whether she could come with him. He was struck by her sensitivity to the circumstances in which they found themselves. He had never once had to say anything to her of the risks of their being together, though that did not prevent him from being continually vigilant.

On arrival, he was directed to the third floor. He took the stairs. This is my last lecture, he thought. After that we will have two more days here before we must return. Two whole days to ourselves.

Perhaps if he had not been thinking of Kate, he might have noticed that there were no lights on in the lecture theatre. Some instinct might have caused him to hesitate for an instant before pushing open the door. By the time he realised something was wrong, it was too late. He was inside the room, and in the darkness someone had moved behind him to close the door and lock it. He felt a gun in his back and a voice said quietly in Russian: 'If you offer any resistance I will be forced to shoot you.'

'I wouldn't be so foolish,' Berlin replied.

The lights came on. The lecture theatre was deserted, except for two men, one guarding the door, the other covering him with a revolver fitted with a silencer.

'I see you have not lost your reputation for punctuality.' The man with the gun was the senior. He smiled grimly. 'Your lecture was planned to take an hour. With questions – and for so distinguished a speaker, there will always be questions – the whole process will take an hour and a half, shall we say? Very well' – he looked at his watch – 'in exactly one hour and twenty-nine minutes we will release you. If you do as we tell you, you will be able to walk from here unaided.'

The girl, Berlin said to himself. For an hour and a half they've got the girl to themselves. They'd set a trap for him, and he had fallen into it without a second thought. Now she would suffer and he would be unable to protect her.

2

The photograph was where he had always kept it, protected by a brown paper envelope and tucked away at the back of his edition of Lenin's *Collected Works* – surely the last place anyone would look. He removed it carefully. He had taken the picture one afternoon at the swimming pool in the Dynamo Stadium. Eva had emerged from the pool, dripping wet and exhausted after a training session. She was laughing, her arm round her friend Julia, complaining breathlessly that she was not fit to be photographed. That hadn't stopped him pressing the shutter release. If he'd had the courage, he would have taken a hundred pictures of her then. There had been another figure in the photograph – Alexei Abrasimov – but Koliakov had long ago cut out his image and thrown it away. If he looked carefully he could just see a disembodied hand around Julia's waist. If only that was all that remained of his memories of Abrasimov.

He looked at the smiling girl, her rich auburn hair released from her bathing cap and tumbling down over her shoulders, the ends wet where the water had leaked into her cap, her skin shining from the pool. He could see the outline of her breasts through her bathing costume, her flat stomach and strong legs. She had the ideal body for a swimmer, compact and muscular, with powerful shoulders and thighs.

What had she been thinking, he wondered, as she posed for him? Did she know that his dearest wish was to photograph her naked? All she had to do was slip the straps from her shoulders and peel off the wet costume – an act that would have taken a moment. Then she would have been standing before him as he wanted her, and he would no longer have had to use his imagination. But she never did take her costume off for him. She never thought of him in that way. That was his tragedy.

He felt a sudden wave of revulsion surge through his mind. How could he imagine for a moment that the girl in the mews cottage was like Eva? What could have possessed him? She bore only the slightest physical resemblance to the woman in the photograph: she had the same colour hair perhaps, the same triangular shape to the face, but that was all, and it wasn't enough. She was a parody of Eva, her skin too pale, her legs too thin, her smile too closed and her eyes – couldn't he have seen that when he first met her? – her eyes were dull and lost, closed doors concealing nothing but a terrible emptiness. How could he have touched her, imagining he was touching someone else? How could he have defiled himself so easily? He felt physically sick with self-disgust. Why had he deceived himself?

He remembered Pountney's expression when he had talked of the girl, how pleased he'd been when he had given his ultimatum – silence for information. Pountney had imagined he would respond to such a crude proposal because an exchange like that was the language of his craft. Well, the Englishman was wrong. He had no intention of entering into any negotiation with him. If Pountney thought he would become their creature, they had seriously underestimated him. Seeing the girl was a bad mistake, he couldn't deny that, and his weakness gave Pountney the upper hand. Now he would have to rely on his own inventiveness to extricate himself from a trap of his own making.

Berlin raced up the stairs, only halting briefly outside the door of their room to listen for voices. There was no sound. He let himself in.

'Kate?'

She was curled up on the bed, hands clasped to her mouth, eyes red, pale face streaked with tears. She was shaking uncontrollably. She tried to speak to him but her shivering was so strong she could say nothing intelligible. He attempted to reassure her, telling her not to speak until she felt better. She was to nod her answers.

'Did they hurt you?'

Her eyes swam with tears. For a moment he feared she had been beaten or worse, and his anger rose like a storm, but she shook her head and murmured, 'No. They didn't touch me.'

He made her as comfortable as he could, covering her with a blanket, rubbing her hands to bring back some warmth. He ordered tea and held the cup to her lips to prevent her shaking hands spilling it over the bed. After a while she fell into a nervous sleep, her body twitching under the blanket, while she murmured words whose meaning he couldn't catch. At one point she hummed a tune he didn't recognise.

He looked at her and wanted to cry. Her innocence had a dark shadow over it now. She had seen for herself that bullying, brutal side of his country that he had worked so hard to conceal from her. She had been frightened in a way she could not possibly have imagined and that he had never felt able to warn her about.

She was our friend, our hope. She could have told the world that we are not the beasts we are thought to be. Now we have lost a friend, and destroyed a small chance to change the world's perceptions of us. How foolish, how wrong-headed our judgements are.

He lit a cigarette and waited by her side as she slept.

Outside, the sky darkened as the clouds moved in and snow began to fall again.

*

For a moment Kate thought the knocking was in her dream but it persisted, more urgently now and louder, and she knew it was real. She got out of bed, put on her dressing gown and opened the door. Three men burst in, one racing past her into the room, the other two taking her by the elbows and dragging her backwards. The door was kicked shut and locked. She was thrown onto the bed, too frightened to scream.

'What did they want?' Berlin asked quietly, as soon as she was awake.

'They asked me where you were,' she replied.

'Did you tell them?'

'How could I? You never told me where you'd gone.'

'What did they ask you?' He was sure they wouldn't have stopped at that, not when they knew they had her for an hour and a half before he was due to return.

'Stupid questions. What I was doing in Moscow. Why I had come here. Nothing really.'

He looked at the pale, frightened figure on the bed and knew that something terrible had happened that she was concealing from him.

'Where is he?' Her captor spoke in Russian.

'Who?' she answered foolishly.

'Your boyfriend.' The man's face was threateningly close to hers and his breath smelled sourly of cigarettes. She saw his pock-marked skin and its awful yellow colour, stained brick red where the irritation was alive.

'He is giving a lecture,' Kate replied.

'There is no lecture,' the man with the sour breath told her, 'and there never was. At this moment your boyfriend is answering questions.' He looked at his watch. 'We have plenty of time to talk. We won't be disturbed.'

He lit a cigarette and stared at her. She saw no humanity in his eyes, only a terrifying emptiness as if conscience and compassion had been burned out of him. There was no quality within him she could appeal to.

'Do you know what he is being questioned about?'

'How can I?' she said.

'His relationship with you. Do you know why?'

'I've no idea.' She felt very cold. She began to shiver.

'We have evidence that you are a British spy.'

'I am a music student,' she said, trying to sound defiant but aware that her voice was hardly above a whisper. 'I'm studying the cello under Vinogradoff.'

'That is your cover. We know you are an agent of British Intelligence, and that you are here to steal secrets from the Soviet Union.'

'Did they ask you about me?' It was her turn to ask questions now.

'No,' he replied. If it is to succeed, the lie must always be close to the truth. 'It was some ridiculous alert about security.'

He was breaking his own rules. Would she believe him? Somehow he feared not.

'It was madness to bring her here.' The man's voice declared neither mockery nor surprise. He had no interest in Berlin. He was here to perform a function. Berlin said nothing. 'Did you imagine you would get away with it?'

Berlin felt the gun being prodded into his side. He remained silent.

'You cannot behave in this way. The risks are too great.'

What difference does my relationship with this English girl make? he wanted to ask. As if he could read his mind, his interrogator continued: 'The girl draws attention to you. Her presence could lead to speculation about your connection to us. We can't risk any disclosure about our relationship with you. The Department still believes you have a value worth protecting. Your actions are thoughtless and stupid.'

The idea of the girl as a threat was nonsense and they both knew it. He could guess what was coming next.

'They must have asked you why you had come to Moscow?' Berlin said.

'I told them about the Conservatoire.'

'Nothing else?'

'Nothing that mattered. They frightened me by being there. They seemed so heartless, so brutal.'

He was sure they had made terrible accusations against her. What he hadn't expected was that she would hide them from him.

'You are an English spy,' the man with the pockmarked face shouted. 'Make it easy for yourself. Tell us what we know to be true.'

'Go to the Conservatoire,' she repeated. It was all she could think of to say. 'Ask Vinogradoff. He will tell you that I am his student. I came to Moscow to study with him.'

She was crying now, any pretence of bravery long gone. She wanted Berlin here to make this horror end. But she knew he wouldn't come. Somehow she would have to get through this nightmare on her own.

'Did they ask you questions about me?' Berlin asked gently. She was grasping his hand as if she were terrified that at any moment he might slip from her grasp, never to be seen again. 'Try to remember.'

'They asked few questions,' she replied. 'They went round and round in circles. They were trying to trick me into saying something I didn't mean.'

'Is this the bed you share with your Russian lover?' She turned away, defiantly refusing to answer. 'Is this the bed where you fuck your Russian boyfriend?' he shouted at her, his face inches from hers.

'What do you want from me?'

'Answer my question.'

For a moment Kate was too frightened to speak. 'Yes,' she said quietly.

The man turned to his companions and they laughed our loud. She felt an icy terror spread through her veins. Once more her interrogator walked round and round the chair she was sitting on, until she thought she would go dizzy.

He bent over her again, bringing his damaged face as close to hers as he could without touching. 'Is he your first man?' he asked.

Kate said nothing. He twisted her face towards him.

'Answer me when I talk to you. Is he your first man?'

'Yes.' Very quietly.

'Does he fuck well, your Russian boyfriend?'

She was crying too much to answer. Once more her interrogator circled the chair until she had recovered her composure.

'We have a present for you. Would you like a present from us? Would it make you feel better?'

'I want you to go.'

He took out a small tape recorder from his briefcase and plugged it in. 'You will like this,' he said. 'It will bring back happy memories.'

The interrogator switched on a machine. For a while the tape ran silently. Then there came sounds of movements, muffled laughter, two voices, both distant and indistinct.

'Do you recognise yourself?'

She heard her own voice murmuring over and over again, *Andrei, Andrei.* There were murmurs from Andrei that she could not understand but which tore into her heart – something so pure was being spied on, eavesdropped, used against them.

'Turn it off,' she shouted, 'turn it off.'

Berlin was standing by the window. It was dark outside. Weeping clouds scraped the rooftops of the city and the snow fell heavily. He felt numbed by what had happened. He knew these people. He had associated with them for years. They were the agents of an authority fearful of threats to its power, though it would never admit to that. They were licensed to terrorise and kill and they had turned their brutality onto an innocent girl. Nothing in her experience can have prepared her for such an encounter. What could they have told her that she now felt unable to tell him? He felt sick. In one encounter the two sides of his life had collided and the girl was suffering. He should never have brought her here. He had made a terrible mistake. What damage he had done to her he could not imagine.

'They must have said something else.'

'What they told me was unimportant.'

'I have listened to the tape a number of times,' her interrogator said. 'I would describe it as a rare pleasure. My only regret is that we do not have it on film. Listen. We have more.'

This time it was different, and she felt a brief moment of relief. She heard a voice like hers but it was not hers, talking about her conversations with someone called Radin, reporting on plans for manned space flights. Then another voice, like Andrei's but not his, asking technical questions about rocket engines, payloads, phrases that the real Kate would never understand in ten lifetimes.

'Do you recognise yourself?' the Russian asked.

'That's not me. That's not my voice.'

'You are in bed, fucking your Russian boyfriend, you are asking him questions and he is telling you secrets which you will give to your contact at the British Embassy.'

'You'll have to do better than that,' she said, trying to sound brave.

'This tape is sufficient evidence,' his interrogator replied. 'You will be arrested, tried, and found guilty of anti-Soviet activity. The punishment for that is ten, fifteen years in a labour camp. We will not expect you to serve out your time with us. After some months, we will release you under pressure from the British Government. A magnanimous gesture, in the interests of good diplomatic relations between our two countries. During your imprisonment, you will meet with an accident. Your hands will be scalded. We will be unable to get you to a suitable hospital in time. That will have put paid to your dreams of playing the cello in the concert halls of the world.'

'The girl is a spy for the British,' the man with the revolver said.

'That's absurd.'

'We have evidence.'

'If she was a spy,' he said, 'I would have told you by now.' He hoped his self-disgust was evident. 'I am expert at that. I steal the secrets of my friends and betray them to you. If the girl was a spy, I would already have betrayed her.'

'Unless you had fallen in love with her.'

Silence. They were locked in the struggle now. This was the turning point. There could only be one winner.

'Are you in love with her?'

What was he to say? 'She's a student.'

'You don't fall in love with students.' Berlin shrugged. 'You fuck them and throw them away, is that it?'

'That's right.' The mockery in his voice would be lost on his interrogator.

'And the English girl is no exception?'

'Why should she be?'

His interrogator did not answer. He unscrewed the cap on his pen once more and wrote in his notebook. He kept his cigarette clamped in his mouth as he did so. His breathing was laboured.

'You will return with her to Moscow tomorrow, after which you will not see her again.'

'Do you know who your boyfriend is?'

'He is a historian. He teaches at the university.'

'Is that what he tells you?' Her interrogator laughed. 'Did you believe him?'

'Why shouldn't I?'

'He is lying to you. Your lover is an informer, a man who betrays his friends, his neighbours, anyone, even his own family. You are sleeping with the lowest form of life. Do you know why he does that? I will tell you. He informs for money. Do you think a man with his tastes is able to live as he does on an academic's salary?' He brought his face close to hers. 'Does that surprise you?'

'I don't believe you.' The suggestion was absurd, ridiculous. She rejected it.

'Ask him. See if he has the courage to tell you.'

'Did they try to poison your mind about me?' Berlin asked. 'Did they tell you stories about me? If they did, you must let me answer their charges. You must hear the truth.'

'No,' Kate replied. 'No, nothing like that.'

He could see she wasn't going to tell him. There was only one possible explanation for her silence. It was the only way she could keep her illusions about him intact. They had told her about him. She knew what he was. He felt sickened and desperate.

★

All she remembered of the journey back to Moscow was that she was cold all the time. Her heart was empty. Her emotions were numbed. Her mind was incapable of rational thought. She was frightened and exhausted and full of foreboding. Again and again she heard the voice of her interrogator in her mind. She felt his foul breath on her, the acrid, musky smell of his body too near her. *What if all he had said about Berlin were true?* She thought of his apartment, the way he lived. 'Sometimes we bend the rules,' he had said.

No, it was impossible. How could this man whom she had come to know so well be two people; how could he conceal his other nature from her? When you loved someone the barriers of camouflage and deception were stripped away. You faced each other as you were, didn't you? She had given herself to him. Had he still concealed some part of himself from her? Was it possible to do that and still love someone? Or was it only possible if you were feigning love? Questions ricocheted around her mind, unanswered and threatening. How was she to find out? Did she want to find out?

'Ask him.' The man had laughed at her inability to reject the doubt that he had so deliberately lodged in her mind. 'Get him to tell you.'

Every time she closed her eyes she saw her interrogator's mocking face leaning over her, smelled his breath again, sensed all too clearly his moral emptiness. How could she ask such a terrible thing? *Is it true you inform on those closest to you?*

The question would tell Andrei that she doubted him. She doubted herself. Better to accept her interrogator's challenge for what it was — a deliberate technique to destroy what she believed because that was all the harm he could do to her — and go on as if he had said nothing. Don't let him control you. Resist him. Forget what he had told you. Don't let him win.

Suddenly she felt an outsider again. In her mind she returned to those early weeks in Moscow when she had felt at odds with this alien city and its strange, disturbing culture. The confidence Berlin had given her was ebbing away. The trust that was so necessary to her — the ability to believe what he told her about himself — had been destroyed in the ninety minutes of her interrogation. That, she knew, was what they wanted. She was determined to ignore what they had told her. But try as she might, her doubts persisted, working their inevitable, intimidating power on what she wanted to believe.

The train roared through the ice-cold night. Berlin was attentive to her. She didn't want to eat. He made her drink tea, laced with brandy, to keep up her strength. If she didn't want to talk, he remained silent. When she shivered suddenly without warning, he covered her with the blanket from his bunk. As she dozed off, he was there watching her. When she awoke, he hadn't moved. He was still there beside her, looking exhausted, not saying a word, holding her hand.

She was grateful for his attention. Her terror at her ordeal had not yet worn off. Her sudden shaking was a physical response to what had happened, Berlin told her. It would pass in time. She wondered if the immediacy of her memories would ever fade. Would she silence the doubting voice in her mind? As the train neared Moscow, she knew the battle was lost — just as she knew that the questions to which she wanted answers lay beyond her power to ask. A terrible damage had been done, and she had been trapped, powerless, in its path.

*

She awoke from a troubled sleep. It was still pitch-black

outside. Berlin was where she had seen him last, sitting by her. She felt like an invalid, emotionally battered and physically weakened, emerging from a dark pit of dreadful dreams.

'Andrei?'

'Another couple of hours,' he said. 'Nearly there.'

'What's going to happen?' she asked. What she meant was: *What's going to happen to us?*

'We'll talk later, when you're better.'

'Now, Andrei,' she pleaded. 'Talk to me now.'

He wouldn't change his mind. He stroked her hair and told her to rest. She felt herself hypnotised by the touch of his hand and her eyes closed. Obediently, she slept. In her dreams she relived new versions of what had happened to her.

★

Berlin left the hostel in Malaya Gruzinskaya Street. He took the metro back to his apartment and on his return poured himself a large glass of whisky. He knew – and he was sure Kate did, though nothing had been said – that the events in Helsinki had brought the secret police into the relationship, and that was intolerable. They would not be left alone now. They would be stalked, harassed, spied on. Kate would lose her nerve or her musical talent would be damaged in the face of what was happening to her. He could think of no way to camouflage that. The police would make sure she was aware of their presence. That was part of the pressure they would exert on her.

Vinogradoff had been right to select her. She had a rare talent. No wonder he had praised her so highly when they had met at the concert at the Conservatoire. He could not put that at risk. Better to end it now before any further harm was done. It hurt him to say that he had seen how frightened Kate had been. He could not allow her to be put into that position again. Whatever the cost to him, he must protect her innocence.

He was surprised at how devastated he felt, how the

thought of losing this beautiful English girl left him gasping and weakened. How close she had come to winning his heart.

*

She watches him disappear into the night and only then does she break down and cry. Will she ever see him again? As she lies awake in bed, she knows in her heart that their relationship can have no future now. Ninety minutes of horror in Helsinki have destroyed it. Berlin has departed from her life for ever. She is heartbroken. What did she do wrong? Could she have stopped him leaving? Only when she dries her tears does she realise that she has done nothing wrong.

There is a mystery to Berlin that she cannot resolve, though in the days that follow she does her best to do so. She cannot pin down his identity nor, after what happened in Helsinki, can she trust him. To that extent, she accepts that her interrogators have won, but there is nothing she can do about it. Sometimes she thinks he is two people – the quiet, studious historian, and someone else, a man with secrets that lead him into a world she wants to know nothing about. Even after the weeks she has known him, she recognises that there is a side of Berlin that she has not penetrated. Whatever it is, he is skilful at protecting it. Helsinki gave her a brief glimpse of that other world, that world he seemed to know about. She hated it because it terrified her. Best, she knows, for her own sake, to keep away.

She dries her tears. She has much to thank him for. Not least, he has taught her how to dissemble.

IVAN'S SEARCH FOR HIS FATHER

Andrei kept his head down between the rows of seats in the cinema, drawn by the sounds he heard: a woman gasping, not in terror as he first thought, but rhythmically, pleasurably. There were small cries of satisfaction, and another sound, a man's voice, words uttered breathlessly, though he couldn't hear what was being said.

Somewhere deep inside him he knew what was going on but he was unable to put a name to it. He felt a strange kind of excitement that he was treading in forbidden territory – adult territory – that what he was about to discover were secrets that would change him for ever because they belonged to a world he had never entered. Part of him wanted to stay where he was, to see nothing, learn nothing, to retain his innocence. Sometimes, he knew, knowing nothing makes your life easier. Sometimes it is better not to know. But another part of him knew that he had to find out, that this was a door that one day he would have to go through – so why not now?

He crept along the aisle at the side of the auditorium, keeping as low as he could, even though it was pitch dark, a sense of mounting turmoil inside him as he did so. Every few paces he stood up cautiously but he could see nothing.

He reached the door at the back of the auditorium that led to the projectionist's box. He opened the door quietly and froze. Had they heard him? Had he been found out? Nothing seemed to disturb whatever was going on. The small cries, the gasps, continued. With relief, he closed the door as quietly as he could and crept up the narrow staircase. It was still pitch dark – he did not dare turn on any lights – and he stretched out his arms so that he could touch both the banisters and the wall. Like a blind man, he felt his way to the projection room and let himself in. He went to the window that looked out over the auditorium. It was no good. There was no light anywhere. All was blackness. There was no vision, only sound. The cries were getting faster, the rhythm picking up.

He never thought about his decision. He had no idea why he decided as he did, except that there was no other decision to make. *He had to know.* He felt for the bank of switches on the control panel. How many hours had he spent up here, watching the projectionist practise his craft? He'd picked up what you did by watching, and then he'd relived it all in his mind as he lay sleepless on his bed during the hot nights. It wasn't hard to remember what was where, even in the dark. He had done this so many times in his imagination. He found the switch for the house lights and pulled it sharply towards him. The auditorium was suddenly bathed in a bright light.

He looked out through the porthole again. At first he could see no one, but he heard a cry of rage from the auditorium, followed by a woman's scream of horror at her discovery. Two people stood up in the central aisle, a man and a woman. Both were naked. The young woman clutched a shirt to her breast. The man was standing up, staring at the projectionist's box, his enormous thing bobbing out in front of him as he shielded his eyes from the glare of the lights.

Andrei Berlin found himself looking down at his own father.

11

1

The lock to his office had been changed. His key wouldn't work. His name-card had been removed from its holder on the door. Perplexed, he looked through the frosted glass. The room had been emptied of anything that identified it with him. He went to the next office. That too was locked and empty, its name-card also removed. The same was true as he looked down the corridor. Empty, nameless rooms were locked in readiness for their next occupants. His whole department had been eliminated. He sat on a window ledge, clutching his briefcase, uncertain of what to do. How long he remained there, he didn't know. If he was dreaming, he had no recollection of what he dreamed.

Then a voice said: 'They did it overnight – cleared out the offices, took away boxes of papers, left nothing behind. I've seen them do it before.' It was the janitor, an old man with a shaven head and few teeth.

In a fury Valery raced down the stairs to the second floor.

'I demand to see Acting Director Grinko,' he said to Radin's secretary.

'Acting Director Grinko is unavailable.' She did not look up from her typing.

'When will he be available?'

She stopped for a moment to consult her diary. 'He is on leave for ten days, then he will be in Baikonur until the end of the month. After that he is fully occupied with budget meetings with the head of the Space Commission. He may be able to see you in five weeks' time, but I can guarantee nothing.'

'I want the keys to my office.'

'Acting Director Grinko has all the keys.'

'And my papers? Where are my papers?'

'I can release nothing without his authority, and he is unavailable.'

He wanted to shout at her but he knew it was pointless. This woman was not his enemy. He had been defeated by a crazy system that allowed a dead man to decide the future, and there was nothing he could do about it. *Did no one understand the damage they were doing to themselves?*

He walked out into the street, dazed and disbelieving. His robotics team had been dissolved and their work impounded. They had worked for months to achieve nothing. No one had warned him, no one had bothered to say that this might happen. He was horrified, dismayed and depressed. How could such a thing happen?

About an hour later Ruth telephoned him at his flat. She had heard about his department's closure. 'How could Grinko do that?' she asked.

'With impunity,' was his sharp reply.

'I'll see what I can do.' Valery did not hold out much hope. The people his mother knew were getting older; they were being replaced by a generation that knew little or nothing of what she had done. He lay on his bed, unable to read, and waited. When the telephone call came, Ruth sounded disappointed.

'I did what I could,' she said grimly. 'It isn't enough. I don't know what to say.'

'Thank you for trying,' he said.

'What will you do?'

'What can I do?'

'All that work gone to waste. I can't bear to think of it.'

He questioned himself continually. Had he been wrong to

push for a decision? Was it a tactical mistake to support his case for robot exploration so enthusiastically? Would it not have been better to work on quietly, and wait for the day when they might be summoned to show what they had achieved? That wasn't how the future would be built. It was the policy of timidity. Ideas demanded boldness. He had tried to keep faith with what his team had produced, and he had failed.

What should he do? He remembered his mother's account of her protest when she was involved, in the months after the end of the war, in the building of the first Soviet nuclear bomb. For weeks she and her fellow scientists refused to work on the project because they had discovered that no provision had been made to move the local population from the area of the test site. Their refusal had succeeded. The test area was cleared. The scientists returned to work. There was no retribution. This had astounded him. His mother had led the challenge to the authority of the state and got away with it. Had she had a protector? She denied it repeatedly and he was forced to accept her verdict without being convinced that she was telling him the truth.

Perhaps he should follow his mother's example, and refuse to continue to work for the Space Commission until his robotics plans had been restored to him. The idea took root. He would protest at what had been done to him.

He stayed at home. He failed to turn up for work. No one came to get him. There were no angry telephone calls. His resistance was ignored. He felt as if he did not exist. Ruth came to see him but for the first time in years they quarrelled, she begging him to return to work, he refusing, quoting her story back at her.

'It isn't the same,' she said. 'We had a position of strength. The Central Committee desperately wanted the bomb. We were the only people who could make it. We had a natural position of power you don't have. That was what we decided to exploit.'

Valery refused to listen. The days passed in depression. He

ate only when he had to, didn't shave, occasionally changed his clothes, smoked continually, drank in bouts, didn't read the newspapers or listen to the radio and refused to see anyone, including Ruth. In his mind, as he lay on his bed staring at the ceiling, the idea of opposing, of standing up for what he believed and saying no, began to take shape.

★

He remembered how, when he was fifteen, Ruth had suddenly insisted that, whatever happened to either of them at school or at work, when they were with friends, whatever lies they told, whenever circumstances demanded that they distort the truth, at least at home there would be no lies, no evasions, no dissimulations. Only the truth, she made him promise – even if they had to whisper it to each other, huddled over the kitchen table with the radio on. His mother didn't disguise from him the daily compromises she had made in order to bring him up as she wanted, 'so that one day I could tell you the truth'.

Valery had been strengthened by her candour but he was made wary too, because knowing more made his life more difficult. For his own safety, he now had to conceal what he knew. To protect him, his mother taught him to create a 'double nature', a duality between the real and the apparent, a technique, she insisted, that sustained rather than impaired her sanity. If truth were to be a necessary secret in his life, then he too would have to develop a double nature, just as she had done. He became her willing pupil. Slowly and patiently he made himself into two people, one public, one private. On occasions, he suffered agonies keeping the two apart, but for her sake he did so. The more he learned about what his mother had survived and how she had done it, the more his admiration for her grew.

'In this country,' she told him, 'belief is a private matter. It doesn't join us to our neighbour, it separates us from him because we have been taught to distrust him. Conscience has no public life because its advocacy can only lead to self-destruction. The time may come when once more it has a value, but that time is surely not now. Do we shore up this bankrupt regime by never protesting its decisions, never speaking out against its acts of immorality, its cruelties and follies? Those who do not understand the conditions of life in the Soviet Union will answer yes, and dismiss us as cowards. Ignore them. They know nothing. Somehow each of us must find our own way to live in this country. What matters is memory. We must never forget the crimes carried out in our name. Like cavemen, we must carve our experiences on dark walls, even if we have to wait a thousand years before the truth of our experience is known. If we cannot write the history of our times, then we must memorise what we know. We must hand down our memories to those who come after us. You cannot conceal truth for ever. *Until that day, nothing must be forgotten.'*

He didn't have her patience. His job had been removed by a man who was dead. Only one person, he was told, could change that policy. There was, he knew, no hope that the decision made against him could ever be reversed. It was wrong, absurd, dangerous. He was not prepared to accept it. In his mind he pushed aside his mother's structures about duality. Those may have been the tactics for the past. The present demanded more direct action. He would stick out his protest. He would force the authorities to test his resolve.

★

Three weeks later he was persuaded by a friend to go to a student concert at the Conservatoire. He had grown a beard by then, and his hair was longer. He was thinner too because he had eaten so little. He heard Kate playing. As he listened, he found he had tears in his eyes. Was this the same girl he had rescued from the Lenin Library? She had a power, a maturity, a command of the music that touched him. He wanted to climb over the rows of chairs in front of him and take her in his arms and kiss her. As he listened, his heart moved inside him and he fell in love.

When it was over he hung back, waiting for her to appear, wondering if she would speak to him.

'Hello,' Valery said. 'You probably won't remember me.'

She turned at the sound of his voice, and for a moment looked puzzled. Then she smiled at him. 'You look different,' she said.

2

'Mascha! Come here!'

The dog was racing away through the undergrowth in pursuit of its prey, and took no notice of the command to return. Marshal Gerasimov looked surprised that his authority should be so easily ignored. In the distance Berlin saw two pigeons rise lazily into the morning air, wings flapping loudly. The tail of the dog was visible above the long grass.

'Damn animal. No discipline at all.'

Berlin followed Gerasimov into the cemetery, presumably once the village burial ground, now long neglected. The gravestones appeared through the undergrowth like the heads of resting animals, the wall surrounding it collapsed in many places through want of repair.

'At my age, a graveyard is a comforting place,' Gerasimov said, 'where I meet old friends.'

Why the old general had brought him to this place miles from Moscow was a mystery. Less than an hour before he had received a telephone message that Marshal Gerasimov wished to see him. A car had been sent. He sat beside the silent, chain-smoking general as they were driven out of the city and deep into the countryside. He was given no explanation for his presence.

'You do not need to believe in any religion to know that after a life of struggle the dead have the right to rest in peace.'

Long grass, ground elder and ivy had overgrown many of the graves; time and the ravages of the Russian winter had damaged and dislodged tombstones and weathered the inscriptions, so that all too often they were unreadable. Occasionally Gerasimov used his stick to attack the undergrowth in his search for a particular grave.

'We should honour those who dedicate their lives to the service of the state,' he continued, 'and not ignore them when they die.'

Was he thinking of his own funeral? Of the huge garlanded photograph of a younger version of himself that would be paraded like a banner before his open coffin, while a long line of whispering mourners followed him into the graveyard for his burial with full military honours?

'Viktor was fiercely proud of his independence,' Gerasimov said. 'He always believed he was the author of his own survival. It wasn't so, of course, but he was too valuable to be told the truth. It would have broken his heart. Even the Central Committee came to recognise that.'

The dog returned and leaped up at Gerasimov, who bent down to stroke her. 'Too old to learn new tricks, aren't you, Mascha? Like your master.' He threw a stick for her and she ran off after it.

'Viktor believed he owed nothing to anyone. He had no idea of the battles that in his absence were fought on his behalf, or he pretended to know nothing because it suited him. He had no favours to repay. Perhaps it is as well that not all of us follow the same creed.'

Did he detect regret in the old man's voice? Did he too have secrets that he could never share, moments when his own life had been dependent on the support of others? Gerasimov had survived so many upheavals since the Revolution. What accommodations had he had to make along the way? What debts were still outstanding, waiting to be redeemed from those who in the past may have saved his life? Or was his power based on the fact that he had outlived them all?

The old general stopped in front of a gravestone and was silent for a moment. Berlin followed his gaze. The name *Yelena Gerasimova* and the dates *1902–1954* were inscribed on a tilting granite slab.

'Today is the anniversary of my wife's death,' he said suddenly. 'It was her wish to be buried where she was born but the village is deserted now, and no one tends the graves. I do my best but it is not enough. Her life was cruelly cut short but she lived long enough to learn of the birth of her grandson. Now he is dead too. My son and I buried the boy next to his grandmother.'

He used his stick to push away the long grass from a newer gravestone nearby. *Nikolai Gerasimov, aged eight*, the freshly carved inscription read. If the old man felt any emotion, he kept it to himself. His dark grey face, eyes buried under enormous jutting eyebrows, stared down at the two graves. He was lost in his private thoughts.

'Sometimes I can hardly remember what Yelena looked like. I can remember the boy as if I had seen him yesterday.'

He must be in his mid-seventies now, Berlin imagined. The deep furrows on his face told of an ingrained weariness, of battles with words as well as weapons, while the worn skin showed that the struggles of a long life were exacting their slow revenge on him. He might look exhausted, but Berlin was in no doubt about the strength of his belief in a creed that for him held the only true answer to the ills of the world. His conviction would remain unshaken until the day he died. He would never doubt the dogma, only those who had failed to live up to its high demands, a weakness to which he was implacably opposed. He saw himself surrounded by men and women who lacked his austere vision, who were too selfish, too weak or too undisciplined to accept the challenge to change the nature of society that he had so readily adopted as a young man.

'Yelena was an artist. Did you know that?'

'You may be surprised to learn that I have one of her early paintings in my apartment.'

Painted on wood when she was in her early twenties, about the time she married Gerasimov, it showed a young man in a fur hat and winter greatcoat, binoculars round his neck and rifle at his side, sitting in a station waiting for the train to take him to war. He stares at the painter, his youthful expression unable to conceal his emotions of alarm and anticipation – there was no attempt to conceal the ambivalence of the young soldier's feelings. From the moment he'd seen it, Berlin had loved its honesty. It had pleased him when Kate had said she loved it too.

'She destroyed too much of her own work,' Gerasimov said suddenly. 'I didn't discover that until shortly before she died. When I asked her why, she claimed she was dissatisfied with what she did. After her death I learned that she destroyed her paintings to protect my career. Too much truth would have damaged my prospects of promotion.'

Yelena Gerasimova was best known for a popular book of drawings the state had published in 1942 entitled *Journey to the Russian Soul*. It in she showed how Soviet citizens coped with the deprivations of war. There was a heroic, sentimentalised aspect to these sketches that Berlin found unconvincing and surprising, so unlike the painting on his wall. What she published was little more than propaganda, which possibly accounted for its extraordinary success. Had she lost that ability to see the truth that he had so admired in her earlier paintings? There was a persistent rumour, which continued even after her death, that for each picture published there was another which showed the true suffering of the people and the ravishing of their land – burned fields, ruined crops, slaughtered animals, destroyed villages, barren faces of raped and widowed women, endless corpses of peasants, women and children as well as men, murdered by the invaders. Berlin knew no one who would admit to having seen any of these drawings, yet references to their existence refused to die.

'Sometimes I think she died of a broken heart. She taught me that you must never sacrifice the truth. It is all we have.'

The old man stared down at the gravestone. He was not praying – an old communist could not believe in an afterlife – he was remembering. Then he resumed his walk. The dog trotted obediently in front of him.

'I have given my life to the cause of communism,' Gerasimov continued. 'I believe that life without social justice is no life at all. Marxist-Leninism is the only doctrine that sets its face firmly towards the goal of liberating mankind from its terrible burdens and creating a just society. We may deviate on the way, we may take wrong turnings, we may even make mistakes, but nothing must deflect us from that single and praiseworthy objective of a fair, equal and open society. That belief has sustained me in my moments of greatest terror in a long and sometimes dangerous life.'

The old man's vision was as strong today as it had been when he was a young communist. Berlin saw that his words were born out of anger and hurt, and his belief that the marchers on the path to progress had taken wrong turnings.

'Viktor was right to blame the politicians for the desperate state our country is in. Our politicians are among the most dangerous people in the Republic today. I have listened to too many of the First Secretary's threats to the West, most recently over the status of Berlin. He is playing with nuclear war as if he were playing with a child's marbles. He refuses to acknowledge the terrible risks he runs. He should remember that just causes are not won by the extermination of civilians but by the strength of belief in the cause.'

Berlin looked back. Were there a hundred graves in this cemetery? Twice that number? It was hard to judge. He felt a certain relief that, as witnesses, the dead were blind and deaf. They could not identify who said what, nor could they repeat what was spoken in their presence. He was beginning to understand why they were walking in this graveyard: the silence of the dead was their security.

'We have built up a huge defensive force. We are not invulnerable to enemy attack, but we have a prodigious ability to defend our homeland. What the First Secretary conveniently forgets is that we lack the ability to strike back at our enemies.'

'Surely that can't be true.' Berlin spoke without thinking.

Gerasimov stopped in the shadow of an ancient cypress. 'Now you see how successful we are at selling propaganda to our own people. Do you know how many missiles we possess with which to attack the West?'

'Thousands.' An imprecise figure, he admitted, but one he was sure of. He had heard it from too many sources for it not to be true.

'Our arsenal consists of less than two hundred long-range missiles, only a handful of which have any capacity to strike at the heart of Europe. None can reach America and most are inaccurate. Our chances of coming within five miles of the target are less than one in ten.'

'Two hundred missiles?' Berlin was incredulous. 'I find that hard to believe.'

'Whether you believe me or not doesn't make what I am saying any less true.'

'What about this orbiting space platform which will launch nuclear weapons?'

Gerasimov laughed bitterly. 'It exists only in the imagination of the First Secretary, nowhere else. There are no plans, no blueprints, no preliminary sketches for such a weapon. It does not exist. Probably it will never exist. It is a complete invention.'

'Does the West know that?'

The old man shook his head. 'The CIA continually overestimates our military capability. Our leader exploits the West's ignorance with his daily threats to use these non-existent weapons. His policy of aggression is a betrayal of the beliefs that have sustained me all my life. The victory of communism must come through example and argument, not aggression and war. We must all share in the achievement we have sacrificed so much for.'

A breeze disturbed the branches of the cypress so that it seemed to bow in honour to the old soldier. Gerasimov walked on, head bent. The dog was way ahead of him now, following her own trail.

'I have sent enough young men to their graves already; I have no wish to see more slaughtered. We will only go to war if we ourselves are the victims of an unprovoked attack from the West, which is unlikely to happen. We cannot wage an offensive war because we have insufficient resources to do so. Yet that is the prospect our leader peddles every day when he makes these wild and dangerous statements. The West believes him, and arms itself accordingly. We are heading for disaster.'

They walked on in silence, the path leading them out of the cemetery and along the edge of a field.

'Last night a decision was taken by the Politburo to sign the treaty with East Germany that will make Berlin into an open city. The attempt by the military to oppose this plan failed utterly. We are now committed to a perilous course of action. By making Berlin part of a sovereign state, we invalidate the legal right of our former allies to remain in the city. Naturally they will not succumb to our demands to surrender their position willingly. They will claim that our absorption of Berlin into East Germany is an illegal act, and in support of their position they will build up their military forces. We will do the same. There will be a steady increase of tension as threat is met by counter-threat, until each side is lined up against the other, ready to resort to force if so instructed. I am sure I do not have to tell you that such a policy runs risks of unimaginable dimensions. When we face each other across the streets in Berlin, the prospect of a local conflict getting out of control will be very great.'

'Would the West risk going to war over Berlin?' What he meant was, would they judge the principle of upholding their position worth the risk?

'Why should they give way before the bullying of a Soviet leader? My judgement is that they will stubbornly resist our plans. They will declare our act illegal and refuse to negotiate. The First Secretary has committed himself publicly. He will not back down. To do so would be to reveal himself before the world as a magician who has run out of tricks. What happens when you have two sides, neither of which will give way to the other? You don't need to be a soldier to predict the outcome. Now do you understand why I fear this situation so greatly?'

'Can nothing be done to prevent a catastrophe?'

'If someone who had lied to you repeatedly came to you one day and said, believe me, this is the truth, would you do so?' The scepticism was all too evident in Gerasimov's voice. 'Through the continual use of lies we have destroyed the meaning of the language we use. Our words have lost their value. We can no longer communicate. If the tension in Germany rises to breaking point, we may have to pay a terrible price for exhausting words of their true sense.'

Berlin remembered the films he had seen at school, propaganda films, he knew, but none the less terrifying, of atomic bombs exploding. The huge cloud bursting out of the earth and slowly forming into a mushroom shape against the dying sky, bleaching itself of colour until it was dust grey and poisonous, and always the neutral voice of the commentator, describing the effects of a nuclear explosion in Zone 1 ('bone and tissue melts and matter vaporises'), Zone 2 ('steel window frames melt, houses collapse like cards in the nuclear wind'), Zone 3 ('you may survive the immediate blast but your body will be burned and poisoned and you will die a slow and painful death'). Watching the blinding glare of the explosion, he imagined the force of the unnatural wind and heard the thunderous roar as matter disintegrated and the nuclear storm destroyed everything in its path, leaving behind only a burned-out wasteland of acidic ash. It was a lasting vision of the end of the world.

'If we are forced into war with the West, the people of this country will suffer dreadfully. They will be ordered to fight on the promise that victory will inevitably be ours because they have been taught that our ideology is invincible and our weapons are superior. They will quickly discover that such promises cannot be kept. The superior weapons will fail to materialise because they do not exist. Ideology is no defence against bullets and shells and bombs. The people will see that they have been betrayed by their own leaders. Millions of innocent men, women and children will die unnecessarily because they have been misled. We will all be responsible for their deaths.'

They walked on in silence. The dog Mascha had returned and was circling them, occasionally running up to Gerasimov and burying her face in his hand as if expecting to find some reward there.

'You can't stand by and let that happen.' Berlin spoke with more intensity than he had expected.

'Do you think I have stood by and done nothing?' The old marshal was becoming angry. 'I have argued against this policy continually, I have supported my case with figures, I have told the truth again and again, but what I have said has not been believed.' He stared at Berlin. 'My warnings have been ignored. What more can I do?'

A sudden breeze set the branches swaying so that they sighed in chorus at Gerasimov's words. 'Without the ability to listen to reason, there can be no hope. We have blinded ourselves to the truth. In this country, reason has lost the battle and the war.'

★

Berlin walked back to the car alone, his mind in turmoil. Why had Gerasimov told him this? What purpose did the old soldier's confession serve? He had no absolution to offer, no comfort of any kind. He was powerless to help. Better to leave the old man to the isolation of his own despair. Best of all to leave this field of death as soon as he could, and return to the secure routines of the Department of History, his students and his lectures.

He remembered the confusion he had felt standing alone in Viktor's study all those weeks ago; how he had wrestled with the sense that he had been brought there for a purpose but had no idea what that purpose was; how he had finally puzzled out a concealed logic that had led him to discover the report on Alexandrof's ill-fated flight. He tried to repeat the process now. There was a clear line – wasn't there? – linking Viktor, the two secret reports he had given him to read, his meeting with Orenko and now this strange walk with Gerasimov in the garden of the dead. The connection was anger, the deep-rooted fury of good and loyal men – Radin, Kuzmin, Alexandrof, Orenko, Gerasimov – who had made sacrifices for their beliefs and had then found their actions betrayed by lesser men.

Disaster follows misgovernment, was the warning in Kuzmin's report, and his warning had been proved right. Viktor's account of Alexandrof's death, Orenko's explanation of the vulnerability of the military were further compelling evidence of a progressive internal collapse. Now Gerasimov had confirmed that the First Secretary wilfully rejected the truth if it did not serve his purpose. The machine of state would run down if abused. As a historian he knew that to be true. Continued abuse would bring the country to its knees, and lies would be no defence against its decline. Rather, they would be proof of its inevitability.

'Historical analysis looks unblinkingly at what has happened and tells us the truth,' he remembered Radin saying to him once, a cigarette stuck between his lips. 'What historian has dared to do that in this country since 1917? You have kept silent when you should have spoken out. You have become the servants of the state, not its critics. You have rejected your true role. When the analysts are corrupt, then there can be no solutions because there are no problems.'

It was the harshest criticism Viktor ever made of him, and it had hurt him deeply. He had never repeated it, but the words had stuck with Berlin, they had lodged deep in his memory. Now they returned to haunt him.

He felt the first drop of rain on his cheek.

*

The rain fell heavily on their journey back to Moscow. The countryside refracted through the rain-drenched car windows had the dreamy appearance of a watercolour. Once more Gerasimov sat beside him, smoking and saying nothing. Berlin felt uneasy, apprehensive. This strange morning had not yet divulged all its secrets.

'If we are to prevent ourselves from being drawn into a war we cannot hope to win,' Gerasimov said suddenly, 'we have only one possible course of action. We must destroy our greatest strategic advantage – the West's vast overestimation of our military capability. We must convince them that we cannot fight an offensive war, that our threat to Berlin cannot be sustained. In particular, we must tell them that an orbiting nuclear satellite in space doesn't exist.'

'How can we do that?'

'We must send them a message.'

'Will it be believed?'

Gerasimov drew heavily on his cigarette before answering. 'We will provide our messenger with supporting evidence to establish that we are speaking the truth.'

'What kind of evidence?'

'Proof that the mind behind our space triumphs, Viktor Radin, is dead.'

'Won't they see that as one more lie, one more trick?'

'That depends on the skills of the messenger.' Gerasimov paused to light another cigarette. 'We want a man who can dissemble, who is used to concealment, yet who carries conviction. Someone who can talk convincingly about Viktor Radin so that he is believed. Someone who knew him well.' He hesitated again, this time fixing Berlin with his dark eyes. 'I understand you are going to England in a few days' time.'

Berlin's mind was in torment. The marshal's purpose was clear. The trap had been set weeks ago by Viktor, and he had allowed himself to be led blindly forward. Now he was caught. What a fool he'd been.

'I knew Radin,' Berlin said desperately. 'I can't deny that. I don't know what he may have told you about me, but I can assure you I am not the man you want. I couldn't do what you ask.'

'What if there is no one else?'

'It would make no difference. I cannot do this. I am the wrong man.'

'You underestimate your abilities. I think you have the qualities to do what we want very well.'

'Please,' he begged. 'I am not a brave man.'

'I am not looking for bravery. I want a man who can keep a secret, who is familiar with the arts of concealment. No one must ever know about this plan.'

'I wouldn't pass your test,' Berlin said quietly. 'So please, tell me no more.'

'Viktor was your friend over many years. He knew you well. He said you were the man for such a task, if ever I felt the moment had arrived. I trust his judgement.'

'What did he tell you?'

'Enough to convince me he was right.' The old general paused, wiping the condensation off the inside of the window with his handkerchief. 'He said that you knew enough about him to be able to convince the British that he was dead.'

Berlin shook his head repeatedly. 'No,' he said, 'I am not the man you want.' It was a last desperate appeal against his sentence. 'I cannot do what you ask.'

'You are not the man I would choose if any choice existed,' Gerasimov said. 'But we have run out of time.'

'There must be many better qualified than me.'

'Don't you think I haven't searched high and low for them?' Gerasimov turned his anger on Berlin. 'This late in the day, you are all I have.'

PART THREE
Autumn 1961

12

1

How would she recognise Berlin? He had sent no photographs – she hadn't asked him to – and only now, waiting at the station, did she realise that she had no idea what he looked like – except he would look Russian, whatever that meant. How would *he* recognise her? She should have worn a different dress, something cooler, certainly – her face felt hot and she knew it wasn't only the heat of the afternoon – or with more colour – red, perhaps, or was that too obvious? Then she would have stood out among the crowd gathered around the exit. Now they'd probably miss each other, and his arrival would be a disaster. How thoughtless she'd been.

*

He knew her at once, even though the arrivals hall was filled with people waiting to meet passengers off the London train. She was tall, slim, dark-haired, and much younger than he had expected. Her face was flushed – was it the heat of the day? – and she studied each arriving traveller with the care he imagined she would bring to the examination of an historical document. The moment she caught sight of him, she took off her glasses, as if to conceal her short sight. She came towards him smiling, her hand outstretched in greeting.

'Dr Berlin? Hello, I'm Marion Blackwell.'

He looked as if he had just woken up. His hair was all over the place, he wore no tie and he was carrying his crumpled jacket and a battered canvas holdall. One of his shirt sleeves had unrolled and was flapping around his wrist. He was grinning at her sheepishly, as if he had no idea what to do next. She felt an immediate desire to take charge of him.

'Dr Blackwell.' He took her hand and bowed over it. 'I am Andrei Berlin.'

'It's so good to see you here.'

'What can I say?' He was smiling at her. 'Thank you for inviting me. You must forgive my appearance. I fell asleep on the train. I almost missed the station.'

She guided him towards the taxi rank. 'Male guests aren't allowed to stay in our college – it's women only,' she said, concealing her embarrassment with a laugh. How absurd he must think this rule was. 'I've prevailed upon a male colleague in our faculty, and he's agreed to put you up in one of his college guest rooms. I hope that's all right.'

'Of course.'

They drove into the city in silence. Berlin stared out of the window with an intensity she found daunting, as if he was trying to draw everything he saw deep down into his memory where it would be preserved for ever.

'You must be tired,' she said when he'd been shown to his room. 'Perhaps you'd like to rest.'

'If you tied me to a chair this minute, like Houdini I would escape within seconds,' he said, grinning again. 'Now I am here, I cannot sit still for a moment. I must walk round this wonderful city. I must breathe its air and touch its ancient stones. Will you accompany me, Dr Blackwell? Perhaps you have other appointments?'

'I'd love to,' she said. 'Where first?'

'King's Parade,' he said breathlessly. 'Then I will look at the books in the window of Bowes & Bowes before we walk down Trinity Street, past the Whim, Matthews' Café, then through the Great Court of Trinity College and on to the Backs.'

Marion started to laugh.

'Have I said anything wrong?' Berlin asked nervously.

'I understood you'd never been to Cambridge before,' she replied.

'That is correct.'

'But you know your way around.'

'In my imagination,' he said. 'Always in my imagination. Now you see why this moment is important. It is when my dreams meet reality.'

'I hope you won't be disappointed,' she said.

'That is already impossible,' he replied. 'Quite impossible.'

★

It was late. Where the evening had gone she had no idea. It seemed only minutes before that she had been waiting anxiously at the station. Now she felt she had known this mysterious Russian all her life. Why mysterious? He said so little, he listened with such intensity, his eyes never releasing you from their gaze, and when he did speak, he chose his words with great care. Was it more than unfamiliarity with the language that prompted his caution? Was he afraid that a misplaced phrase might carry some kind of risk about whose origin she could only speculate? His hesitation made her want to touch his hand all the time to reassure him that now he was in Cambridge, he was safe, no harm could come to him. He had nothing to worry about.

Fearing that he might be tired of her company, she had offered to bring him back to college in time for dinner in hall. He had declined, insisting that they have supper together – unless she had some other appointment. She had asked, jokingly, if in his dreams of Cambridge he had a favourite restaurant.

'The Koh-i-Noor,' he had replied. 'I have never eaten Indian food.'

Over dinner she told him about her childhood in a quiet suburb of Northampton where she'd been brought up by her widowed mother – her father had been killed during the battle of El Alamein – the grammar school she had attended (why was the English school system so difficult to explain to someone who hadn't been born to it?) and her overwhelming sense of arrival on her first day at Cambridge, of one journey ending and another beginning, and why since childhood she had wanted to be a historian.

'Curiosity, really,' she explained. 'I've always wanted to understand why things happen the way they do.'

'The truth and meaning of events.' Berlin smiled. 'Have you come to any conclusions?'

'Not yet,' she replied laughing. 'But I'm working on it.'

Throughout the evening his dark eyes interrogated her, and she felt a compelling need to answer questions that he had not asked. For some reason she was justifying herself to him – it was absurd, she knew, but she was unable to stop herself. He listened intently, prompting her to continue if she faltered, occasionally smiling at her jokes – why were they always so self-deprecating? She had questions of her own: what was it like living in Soviet Russia? What was going to happen over the crisis in Germany? Why was the Soviet leadership always so aggressive towards the West? Was there going to be a war in Europe? Surely some kind of reason would prevail? But for reasons she didn't understand, she found herself inhibited from asking him anything about himself.

They walked back through the deserted streets. She was ashamed of monopolising the conversation. How unfriendly she must seem. What could she have been thinking of? But she was powerless to do anything different. There was something in those dark, hypnotic eyes that made you want to confess your innermost thoughts. She had never met anyone who made her feel like that. She was defenceless before his gaze, and she found herself surrendering willingly.

'Two days ago,' he said suddenly as they walked past the Round Church, 'I stood on the Lenin Hills that overlook Moscow and tried to convince myself that in forty-eight hours I would be standing in this street and that everything would be

312

as I imagined. What I find hard to believe is that I am not dreaming, that I am actually here.'

'Have we met your expectations?' she asked. 'Or have we failed the test?'

He took some time to reply. For a moment she wondered if she or the university had disappointed him.

'I have no words. It is much more than I am able to describe. So much more.'

★

He lay awake listening to the college clock chime every quarter-hour. He felt exhilarated, his mind buzzing with conflicting sensations. He found it impossible to believe that he was no longer in Moscow, that he had actually arrived in Cambridge, that in the last few hours he had walked the streets of his imagined city. He had breathed the pure air of intellectual inquiry that over the centuries had nourished so many great minds; he had walked in the Great Court of Trinity – whose feet had trodden those very same cobbles before him? He had looked up at the windows of the Wren Library, he had wondered at the majestic spires of King's College Chapel, he had watched punts gliding on the Cam, and he had done all this with a companion who was not the bearded monster of his imagination but a slim, shy, studious English woman in her thirties, who seemed wholly unaware of her attraction.

He was relieved that she talked over dinner. He found himself without words, his mind suddenly locked in a frenzy of fear and embarrassment. He did not want her to sense his uncertainty. He needed time to come to terms with the simple but extraordinary notion that this new world he was discovering had no dark mirror. What it reflected was itself, nothing more, nothing less. He could walk its streets and he would not be followed. He could speak its language and not be overheard. He could say what he believed and not fear arrest. As they sat in the Koh-i-Noor and strolled home afterwards, he reminded himself repeatedly that nothing he did or said could put himself, or anyone else – certainly not his companion – at any kind of risk. He was free – and the realisation terrified him.

He had kissed her hand when she had left him because he did not dare to kiss her on the lips. He was as surprised as she was by his gesture. He had bent low over her white skin and smelled coriander and other spices on her fingers, and when he had looked up into her eyes he had known all too well what he had seen there.

'The sensuality of innocence,' he said aloud, and laughed. Was that what attracted him? Whatever the body or the mind may try to deny, it is in the eyes of those untutored in the dark arts of self-concealment that the truth can so easily be found. Nothing was hidden in Cambridge, she was telling him with every word she uttered. Not even the truth in our hearts can be concealed. In the country I come from, his silence was telling her, nothing can be revealed. Would she understand? Would she realise that he was a stranger to the habits of self-expression, that it was a language he had never learned, a cultural norm he had never experienced? If he were to use the words and expressions that he so desperately wanted to, he would have to learn a new language. And he had only a few days in which to do so.

The possibility of speaking without restraint, the opportunity to cast off the disciplines of a lifetime was confusing him, and his confusion was preventing him from sleeping. If such turmoil was the gift of freedom, he had no idea how to make use of it, nor did he know whether it was wise to do so, given the short length of his stay. Would it be possible, on his return to Moscow, to unlearn a recently acquired skill like telling the truth? Tonight Marion's kindness in talking about herself had given him some breathing space in which to bring order into the chaos of his troubled mind. But what about tomorrow? Or the day after? He could not stay silent all the time. Perhaps during these few days in Cambridge he would begin to appreciate how the complexities of freedom worked. Perhaps he would begin to like it; perhaps not.

Outside, the clock on the small tower over the hall chimed the hour. He counted the soft hammer blows five times.

★

The gesture had surprised her. The man was a communist, what Michael Scott would call, in his unguarded moments, 'a bloody Bolshevik', not someone you would associate with old-fashioned courtesy. For an instant she had felt his lips, soft and warm, on the ends of her fingers. She had pulled her hand back because it was so unexpected, and now she was furious with herself. What must he have thought? How could she have been so ill-mannered? She knew it was not the kiss that had alarmed her. As she withdrew her hand he had stared deep into her eyes. She had not expected him to look at her in that way, as if he was shining a light into her mind and forcing her to reveal thoughts so secret she was barely aware of them herself. She was afraid of what he might have found there.

What was happening to her? Where was the self-control on which she prided herself, and which had never let her down before? How could she have let such a moment happen? Why had she been so unprepared? Her mind was bursting with memories of their conversation, of sentences she wished she'd been quick-witted enough to come out with. She was painfully aware that some of what she'd said had been embarrassingly banal. If Berlin had noticed – and surely he must have – then what did he think of her? Her face flushed at the recollection. She'd talked too much tonight, no question. She'd made a fool of herself.

Too disturbed to sleep, she got out of bed, wrapped herself in her dressing gown and watched the dawn come up over the roofs of Cambridge. Somewhere in the distance she heard a clock strike five.

Kate had never warmed to the Polish girl. She was knowing and overconfident, and frequently criticised the playing of the other students. It was a surprise when, one morning, Agniewska suggested they practise together. Despite herself, Kate agreed. It would have been churlish to refuse. Her own playing had never been the butt of any of Agniewska's comments. The experience proved to be exciting. They had played a series of cello pieces with piano accompaniment with real enjoyment.

'We must do this again,' Agniewska had said. A week later she suggested they repeat their experiment. By this time a few of the other students had spoken to Kate.

'We do not trust her,' they said. 'Be careful.'

Kate took this to mean that they were jealous of her ability, and ignored their warning. Agniewska was unquestionably one of the best musicians at the Conservatoire. She was benefiting from the experience. Each week they played together, discussed the music and parted. Nothing unusual occurred.

'She is watching you,' Kate was told when her friends asked how the practice had gone, and Kate had reported positively. 'Waiting to choose the right moment.'

The right moment for what? she asked. No one had a convincing explanation. Kate waited. Nothing happened, and she forgot the warnings. Then, one morning, as they were clearing away their music stands, Agniewska asked, 'Have you heard about Vinogradoff?'

The Conservatoire was full of gossip. Kate assumed she would be told how Vinogradoff had scored a triumph at the expense of one of his rivals.

'He is being investigated.'

'Investigated?' Kate was incredulous. 'What for?'

'Maybe it is not true,' Agniewska said.

'What have you heard?'

'You are his pupil. Perhaps it is better if I say nothing. I do not want to upset you.'

'Tell me what you know.'

Agniewska closed the door and came and stood close to Kate. She spoke in a hushed voice. 'Apparently he has composed some music which the censor has judged to be subversive. There is a rumour that some of our students have been to his flat to perform for him. That is what drew the attention of the authorities.' She smiled. 'It seems unlikely, doesn't it? Vinogradoff is establishing himself as an international artist. He would hardly risk that kind of freedom, would he?'

'How can music be subversive?' It was no good asking Agniewska such a question. She would only reply with the official answer.

'Music that undermines our moral beliefs is always subversive.'

Keep off politics. That was the advice she had followed until now. She had to control her instinct to argue the case. 'What I meant was, how could Vinogradoff do such a thing? He's so' – she was suddenly lost for words – 'so mild.'

'It is the mild ones you must watch out for.'

'What has he written?' Kate asked.

'I do not know exactly. Has he not mentioned it to you? Has he never asked you to play some of it? You go to his house for lessons. You would have the perfect opportunity. No one would be able to hear you.'

If this wasn't an interrogation, it was the next best thing. Her friends had been right. Agniewska was an informer. Kate should not have disregarded their greater experience.

'I am here to learn the cello,' Kate said stiffly. 'Vinogradoff would never ask me to play any of his own music – presuming of course that he has written any, and he has never told me that he has. We agreed the pieces I would study before I came to Moscow. Nothing has changed. I would not let it change.'

There was nothing more to say after that. They put away their instruments in silence. It was the last time they practised together. The question on Kate's mind was, should she tell Vinogradoff or not? In the end, she decided it was not her business. She had no evidence that the Polish girl was acting on anyone else's behalf. She said nothing. For all she knew it was a case of deliberate provocation. Agniewska had wanted something from her and had failed to get it. Kate experienced a brief moment of triumph.

3

Koliakov looked at his watch. It was too early. He would wait until dark. He would not telephone to say he was coming. He didn't think her telephone was bugged, but it was better to take no risks. He sat in a café in Victoria Station for an hour and had a cheerless plate of bacon and eggs and a milky cup of tea. He read the evening paper from cover to cover. As soon as it was dusk, he took the Circle Line to South Kensington. He emerged from the rumbling depths of the underground to find that it was now fully dark. He walked the rest of the way, doubling back on himself to make sure he was not being followed.

All the time the tumult in his mind beat like a drum, its rhythm driving him relentlessly forward against the lights that seemed to explode in his face from street lamps, shop windows and passing cars. These lights were his enemy now, each reflection a beam that was trying to blind him so that he would never find the girl. He was surrounded by hostile forces whose sole purpose was to prevent him from doing what he had to do. He shielded his eyes with his hand and struggled on, fighting the storm in his mind.

To his surprise the front door was unlocked. All he had to do was push it open. The living room was a mess: bottles and glasses were everywhere, on the window sills, the mantelpiece, the floor, any available surface. He saw wine stains on the carpet and on the furniture. Cushions had been thrown on the floor. He righted an overturned chair. He saw full ashtrays and he smelled the stink of dead smoke and cheap scent.

'Georgie?'

There was no answer. He was sure she was there, he could sense her presence.

'Georgie?'

He went upstairs. The curtains were pulled in the bedroom. When were they ever open? One dressing-table lamp was on. She was lying on the bed, an orange paper streamer tied around her hair and a pair of white high-heeled shoes, at least two or three sizes too big, on her feet. Otherwise she was naked.

'Alexei?'

Someone – he could not believe she could have done this herself – had drawn on her skin all over her body in lipstick the impressions of kisses, small rosebud lips in clusters on her neck, round her breasts, across her stomach, at the tops of her thighs, there was even one large smudge between her legs.

'What have they done to me, Alexei? I feel so ill.'

There were bruises on her arms and body, and a swelling on her temple. She had been attacked, but by whom? A lover, perhaps? There was never any tenderness in her lovemaking. Tenderness was a world that had passed her by without touching. Reality for her was tricks and pretence. Perhaps the games she played had got out of hand.

'Help me, Alexei. Help me, please.'

He heard her appeal. The burning pain in his mind faded, the drumming dimmed and an unexpected calm spread over him. He no longer saw a poor imitation of Eva, or the cold heart of a woman who sold herself for money. Whatever he may have felt about her, this woman on the bed was young and frightened and in desperate need of comfort. If he helped her, he might smother the demons that lived in his conscience and attacked him for not rescuing Eva from Abrasimov. He found a blanket by the foot of the bed and covered her.

'Tell me what happened.'

He knelt by the side of the bed. She spoke slowly and with difficulty, as if she had been drugged. 'There was a party last night. The bell went after midnight. These two men were at the door. They said they'd been invited. I thought they were friends of friends. I let them in. When everyone had gone, they came out of the kitchen and attacked me.'

Her pupils were huge and unfocused. She wasn't drunk, though there was an empty champagne bottle by the bed. She had taken something else. He knew she used Benzedrine but this was different, as if she were being slowly anaesthetised in front of him.

'What did they do to you, Georgie?' he asked quietly. 'Try to tell me.'

Her eyes were rolling now, and she was speaking so quietly that he could neither hear nor understand. He held her cold hand against his cheek and saw the speck of blood on her arm and the mark on her skin. He knew at once that she had been forcibly injected, though he had no idea what with. What if she'd been given an overdose of some drug?

'I'll call an ambulance.'

'Alexei!'

Suddenly she sat up, tears bursting from her eyes, a scream of pain torn from her lips. She clutched her stomach and writhed in agony. 'I'm hurting, Alexei. I'm hurting so bad.'

He tried to take her in his arms, but she screamed as if the touch of his fingers was burning her. He had the impression her body was on fire, inside and out. Suddenly the screaming stopped. She opened her eyes very wide in surprise and stared at him as if she had never seen him before. Then she fell back against the pillow. He reached for the pulse in her neck. There was no movement. She was dead. Someone had done his job for him.

Hart had returned home late and exhausted from the office. It had been an uneasy day. The morning had lost its shape almost as soon as he arrived – there was no news from Pountney and he couldn't reach him on the telephone – and the afternoon hadn't ended much better. Within the last hour he'd received a report that told him little he didn't already know. Dr Berlin was a Russian academic from the Institute of Contemporary History in Moscow, author of a number of books, one of which, *Legacies of History*, had been published in translation by Fischer Stevens. He had been invited by the Blake-Thomas committee of the University of Cambridge to give three open lectures over a period of ten days. His first two days in London had been organised by his publishers, who had arranged interviews with the press and radio. When asked about the current crisis in West Berlin he had declined to comment, claiming that he was an academic, not a political visitor. He had now arrived in Cambridge, where he was expected to stay for twelve days before returning to Moscow.

Was it possible, Hart wondered, that Berlin might be some kind of messenger, bringing from Moscow an offer to negotiate over Germany? Secret information that might allow the world to draw back from the edge of war? Possible but unlikely, he concluded. The man, as he himself had made clear, was a university teacher. Hart doubted that he would have political contacts, at least not at the level required if he was to be entrusted with an important message from, say, the Politburo or a senior member of the armed forces. A little digging around in the Registry established that Berlin had received his invitation to speak long before the current crisis in Germany had begun to simmer. His arrival in Cambridge now was little more than coincidence.

None the less, as a precaution, Hart had ordered twenty-four-hour surveillance on the Russian from the moment of his arrival. If there was a motive for his visit other than the one he had declared, then his behaviour might reveal his intentions. So far, the watchers had seen nothing.

*

Pountney telephoned at six-thirty to say that since his meeting with Koliakov, he'd not had a peep out of him. He didn't answer his phone calls and he wasn't at work. The embassy explained his absence by claiming he was unwell. If he didn't know better, he'd say that Koliakov had disappeared into thin air. Worse, the deadline he'd given him had been and gone without a murmur from the man. What was he to do?

'He'll turn up,' Hart insisted. 'Keep after him until you get an answer.'

'Can't you get your people on to him?' Pountney pleaded. 'They're better at this sort of thing than I am.'

'If the Soviet Embassy isn't worried about his whereabouts, we're powerless,' Hart replied. 'You're all we've got right now.'

'I don't know what the hell I'm going to do.'

*

The train was late and crowded and he had to stand from Waterloo. He turned over the pages of his evening paper with difficulty. There, facing him, was a photograph of a man in his early forties, dark-haired, aesthetic-looking – Andrei Berlin, the caption told him, the Soviet historian. The article, by the Literary Editor, discussed Berlin's standing among historians. Hart skipped these paragraphs and went to the end of the article.

It was clear that Dr Berlin was reluctant to answer any political questions. Instead, we discussed the prevalent attitudes towards the West in Moscow today, particularly how the increase of tension over the future of West Berlin was seen by the average Muscovite. Berlin considered his reply. 'Of course there is tension,' he said. 'In such a situation, how could there not be? No civilised person wants to go to war. Our people are not belligerent. They have sons and daughters and worry about the future, like anyone else. Perhaps if the voice of the people could be heard, then we would all be sure of a peaceful solution to this crisis.'

Hart didn't wait to get to Richmond. He got out at Putney and caught the next train back to Waterloo.

5

Berlin's lecture had drawn a larger audience of dons and undergraduates than Marion had expected. From her vantage point at the back of the university church, she was able to see Michael Scott and Bill Gant. They had both avoided her before the lecture began, Michael Scott looking sour and disdainful, while poor Bill was more drained and exhausted than she could believe. Not that their feelings mattered. Her preoccupation was to ensure that the evening was a success, and that allowed her little or no time to worry about either of them.

At the drinks party afterwards, in a room in the Senate House, she was thanked repeatedly for 'putting the Blake-Thomas lectures back on the map'. Shyly, she replied that it was not her doing: they owed the success of the evening to Dr Berlin.

'Take the glory while it's offered, my dear,' the Master of St Catherine's said. 'Too few of us ever sip that cup. Enjoy it while it lasts, which is never for long.'

'I congratulate you, Marion.' Michael Scott's smile, she noticed, did not spread beyond his eyes. 'A veritable *succès d'estime*. But a little word in your ear. Beware *folie de grandeur*.

There are still two more lectures. Plenty of time for your good fortune to go into reverse.'

'A splendid occasion,' Geoffrey Stevens grinned. 'You must be very pleased.'

'I'm more relieved than anything,' Marion replied. 'I had this recurring dream that no one would turn up.'

'When news of this evening's success gets out, it'll be standing room only next time, you mark my words.' Stevens laughed. 'There's nothing so sweet as blacking the opposition's eye, is there?'

'I'm ashamed to say I agree,' Marion said.

'Nothing to be ashamed of,' Stevens protested. 'It was a fair fight and you won.'

'You gave me the courage to go on,' she said, taking Stevens's hand in hers. 'I was near to throwing in the towel that day I came to see you.'

'That's not how I remember it,' Stevens replied. 'Now,' he added, pointing her towards Berlin. 'Go and rescue your Russian, Marion. If you ask me, he looks as if he's had enough of being harangued by Colin Whitley.'

As she went to find Berlin, a fellow historian from Girton came up to her and said, 'He's so dishy, darling. You are lucky. If you don't want him, pass him on to me.'

★

Throughout the evening, Marion had been attentive, introducing Berlin to a list of academics whose names he soon lost track of, and occasionally protective: she had rescued him from being bored to death by an opinionated don, who seemed intent on explaining to him how communism would ultimately fail because of the inherent flaws in its system, though what those flaws were he appeared unable to say. She had stood beside him for no more than a few seconds at a time. Like a butterfly, she had fluttered all evening, just out of reach.

He was aware too of the congratulations showered on

Marion. Again and again he saw people shake her hand or kiss her. Why should she be congratulated? Perhaps his invitation to speak had not had an easy passage through the Blake-Thomas committee. Perhaps her support for his candidacy had attracted opposition. He saw Marion in a new light. She was a determined woman who knew her own mind and was prepared to fight an established opposition for what she believed in. Who of those present tonight, he wondered, looking around the room, had voted against him?

He had watched Marion throughout the evening. He had seen her changing moods, vivacious one moment, solemn the next, diplomatically seeing to her guests while supervising first the drinks and then the dinner. He admired her energy and sparkle. Most of all he had been beguiled by her eyes, by those wonderful if rare moments when she took off her glasses to smile reassuringly across the table at him. It was as if they had already established their own private language of conspiracy.

Towards midnight, when only a few guests remained, she asked if he wanted a taxi to take him back: he must be exhausted by his ordeal. No, he replied. It was a lovely night. He preferred to walk. The exercise would do him good. He had dearly wanted to ask if he could accompany her home, but he was never alone with her for long enough.

'You've made a lot of friends tonight,' she said, resting her hand on his arm. Once more he felt that sense of conspiracy between them. 'An exhausting but wonderful evening. I haven't been as nervous as this since the day I took my finals. It'll all be much easier next time. I hope you're pleased.'

'How could I be otherwise? I am overwhelmed by your kindness. Everyone's kindness.' He was aware that a small group had gathered round him. The prospect of intimacy with Marion vanished. 'Goodnight to you all. Thank you. Thank you.'

He bowed to them and they burst into spontaneous applause. For one terrible moment he thought he might cry.

He opened the window and gazed out. Milton Court was in darkness, the college asleep. It was a still, warm night: there was no movement, no sound. He looked up at the stars, tiny specks of icy light flickering in the darkness – it was the same sky that looked down on Moscow, but how different its context. In this quiet, contented landscape there were no secret terrors. Even so, he was unable to relax. Where was British Intelligence? Why had he heard nothing from them? He had been in the country for four days, and there had been no approach. Perhaps they would never contact him. Perhaps they had dismissed him as an academic who could say nothing of importance.

He had voiced his concerns to Gerasimov, who denied them. 'For two, maybe three days, there will be silence. They will watch you from the moment you arrive. They will read the interviews in the press, listen to the radio, attend your lectures and study what you say for clues. At first they will reject the possibility that you have anything of value for them. Why would we employ someone like you to bring a message to the West? They will think about it and slowly, carefully, they will change their minds.'

How could Gerasimov be certain that that's what would happen? Berlin had asked.

'I know them,' had been his enigmatic reply. Did he mean the British, or Merton House? 'Sometimes I think I know them better than they know themselves.'

If it was meant to be helpful, it was having the opposite effect now. Why hadn't someone contacted him? What was he doing wrong?

IVAN'S SEARCH FOR HIS FATHER

Andrei unlocked the door to his father's studio and went in. The morning light poured in through the tall windows, illuminating the huge plaster head that, two or three times life-size, was like a monument from an ancient civilisation. The details were instantly familiar: the thick hair *en brosse*, the narrow forehead, bushy eyebrows, full moustache, forceful chin, the expression 'caring and purposeful' as the leader of his Pioneer Group had once described it, and the eyes staring ahead at the golden path that led to the distant horizon that only he could see. These were the unchanging features of wisdom and foresight of the 'Man Sent to Lead'.

To his right he recognised a 'Kindly Father'. Here the eyes of the Great One were lowered so that, when the bust was joined to the torso, a hand would rest on the head of a smiling child on whom the Great One's expression would be fixed, an affirmation that the task of the Momentous Undertaking would be inherited by the next generation. Next was a 'Great Leader', a massive bronze structure, ready for transportation to the main square of a provincial city. Now the eyes looked sternly ahead as the People's Leader pointed the way to the future, the uncompromising image stating clearly that the journey into the glorious unknown could follow only one direction.

Did the Great Leader look like that? The sculpted version of his face was no different to all the photographs Andrei had ever seen – eternally youthful, defiantly ageless. Was his skin smooth and unmarked, his face unlined? Was his hair as thick as a young man's? Was he made so differently to the rest of us that he never got old?

Finally to his left were two 'Friendship Monuments', each featuring a worker holding a hammer aloft and a woman with a sickle in one hand and a child in the other, greeting a Soviet soldier. One group was dressed in winter clothes, wrapped up against the ice and snow, the other in the lighter clothes of summer. The woman wore a full skirt, her hair flowing behind her; the peasant's sleeves were rolled up, his cap set at the back of his head. The joyous moment when the people of the world met their Russian saviours, where one journey ended, and another began, had been caught for ever in bronze. These images were popular in the more distant parts of the communist world, so his father had told him, where the people liked to be reminded of how they had been rescued by the Soviet Army from enslavement to their own leaders and their mistaken, error-ridden philosophies.

He examined the portrait of the woman. The inspiration for her face, indeed for all the faces of all the women his father had ever sculpted, was his mother. It always gave Andrei a great sense of pride when he looked at a sculpture in a public place and recognised that beautiful face so faithfully reproduced. His father's early portraits of her were more than just a likeness, though the likeness was striking. What they showed was his mother's innocent beauty, her open and trusting nature, and above all her unhesitating belief that the future would be better than the present. It was that hopeful, confident expression that his father's loving hands had captured so well. He looked for the familiar inscription. On the base of the sculpture, beside his father's signature, he read the words, 'The Radiant Years'.

There was a bitter irony about the title now. The figure his father had made was anything but radiant. The woman was no longer beautiful; she was coarse, hardened, hollow, devoid of destiny. Where was that special beauty, where was the bloom of her skin, where was the lustre in her thick hair that in some miraculous way his father had found in all his early pieces? Where was the youthful hope that he had captured in clay when he first set eyes on her?

What Andrei saw now, cruelly cast in bronze for all the world to see, was his father's fading memory of his mother. How frightening, he thought, that the intensity of your feelings can fade so fast, that you should care so little that you no longer even bother to conceal your lack of interest. Was that what happened when you grew older? Was love not meant to last? But even if love did die – an idea he found hard to understand – even if his father's heart was no longer in his work, couldn't the hands that moulded the clay still honour the beauty that had faded throughout her life with him? Wasn't that a justifiable lie?

He found another door smeared with plaster marks and pushed it open. This room was dominated by a single huge plaster statue of the 'Father of the People', surrounded by platforms that allowed his father and his assistants to work on it. Scattered all over the floor were spare hands and feet: the hands holding a machine-gun or a rifle, outstretched or bent in salute; the feet always in boots, huge boots, boots for all weathers, boots worn and scarred by years of activity guarding the state and the lives of all those who lived within it.

Andrei climbed the ladder that had been tied to one of the platforms, and found himself level with the Great One's eyes. The irises had yet to be cut in the plaster. This figure was neither watchful nor vigilant – it was blind. Andrei was suddenly aware of its vulnerability, its ordinariness. He felt neither awe nor fear in its presence. Blindness robbed the statue of its power. It gave Andrei a freedom he had not felt before in the presence of the Great One. He looked at the statue, his vision shorn of the myths that up to now he had accepted without question. The Great Leader aged because he was a man like any other. His face became lined, his hair thinned, his shoulders sagged. His father could allow his images of women to show that he had tired of his mother, but he lacked the courage to sculpt a Leader who was growing old. Suddenly he saw his father's work as a continuous lie.

A huge anger rose up within him. He wanted to strike back at his father, to hurt him for the terrible things he had done to his mother's beauty and youth, for bruising her face, for leaving her sobbing helplessly on the bed, for sticking his red bobbing thing into that ugly girl, for all the ways in which his cruelty had driven the spirit out of her, and for portraying the Great Leader with lies and not with truth. Suddenly he was in the grip of an irresistible force that told him what he had to do. He snatched a chisel and went to work.

Cross eyes, wall eyes, wandering eyes, lines on the face, pock-marks on his cheeks, furrows on the brow, tears on the cheeks of the women – *no more lies*, he shouted out loud as he ran from statue to statue in the studio, defacing his father's work.

Then, using the wet clay he found wrapped in a sheet, he stuck enormous hooded things onto every torso and into every hand he could find.

Only the truth, he shouted into the empty room. *From now on, only the truth.* Witnesses to his desecration, the damaged statues neither stirred nor spoke.

13

1

'Dr Berlin, sir.' The porter hurried after him. 'There was a man asking for you this morning, sir, when you were out. Wouldn't leave his name. Very insistent about that, he was.'

'What kind of man?' Berlin enquired.

'Youngish man, sir. Not an undergraduate. Thirties, I'd say, though it's hard to tell these days. They all look alike when you get to my age.'

'Was he English?' How absurd the question sounded.

'He wasn't a foreign gentleman, sir. He was English all right. Quite tall.'

'Did he say when he would call again?'

'No, sir. Nothing like that.'

'Thank you—' He realised he had no idea of the porter's name.

'Wilkins, sir.'

'Thank you, Wilkins. If he comes back, I'll be in my room.'

'I'll let you know at once, sir. Don't you worry.'

British Intelligence had called – who else could it be? – and he had missed them. He cursed his luck. He'd have to wait now – surely they wouldn't give up after one attempt? He was desperate to be rid of his burden. He disliked responsibility, and the weight of his mission oppressed him. He was sure that was the reason for the nightly hauntings that dragged him down into the mire of his life. When his message was delivered, he would be free of these terrible memories, able to enjoy to the full these glorious days in Cambridge, this beautiful Indian summer, as he had learned to call it.

*

A knock at his door awoke him with a start. 'Dr Berlin, sir?' It was Wilkins, the porter.

'Yes?'

'Your visitor, sir. He's back.'

Berlin opened the door. 'My visitor?' For a moment he was perplexed.

'He came this morning, sir. Remember? Wouldn't leave his name. Shall I show him up?'

'Please.'

A youngish man, mid-thirties, with bushy fair hair, looking fresh-faced and eager came in, carrying a newspaper. He wore a tweed jacket with leather patches on the elbows, baggy grey trousers and battered suede shoes.

'Hello. I'm Hugh Hart,' he said smiling.

'I am Andrei Berlin.' They shook hands.

'Yes,' Hugh Hart said. 'I know who you are.'

'How did you find me?' Berlin asked.

Hart smiled. 'You can't keep a secret in this place longer than you can hold your breath. Isn't it the same in Moscow?'

No, in Moscow we keep our secrets to ourselves because to betray them might mean imprisonment or death. But I would not expect you to understand that.

'Well, now you have found me, what can I do for you?'

He felt an overwhelming sense of relief. His ordeal was nearly over. An hour, perhaps two, surely no more. Then he would be free.

'It's a beautiful day, very unexpected for this time of year. We should make the most of it while we can, don't you think? I wondered if you'd care for a walk.'

And what shall we talk about, Mr Hart? Berlin wanted to ask, but Hart was already out of the door. All Berlin could do was follow him.

★

'Am I allowed to ask a question?'

'Please,' Hart said. 'Fire away.'

'Why have you come to see me?'

'It's very simple, really. We were wondering if you had anything to tell us.'

'I am a history teacher and you, I assume, are an intelligence officer.'

'In a manner of speaking.'

'What would you expect me to tell you?' Don't blurt out what you have to say too soon, Gerasimov had instructed. Make them work for their prize, then they will value what you tell them more highly.

'That's up to you,' Hart said.

'Why do you think I have a message?'

'You're the only Russian visiting these isles at the moment. Given present circumstances, it was worth a try. Call it a hunch.'

'A hunch?'

'An idea. An instinct that you might have brought something with you.'

Berlin walked on in silence. This was it. This was the secret moment when he played his part in history, when the message that he brought was passed from one side of the Iron Curtain to the other so that an unnecessary war might be avoided, human lives might be saved and evidence of European civilisation preserved. His own part in the drama would never be recorded. If he were to claim it for himself, it would be denied. He didn't care. It was enough to know what he had done, and that because of his action, there was a greater possibility that life – the lives of many people in many countries – might have a chance of survival. This single act would redeem the years of betrayals.

'Your instinct is correct,' Berlin said.

'I'm pleased to hear that.'

Berlin saw no excitement on the man's face. It was as if he had offered him a cigarette and he had accepted it.

'How do I know I must give my message to you?' Berlin asked.

'You want my bona fides, do you?'

'I'm sorry. I don't understand.'

'You want to know who I am. My official status.'

'Some form of verification. Yes, that would be helpful.' Be careful whom you give your message to, Gerasimov had warned. Status confirms authority. If you give it to the wrong person it will never reach those who make the decisions, it will get lost in the undergrowth of bureaucracy and our efforts will have been wasted.

'Will this do?' Hart pulled a card out of his wallet and showed it to Berlin. His name, his job title – Senior Controller, what was that? – and his Department, 'Ministry of Supply Resources Management'.

'Call this number if you want to. They'll confirm who I am. There's a phone box over there. I've got some pennies if you need them.'

'It is not your identity that concerns me,' Berlin said. 'I must trust you because I have no other option. It is your position. How can I be sure that you are powerful enough to be listened to? How can I know that you will pass my message upwards to the appropriate people?'

'It's that important, is it?'

'I bring a message from Marshal Gerasimov, commander of the Red Army. You may have heard of him.'

'Last time I saw him, he was standing on a podium in Red Square applauding your spaceman and looking pleased with himself.'

'You have not answered my question.'

'Any communication from Marshal Gerasimov will be sent to the Cabinet Office.'

'This Cabinet Office – is it powerful?'

'It's the committee that reviews all intelligence in this country. It reports to the Cabinet, and the Prime Minister chairs the Cabinet.'

'You understand my concerns,' Berlin said. 'I am not familiar with your country.'

'That is why I came to Cambridge to see you. Now, what's the great man got to say for himself? I trust he's as well as can be expected, given his age.'

2

The news that Medvedev had been appointed the new head of the Directorate came without warning, and filled Koliakov with foreboding. He had heard nothing while he had been in Moscow. Had his usual contacts failed him? Or was the reason more sinister – that they knew more than they dared tell him? He waited anxiously. Four days later he received a letter from Medvedev ordering him to return to Moscow within fourteen days, where he would be reassigned to 'other duties', though as to what those other duties might be he was given no clue. His successor in London was named, a man he didn't know, presumably one of Medvedev's placemen. He was not wrong about the hostility between them. Medvedev had wasted no time in getting his revenge for his failure to support him all those years before.

He experienced a feeling of bleakness at the prospect of leaving London. He liked the freedom of his role, how it took him close to the heart of power in this strange country where political leaders believed that, shorn of empire but supported by the weight of history, they could still exercise influence on a world that had long moved past them. Were they arrogant, blind or misguided? He would never know. The British disease, he thought, was too strong a belief in their own past – a past they could never shake off because it surrounded their present, like a cloak around their shoulders. How self-conscious they were about the distinction of their old buildings, the value of their institutions, the permanence of their monarchy, the importance of their aristocracy. How they adored their capacity for ceremonial pageant. Did they truly imagine that these historical tableaux were an alternative to the vast technological power that lay at the heart of the two great systems whose life-or-death struggle divided the world? Foolish, self-deceiving and arrogant the British might be, but he had come to have an affection for them. Their faults were born of innocence, not of terrible violence and cruelty towards their own kind. Such a verdict could never be delivered in his own country.

The more he thought about his impending departure, the more his anger rose, and symptoms he had not experienced for years returned. He developed a permanent headache, a searing pain behind the eyes that no analgesic could mollify. His eyes became sensitive to bright light, forcing him to wear dark glasses. Light once more was his enemy – its purpose was to melt his eyeballs, to blind him.

He had suffered like this once before, in Budapest in 1956 after the fighting had ended, the day he learned that Eva had gone missing. In his obsession to find her, his connections with the reality of his daily life had become flimsy, insubstantial. The world he inhabited no longer belonged to him but was peopled by hostile presences that he had to outwit. For days he felt he had lost his identity, that his mind was governed by forces he neither welcomed nor understood, but whose demands he was unable to resist.

He searched for Eva everywhere. He watched them clear the streets and houses of bodies, he asked questions about the identities of the corpses, were they male or female, young or old, did they have a name? He stood by as they dug them out of the rubble. He visited the mortuaries and hospitals, checking the lists of the dead and wounded. He saw the pain in the faces of parents searching for their lost children, but

336

despite the human devastation he had witnessed, he felt no pity for them. He had no doubts about the rightness of what had happened, about the violent suppression he had witnessed. The idea of a satellite state securing its own freedom from Soviet control was unthinkable. Any means were justified in keeping the Soviet empire intact. What had been done was necessary.

Wherever he looked, the answer was the same. Eva and her daughter Dora had not been heard of since the fighting began. Her apartment remained deserted. When the schools re-opened, Dora's absence went unexplained. Martineau, too, he learned, had disappeared, but there was no word from the British Embassy about a missing diplomat. Twice Koliakov attempted to make contact with Hugh Hart but each time his approach was ignored. What could have happened? How could three people vanish? Looking at the ruined city, it was only too clear. It might be weeks or months before their bodies were discovered – if they were dead. That was his predicament. He had to know the truth. Against all advice, he hung on long after the time for leaving was past.

He took to wandering the streets by night in the vain hope that he might come across Eva. How many times he thought he'd seen her, only to be disappointed. His behaviour was reckless and out of character. If his colleagues were aware of what he was doing, they were too preoccupied to report his strangeness. If he knew it – and by now he hardly recognised himself, so deep was his obsession – he didn't care. His life had one purpose. The days after the end of the uprising became a time of madness.

Then from one his agents came a rumour that the Hungarians knew he had sent the signal to Moscow that had led to General Abrasimov's arrival in Budapest and his brutal suppression of the uprising. Koliakov had been betrayed by someone in the embassy, though by whom he never knew. He was advised to leave. He ignored the warning. He would not be seen to run because he had received a threat against his life. His visible contempt for those who threatened him concealed the fact that he still had unfinished business in Budapest.

Only a chance encounter with a member of the Soviet Embassy who lived in the same block of flats saved him from certain death. He fled from those who lay in wait for him. For three days he disappeared into the ruins of Budapest before he was able to get word to Abrasimov and arrange for a flight to Moscow on a military aircraft. What happened during those three days he never told anyone, not even the psychiatrists at the KGB sanatorium to which he was sent on his return. He hated his time in hospital but he never gave way to impatience. Survival, he knew, depended on his ability to convince his doctors that he had recovered sufficiently so they could release him. Then he would be able to resume his search. He turned the interviews and the treatment into a secret game. He would outwit the specialists. After four months he was allowed to return to normal duties. In Moscow he scanned the lists of the Hungarian dead. He never found Eva's name. Discreet enquiries at the Budapest Embassy confirmed that her flat remained unlived in. She was not dead, but she was not alive. He was mystified. But he learned nothing about Eva's fate, either then or later. He forced himself to accept that she was dead. He shut her out of his mind. The madness retreated. He knew it had not left him. It was biding its time, lying in wait, ready to seize him once more when it chose to.

*

His eyes hurt from the lights in his bedroom. He turned them all off except for the bedside lamp. How bleak this room was. There was nothing in it to suggest his presence. It was as anonymous as he was. Perhaps that was why Eva had never noticed him – there was nothing to notice. In a world of colour and movement, he was transparent, invisible. Perhaps he didn't exist.

He packed a small leather holdall that he kept under his bed with a change of clothing and the envelope with money he had put by for just such an emergency. Over the months he had marked out the boarding houses he would use if he needed to: one in Pimlico, one in Kentish Town, one in White City, inconspicuous places where he could hide for a day or two under an assumed identity. He knew where he would be going even if he was unsure what he would be escaping from – but escape he must. His enemies were once more loose on the streets, and they were looking for him.

The burning sensation behind his eyes told him that he had to escape into the dark, as if he were running into a long tunnel, and only then would the direction of his future become clear. Perhaps this was a time of madness again. If so, its strength was as great as before and there was nothing he could do to control it. He was governed by forces more powerful than his own will.

He zipped up the bag and secured the straps. It was heavy with the weight of his typewriter. There was one last thing. He opened a drawer and took out a revolver. Why he might need it he wasn't sure. But he felt better taking it with him, so he tucked it into his bag and went out into the night.

3

'Who's this?'

Kate showed him a framed photograph of a man in his sixties she had found tucked behind a pile of books stacked in the empty fireplace.

'My father,' Valery said.

'Why do you keep his picture hidden?'

'I do that when I'm angry.'

'What's he done to deserve banishment?' she asked.

'You haven't got enough time left in Moscow for me to explain.'

It was not the first time he had shown a reluctance to talk about himself. Despite her questions, he had only recently explained why he didn't work, and even then his answers had left her perplexed. His department had been disbanded, he said, when the project he was working on had come to an end. He was waiting for the next project to materialise. Until then he had nothing to do. She didn't believe him for a moment but with so few clues, what was the point in trying to deduce the truth? Why was he so evasive? Her only explanation was that he was engaged in some kind of conflict with himself and that he needed time to resolve that conflict. Its nature and the shape of any possible resolution remained mysteries to her. She would show patience. He would tell her the truth, she was sure of that, but only when he felt he was ready to do so, not before.

*

Sunday dawned clear and bright, the city shining under an arching blue sky. Why not take a bus and go into the country? Kate suggested. It would do them good to escape Moscow for a few hours. Valery had agreed. There was a place he knew, he said. Two hours later, they were sitting beside a river at one end of a long field that sloped gently down from a birch wood. There was no sound except for the water washing over stones and the humming of insects.

'Is your father still alive?' Kate asked.

'When I last heard, yes.'

'Don't you see him much?'

'I haven't seen him for years.'

She sensed the tension in his voice. He wanted to tell her but did he have the courage?

'I didn't know he was my father until I was fifteen.' The words burst from him as if he was surprised to find himself

340

saying anything. 'One day this man I'd never seen before turned up, and my mother told me he was my father. He stayed for a few weeks, then he vanished from my life again. I've not seen him since.'

'Are you angry with him because he deserted you?'

'I don't blame him for that,' he replied. 'It was obvious he couldn't stay here. I'm more angry with myself.'

'Why?'

'For not understanding who I am.'

She waited for him to continue but he said nothing.

'My mother died when I was fifteen,' she said suddenly. 'I know what it's like to want someone who can never be there. I know what it does to you.'

She saw the look of relief on his face, as if her sudden admission had broken a barrier inside him.

'My father is English,' he told her. 'That's why he could never stay in Moscow. He lives in Cambridge. He's a professor of nuclear physics. Now you probably understand even less than before.'

*

'How do you come to have an English father?' she asked later.

'I have to tell you sometime, don't I?' He lay on his back on the grass and gazed up at the sky. In the early thirties, he said, his mother had gone to a conference on nuclear physics in Leyden. She was an ambitious scientist, newly married, and she had never been outside Russia before. It was her first conference and she didn't know what to expect. The first lecture she attended was given by the English physicist, Geoffrey Stevens. She was swept her off her feet.

'She had never met a man like him, she said. He was like a gale. He knocked everything she had believed in completely flat. He gave her new ideas, new energy, new enthusiasms. He showed her all the possibilities that sprang from the extraordinary discoveries they had made.'

Their affair lasted the week of the conference. Six weeks later she knew she was pregnant. She never told her husband he was not the father. It was just as well: the marriage hadn't lasted. In those days many didn't.

'In all those difficult years before the war she longed to see my father, she longed to tell him about their child, but she was afraid. Those were dangerous times in Moscow. Had she succeeded in making contact, she would probably have been arrested and shot for spying. So she did nothing.'

'Was that when she told you about your real father?'

'No,' he said carefully. 'Not then. Later.'

He was silent for a moment. Would he continue? Would this be one more tantalising glimpse, or would he continue to unravel what happened?

'In the years after the war, my father had a kind of conversion. He was in charge of the building of the British bomb. During this time, for reasons I have never really understood, he changed his mind and opposed the manufacture of nuclear weapons. He came to Moscow to try to persuade the Soviet government to make public all their nuclear secrets, so that no side would have any advantage over the other. It was naive of him to think it would work, and of course it didn't. But if he hadn't done so, I would never have met him. So something came from his madness.'

4

Marion hurried across the court, wishing that she had made some kind of plan last night before Berlin had gone home after dinner. It had been impossible to get him on his own for more than a moment after the lecture, and she had not wanted him to feel she was monopolising him. Yet she was the one who invited him, fought for him. Not surprisingly, she felt responsible for his presence. That was why, she told herself, the lack of arrangements for the day concerned her. She had to see him.

She ran up the wooden stairs, her cheeks burning – what would he think of her, out of breath and blushing? She knocked on the door of the guest room. There was no answer. She knocked again, waited and then went in. The room was deserted. The only signs of occupancy were a few clothes thrown over the back of a chair, a copy of yesterday's newspaper spread across the bed and an opened bottle of whisky on the chest.

She went back to the porter's lodge. Had anyone called for Dr Berlin? Not since this morning, she was told. This morning? A man had called for him twice, Wilkins had mentioned that, and they'd met up on the second occasion and gone off together. And no one since then? He'd only come on duty an hour before: he couldn't say for sure, but he didn't think Dr Berlin had returned. Wilkins might know but he wasn't on again until five. If she could try again later.

'I'll leave a note,' she said.

Please call me, she wrote. *We need to discuss arrangements for the second lecture.* It wasn't true but Berlin wouldn't know that.

'Good morning, Marion,' Michael Scott was walking across the grass towards her, his gown draped casually over his shoulder. 'How is our Soviet friend today? Nursing a sore head, if there's any justice. They can certainly drink, these Russians, can't they?'

'You'll have to ask him yourself, Michael,' Marion said testily. 'I've not seen him since last night, so I've nothing to report.'

'I saw you emerging from his staircase just now, didn't I?'

'He's not in, Michael.'

'Not done a bunk, has he?'

'Why on earth should he?'

'It can be quite a shock to the system, crossing from one side of the Iron Curtain to the other. Too strong a dose of freedom can be hard to swallow. I sometimes think it's a taste that some of us are not meant to acquire.'

'I would have thought he was well able to take care of himself.'

'Keep an eye on him, Marion.' He was standing close to her. 'We don't want to gather before an empty podium for lecture number two, do we?'

5

'It's an interesting story,' Hart said, 'no question about that.' He pushed aside his lunch tray and gazed out of the window. He appeared to be talking to himself. 'Intriguing.'

Their walk had ended the moment Hart had suggested they find a better place to talk. He waved his arm and a minute later a car appeared. For a while Berlin wondered if he was being kidnapped, but there was no coercion, no threat, just a smile and an open door, and that extraordinary charm with which the English seemed to get their way. For all the choice he had, Hart might just as well have held a gun. The only weapon he used was courtesy.

They were driven a few miles outside Cambridge, along a twisting country road that linked a succession of hamlets with strange-sounding names. He passed an observatory, a war cemetery, a few isolated farms and the occasional grand house, but mostly he saw the flat empty landscape of East Anglia, endless fields ploughed ready for winter and poplars on the horizon. After thirty minutes or so, they turned down a rutted drive and drew up in front of a Victorian mansion of patterned red and grey brick, with oak doors and a bewildering number of turrets and towers with leaded windows.

They walked into an oak-panelled hall. Berlin saw a coat of arms above an open, empty fireplace, and a staircase leading to a gallery. A suit of armour had been placed at the turn of the stairs. Swords and spears and ancient firearms were fixed to the walls. Hart led the way, his feet echoing on the wooden flooring, to a sunny room overlooking a formal garden at the back. Lunch was brought on trays: cold chicken, salad, bottled beer and cheese. It was Tolley's beer, Berlin noted. And it was as good as the guidebooks had stated. When they had finished eating, they were joined by a tall, silent man to whom he was not introduced. Berlin was asked to start again, to retell the whole story with as much detail as he could remember. It took him almost an hour to complete his account.

'In many ways what you say is plausible,' Hart said. 'But is it credible? Do I believe you?' He turned to face Berlin. 'That's the difficulty, isn't it? Are you telling us the truth, or are you deliberately trying to mislead us?'

Berlin was perplexed. He had followed Gerasimov's instructions to the letter. He had given the series of codes that the old general had said would put it beyond doubt that the information he brought was authentic. Uncertainty was not a reaction either he or Gerasimov had anticipated. He felt a growing sense of alarm.

'I have told you what I was instructed to say, everything I know. There is nothing more.'

'That may be so,' Hart said, 'but if you expect us to take your message seriously, you're going to have to work a lot harder. You'd agree with that, wouldn't you, George?'

The silent man looked up from the notes he was making and nodded.

There was an edge to Hart's manner now. Gone was the bonhomie encouraged by their lunch together, when they had talked openly about anything that was not political, when Berlin had relaxed, enjoying the younger man's company. Now he saw that though the manner might be different, beneath the surface there were more similarities than differences with Hart's opposite numbers in Moscow.

'Let's go through the details again, shall we, and see where we run into trouble.'

Remember why you are here, Berlin told himself. When

you answer their questions, tell them everything you can be sure of. If you don't know the answer, say so. Invent nothing. Above all, don't lie.

'Where were you when Gerasimov gave you these instructions?'

'In his car on the way back to Moscow.'

'Was there anyone else in the car?'

'Only the driver.'

'Could he hear what you were saying?'

'It's unlikely. The glass partition was closed. I am sure it was soundproof.'

'No hidden microphones?'

Berlin shrugged. 'How would I know? It's always possible, but I doubt it.'

'Where had you been?'

'I'd accompanied Marshal Gerasimov to a cemetery in a village some miles outside Moscow. We visited his wife's grave.'

'Are you a close friend of his?'

'No. I'd never met him before.'

'Why do you think Gerasimov took you on this pilgrimage to his wife's grave?'

'I have no idea.' Berlin shrugged his shoulders. How could he explain to them in ways they would understand the significance of the homage Gerasimov had paid, in Berlin's presence, to his wife's unrelenting eye for the truth? Hart and the silent man would never comprehend that. 'All I can tell you is what happened. I am here as the voice of others.'

'Doesn't it strike you as odd, Dr Berlin, that a man you don't know takes you on a visit to his wife's grave and then asks you to betray your country's best-kept secrets to the West?'

'He asked me to betray nothing,' Berlin said sharply. 'He instructed me to bring to the West the truth about the Soviet inability to wage an offensive war. He did so out of a deep sense of patriotism. He has no wish to see once more thousands of his citizens slaughtered. We suffered enough in the last war. I think that is sufficient reason to give you information. If you are looking for traitors, then I suggest you look elsewhere.'

Hart's expression gave no indication of his response to Berlin's appeal.

'All right, let's try another tack,' he said. 'Let's paint the picture as we see it.' He was walking around the room, his hands in his pockets. The silent man wrote relentlessly in a notebook. 'The Soviet government appears intent on going to war over West Berlin. However, the head of the Soviet armed services, the austere Marshal Gerasimov, opposes this policy. He is in possession of important information about the real state of the Soviet Union's readiness for war. In particular, he tells us that the much-vaunted nuclear satellite does not exist, that it's a figment of someone's imagination, and that Professor Radin, the architect of your space programme, is dead. Two very significant statements which, if true, will have enormous repercussions on what happens in Berlin. He decides to share this information with the West because he believes it may prevent such a catastrophe. All correct, so far?'

Berlin nodded. 'All correct, yes.' Hart turned to stare out of the window. For a moment or two he was silent.

'Here's this man, probably one of the most powerful in the Soviet Union, who can snap his fingers and have any number of professionals do his bidding – so what does he do? Does he take his concerns to the Central Committee? In your version of events, he doesn't. Does he face the wrath of the First Secretary by telling him a few home truths? Again, no. He's tried that too many times in the recent past, you tell us, and on every occasion he has failed. Does he choose a KGB professional to bring this most important of messages to the West, someone who would carry conviction? Or does he employ someone from the Soviet Embassy here? Strangely, he does neither. Does he send a soldier, a senior officer, perhaps someone known to us from some previous contact whom we can easily verify to bring this message to us? Again, to our bafflement, he doesn't. What does he do? He chooses an academic historian who has never done anything like this before and whose only claim for the job is that he happens to be travelling to Cambridge at the right time. He entrusts this inexperienced man with information of the very highest importance.' Hart paused and looked at Berlin. 'Surely you can see our concerns.'

'What can I say?' Berlin replied. 'I do not know his reasons, I can only speculate.'

'Speculate, then.'

'He came to his decision that this information should be given to the West quite suddenly. The political situation in Berlin is deteriorating rapidly. He sees the West and the East sliding towards war. He knows that if he approaches any official organisation like the KGB, he risks betrayal. His only certainty then is that his message will never reach the West. He will have achieved nothing. So what does he do? He looks around for someone no one will suspect, the last person anyone would imagine acting as a messenger for him. He learns that I am travelling to the West. He approaches me in secret. If I can be persuaded to perform this task for him, he has more than an even chance of getting the truth to you. That is a risk he is prepared to take.'

'Do you have any evidence to sustain your theory?'

'Only a chance remark the marshal made.'

'What was that?'

'He told me I was not the right person to do this job but that he had no choice. There was no one else.'

'Why did he say that?'

'I suspect the reason he said it and the reason he chose me are one and the same. I am the least likely candidate. My visit to England already had the official sanction of both the British and the Soviet authorities, therefore my departure would arouse no suspicion, least of all from his political enemies. There is nothing to link my name with his.'

'Who are these enemies?'

'I am sure there are people both here and in Moscow who he would rather did not know what he was doing.'

'His fellow officers?'

'Possibly.'

'Politicians?'

'Certainly. The army has lost a great deal of political influence recently.'

'And presumably KGB officers, either in Moscow or at the embassy in London?'

'Gerasimov specifically instructed me to make no contact with the Soviet Embassy here.'

'Why did he say that?'

'I think he suspected that some of them are less trustworthy than we would like them to be.'

'They might betray him to his political masters, is that it?'

'Yes.'

Hart pondered Berlin's reply.

'We hear rumours that there is a group in Moscow opposed to the First Secretary.'

'I know there is a growing body of opinion opposed to the First Secretary's methods and pronouncements.'

'How powerful is this opposition?'

'There is no such thing as a formal opposition in my country.'

If Hart heard his answer, he ignored it. 'Is Gerasimov its leader?'

'Leader of what?'

'You're not being very helpful, are you?'

'You are asking me questions I am not qualified to answer.'

It was the first antagonistic exchange they had had since the interview began. Hart waited for the moment to pass.

'Let me put it to you a different way. Is Gerasimov a member of a growing body within the Soviet élite who oppose your leader's publicly declared policies?'

'I cannot answer that because I have no information.

Gerasimov is a humane man. There are others like him in my country, some of them in positions of power. He will not waste human life to no purpose. That is why he has always been popular with his troops. They know he will not ask them to sacrifice their lives needlessly. He made it clear to me that he opposes the official Soviet line on West Berlin. He believes it to be wrong. I know of no evidence to suggest that in this case he is acting other than on his own initiative. He wants to prevent people from dying. He wants to save lives. Is that so hard to understand?'

'All of which is very laudable. But I come back to my point. If this is so important, why you? Why not someone known to us? He must know you would carry no credibility here. You can understand our difficulty, can't you?'

Berlin shrugged his shoulders. There was nothing more to say. Hart's questions lay beyond his competence to answer. The room was still. Outside he could hear the distant sound of a motor-mower.

★

Tea was brought, three mugs on a tray, all sweetened with sugar which Berlin found hard to swallow, but his throat was dry and he needed liquid. The silent man – Berlin was sure he was American – whispered something in Hart's ear and left the room. Hart smiled at Berlin, a wistful, distant smile. They drank their tea in silence.

As soon as the silent American returned – his tea remained untouched, Berlin noticed – the interrogation began again.

'On many occasions in recent weeks,' Hart said, 'your First Secretary has been publicly very belligerent towards the West. He's made remarks like, "I want to bury imperialism", and "I will bring the West to its knees." He boasts of the huge Soviet missile advantage over the West. Your engineers have put the first man into space. Now they are about to surprise us with an orbiting craft that will be able to fire nuclear missiles at any target in the Western world. He has signed a treaty with the

GDR that threatens the position of the Western Allies in Berlin. He is your leader. He knows your military capability better than anyone. If the situation were as dire as you and Marshal Gerasimov claim it is, I very much doubt that he would take the line he does. He would temper his aggression to bring it in line with reality.'

The more Hart spoke, the more Berlin felt what small advantage he had slipping away. Somehow he had to wrest control of this meeting from his interrogators.

'It is the First Secretary's wild and unjustified statements that have built this opposition to him,' Berlin said. 'That is what has forced Marshal Gerasimov to send me to you.'

'You say that, when only a few months ago you were celebrating sending the first man into space.' Hart sounded incredulous. 'It doesn't fit, does it, this modest approach, this sudden burst of truth about the few weapons you have at your disposal.'

Berlin remained silent. He could guess what was coming next.

'That brings us to the notoriously invisible Professor Radin. How is the professor? We hear he's not been in the best of health lately.'

'Viktor Radin is dead.'

'That's not what your people are saying. Very much the opposite, in fact. The message we're getting is that he's alive and well and working on this orbiting platform.'

'He was my friend for years. I knew him very well. I can assure you he is dead.'

'Why should we believe you?' The silent man uttered his first words since they had come into the room. He spoke with an American accent. Berlin felt he was under attack from both sides. 'What proof have you got?'

'Radin was suffering from cancer of the liver. The disease was diagnosed as terminal in May. He was not given long to live. None the less, the Kremlin ordered that a number of different cures be tried, some of them extreme. Viktor suffered. He begged the doctors to stop experimenting on him. They were not allowed to do so. He died two months ago.'

'Our evidence contradicts everything you say.' The American again. 'All our intelligence suggests that Radin is very much alive and at work.'

'Your intelligence is wrong.'

'Did you go to his funeral?'

'He did not have a funeral. There has been no public announcement of his death in the Soviet Union. This was deliberate policy to conceal the fact of his death.'

'Why would you want us to believe he is still alive?' the American asked.

'In order to sustain your belief in the threats that the First Secretary has made. I can assure you, the orbiting space platform is a dream, and whoever dreamed it up was not Radin. I know for certain that he did not even embark upon any preliminary studies for such a vehicle. If Viktor Radin were here now, he would tell you that such an idea is years away from realisation.'

'Then why did the First Secretary boast in front of the world that you are close to making this space platform a reality?'

'To intimidate the West. It would appear that he has been successful.'

'And to keep the opposition at home at bay?' the American suggested. 'To show he's not soft on the Americans?'

'Quite possibly,' Berlin said. 'Quite possibly.'

He was suddenly overcome with a desire to sleep, to close his eyes and drift away out of these men's cynical power, to escape the constant battering of questions to which he did not know the answers.

★

The light was fading. Berlin had lost all sense of time now.

The urge to sleep was overwhelming. But the questions continued. Hart was tireless in his interrogation.

'I want to return to your relationship with Viktor Radin. You say you were a close friend of his. How close?'

Berlin hesitated. What was he supposed to say? 'I saw him when he was in Moscow. We would eat together sometimes in his apartment. Viktor was divorced. He never remarried. He liked company in the evenings, when he was not working. He took an interest in my career. He encouraged me.'

'Did he talk to you about his work?'

'No. He never mentioned anything he was engaged in.'

'He never complained about the bureaucracy, about his impatience with red tape? Nothing like that?'

'Never to me.'

'So you'd meet in his apartment, have something to eat, talk about history, and politics too, I suppose?'

'Viktor had little time for politics. His whole life was driven by a single vision, to get men into space. His relaxation was to discuss history with me. I would test my ideas on him. He was a very well-read man.'

Hart leaned forwards and handed Berlin a photograph. 'If I am not mistaken, this is a photograph of a meeting you had with Radin when he was ill.'

He saw himself sitting on the grass beside Viktor in his wheelchair. How ill Viktor looked. He wondered how British Intelligence had got hold of the photograph.

Berlin nodded. 'Yes. That was the last time I saw him alive. He died a few days later.'

'What did you talk about? Were there any last things he needed to say to you?'

Last things. Why did that phrase keep recurring?

'He knew he was dying.' He hesitated. What should he say? Nothing mattered more than that they should believe him. Should he mention Kuzmin's report? 'He gave me a document. He made me swear I would show it to no one.'

'What kind of document?'

'It was a report by a senior engineer at the Baikonur Cosmodrome on a number of design failures in Radin's new rocket that had not been fixed before the scheduled date of the rocket launch.'

'Can you explain that further, please?' the American asked.

'Peter Kuzmin was the Flight Engineer on Viktor's last project. They had worked together for a number of years. They trusted each other. Kuzmin was alarmed at the drop in standards since Viktor's absence due to ill-health. He was concerned for the safety of the launch. He wrote a secret report to Viktor to bring this to his attention.'

'Was he right to be concerned?'

'Viktor told me that afternoon that his rocket had blown up on the launch pad. Kuzmin died in the disaster, along with nearly two hundred other people.'

'When did this occur? Can you put a date on it?'

'In May of this year.'

Hart looked at the silent American. 'May, George. Do you hear that? May.' He turned back to Berlin. 'What can you tell us about the rocket that exploded?'

'I can only describe it as Viktor described it to me.'

'Go ahead.'

'He said it was the biggest rocket in the world, far bigger than anything that had flown before, and at least twice as powerful as that which lifted Gagarin into space. He knew it was the last launch he would ever see, and he wanted it to fly. He was greatly distressed at the disaster. He said this disaster would set Soviet plans back by at least a year, probably more.'

The room was silent. Hart walked away to the window and looked out into the evening darkness. 'What exploded that day,' he repeated, 'was the biggest rocket in the world.'

Berlin knew that, in some way he did not understand, his attempt to tell the truth had destroyed his case.

*

He had supper alone. Hart had explained that he and George

had 'to put their heads together'. He imagined they would return after he had eaten but they didn't. He waited. He skimmed a magazine about life in the English countryside, full of houses for sale and pictures of young women announcing their engagements. He tried to examine his responses, to see where he had gone wrong, whether his mistake had been avoidable – 'all mistakes are avoidable', a voice from his schooldays repeated in his mind. 'Our task is to achieve perfection.' To his surprise he found that he was unable to reconstruct his interrogation. Mysteriously, his memory seemed to have been wiped clean. After a while, he was overcome once more by a feeling of intense fatigue. His eyes closed and he slept

*

The lights came on and Berlin awoke suddenly. For a moment he could not remember where he was. He heard Hart saying, 'We're sorry to have kept you so long. Do you realise, it's after midnight, George. You gave us a lot to think about.'

'Well?' It was all Berlin could find to say. He felt like a man about to receive a sentence for a crime of which he was innocent.

'Do we accept your story? That is the big question that has been preoccupying us. Do we trust you as a bona fide messenger from the Marshal of the Red Army? The short answer, Dr Berlin, is no, we don't. We believe that you are faithfully giving us the story you were told to give us. Our difficulty is, we don't accept the motives of the man who sent you, therefore we don't accept your story. That's our difficulty in a nutshell, isn't it, George? What you've told us doesn't add up. We think it's a nice try to make us lower our guard at a moment of great political tension but it's not one we're going to fall for.'

'Nice try,' George repeated. 'That's right.'

He found it impossible to sleep. It was not just the heat, though there was not a breath of wind and the humidity was high, it was a sense that something significant was about to happen, an event of such magnitude that he knew it would change his life for ever. He was afraid to tell anyone about his sudden premonition, certainly not Anton, who would have mocked him mercilessly in front of all his friends, especially Igor, and they would have joined his brother in laughing at him.

For a day or two his mother watched him closely as if he was sickening for something. She fussed over him more than usual, touching his forehead to see if he had a temperature. 'You look flushed, Andrei. Are you all right?' She brushed his hair away from his forehead, and left a glass of water by his bed. Once, in the middle of the night, she crept into his room and for a few moments lay beside him. He pretended to be asleep.

For two days and nights nothing happened. He fell asleep at dawn and had to be woken by his mother, who worried about his pale appearance and the darkening shadows under his eyes.

'It's the heat,' he told her. 'It's so difficult to get to sleep.'

On the third night, he was sitting up in bed holding the glass against his cheek – even that was warm now – when he heard the sound of a car drawing up in the street below. Doors opened and slammed shut. Boots rang on the pavement. Voices came, though he couldn't make out what they were saying. He crept to the window and looked out. He counted four men in dark suits before they disappeared into his building.

He went to the bedroom door, opened it quietly and listened. The flat was silent, The only sound he heard was that of his brother Anton snoring heavily in the other bed. Then he heard footsteps running up the stairs, fists hammering heavily on the front door of the apartment. Someone pressed the bell continuously. He heard his father's name called. The light went on in his parents' bedroom. His father came out, followed by his mother. How young she was, he thought, how delicate and vulnerable.

His father opened the door. The men – he was sure they were policemen – rushed in. They behaved as he expected them to. They told his father to get dressed. He was to come with them at once. Why? he heard his father ask. What for? But he got no reply, only the order to do as they said and quickly, they were in a hurry.

His mother was crying, clinging desperately to his father's arm. He saw his father push her away. It was not rejection but the gesture of a frightened man. One of the policemen would stay behind, they were told. In an hour or two they would come back to search the apartment. In the meantime, nothing was to be disturbed, nothing removed. The front door slammed. Andrei heard footsteps clattering quickly down the stone steps, and his mother crying in her room.

He crept back into bed, covering himself with a single sheet. Later, his mother came in and lay on the bed beside him, holding his hand against her, kissing his hair and crying softly but saying nothing.

All the time, in the bed opposite, Anton snored.

*

His father's trial lasted less than half an hour. Photographs were produced of the defaced sculptures. His father, white and unshaven, denied any desecration. Why would he damage his own work? What was the point? He was a sculptor, an artist.

He was privileged to create the likeness of the Great Leader and other heroes of the Soviet Union. They were the work of his own hands. It was madness to suggest that he would destroy what he had so painstakingly made. Repeatedly he said he was not the perpetrator of this terrible act.

If he had not defaced the statues of the Head of State, the prosecutor asked in a menacingly quiet voice, who did? The court waited. His father had no answer. He could only shake his head, sob and protest his innocence. Without evidence of these acts of desecration, brought to the notice of the authorities by a loyal citizen of the Soviet Union, the judge said in his summing-up, this case would have gone undetected. He praised the writer of the anonymous letter that had revealed the depths of the crime against the Great Leader. Andrei felt his mother tighten her grip on his arm.

His father, trembling as he waited for his sentence, never once looked back at his wife and son.

*

When he saw his father again he did not recognise him. In five years he had become a shrunken old man. The stocky frame was gone. His arms and legs were like sticks now, and the lines of his skull showed through his prison-pale skin. He had lost his hair and his teeth and his eyes had a frightened look about them. He refused to speak of his experiences, except to say that they were too terrible to repeat. In her horror at what his time in prison had done to him, his mother hardly spoke to her husband. She could not bring herself to touch this diminished man, this husk who bore little resemblance to the artist who had been taken from her. His father seldom went out, preferring to remain within the narrow confines of the apartment.

He refused to return to his studio, and disowned all his sculpture. He asked Andrei's mother to remove the bust he had sculpted of her, and she hid it in a cupboard. He had no profession any more, he said, because he had no life. That had been stolen from him by the injustice of the charges against him and the sentence he had been given by the court. The years in prison had killed his soul. He no longer shared his wife's bedroom, but slept on a low sofa in the living room of the small apartment. He drank and occasionally, in a drunken stupor, he would try to hit Andrei's mother. He no longer had any strength and she was able to push him away. She said nothing in his presence, living in a private world of her own silence. Andrei spent as much time as he could away from the apartment. His brother had already left home to train on submarines in Murmansk.

When he was home, his father hardly acknowledged Andrei's presence. On the few occasions that he did look at him, Andrei had the unmistakable feeling that he knew what he had done and that he would never forgive him.

14

1

'Today the Soviet government detonated a one-hundred-megaton nuclear bomb in the atmosphere, breaking the treaty with the West to ban all such tests.'

Pountney is in Berlin. It is a cold autumn evening. He wears a dark overcoat. As he talks to the camera, people pass him on the pavement and cars with headlights blazing race down the street.

'There can be little doubt that this was a deliberate act to increase international tension and put pressure on the West to give in to Soviet demands over Berlin.'

The camera moves past Pountney to a checkpoint where, under bright lights, American troops stand with automatic weapons at the ready. In the background, armoured personnel vehicles can be seen.

'Today the city has gone about its business as usual. But the people are understandably nervous. The talk is of the likelihood of war, brought that much closer by the news of the Soviet nuclear test. American reinforcements, under the command of General Clay, have been arriving over the past two days. There are growing signs of battle readiness here. Have they brought nuclear warheads with them? That is the question most in need of an answer. Speculation is rife. There can be little doubt that this is a city preparing for war.'

'What time is it?' Kate asked.

'Time to get up.'

'It can't be.'

'Come here.' He took both her hands and pulled her gently from the bed, enveloping her in his arms as he did so. 'Remember this little room,' he whispered. 'Fix it in your mind. This is our room. Remember that we were happy here.'

★

Kate knocked on the door a second time, but still there was no answer. Could she have made a mistake? She put down her bag and looked at her diary. No, she was right. She was meant to be at his apartment at ten-thirty today, Thursday. She knocked again, this time louder. Silence. She waited. The door to the next apartment opened slightly. She saw an elderly face staring one-eyed at her.

'I've come for my lesson with Mr Vinogradoff,' Kate said in Russian. Why did she sound apologetic? 'I wondered if you knew where he was.'

The door was closed and the lock turned. She waited. She could hear whispers. The door opened again.

'Come in, please.'

The curtains had been pulled against the strong sunlight, and at first she found it hard to adjust her sight. The flat was smaller than Vinogradoff's and decorated with a few heavy pieces of furniture, some photographs, though of whom she couldn't make out, and thick carpets. The old woman was dressed in widow's black and ancient slippers.

'In here.' Kate was led by the hand into another darkened room. She sensed rather than saw the presence of someone else.

'Kate, I'm sorry. I'm so sorry.'

Vinogradoff stood up. His suit was more crumpled than before and his expression was a mixture of depression and fear. She had never seen him like this.

'What's happened?'

'I cannot tell you in my own words,' he replied. 'But I know you will not be satisfied until I have given you an explanation. Better that I take you there. What you see will speak for itself.'

'Is it safe?' the old woman asked.

'What's the difference between a moment of safety and a moment of risk?' Vinogradoff said sharply. 'There are no safe times any more. We live in permanent danger.'

He put his hands on the old woman's shoulders and bent low to kiss her on both cheeks. 'Thank you for sheltering me, Mrs Markova. I am grateful.'

She touched his cheek with her hand. Kate could see that there were tears in her eyes. Vinogradoff turned to Kate. 'Come,' he said. 'Let me show you what they have done.'

The flat had been devastated. The contents of drawers littered the floor, chairs and tables had been knocked over, crockery smashed, cushions and mattresses ripped open with knives, the carpet and even some floorboards had been torn up in a frenzied search. In one corner, propped up against the wall, lay the remains of a cello. Its strings had been torn from it and someone had kicked in the side. The bow had been snapped in two.

'Who did this?' Kate asked.

'The KGB,' he replied.

'Why? What do they want?'

'They fear witnesses to the truth,' Vinogradoff said. 'Because it can take so many forms, they must search everywhere for the smallest sign of its existence and then destroy it.'

'What were they looking for?' she whispered.

'A few sheets of paper on which some notes were written.'

'Your music?' Vinogradoff nodded. 'Did they find it?'

'No.'

'That's good, isn't it?'

For a moment he seemed to struggle for words. 'There is nothing to find. My score no longer exists. I have destroyed it.'

Destroyed – the lovely piece he had asked her to play. How could he do that to his own music? What could have driven him to such a desperate action?

'Why?' It was all she could say. 'Why?'

'They want to silence me. My music was disloyal.' He laughed drily. 'Take away my music and I am denied a voice. I am made safe. I would rather destroy what is mine than have others do it for me.'

'How can music be disloyal?' It was so ridiculous she wanted to laugh.

'In this country,' Vinogradoff said quietly, 'art's sole function is to proclaim the glorious virtues of the Soviet way.'

'That is the greatest lie of all,' she said.

The radiant future. The promise that could never be delivered. She saw clearly then for the first time the scale of the deception practised on the people. You cannot play the music of Bach, Brahms, Dvořák, and then submit your own music to people with no understanding of art, who respond to barren instructions from those in command who in turn are as ignorant as those who carry out their orders. You cannot fix music to the mast of socialism, call it to account against tenets that have nothing to do with musical form and expect it to have any originality. Music comes from the heart, and what the heart says must be true. It was the human heart they feared.

'Why are they afraid of what you have written?' she asked suddenly.

'Won't my answer place you in danger too?'

'I don't care about that,' she replied, not knowing if she meant it or not.

Vinogradoff thought for a moment. 'Since it is over now, I see no reason why you should not know.'

He had composed an oratorio, he said, the setting to music of a long poem written over the years by unknown prisoners in the gulags, the secret system of concentration camps that Stalin had set up across the country in which to incarcerate anyone who opposed his way.

'My father spent ten years in one of those terrible places. His only crime was to play the violin. When he was released, he recited that poem to me one night and I wrote it down. Weeks later he died. He had lost the ability to play his beloved violin and it broke his heart. I promised myself then that one day I would raise a memorial to him in the only way I knew how, through music I would write.'

He paused for a moment, overcome with emotion. 'The existence of these camps is an open secret never officially acknowledged. You will find them listed on no maps, you will never read their names. Yet it is to this state within a state that the so-called enemies of socialism are sent. It is fear of these terrible penal colonies, where human life no longer has a value, that makes liars and cowards of us all. These forgotten cities in hell,' he added, 'embody all that is worst in our nature. They are vile, cruel places where men are reduced to a status below that of animals. They become slaves. Yet out of these camps of evil and degradation has come something unexpected and wonderful, words that redeem the daily humiliations and violations of the camp guards on their victims. Words of hope and trust in the future from those who cannot speak for themselves, that proclaim a vision of the world as it was and perhaps as it one day might be again. Words whose knowledge is a crime, whose repetition is an act of hostility towards the state. That is what I set to music.'

'What would they have done if they had found the score?' Kate asked.

'I would not be here talking to you now.'

He would be in a cell somewhere, facing the prospect of a rigged trial, years in some distant, forgotten, undiscoverable prison like his father, where he would not be allowed his cello, where he would be made to do manual work that would ruin his hands so that when he was freed, old before his time from malnutrition and the terrible conditions in which he had lived, like his father he would never again be able to take up his profession.

'You may think that destroying my music to spare my life is an act of moral cowardice. But I could not survive in one of those camps. My decision was that it was better to hope that one day I would be able to return to composing than suffer now as a martyr. I hope you will not think badly of me.'

'How could I?' she said. 'What right have I to judge you?'

What she wanted to say was that she felt insulted and sullied by what he had told her, and outraged that the world would now never hear the beautiful music that, for a few moments one afternoon, it had been her pleasure to create.

'Unless I had seen it with my own eyes,' she said, looking round his devastated apartment, 'it would be difficult to believe that this had happened.'

'You have now seen us at our worst. You have met the evil that lives in the heart of this country. You now know the most awful truth of all, that to survive in this madhouse, we must all collaborate in the destruction of truth. I am no more courageous than my neighbour. I am ashamed to tell you that I have destroyed my manuscript to save myself, but it is true. If we are to live until tomorrow, we must all deceive ourselves every minute of the day. We have no strength to resist, only to survive. That is why we are a compromised people. The life we try to lead is not the truth, and so long as we live in these conditions it never will be. The truth is black and bitter and concealed. It is suppressed by those who control our lives because they fear that if we come too close to it, we will see them exposed for what they are – cruel guardians of a worthless dogma.'

She was no longer listening to him. All she could hear was the lilting notes of the piece she had played: the sound of water racing over stones, the humming of insects, the rustle of the breeze through grass, the stillness of a summer afternoon. How could such beauty betray anyone?

'Is that right?' she asked, humming a bar or two.

'Yes.' He hummed the melodic line with her and developed it.

'You see,' she smiled. 'Your music is not dead.'

'You must explain that to me,' he said.

'You can remember the piece, can't you?'

'Every note. So long as I can breathe, it will be here, locked in my heart.'

'Then sing it to me. Sing it to me now.'

He looked at her, with no understanding of what she was saying. She saw a poor, diminished, desolate man, standing among the ruins of his apartment, holding in his hand a broken cello bow and staring at her without knowing what she was saying.

'I want you to sing your piece to me.'

For a moment he did nothing. Then out of the silence came the sound of his voice, and the first notes of the hymn to the unbreakable dignity of human life that he had composed.

'Do you understand now?' she said. 'I will learn your music, the words and the notes. When I leave Moscow I will take your music with me. No one will know because no one can see into my head – not even an X-ray can find this. When I get home I will transcribe it, then I will get it played.'

'You must not put my name to it,' he said, suddenly terrified. 'If you do that, they will arrest me, my wife and child. They will separate us and send us to different prisons.'

'Then it will be music without a name, without a composer, an anonymous cry of truth from a distant country. No one will know who composed it, nor where nor when.

The mystery will remain until the day when you can identify yourself with what you have written.'

He reached across and, taking her hand, held it to his lips. She felt the warmth of his tears on her fingers.

'If there is a God,' he said quietly, 'he must have sent you to me.'

3

Koliakov saw the headline on a newsagent's stand as he came out of the tube. He bought an evening paper and read with incredulity that the Soviet government had exploded a nuclear device in the atmosphere. This was madness, he kept repeating to himself, sheer madness. If it was scare tactics to heighten the tension around Berlin, then the risk was out of all proportion to the gain. Use Soviet troops, as they'd been used in Budapest, fight if you have to, but reject weapons of mass, indiscriminate slaughter. What hope can there be if you make a poisonous, uninhabitable desert of the world you wish to conquer?

Was this act a consequence of Medvedev's appointment? He could hear that shrill, coarse voice arguing that the Test Ban Treaty should be ignored, that the West must be frightened into a corner by a show of Soviet strength. He could imagine the smile that would touch the corners of his mouth as he saw his argument gaining ground. By the time Koliakov reached Victoria, he was certain that Medvedev was the author of this outrage.

Once more the image of an old man lying dead on the hard earth flashed before his eyes. He felt again the pain in his head, as if something was trying to melt his eyes. He rubbed his face frantically with both hands to get rid of it but without success. The only relief, he knew, was to be found in the darkness of his room.

He walked back to his lodgings in his usual manner,

doubling back on himself and setting traps for anyone who might be shadowing him. He warmed some soup on the gas burner in the fireplace and drank it while skimming the rest of the paper. Somewhere inside he read a short paragraph about the discovery of a woman's body in a mews house in Knightsbridge. Police, it said, were pursuing their inquiries.

Then he broke open what he called his emergency supplies, a bottle of vodka he had brought with him from his flat. He drank while he considered his next move.

4

It took a long time to get through but Berlin hung on because he was desperate. He had got a handful of sixpences and shillings from the porter Wilkins. He had found the number from directory enquiries. He dialled, waited, inserted his coins.

'I would like to speak to Mr Pountney please.'

'Trying to connect you,' a girl's voice said.

There was a ringing tone but no one answered. He waited. If he hung on long enough surely someone would have to answer. Be patient.

'Hello?' Another woman's voice.

'Mr Pountney please.'

'I'll try to find him. Just a moment.'

He heard a muffled conversation. He heard someone ask: 'Is Gerry back from Berlin?' 'Last night,' came the reply. Then silence. Suddenly a new voice asked: 'Who do you want?'

'I am waiting for Mr Pountney.'

'I don't know if he's here. Who shall I say is calling?'

'Say a friend from his past. He won't remember my name.'

'All right.'

More muffled conversation. Then a series of clicks. For a moment he thought he'd been cut off. Patience, he said to himself again. Someone picked up the receiver.

'This is Gerald Pountney.'

Berlin felt a moment of intense relief. He had found Pountney. He was his last hope.

'Hello? Are you still there?'

'I am Andrei Berlin.'

'Who?'

'We met in Moscow some years ago. We were introduced at a concert by Annabel Leigh. Does that jog your memory?'

'Good heavens. Where are you? Not in Moscow, surely.'

'At this moment I am in Cambridge as the guest of the university. I am here for a few days to give a series of lectures.'

'We must meet,' Pountney said. What was Berlin up to? Was he allowed off the leash at all? Berlin didn't understand. Did he have any free time? What about lunch tomorrow? Yes, he would like that. Pountney would come to Cambridge, he hadn't been back for years, it would be a pleasure seeing the old place again. They'd go to one of his favourite pubs where the beer was good and the food was passable.

'All set then,' Pountney said.

'It would seem so, yes.'

'One question before I ring off. How did you know where to find me?'

'It was not difficult,' Berlin said. 'I saw you on television. You haven't changed a bit.'

5

Hart tried the Television Centre but Pountney wasn't there. He'd gone to Cambridge for the day, he was told. He'd be back later in the afternoon. Hart tried his flat on the off chance but the phone rang unanswered. Damn. He needed to alert Pountney that the girl had been found dead and Koliakov had gone missing. The Soviet Embassy was denying this, but his own people had reported that the Russian hadn't been back to his flat for two nights now. Had he killed the girl? Until they knew the cause of death, it was hard to say. Murdering a prostitute wasn't Koliakov's style, but then visiting her wasn't either. Was it likely that he would have killed her to destroy the evidence Pountney might give Smolensky? The Russian had always struck him as a circumspect man who did nothing instinctively. Every act was carefully weighed. Maybe somewhere along the line he had missed a vital clue about Koliakov and he was misreading him. Somehow, though, he did not see the Russian as a murderer.

Why had Pountney gone to Cambridge? Then he remembered. Pountney had met Berlin in Moscow. He'd identified him in the photograph as the man talking to Viktor Radin. Why would Pountney want to see Berlin? What was the connection – unless Berlin had asked to see him.

He telephoned the college. Dr Berlin was out, he was told. They had no idea when he would be back. Hart left a number Berlin was to ring when he returned. He didn't hold out much hope that he would call back, not after his rejection of Berlin's message. But it was all he could do.

6

'Why did you contact me?' Pountney asked. They were sitting outside the Anchor, watching the water spill over the weir.

'You are the only person I know in this country.'

'You sound as if you need help.'

'I do,' Berlin said.

'Fire away.'

'It is a long story. You must be patient with me. It begins weeks ago with an invitation to lecture at Cambridge, which I accept because to come here has been my dream for many years. I am an academic historian, as you know. I teach students in Moscow, I do research. I live a normal life.' He grinned sheepishly. 'Normal, you understand, by Soviet standards. During the summer, this crisis builds up in Germany. The political situation gets worse. The Wall is built dividing Berlin. The First Secretary announces this orbiting satellite from which no city or installation in the West will be safe. I become very pessimistic about my visit. I fear my invitation will be withdrawn for political reasons. I continue to prepare my lectures. Nothing happens. No one says to me, no, you may not come. Suddenly here I am and everyone is very kind. I am grateful for that.'

'The university would resist any pressure from the government, but it's unlikely the government would want to get involved.' Pountney smiled at him. 'Our universities are very independent, you know.'

'A few days before I leave Moscow, I am summoned to accompany the Commander of the Army, Marshal Gerasimov, in his car. I am mystified. I do not know Gerasimov. I am not told why he wants to see me.'

'I've heard of Gerasimov,' Pountney said. 'Isn't he a communist of the old guard?'

Berlin nods in agreement. 'When we are alone in his car, he says that when I go to the West, I must deliver a message from him to a senior member of British Intelligence. It is important information about the Soviet readiness for war.'

'You want me to help you make contact with our Intelligence Service, is that it?'

'No, no,' Berlin says. 'I have delivered my message to your people as I was instructed. I have already fulfilled my obligation. The problem is, your Intelligence Service does not believe that the message I bring is true. They have rejected what I have told them. That is why I contacted you.'

7

Koliakov woke refreshed. He looked at his watch. He had been asleep for nearly an hour. The reflection from the street lamp cast a square of light onto the wall of his room above the bed. He gazed at it for a while. Then he yawned and got up. It was time to begin. He sat down at the small table, switched on the light and fed the first sheet into his typewriter.

Minutes of the 107th Meeting of the Disinformation Committee, dated 11 July 1961.
Present: Major-General N. I. Sharankov (chairman), Col. V. Medvedev, Col. G. Koliakov (observer).

Could he remember all the names of the committee? There were nine of them present that night. He thought hard: 'Major L. Simonov, B. I. Chuikov, M. Shtemenko, P. Rotmistrov, A. Sokolov, G. Vasilevksy.'

The chairman said it was his sad duty to report the death the previous day of the Chief Designer of the Soviet space programme. The members of the Committee offered their condolences to the First Secretary on the loss of this great servant of the state.

He thought back to that stifling, interminable evening, reliving his feeling of near-suffocation, his frustration at the inactivity of the committee, how the passivity of his fellow Committee members, so afraid of sticking their necks out, had extended the evening into the early hours while the intensity of the heat had built up. He remembered Medvedev's assured performance – he already clearly knew of his impending promotion – and the way he pushed himself forward into the limelight.

The chairman reminded the Committee that, although little was known of the identity of the Chief Designer outside the Soviet Union, all their intelligence confirmed that the West ascribed the overwhelming successes of the Soviet space programme to his genius. His reputation was a major strategic advantage in the battle against the enemies of socialism. The First Secretary had instructed that the Chief

Designer's death should not rob the Soviet Union of this unique advantage. It was the Committee's task now to devise strategies that would convince the West that the Chief Designer was still alive and working on new projects.

Koliakov smiled with a grim pleasure. As minute-writer, he was the master of his own universe. He could make his players perform as he chose. He would switch roles. What *he* had actually proposed, he would now ascribe to Medvedev. He would rewrite his own part in the proceedings as that of a passive member of the Committee, anonymously nodding through the proposal when a show of hands was called for. Medvedev would take the glory as the architect of the deception. How that would please him – if he ever came to hear of it.

Col. V. Medvedev reminded the Committee that in 1947 he had uncovered the 'Peter the Great' plot against the state, and that subsequently he had successfully poisoned the line of communication established by the traitors to convince the West that the Soviet Union was far behind in the development of a nuclear bomb. This disinformation had had its effect. For months, the West had slowed its efforts, to the great advantage of the Soviet bloc. Meanwhile, social opposition to nuclear weapons had blossomed in Europe, making the management and deployment of nuclear bombs much more difficult.

He would like that, Koliakov thought. His career was based on his one moment of glory. It was always in his interest to remind others of what he had done.

On the same basis, Col. Medvedev now proposed that false information be passed to the West about the imminent launch of an orbiting satellite capable of firing from space missiles fitted with nuclear warheads, from which no location in America would be safe. Such an ambitious project, he stated, could only come from the mind of the Chief Designer. The West would assume, he was sure, that the announcement had the sanction of the Chief Designer. What further proof was needed that he was alive and working?

The Committee asked if this was a project under consideration by any department within the Space Commission. Col. Medvedev assured the meeting that it was not. The idea, he declared, was his own invention. After a thorough discussion, the Committee endorsed the deception and suggested that it now be forwarded to the policy-making group. The chairman confirmed that this would happen within forty-eight hours and that the proposal would become policy immediately thereafter.

Forty minutes later Koliakov had finished. He had embellished the detail of the proposal with some new ideas of his own. He reread his text with quiet satisfaction. Nothing he had written was inauthentic. It was as close to the truth as he could go. He smiled to himself. Only the names had been changed, to incriminate the guilty.

He extracted the carbon copy and laid it carefully face down on the table. He burned the top copy of the minutes together with the carbon paper, crushing them in an ashtray before sluicing the blackened remains into the basin.

He wrote at the head of the copy of the minutes: 'Mr Pountney. The information you have been waiting for.' Then he folded it, sealed it in an envelope on which he wrote Pountney's address, attached a stamp and, locking his door behind him, went out into the night in search of a postbox.

Berlin heard the sound of her shoes on the wooden stairs, a quick knock at the door and she burst in.

'Thank God you're here. I was so worried yesterday.' She was in his arms, kissing him. 'I began to think something had happened to you.' She drew back from him, embarrassed by her impetuosity. 'I'm so sorry. I don't know what you must think of me.'

He looked at her worried expression. Was that the sum of the complications in her life – anxiety about where he'd been? It was her innocence, the simplicity of this woman that made him draw her to him and kiss her. He felt her arms around his neck, and the passion within her.

'I had to see someone yesterday. I should have told you. I'm sorry.'

'I was in a panic all day. You must think that ridiculous.' She stood back, holding both his hands. 'I convinced myself something awful had happened to you. I imagined our Intelligence people had found you, and whisked you away to some secret location for questioning.'

'Nothing like that.' He smiled at her. 'I had to do a commission for a friend. I had a gift to deliver.'

It was a familiar pattern, half lie, half truth. Was there no escape from a world of deceit?

'And today?' she asked.

'Today?' He smiled. 'I have no plans for today.'

'Then I claim the rest of today as mine,' she replied.

*

'Come in.'

Her apartment was on the first floor of a row of Victorian houses in a part of Cambridge that his imagination had never reached. He was, he realised, out of his depth. He knew no landmarks: this was unknown territory. It was light, filled with books, sparsely furnished, and yet it was completely hers. What she needed she had, no more, no less.

'Can I get you something?'

Before he could answer she was in his arms again, pulling him through the room, pushing her hand through his hair, murmuring his name and other words he could not distinguish, her eyes half closed, her lips all over this face, his hands, his fingers. For a moment, until he overcame his surprise and succumbed, she was fighting for him. Then, as she sensed that she had won, her gestures became less frantic and more assured, the desperation replaced by warmth.

He undressed her slowly, touching her body with care, as if too sudden a movement might damage it. Her skin was very white, like china, and she trembled under the touch of his fingers. Her eyes were closed, she was alive only in the world of her senses. All inhibitions, all barriers had fled. She was his completely.

*

The morning sun poured in through the open window. The warmth made her stretch herself as she woke up.

'Hello?' she said smiling. 'Was that a dream, or did it really happen?'

'I would be disappointed if it were only a dream,' he said.

'Oh, Andrei.' She held him tightly in her arms. 'I will never let you go now. You know that, don't you?'

I never want you to let me go, he thought. But I know I will have to.

*

He heard a clock chiming, and the strange echo that he was getting used to of other clocks chiming across the town but never quite in harmony. He forgot to count the number of strokes. He no longer had any idea of the time.

He slept after that. If he had dreams they left him unscathed. As he awoke he felt that he had been washed clean, like standing naked under a fountain as the water streamed over him. He was renewed, and for the moment at least, the cares of the world that he carried with him were pushed aside. Not for long, he told himself. To escape for ever was impossible. But for now – for now he must celebrate his moments of freedom.

'I fell in love with you the moment I saw you,' she said suddenly. 'The moment you came through the barrier.'

He laughed and said: 'I knew something had happened.' He regretted what he had said immediately. How arrogant can you be?

'I couldn't believe what I felt. You appeared, and the next instant I was in the control of a force more powerful than any I have encountered before. After I left you that night, I couldn't sleep. I kept worrying what you must have thought of me. I know I didn't stop talking. I feel very ashamed of my behaviour.'

'It was the kindest thing you could have done,' he said. 'I was too overwhelmed to speak.'

'Overwhelmed?'

'By what was happening to me.'

'Tell me,' she said. 'Tell me everything.'

He sat up against the pillow. 'I have always known that Cambridge held my destiny. That is why I tried so hard to come here, and I was always so disappointed when my attempts failed. Even when you wrote to me with your invitation, I did not allow myself to believe it would happen. I expected some malign force to intervene and prevent me from leaving Moscow. Now do you understand why I could hardly speak when we had dinner in that restaurant, with all those people around us? I could not believe that what I had dreamed of for so long was happening to me. It was a very emotional moment. That is why I was happy to listen.'

She kissed him, and he felt her body against him.

★

'Are you hungry?' she asked.

He laughed. 'I was hoping you would ask that.'

'Stay there,' she commanded.

He watched her get out of bed. There was an unrealised beauty about her. It was not the slimness of her body nor the whiteness of her skin, it was her unawareness of what she was. How strange that this woman should hide herself behind her glasses and the full clothes she wore, loose skirts, loose shirts, as if she were concealing herself among so many layers of disguise. Who was she when she was naked? He knew now. He understood. She was a woman who had satisfied so much in her life but not her craving for love. She yearned for affection, for companionship. That is what he had felt when he first saw her. They were both lonely people for whom love had brought no happiness.

Until now.

*

She knelt down beside the bed and put the tray on the sheets.

'I hope it'll do,' she said. 'I wasn't really prepared for this.'

'It's wonderful,' he said. 'Thank you.'

She poured him a glass of wine from an opened bottle – had she been drinking alone? She put salad and cold meat on his plate. She got in beside him, kissed him lightly on the lips and then more deeply on the shoulder. She laughed and pushed the tray away.

'I don't mind how hungry you are,' she said. 'You're going to have to eat later.'

*

By the time he awoke, the sun had moved and the room was in shadow. He did not dare to look at his watch. Time is the enemy of happiness, he thought. All joy is short-lived. The trick is to live as intensely as you can within the moment. This moment must last for as long as it could. He must absorb every second into his memory, he must be able to recapture every moment of this extraordinary day when this woman had revealed herself to him, holding nothing back. There was no concealment in what she felt for him. He knew that she loved him, he had known it before he had kissed her hand on that first day and looked into her eyes and seen the words imprinted there, as clear as if they had been a poster on a wall enjoining him to sacrifice now in order to forge a path to the radiant future.

9

The news of the successful launch of a new Soviet satellite broke just before lunch. It was circling the earth every ninety minutes, and its trajectory took it menacingly over Washington.

'Is it armed?' Hart asked.

'We don't know,' he was told. Nor did it appear that there was any way in which they could find out what kind of threat it posed. The Russians were saying nothing – they didn't have to. It was either a brilliant bluff aimed at making the West believe they had made good the First Secretary's promise, or a very genuine threat – either way, their timing, Hart had to admit, was near-perfect. The Soviets had cleverly succeeded in increasing the tension over Berlin by pushing up the stakes once more.

Hart ran his fingers through his hair. Slowly but inevitably the situation in Berlin was slipping out of control.

'You were the one, weren't you, Andrei?' His mother was shaking her head as if she desperately wanted him to deny the accusation. 'You of all people. You did this terrible thing.'

They were in the small apartment in Moscow. Andrei had known his mother was upset because in the last few days she had hardly spoken to him or his brother Anton. He had tried to keep out of her way for as long as he could but now she had got him alone in the kitchen and she was shouting at him. She was too angry to care if she could be heard in the next-door apartment.

'You defaced his sculptures, didn't you?'

It was impossible to lie to her. 'Yes,' he admitted. 'I did.'

His mother's scream of incomprehension and distress came from deep within her. 'How could you betray your own father?'

'He didn't love you,' Andrei said simply.

'You don't know that.'

'He did it with that girl when we were at the Black Sea. I saw them together. They were lying on the floor of the cinema naked and he was sticking his thing into her. I saw them doing it, Mother. I know it happened.'

'That doesn't mean he didn't love me,' she said in an agonised voice.

Andrei was confused. His mother was not reacting as he had expected her to. He'd imagined she'd be grateful for what he'd done.

'If he did that to her, how can he love you any more?'

'Oh, Andrei.' She put her head in her hands. 'Why didn't you come and tell me about it?'

'I was too ashamed. I didn't know what to say.'

He had tried to find words that would allow him to explain what he'd seen, why he was angry, why he felt this burning compulsion to hurt his father. But he didn't know how to tell her what he wanted to say. His emotions outran the words he could command; they were too overwhelming to be described with any kind of coherence. Words no longer governed his thoughts. He had lost the power of self-expression. And what good would telling her do? She was weak with his father, she never stood up to him. She accepted what he did to her without complaint. Each time she did so, the life in her eyes dulled a little more. He had seen it happen too often. This was too serious to be left to his mother to deal with. That's why he had behaved as he had. This time, he told himself, his father would not get away with it. This time he would protect his mother.

'You're old enough to know that what you'd done was bound to be discovered and your father arrested.' She wiped her face with the corner of her apron but it made no difference to the tears.

'Yes,' he admitted. 'I knew what would happen.' Why couldn't she understand that his father deserved punishment for what he'd done?

'You knew that and still you went ahead. What possessed you, Andrei?'

He's the guilty one, he wanted to shout. *He betrayed you. All I've done is to save you from him. He can't harm you now, he's well out of your reach. Why can't you be happy? Why are you angry with me?*

'How could you stand beside me in the courtroom and watch them send your father to prison, knowing the charges against him were false?'

What was the point in saying anything to her? She wouldn't listen. Say nothing and the storm would pass, it was bound to. It always did with her.

'You saw him trying to defend himself,' she continued. 'You heard him protest again and again that he had done nothing. He swore he'd not been in his studio that day. You saw how the judge wouldn't listen to him. Yet you stood there, knowing he was innocent, not saying a word, not showing any emotion. How could you be so cold-blooded?'

She understood nothing, which made explaining what had gone through his head an impossible task. All she saw was the husband she had lost and the empty years stretching ahead. Why wasn't she glad that he had gone? After all his father had done to her, how was it possible that she should still care for him?

He had another reason for keeping silent. In the courtroom, the prosecutor had held up enlarged black-and-white photographs of the defaced sculptures. He had been shocked by what he had seen. The damage was far worse than anything he had done himself. Someone must have gone in after him and completed the task with a thoroughness he had not dreamed of attempting. The discovery froze him, denying him movement or speech. He felt a spasm of fear spiral through his veins. His father had enemies and they had seen the opportunity that he, Andrei Berlin, had unwittingly given them, and they had used it to destroy him. He had remained silent during the trial because he had lost the power of speech. He found himself up against powerful invisible forces, and he had been almost too frightened to breathe.

'I saw how he treated you,' he told his mother, defiance creeping back into his voice. 'He didn't love you any more.'

'Wasn't that my business?'

'I couldn't bear it any more.'

She went to the sink and poured herself a glass of water. She drank it slowly. She was calmer now, perhaps in her mind coming to terms with her loss.

'When I fell in love with him I knew what sort of a man he

was. Even if I were the most beautiful woman in the world he would still have had other women. That was his nature. I didn't like it, but I couldn't change it. I couldn't even try. But if I loved him, and I did, then I knew that he would always come back to me, and I was right. He always did. That girl you saw wasn't the first. There'd been others before and there were others afterwards. I knew all about it — sometimes he would tell me what he'd done. If I could accept that, why couldn't you?'

Andrei looked at his mother in astonished silence.

'You sent him away, Andrei, and left me with nothing. Can you understand that? You have left me with nothing and ruined my life.'

You've still got me, he wanted to say. *You've still got me*. He wanted to go up to her and put his arms round her, to comfort her, to say that things would improve now they were without him. He found he was rooted to the spot, unable to move and unable to speak. He gazed at his mother with horror in his eyes.

15

1

Pountney is standing near Checkpoint Charlie. He wears an overcoat against the cold, and the wind blows his hair over his face. It is nine p.m. West German time. Behind him, powerful searchlights turn day into night. The area is full of heavily armed American soldiers. Pountney is providing a live televised report from what he describes as 'the front line in this latest and most serious clash between the free world and the Soviet Union'. His coverage of the situation in Berlin is the first part of Julius Bomberg's current affairs programme. It will be followed by a studio debate about whether the defence of the West's right of access to Berlin is worth a war.

'This afternoon I was privileged to watch an American Marine Division practising an assault on a mock-up of the Berlin Wall under the eagle eye of their commanding officer, General Clay. I cannot tell you where this exercise took place, nor how the Americans overcame the natural obstacles that such a Wall poses an attacking force. I can tell you that the efficiency of the Marines was impressive, as was their clear determination to take the offensive in any conflict. We can deduce from this that the Western Alliance is assembling a formidable fighting force as it prepares to resist Soviet claims on the city of Berlin.'

His voice is momentarily drowned as a troop carrier passes behind him. He waits until the roar of its engines dies down before continuing.

'The increase in the military presence here is not one-sided. Over there' – he points towards the darkness beyond Checkpoint Charlie – 'we know because in daylight we can see them, the Soviets are assembling a huge force. They too are engaged in exercises behind the lines. The tension here is electric. You can see it in the strained faces of civilian and soldier alike as West and East face other in the final preparations for war. Every hour the danger of conflict mounts.'

2

'What is it? What's wrong?'

Berlin was sitting in a chair gazing out of the window at the moonlit night. Marion had heard him get out of bed. She knew him well enough now to realise that he was in some kind of distress. At first she was reticent about questioning him. Did this strange man whom she was slowly getting to know want her to get involved with his life? Or was he better off alone? As she stared at his hunched, withdrawn figure, she felt his silent appeal for help.

'What is it?' she asked again.

'I am in trouble,' he said.

'What kind of trouble?'

'It would take a long while to explain.'

'It's a long time till dawn,' Marion said.

'Then we shall see if it is long enough.'

*

Had he intended to tell her? He knew he had woken her when he got out of bed. Was his clumsiness deliberate? He had no way of knowing. But when she spoke to him, he felt a wave of relief at the prospect of confessing the burden he was carrying. He had reached the limit of what he could support alone. The weight of his responsibility since his arrival had become intolerable. If she would listen, he would talk.

When later he tried to recall what he told her, he could not remember. How honest was he? This was a confession to lighten a burden, not to cleanse him morally. He told her about the politics in his country, the recklessness of the First Secretary's unscripted pronouncements, how his belligerence towards the West sickened him. He spoke of how the state could not accept the death of his friend Viktor Radin, and how Marshal Gerasimov had given him a message which no one in the British Intelligence Service would believe was true, how every word he said was met with suspicion. He described his desperation at his failure, how he could not sleep because he was haunted by the consequences if the situation in Germany should suddenly explode into war.

★

She said nothing while he talked. She did not question him when he had finished, though her mind was teeming with questions. She accepted his story unequivocally because she could not imagine him not telling her the truth. Throughout the hour or so it took him to describe what had happened, she willed him to leave nothing out, to open his heart.

When he had finished she said: 'I think I know someone who might help.'

When it was light, she telephoned Michael Scott.

★

'I believe your story,' Michael Scott said. 'I am merely a servant, a voice representing others. I have no power to convince, or to promote a case. All I can do is try to persuade others to talk to you and listen to what you have to say. You understand that?'

★

They walked through St John's and sat on a bench near the

387

Bridge of Sighs. In the distance a young man and woman were playing tennis. The river was deserted, the willows trailing in the slow-moving water as they looked upstream towards Magdalene Bridge. Marion held his hand and felt his tension.

'Three more days,' Berlin said suddenly. 'Then I return home.'

'I know,' she said. 'Three days, one more lecture. Then what?'

They sat in silence. What happens now? She wanted to know. What becomes of us? Is this one of those brief affairs that lights up your life like a flaring match, then dies and is forgotten? Surely it was more than that.

'I came here with a dream of what I imagined freedom would be. I was wrong, of course, my ideas were quite wrong. I have had to learn to be unafraid of the sound of my own voice, even of the sound of my own heart. I have had to learn to trust my instincts. That is very new for me.'

She drew his hand to her lips and kissed it.

'In Moscow, my friend Viktor Radin used to push me to write articles and books. For years I did so. Then one day my inspiration dried up. I was no longer able to write. I had run out of ideas. I know now that it was because I no longer had any beliefs. I doubted everything, especially myself, my own judgement. That is a terrible abyss into which to fall, not any longer to know yourself. I became very frightened. My mind locked itself away and I froze. My life has been suspended for years.'

'Is it suspended now?' Marion asked.

He looked at her and shook his head. 'You have given me back my belief in myself. You have shown me that I am not as worthless as I believed myself to be.'

'When you leave,' she said suddenly, 'my heart will break.' For a moment she felt tears pricking her eyes and she fought to hold them back. 'I have never loved anyone before. For me, love has always been a dismal failure. Then one hot afternoon at Cambridge Station, before we had even spoken to each other, I discovered I had given you my heart.'

★

'Good news,' Michael Scott said. 'At least I think it is. They want to interview you again. My friends would like you to meet a man named Carswell this afternoon. Is that all right?'

★

At four o'clock Koliakov telephoned Merton House. 'I would like to speak to Mr Hart, please,' he said.

3

Hart was furious at the instruction that Nigel Carswell be brought in to interview the two Russians. 'Carswell retired years ago,' he objected. 'We're perfectly capable of dealing with this ourselves. We don't need to dig out relics of the past.'

Carswell was thought to have the necessary background – whatever that meant – and sanction for his recall had been given at the highest level. The argument, Hart saw, was lost before it began. He remembered Carswell. His appearance hadn't lived up to his reputation as a feared inquisitor. He was a large, florid man, painstaking in his method, but there was no spark, only a relentless steadiness as he built up a picture with the care of a miniaturist.

People talked to him, that was his gift. He looked so helpless sometimes, so lost, that you wanted to help him out. It was all a clever disguise, of course, but it got results. He'd come out to Budapest to interview Bobby Martineau the summer before the Revolution. Something had happened between them – Hart didn't know what – because in some unexplained way, after the visit, Martineau was a diminished man.

389

He might make mincemeat of Berlin, but Koliakov was of a different mettle altogether: he was a hardened professional playing a mysterious solitary game. Getting anything out of him other than what he wanted you to know was going to demand more than a light dusting off of old skills.

'Nigel, how are you?' He could hear music in the background. It sounded like Dixieland jazz.

'Struggling with the diminishing capacity of old age, but otherwise not bad. What brings you back into my life after so long, Hugh?'

'We have a problem, and we think you might be the man to help us.'

'I retired five years ago. What possible interest can I hold for you now?'

'We have someone we'd like you to talk to.'

'A Russian?'

'Two Russians. One's a KGB colonel. The other's a historian.'

'They want to talk?'

'The historian already has. It's the other one that interests us.'

'When would you want me?'

'As soon as you can get here. I'm sending a car now.'

'It'll mean missing a game of golf.'

'The course will still be there tomorrow, Nigel.'

'I can see you aren't a golfer, Hugh.'

*

'How about a sandwich?'

It was well past one when Hart completed his briefing. Carswell had listened carefully, taking a few notes and asking the occasional question. The room was filled with the sweet, sickly smell of his pipe tobacco.

Carswell shook his head. 'A cup of tea would do me fine. No milk, no sugar. Doctor's orders,' he added ruefully. He pushed his spectacles onto his forehead and leaned back in his chair to stretch. 'I'd be teeing off about now if you hadn't called me.'

'What do you make of it?' Hart asked.

'Radin's the hinge, isn't he?' Carswell seemed to be talking to himself. 'If we can convince ourselves that he's dead, then we can be reasonably certain that recent Soviet actions – the testing of the bomb, the launch of the satellite, the build-up of their military forces in East Berlin – are all intended to deceive the West into believing the Soviets are more powerful than they actually are. The aim is to get the West to concede to Soviet demands before a shot gets fired. On that basis, we hold our nerve and push the Soviets to the very edge.

'On the other hand, if we believe the official Soviet line that Radin is alive, then our reading has to be very different. The Soviets have a huge military advantage over the West on the ground and in space which, from what we know, it would be foolish, not to say catastrophic, to try to resist. On that interpretation, Berlin is not worth a war. We should be conceding as little as we can get away with, but we should certainly agree to let them have the city of Berlin.'

'In other words,' Hart said, 'do we give in or do we outface them?'

'The dilemma hasn't changed over the years,' Carswell said thoughtfully. 'The difference is, the stakes have been raised to a very high level.'

'And time is now very much against us.'

Outside a clock chimed the half-hour. Both men were silent, troubled by the judgements they would have to make before the day ended.

'One last thing,' Hart said. 'I'd like you to take a look at this.'

'What is it?'

'Our unexpected present from Koliakov which arrived yesterday. It's the minutes of a meeting of a KGB planning committee that took place in July. The document asserts that Radin is dead and outlines the Soviet strategy to keep us thinking that he remains alive. It explains much of what is happening now.'

Carswell held the paper up to the light and studied it. 'Consistency of blotting paper. Unmistakably Soviet.' He held it under his nose and sniffed. 'It's got that familiar gluey smell. Nothing changes, does it?'

'Is it genuine?'

'The paper's genuine. So is the typewriter. If it's not the real thing, it's a bloody good imitation.' He took his pipe out of his mouth to inspect the bowl. It appeared to have gone out. 'Do you have a translation?'

'Right here.'

Carswell skimmed it. 'Good God,' he exclaimed. 'Peter the Great. I never expected to hear that name again. There can't be many Soviets who know about Peter.' He lit his pipe again, disappearing briefly behind a cloud of blue smoke. 'I'd better get down to work. I'd like a word with Koliakov first, if I may.'

4

'Over there.'

Pountney raced forward. His cameraman and soundman followed, struggling with their equipment. From their vantage point, they could look down Friedrichstrasse to the crossing point as the Soviet tanks hove into view in the distance and rumbled towards the border.

Pountney spoke breathlessly into his microphone. 'The main force of thirty or more Soviet tanks has halted near the Brandenburg Gate. A smaller force of ten has peeled away and is now advancing menacingly up Friedrichstrasse towards the crossing point at Checkpoint Charlie. They appear to be halting on either side of the street only yards from the border between East and West Berlin.'

From below he heard the rumble of American tanks as they prepared to move into position.

'Below me, I can see the Americans mobilising in response. They too are advancing up Friedrichstrasse.'

As he spoke, ten American M-48s rolled forward into view, the earth throbbing to the sound of their engines.

'The roar of the engines is deafening.' Pountney was shouting now. 'There are blue clouds of diesel smoke on both sides of the crossing point. The Americans too are moving up to the border. There is less than a hundred yards between the two forces as they face each other.'

They were like athletes, he thought, waiting in their blocks for the gun to sound to start the race. Only now, the sound of the first shot would precipitate a war.

'All forces in Berlin are now on full alert. The situation is fraught with danger. This is a real confrontation. The gun barrels on each side contain live ammunition. If someone does not pull back soon, we may be only minutes away from the start of war.'

5

'If these minutes are genuine,' Carswell said.

'Of course they are genuine.'

'They would appear to be convincing evidence that Viktor Radin is dead and that therefore the present show of Soviet strength over Berlin may be no more than bluff.'

Koliakov lit a cigarette. 'I cannot tell you what is bluff and what is not. All I can say is that I was present at the meeting described in those minutes. I can confirm that what you have read is an accurate record of what happened. The policy proposed by Colonel Medvedev was agreed.'

'There is no doubt therefore that Professor Radin is dead.'

'No doubt at all.'

'Why is the Soviet Union so keen to conceal his death?'

Koliakov laughed. 'I would have thought the answer was obvious.'

'I would still like to hear your explanation.'

'With Radin gone, our space programme no longer has its visionary driving force. Power will now move from a courageous and inspired leader to the bureaucrats. Do I have to describe the consequences?'

Carswell wrote on the paper in front of him. Koliakov waited.

'What puzzles me,' Carswell said quietly, 'is why you are prepared to tell us this. Aren't you giving us a very valuable secret?'

'Of course.'

'You don't strike me as a defector or a traitor.'

'I am neither.'

'Then why are you doing this?'

'I am giving you this information because I am a patriot.'

'Some of your colleagues might find that hard to accept.'

Koliakov shrugged his shoulders. 'That may be so.'

'That doesn't answer my questions.'

'I am opposed to senseless slaughter.'

'You believe that Soviet policy will lead to senseless slaughter?'

'If Berlin explodes, yes.'

'What brought you to such a view, Colonel?'

'If I convince you, you will believe me. Is that it?'

'Probably.'

'Very well.' Koliakov stubbed out his cigarette and immediately lit another one. 'I must take you back a few years. In 1947, the Soviet Union was building its first nuclear bomb. It was a slow and difficult process. Our politicians were very unhappy at the pace of progress. We had to do something to make the West feel safe enough to slow its own hectic rate of development. So we manufactured an explosion in the laboratory where the bomb was being built. Many died, not just technicians, civilians too. The news was deliberately leaked to the West through the spy Peter the Great whom, by this time, we had turned. The West's assessment was that the Soviet Union's nuclear policy was in grave difficulty. That was what we wanted you to believe, and for a time you did. And much to our advantage.'

'I remember,' Carswell said. There was an edge of bitterness in his voice.

'Our deception was very successful. Its effect lasted for months. You slowed your nuclear development while we hastened ours. A sense of complacency emerged in the West. Little need to worry about the Soviets. They were far behind.'

'The question I asked was what brought you to your current position,' Carswell reminded him.

'I am coming to that. Let me take you back to the so-called explosion. It was set up by members of the KGB at the instructions of certain members of the Central Committee. The men and women who died were real people, civilians. Old age pensioners mostly, who lived in a block of flats near the laboratory. They died in a separate explosion which was made to look as if it had been caused by the explosion in the laboratory.'

'What happened?'

'The old people were rounded up one night, driven to a forest clearing outside Moscow and murdered in cold blood. Their bodies were buried in a trench near where they were killed. My father was one of those who died that night.'

'I see.' Carswell puffed at his pipe.

'I am a communist because I believe in the teachings of Marx and Lenin. I am opposed to the realisation of their goals through the senseless slaughter of civilians.'

'A conflict in Berlin would come under your definition of senseless slaughter?'

Koliakov nodded. 'Such a conflict would rapidly become nuclear. Many millions of our peoples would die unnecessarily. It is a sickening thought – particularly when one man's hubris will have caused so much destruction. Now do you understand why I call myself a patriot?'

'Thank you, Colonel. You've been most helpful.'

★

'Does the name Peter the Great mean anything to you?' Carswell asked.

'As a historical character?' Berlin replied.

'As a code name.'

'Nothing, no.'

'You're sure?'

'Yes.'

Carswell wrote in a notebook. 'I understand you know Marshal Gerasimov.'

'I have met him once.'

'In a graveyard – am I right?'

Berlin nodded.

'Tell me something about him that will convince me that what you are telling us is true.'

Berlin took his time to reply. 'He is a convinced communist, an idealist. Communism for him is the only way to universal human justice. His wife was an artist. He discovered, after she was dead, that she destroyed many of her pictures to protect him.'

'How?'

'Because they showed too much truth. She painted life in our country as it is, not as our government would have us believe it is.'

Berlin saw the old man clearing the undergrowth from his wife's grave and standing in silence before it. He knew now that Gerasimov was not remembering Yelena. That was not why he visited her grave. It was to rededicate himself to the need to act on the truth, not to be deceived by lies.

'Every year he visits her grave to remind himself of what she sacrificed for him.'

'What did his wife die of?'

'Gerasimov would say she died of a broken heart. She sacrificed her painting to her love for him. In fact it was cancer.'

He thought back to the painting of the young man on his way to the front, and the mixture of anxiety and anticipation on his face. His father had disliked the picture. It had been too real for him. It brought back fears he had tried to banish from his life.

'Gerasimov, you're saying, is a humane man.'

'He is opposed to the indiscriminate killing of civilians. He says our people have suffered enough.'

'That certainly is true,' Carswell said. He looked up at Berlin. 'Thank you. You've told me all I need to know.'

★

'What's your verdict?' Hart asked.

Carswell took his time to answer. 'I think on balance Koliakov is telling the truth. He has a motive.'

'And Berlin doesn't?

'I think he is lying. I have no doubt that he is who he says he is. I do not believe for one moment his story about Marshal Gerasimov. Nothing rings true. I think Berlin is a vain man who saw an opportunity to gain himself a role. The sooner he clears off back to Moscow, the better.'

6

Berlin looked out at the deserted court: the soft red-brick buildings, almost pink in the sunlight, were covered in places by dark green ivy, and flanked by neatly trimmed flower beds filled with late summer flowers, deep red roses, purple Michaelmas daisies and pink anemones; the well-cut grass was bisected by a worn stone path tucked in with cobbles; a clock over the entrance to the hall struck the half-hour, sounding the same note it had struck over the centuries.

'Dr Berlin, sir? You're wanted on the telephone.'

He came down the stairs two at a time and followed Wilkins into the porter's lodge. He was sure it was Pountney.

'Andrei? Gerry Pountney. Not good news, I'm afraid. I've seen Hugh Hart. In fact, I spent most of last night with him. I can't get him to budge. I'm sorry about that. I think the Americans have got at him. It's a setback, but it's not the end of the line. Give me a few hours. I'll be in touch, all right?'

'Thank you for trying,' Berlin said. 'I am grateful.'

He put the phone down. The message was unequivocal. He had failed. His heart felt like stone.

7

They sit on steel-framed chairs in the airport lounge, holding hands. Occasionally she leans her head against him and he puts his arm round her. They say nothing – there is nothing new that can be said.

I am a convicted prisoner, she thinks to herself. I am waiting for the last minutes of my life to pass before my execution. Soon a voice will summon me and I will stand up, kiss the man I love for the last time, hold him briefly in my arms, and then I will walk away and that will be it, the end of everything. No more light, only darkness.

'Will you write to me?' she asks suddenly.

'Yes.'

She squeezes his hand, a gesture of reassurance that she doesn't feel. He may write but will the letters reach her?

There is an announcement over the tannoy that she cannot understand. He looks up at the board. The boarding sign is flashing against her flight number.

'Is it time?' she asks, knowing it is, but hoping for a reprieve.

'Yes.' He stands up. 'You must go now.'

She has thought of this moment so many times, rehearsed it

in her mind with a thousand variations. Should she be brave and embrace him without crying? Should she break down with declarations of undying love? But what she has imagined is not what happens.

'Come here,' he says, gathering her in his arms. She feels his warmth around her. His lips are close to her ear and he is whispering urgently to her. 'When you are alone, remember this. You made me understand who I am. There is no greater gift than that. I can never thank you enough. Never in a hundred lifetimes. I dedicate my life to you.'

Why do you tell me this now? she wants to ask. *You've never said anything like it before. What does it mean?*

Before her lips can frame the questions, she is walking away from him, holding her passport and her boarding card and a Russian bag that he has bought her. She refuses to turn round. She knows that if she does so something terrible will happen. All her energies must be concentrated on getting onto the plane. Nothing is more important than that.

'Tell my father you've seen me,' she hears a voice call after her. 'Tell him I'm alive.'

As she walks across the tarmac, she hears the wind in the grass, sees the river flashing in the sunlight as it breaks over the stones; she watches dragonflies hovering above the reeds, fishing darting into the shadows, birds wheeling above her.

Suddenly she starts to sing quietly to herself.

8

For hours nothing has happened. The two sides have faced each other. But there has been no movement, no sound. Suddenly the eerie silence is broken by the firing up of an engine on the Soviet side. Will the tank move forward or back? Nerves are stretched to breaking point.

Pountney whispers into his microphone, as if any sound might cause the stand-off to end in a withering hail of file. 'I have lost count of the hours we have waited here, certainly twelve. But it's more like fifteen, sixteen. Each side has stared down the gun barrels of the other. But no shots have been fired. There is total stillness. Now one of the Soviet tanks has started its engines. What will it do? Will it move forward or back?'

He watches. The Soviet tank remains where it is, its engine turning over. Then it is put into reverse, and it moves back five yards. It is no more than a gesture, but it is enough.

From somewhere a faint cheer breaks out.

9

'Professor Stevens? Hello. You won't know me. My name is Kate Buchanan. I've just returned from Moscow. I met your son while I was there. He asked me to tell you that he is well. I would like to come and see you, if I might. I wondered if we could arrange a time.'

*

Our policy (*Valery Marchenko writes, addressing his open letter to the First Secretary and to the Soviet newspapers*) is based on the myth that the Chief Designer of our space programme, Viktor Radin, is still alive. He is not. He died of cancer last July. Since then, no appointment has been made to replace him. Instead, the attitudes he held have been allowed to govern our policy decisions *as if he were still alive*. That is wrong, naive and certain to be catastrophic in the long run. I am a victim of this refusal to face the truth. My own project – to use robotics rather than humans for the exploration of space – which saves lives and money – was rejected because it opposed Viktor Radin's profoundly held belief in the value of the human cosmonaut in performing every task, and reflects his scorn for the remarkably versatile machines we have built. My project was not rejected on the grounds of its merits nor its costs, but on the basis that, since it did not emanate from Professor Radin, it could have no validity at all.

This letter calls for the urgent reform of our space administration, the appointment of a new Director and the adoption of a new policy based on reality as we perceive it now.

10

What shall I tell Gerasimov?

Berlin stares out of the window. The plane has not moved. He looks at his watch. They are delayed, though no one has explained why. He tries to concentrate on what he can see from his window seat of the life of the airport but he sees nothing. His thoughts return to Marion and his eyes fill with tears. His arms are still warm from Marion's embrace, his lips still burning from her kisses. How impossible it was to leave her – she had tears in her eyes and a startled, hopeless look on her face.

'Come back,' she had begged, 'please come back. Don't leave me alone.'

With each step he took as he walked away from her, he felt as if he was dragging the world behind him.

What shall I tell Gerasimov?

He has failed in his mission. Whoever caused those tanks to withdraw, it was not him. A historic moment that he wanted to claim as his own has nothing to do with him. He has saved no one, not even himself. That is the truth he will have to live with.

'Well,' the old general will say when they met in Moscow, 'it worked, didn't it?'

'I didn't think it was going to,' he will reply. 'For a long time I had my doubts. The British were slow to recognise what I was saying. But in the end it was all right.'

'I warned you they would be,' Gerasimov will reply.

'They believed me,' Berlin says. 'That's all that matters, isn't it?'

'The world saw us retreat from that moment of confrontation,' the general says. 'Only you and I know the truth.'

Then, as if in slow motion, Berlin sees the general draw a revolver from his pocket and aim at his heart. He sees the old general's finger squeezing the trigger. He is too frightened even to beg for his life. He knows that he has to be sacrificed because Gerasimov believes he has fulfilled his duty, and no one must know the role either man has played. He knows he has lied to Gerasimov, and the price of the lie is that Gerasimov must kill him to keep a secret that doesn't exist.

He feels a terrible pain in his heart. He is dizzy, short of breath.

'I'm sorry,' he says to his neighbour. 'I must get out of the plane. I am not well.'

IVAN'S SEARCH FOR HIS FATHER

It had seemed so simple in the film. Once Ivan had got into the Kremlin, he had been passed on from hand to hand like a baton in a relay race, until finally he reached the presence of the Great Leader, to be rewarded for his courage with fame as a youthful hero of the Soviet Union.

He was the same age as Ivan. Why couldn't he do the same?

Reality and illusion, Andrei came to realise, are never the same. In dreams one knocks obstacles aside that in life are as solid as rock. The grim faces on the Kremlin guards − so unlike the grinning men Ivan had met − told him he had no chance of winning their support before he had said a word. Twice he tried to sneak past the guards but on both occasions he was stopped. He was struck on the head and told to get lost, or his treatment next time would be a great deal worse.

How was he to get into the Kremlin? If there were any doors he might force, he had no chance of getting near them. The walls were too high to climb and he was sure there were guards watching and an electronic surveillance system. But if Ivan could get in, then he could do so. It was simply a matter of finding a way.

Two nights later he crept out of the apartment after his mother had gone to bed and ran the mile to the Kremlin. There he watched the guards march up and down, he noted the times they were relieved and the procedure by which the new guard took over. Once or twice official cars entered. It was too dark to see who was inside. Only just before dawn did the routine change. Garbage trucks stopped on the apron before the gate, the guards checked the drivers' passes and waved the trucks in.

The following night, his heart racing, he ran across the huge forecourt as the rain poured down and jumped into the back of a lorry that had halted briefly at the gates. A short ride and he was in. He jumped off as the lorry slowed and hid in a doorway. So far so good. But now where?

He tried a door. It was locked. Another: locked again. The windows? Secure on the inside. There was no chance of entry there unless he broke a window and forced the catch but the noise would give his presence away. He ran across the road, the rain lashing him as he did so, and tried another building. Again the doors were locked. No lights were on anywhere. There was no sign of any guards.

He found a door that yielded to his push and went into a warm room filled with brooms, buckets and cleaning fluid. It smelled, but at least it was dry. He lay down on the wooden floor. In his excitement and exhaustion he fell asleep.

★

'He was sleeping in a cupboard,' the guard said. 'His clothes were dry so he must have been there some time.'

'What is your name?' the officer asked.

'Andrei Berlin.' He toyed with calling himself Ivan, but decided that was too great a risk.

'What are you doing here?'

'I am a representative of the children of the Soviet Union,' he said, quoting Ivan. 'I am here to see our Great Leader.'

Was the officer smiling? 'Why?'

'He is the Father of the children of the Soviet Union. I have come to thank him for his great leadership, and to tell him of the bright future we will build under his guidance.'

Had Ivan said that? He could no longer remember.

'Would you like to write a message for him?'

'I must see him,' Andrei persisted.

'That may not be possible.'

'I am sure if he knows I am here he will want to see me.' How easily the words came back to him. They had worked for Ivan. He felt braver now.

The two men turned away and talked in whispers. He was unable to catch what they were saying. The officer picked up the telephone and spoke sharply.

'Someone's coming for you in a moment or two.'

'Thank you.'

He was escorted down a long, well-lit corridor, just like those Ivan had travelled along before him. A knock on a door, a summons to enter, and he was shown into a darkened room.

'Come in. Sit down.'

He couldn't see the speaker but he responded to the command and did as he was told. He was in a small private cinema. He could hear a faint clicking as the film ran through the machine. As his eyes got used to the dark, he could make out three or four people in the small room. He looked at the screen. Two naked bodies were writhing around, one on top of the other, both were groaning, the woman making short rhythmic cries as the man lunged at her. They seemed to have no heads, only torsos, the camera focusing on the man's enormous thing which was plunging in and out of the woman. Andrei looked away.

'No, look at the screen. It is important you look at the screen.'

He felt no desire to do so. He stared straight ahead and covered his eyes with his hands. A man came up behind him and pulled his hands away.

'Do as you're told.'

He knew without looking who the man on the screen was. He had never seen the woman before. An old mattress had been dragged out from somewhere onto the floor of the studio and his father was sucking at the woman's thing – how could he do that? He looked away, horrified. The men around him were laughing.

Suddenly the bodies were gone and the studio was deserted.

Night became day. Why was the camera running when there was nothing to record? The door opened. He saw himself entering the room. The next minute he was defacing the statues, modelling the clay. He watched himself, astonished. They knew all along that he had done it. There had been a secret camera and they had captured him on film. He felt sickened, dirty, horrified. He was their accomplice, and they were all around him now, laughing at his horror, knowing he was their captive and there was nothing he could do to escape. He put his hands over his ears, but by now the sound of mocking laughter was inside his head and a voice was saying, 'Now you'll never escape from us. Never, never, never.'

17 March 1962

The Soviet news agency TASS today reported the death of the great Soviet realist film director, Grigor Penkovsky. He was seventy-three. The director of more than twenty films, he was best known for his production *Ivan's Search for His Father*, which many critics saw as setting the style for the heroic sacrifices of the Soviet military in the war against fascism.

The death of Viktor Radin, space engineer, was reported. He was sixty-two.

Gerry Pountney devoted the whole of his weekly current affairs programme to a televised reconstruction of the Moscow trial of the dissenter, Valery Marchenko, who had been sentenced to five years' hard labour for anti-Soviet activities. The production was based on transcripts of the trial which had been smuggled to the West. The programme concluded with a moving plea for Marchenko's release by his father, Professor Geoffrey Stevens of Cambridge University.

The cellist Kate Buchanan, recognised as one of the country's leading young musicians, who had made her name in a remarkable solo performance, *Song of Freedom from an Unknown Land*, by an unknown composer, today began a solitary vigil outside the Soviet Embassy in London in support of efforts to release Valery Marchenko.

KGB Colonel Vadim Medvedev was taken from his prison cell at four in the morning and shot for betraying Soviet secrets to the West.

Vassily Vinogradoff left hospital after a fourth operation to restore movement to two fingers of his left hand which were damaged when the car in which he was a passenger was hit by a lorry.

Hugh Hart received a letter from Bobby Martineau saying that he and Eva Balassi were living under an assumed name in a small town south of Stockholm. Eva's daughter, Dora, was studying to be a doctor at the medical school in Lund.

The First Secretary of the Communist Party of the Soviet Union secretly approved the first planning document for the installation of Soviet missiles in Cuba. He commented at the time: 'The rehearsal is over. This time we mean business.'